Wordless

A Novel

SABRINA STARK

CHAPTER 1

Becka

For someone I'd known less than four hours, he sure was bossy.

"Pack your stuff," he said. "We're leaving."

I stared up at him. "We?"

His hair was thick and blond, and his eyes were so blue, they made the ocean look dingy in comparison. "Well you're not going alone," he said.

I struggled for a reply and came up empty. *Honestly, what was I supposed to say?* The guy in front of me wasn't *just* a new acquaintance. He was also Jack Ward – my favorite author, a total hottie, and a billionaire several times over.

Unfortunately, he was also just a little bit scary. Ask my roommate. *He'll* tell you – well, unless he's already escaped through his bedroom window, that is.

I glanced around the condo where I'd been living for the past two weeks. To say the arrangement had gone to crap would be giving crap a bad name.

Turns out, my roommate was a druggie *and* a dude. On top of *that*, he wasn't terrific at keeping his horse in the barn, if you know what I mean.

Until just five days ago, I'd never even met the guy, much less realized that "Nicky" wasn't short for Nicole, but rather Nicholas. But in my own defense, the gal who'd rented me the place had neglected to mention this little detail, along with a whole bunch of other stuff – on purpose, no doubt.

And me? Like a total sucker, I'd actually trusted her.

Now I didn't know *who* to trust. I bit my lip. *If only my sister were here.*

Jack's voice interrupted my thoughts. "If you need boxes, let me know. I'll have some delivered."

I blinked. It was nearly ten o'clock on a Sunday night. This was a small town. Nothing was open. I shook my head. *And was box delivery seriously a thing?*

Not in my world, it wasn't. Then again, *I* wasn't a billionaire. In fact, my bank balance was dangerously close to zero.

I just had to ask, "Who'd do that?"

"Do what?" Jack said.

"Deliver boxes. I mean, nothing's open."

He gave me a look. "Do you need them or not?"

"No," I admitted.

"Good," he said. "Then get packing."

I didn't appreciate his tone. "Don't you think that's kind of bossy? I mean, I never said for sure that I'm moving."

His jaw tightened. "Well you're not staying here. I can tell you that."

Yup, he was definitely bossy. I wanted to argue. But I couldn't. *And why?*

It was because he was right.

I couldn't stay. Not anymore. But I'd known that already.

Stalling for time, I glanced around the condo. The place was surprisingly nice. It had come pre-furnished, too, which meant that nearly nothing was mine.

Sure, I had some clothes in the bedroom along with my notebook computer and a few essentials. But the sad truth was, I could probably cram everything I owned into my cheap compact car.

No boxes needed.

Still, I shoved a hand through my hair and tried to think. Leaving sounded easy enough, but where would I go?

A hotel?

As if I had the money.

My sister's place?

That *would've* been the plan, if only she were in town.

I was still running through my options when Jack said, "Becka."

I jumped at the sound of my name. "What?"

"You're not packing."

"I know, because I'm thinking."

"So do both," he said.

I sighed. On this, he was right, too. After all, it would take me at least a half-hour to gather up my stuff. Surely by then, I'd know where I was going.

But for now, I was simply going crazy.

Some of this was Jack's fault. Not only had he just assaulted my scuzz-bucket of a roommate, he was distracting the heck out of me.

Some people go for movie stars. Or rock stars. Or hell, even reality TV stars. But me? I'd had my nose crammed in one book or another for as long as I could recall. Some of those books were better than others.

But seven years ago at the ripe old age of seventeen, I'd fallen head-over-heels in love – with *his* books, sprawling medieval tales that were beyond brutal, and yet sometimes so beautiful they almost made me cry.

It was totally insane. Jack was only a few years older than I was. In fact, he'd just turned thirty-one last month. *And how did I know this?*

I'd read it on the internet, of course.

Now, he was glowering down at me like I was a bratty kid refusing to clean my room.

I wasn't bratty. I was just confused.

Hell, I'd been confused ever since showing up on my sister's doorstep four hours ago, only to encounter someone who definitely didn't belong.

And *that* was putting it mildly.

CHAPTER 2

Becka – Four Hours Earlier

Un-freaking-believable.

I stared up at the half-naked floozy who was blocking the mansion's front door. Okay, floozy was an old-fashioned word, but that's exactly what she was – a total freaking floozy – unless I was planning to dive for the gutter and call her something a whole lot worse.

Slut.

After all, she *had* to know exactly who she was screwing – Flynn Archer, a guy who was already engaged – to *my* sister.

The bastard.

Not her. *Him.*

Obviously.

I felt my jaw clench. *Boy, was he gonna get it.*

Again, I moved forward, intending to yank open the massive front door and barge my way into the house, *his* house, the glorious secluded mansion where my sister had been living since sometime last year.

Unfortunately, my sister was out of town. She'd been away for the past week, helping our mom get settled into a new place. That place was in Wyoming – several hours away, even by private jet. *His* jet.

The jerk. Probably the whole private jet thing was his way of keeping track of her – making sure that my sister didn't return early while he was doing – well, *her*, whatever her name was.

I'd been arguing with her for several minutes now, and so far, she'd refused to tell me her name, much less what she was doing here.

But hey, it was easy to guess.

When she moved sideways yet again to block my path, I took a single step backward and let my gaze drift rudely over her nearly naked form. She was wearing a lacy black bra with matching black panties. The lace of both undergarments was so flimsy it was practically transparent, giving me an intimate view of her perky nipples and shaved – well, you know what.

The undergarments – what little there were – perfectly matched her long, ebony hair and thick, dark eyelashes. I squinted upward and gave them a closer look. They couldn't be real. *Could they?*

Without thinking, I looked down to her ample chest and mentally repeated the question. Were *those* real? If so, it was hard to fathom, given the tiny circumference of her waist.

I knew one thing for darn sure. She *wasn't* from around here. This was my hometown, not hers. And yes, I *would* know. After all, this wasn't New York or even Detroit. This was Sugar Falls, Michigan, where, depending on the season, tourists might outnumber actual residents several times over.

I was still staring when her voice – in that upscale English accent of hers – interrupted my thoughts. "Maybe you should take a photo. It will last longer."

"Oh yeah?" Suddenly inspired, I blurted out, "Well maybe I did."

It was a total bluff. In truth, I'd been too surprised to do much of anything after pulling onto the property only to see a scantily clad stranger standing in the open doorway.

The door wasn't open anymore. *And why was that?* It was because the moment I'd stalked up to the front porch, she'd slammed it behind her faster than you could say, *"Where the hell is Jonathon Flynn Archer?"*

That was his full name – the guy who was going to get a piece of my mind, as soon as *she* moved aside.

In front of me, she gave a mean little laugh. "Oh, please. You did not."

Take her picture? She was right. I hadn't. Still, I pulled out my cell phone and gave it a random wave. "Are you *sure* about that?"

"Of course I'm sure." She glanced toward the phone. "I would've seen."

"Not if I took it from my car." I forced a smile so evil, it made my face hurt. "And just so you know, it *wasn't* flattering."

She gave a little gasp. "What?"

When my only reply was a loose shrug, she sputtered, "You are such a liar!"

I kept my smile plastered in place. "If you say so."

Okay, so maybe I was lying just a little. Even if I *had* taken such a picture, she would've looked impossibly gorgeous. In fact, I couldn't imagine any angle that wouldn't make her look like some sort of goddess, sent to make normal girls like me feel short and frumpy in comparison.

Then again, she *was* wearing high heels. That had to account for at least a *few* inches, right?

Her eyes narrowed as they zoomed in on my phone. "Show me," she commanded.

I took another step backward. "No."

She stepped forward. "Why not?"

Again, I backed up. "Because you're too far away."

"So stop moving."

I jerked my chin upward. "Make me."

Finally, with a long-suffering sigh, she strode forward as if she *weren't* wearing nearly nothing. Even worse, she managed to look stupidly elegant doing it, almost as if she were walking down some fashion runway in Milan – and not some porch in northern Michigan.

It was *this* twisted observation that made me suddenly realize why she looked so annoyingly familiar. *Holy hell.* She was a model – an *underwear* model. Swimsuits, too. Her name was Imogen St. James, and I'd seen her on television just last month as part of some prime-time lingerie extravaganza.

Well, this was just great.

Not only was Flynn cheating on my sister. He was doing it with one of the hottest models in the world. *What a total cliché.*

But what did it matter?

Cheating was cheating, right?

As she strode forward, I kept backing up until I was in serious danger of toppling backward down the front steps. But then, just as she nearly reached me, I sidestepped around her and bolted straight for the front door.

From behind me, she squealed, "You little bitch!"

Hah! She was ten times bitchier than I was, because unlike her, *I'd* never sleep with a guy who was taken.

Already I could hear her scrambling up behind me. *Too fast, even in high heels.*

Crap.

In a burst of raw desperation, I took a flying leap for the handle of the front door, only to have the door itself swing magically open just as my fingers stretched out toward it.

With an embarrassing little scream, I soared through the open doorway, and landed with a thud on the ornate entrance rug. On impact, the stupid thing slid forward across the glossy wooden floor, moving like a bobsled on ice – and carrying me along for the ride.

Damn it.

When the rug finally stopped moving, I flopped over onto my back and lifted my head, looking up at the guy whose hand was still on the interior door handle. He was tall and muscular with thick blond hair and piercing blue eyes.

He was frowning and shirtless above his faded jeans. His waist was lean, and his torso was a mouthwatering work of art – not with ink, but rather with muscles cut so fine that I couldn't help but stare.

When my gaze dipped to his abs, I swallowed with an audible gulp – and *not* because I'd just had the wind knocked out of me.

Trying not to drool, I jerked my gaze upward. From the look on his face, he was just as surprised to see me as I was to see him.

I knew exactly who he was.

But he *wasn't* my sister's fiancé, which meant...*what, exactly?*

CHAPTER 3

Becka

I could hardly believe it. I was looking at Jack Freaking Ward, my all-time favorite author.

He was still frowning – except now he was frowning at Imogen, who was standing in the open doorway, griping up a storm. Even worse, she sounded stupidly elegant doing it.

It was the accent. It *had* to be.

She concluded her little tirade by saying, "And I don't appreciate the intrusion."

At this, I couldn't help but snort. "Yeah, right."

Her gaze snapped in my direction. "Pardon?"

Like an idiot, I was still lying on the rug. As I scrambled to my feet, I said, "I guess I'm just wondering why you'd be standing outside in your underpants if you didn't want any attention."

She was glaring again. "I said *intrusion*, not attention."

"But isn't that the same thing?" I asked.

"Hardly." Through gritted teeth, she explained, "I wasn't *outside*. I was in the doorway."

To me, that seemed like a distinction without a difference. "Yeah, but I could still *see* you from outside."

"It was an oversight, I assure you." She turned accusing eyes to Jack Ward. "You said his estate was private."

"Yeah? And *you* said you were going to the bathroom."

She frowned. "What?"

"The bathroom," he repeated. "So unless you were planning to pee off the front porch–"

"What?" she sputtered. "I'd never!"

He looked unimpressed. "If you say so..."

"You're barbaric. You *do* realize that, don't you?"

"Hell yeah," he said. "But at least I do my business in the house."

I almost snickered. He was goading her. That much was obvious, even to me – a total stranger. But the way it looked, she was totally missing it.

I watched in silent wonder as she launched into a long explanation of how she only opened the door because she thought she heard a noise on the front porch.

Oh, please. It was the dumbest excuse I'd ever heard, unless of course, she was starring in a slasher movie, in which case her logic made total sense.

When he didn't bother with a reply, she demanded, "And what about *this*?"

His eyebrows lifted. "This?"

She extended an arm and pointed a bony finger in my direction. *"Her."*

He looked to me, and then to the rug that lay twisted at my feet. "Yeah, well..." He shrugged. "These things happen."

At this, even *I* had to frown. If people soaring through the open doorway was a regular occurrence, this guy's life had to be a million times more exciting than mine.

Then again, he *was* Jack Ward. I'd seen his picture on the back of all those books. They were the same books that had formed the foundation for some of the most popular movies in the world.

In what couldn't be a coincidence, my sister's fiancé had starred in those movies. In fact, the newest flick was still killing it at the box office – here *and* overseas.

Near the door, Imogen was still sputtering. "These things happen? Not to me, they don't."

Yeah. Well, they did now.

But I didn't say it. Instead, I glanced around while she continued to complain, even as Jack Ward continued to look oddly unconcerned.

He hadn't even bothered to shut the door.

I spoke up. "Maybe you should shut that. You know, to keep the bugs out." It was, after all, nearly summer, and the place was surrounded by acres of dense forest. *Bug Central, right?*

Imogen gave me an irritated look. "What an excellent idea." Stepping aside, she made a grand sweeping gesture toward the open doorway. "Off you go."

I glanced toward the door. "Sorry, what?"

She smirked. "It's called a hint, dearie."

Dearie, my ass. She could hint all she wanted, but I wasn't leaving, not without making sure that my sister hadn't been screwed over. "Just to make sure," I said, "you're with Jack Ward? And *not* Flynn Archer?" I looked from her to him and back again. "Right?"

She eyed me with open hostility. "That's hardly your concern."

"It is, too," I insisted.

Through clenched teeth, she replied, "And why is that?"

Jack Ward spoke up. "Because that's her sister, Becka."

At the sound of my name on his lips, I sucked in a quiet breath. *He knew my name.* I didn't even care how he knew it. I just wanted him to say it again. *How stupid was that?*

She turned to face him. "Whose sister?"

Finally shutting the door, he answered, "Anna's."

At this, Imogen gave an annoying little laugh. "You can't mean the waffle waitress?"

I stiffened. "Hey! There's nothing wrong with being a waitress."

With a lingering smirk, she turned back to me and said, "If you say so."

My jaw clenched. "I *do* say so." But what I *didn't* mention was that I was no stranger to food service myself. Not too long ago, I'd been working at a burger joint that wasn't terribly different from the waffle place. I hadn't even been a waitress. I'd been a part-time cashier, which meant that I'd been earning even less than my sister.

But in my own defense, good jobs were hard to find, especially when someone's stepdad had been sent away to prison for a whole slew of financial crimes.

Considering my family history, it was amazing they'd let me near the cash at all.

With a final snicker, Imogen turned back to Jack Ward and said, "Well? Aren't you going to tell her to leave?"

He crossed his arms, making his biceps pop in a way that was stupidly distracting. "No."

She sighed. "Why not?"

"Because she's here for a reason."

"But you don't know that," she protested.

"Then neither do you."

"What does *that* mean?"

Jack looked to me and said, "Go on. Tell her."

I wasn't quite following. "Tell her what?"

"That you're here for a reason."

He was right. I *was* here for a reason. But his confidence was unnerving, and I didn't want to discuss it, or at least, not with Jack Ward or his bitchy sidekick.

Still, I *was* curious. "But wait, how would you know?"

He gave me a penetrating look. "Let's cut to the chase. Your sister's out of town. You knew this, right?"

I nodded.

"So why are you here?"

I drew back. *Talk about blunt.* I'd read all of his books, multiple times. Maybe some of his *characters* were blunt, but I'd always imagined that in real life – assuming that I ever got lucky enough to meet the guy – he'd be a lot more eloquent. *And definitely nicer.*

My fangirl enthusiasm was fading fast. "I don't know," I said. "Why are *you* here?"

Okay, maybe it was a snotty thing to say, but his eyes weren't just amazingly blue. They were so sharp, they made me feel like he could see straight into my brain.

I should've looked away, but my own eyes refused to cooperate. Under my breath, I mumbled, "I'm just saying, it's not *your* house either."

Next to him, Imogen gave a little huff. "Speaking of houses, are you going to be leaving *this* one any time soon?"

Well, that was nice.

But whatever. I wasn't here to see her goodies, or even Jack Ward's amazing abs. I was here to see Flynn Archer, my future brother-in-law.

I was in a tiny bit of trouble, and he was the closest thing I had to family, at least nearby.

Pathetic, I know.

Ignoring her question, I looked to Jack and said, "So where's Flynn?"

"Out."

I glanced toward the rear of the house. "You mean he's hiking out back?"

"No."

I hesitated. "So…is he running an errand or something?"

"No," he repeated.

I made a sound of frustration. "So, where is he? I *know* he's in town."

Jack's eyebrows lifted. "You sure about that?"

"Definitely," I said. "My sister told me so."

"When?"

I recalled our recent phone call. "Maybe an hour ago."

"Yeah, well, maybe your information's outdated."

I gave a confused shake of my head. "What does *that* mean?"

Jack studied my face. "So, are you gonna answer my question or not?"

"What question?"

"Why are you here?"

Next to him, Imogen chimed in, "And *when* are you leaving?"

Slowly, he turned to face her. In a surprisingly calm voice, he said, "Zip it."

She blinked. "What?"

"Zip it," he repeated. "Or leave. Your choice."

She glanced down. "But I'm not even dressed."

He gave her clothes – or lack thereof – a dismissive look. "That's your problem. Not mine."

His words were so cold, I stifled a shiver. With growing unease, I said, "All right, just tell me one thing. When will Flynn be back?"

"My guess?" Jack said. "Next month."

My jaw almost hit the floor. *Next month?*

I shook my head. *No, that couldn't be right.* I'd literally *just* talked to Anna. She'd said nothing about Flynn being gone, much less for a whole month. *And she'd surely know, right?*

I'd need to call her again.

But in the meantime, I had to face facts. Whatever the situation, Flynn definitely wasn't here at the moment.

This posed a disturbing new question.

Now what?

CHAPTER 4

Jack

In the end, Anna's little sister wouldn't tell me dick. Instead, she'd turned and stomped out of the house, leaving the door wide open behind her, like she was looking to make a point.

What the point was, I could only guess.

I watched through the open front doorway as she stalked to a small beat-up car parked haphazardly in the driveway. She got inside and fired up the engine. The car lurched forward, circled the turnaround, and then sped out through the open front gate before disappearing in a cloud of dust and disappointment.

Not *her* disappointment.

Mine.

This trip had been a giant cluster, and it wasn't getting any better. I'd been planning to stay at Flynn's for two solitary days until starting the upcoming book tour – *and* the secret side missions I'd been planning for longer than I cared to consider.

But Imogen had surprised me an hour ago, showing up outside Flynn's gate as if I'd be happy to see her.

I wasn't. Hell, if I'd known she was coming, I'd have gone somewhere else to finalize my plans.

Six weeks earlier, Imogen and I had ended our relationship. We'd been together for several months, but it seemed like longer, and not in a good way. To me, the split was permanent. But Imogen wasn't seeing it the same.

She'd spent the last hour trying to get me into bed. *No surprise there.* It was her answer to everything – distract me with sex and gloss over the rest of it.

As for myself, I'd spent the last hour wondering how the hell she'd learned where I was.

There was a reason I'd come out to Flynn's place, and it wasn't to be hounded by a girl who refused to take no for an answer.

But I wasn't thinking of Imogen *now*. I was thinking of Anna's little sister. She was in some kind of trouble, even if she'd refused to admit it.

When the dust in the road finally cleared, I shut the door and turned away. As I did, Imogen sidled closer to say, "I thought she'd *never* leave."

With a flirtatious smile, she reached up and laced her icy fingers around the back of my neck. She leaned into me, and her voice grew husky. "So, what shall we do now?"

Shall?

Oh, for fuck's sake.

Imogen had more than her share of secrets. And guess what? I knew them all. Her accent was faker than her eyelashes, not to mention any of those other attributes that had made her famous.

During our time together, I'd never called her on any of it – including the fake accent *or* the fake history. *And why?* It was because she didn't know that I knew. And I was fine with keeping it that way.

If I ever wanted to swap secrets, it *wouldn't* be with Imogen St. James – aka Rachel Krepke from Cincinnati.

I pulled out of her embrace and said, "You need to go."

She frowned. "But why?"

"Because it's not my house."

"So?"

"So I'm going out, which means you can't stay."

"So I'll come with you."

"Trust me, you're heading out," I said. "But not with me."

She tried for a flirtatious laugh. "But I can't just leave, silly. I'm all dressed up."

Silly?

Silliness was inviting yourself on an errand while insisting that you can't leave the house. Then again, Imogen wasn't known for her consistency.

I gave her outfit – what little there was – a quick glance. "Dressed for what?"

She cocked a hip. "For you, of course."

Yeah. Me and a few million other people. I knew damn well what she'd been doing in the open doorway, and it had nothing to do with me. It had to do with her millions of fans on Instagram and wherever else.

If I knew Imogen, she'd been setting up a selfie – some pseudo-candid shot of her nearly naked body, framed in the open doorway of Flynn Archer's secluded mansion. Flynn was a big movie star, which meant that in Imogen's world, his was a name worth dropping.

Not to me.

To me, Flynn was the closest thing I had to a brother. I'd known him before either of us guys had become famous – me with the books and Flynn in the related movies that had made him a star.

But to Imogen? He was just a name – a good one to drop on her slobbering fans. That's how she worked.

I should know. She'd been dropping *my* name non-stop since early this year, when we'd somehow become an item.

I said, "Where's your coat?"

She shook her head. "What coat?"

"The one you arrived in."

She'd shown up in a limo, wearing exactly what she was wearing now, plus a long trench coat – some tan retro thing that had probably cost more than the vehicle that had carried her here.

Her lips curved into a slow smile. "I don't know." She made a show of eyeing my bare chest. "Where's your shirt?"

She knew damn where it was. I'd yanked it off after she'd "accidentally" spilled a bottle of soda water down the front of me.

Wet T-shirts – she had a thing for them. Or maybe she'd just wanted to get the ball rolling as far as getting me out of my clothes.

That was Imogen – subtle to the core.

Ignoring her question, I pulled out my cell phone and started scrolling across the screen.

She asked, "What are you doing?"

"Calling the limo."

"Why?"

"So they can come and get you."

She frowned. "But where would I go?"

"Back."

"Back where?"

I didn't know, and I didn't care. "Wherever you came from."

She made a sound of protest. "But I don't have a flight."

"Sorry, not my problem."

"Can I at least borrow your jet?"

"No."

"But why not?" she said. "It's just sitting there, waiting at the airport, right?"

Yeah. It was. But letting her use it would only encourage further visits – visits that I didn't want *or* need. "Whether it is or not," I said, "the answer's still no."

She gave a dramatic sigh. "Forget the jet. I can't leave yet anyway."

She was wrong. *She could. And she would.*

When my only reply was a cold look, she added, "I mean, we haven't had the chance to talk."

I didn't bother to hide my impatience. "About what?"

"Us."

"There is no us," I reminded her. "We're done. Remember?"

She *should* remember. It was *her* doing. She'd wanted to take our relationship to the next level, and when I'd balked, she'd responded by trashing her own kitchen and storming off to Tuscany or wherever, expecting me to follow.

I hadn't.

She tried for a laugh. "Oh come on. It was just a disagreement.

That's all."

A stack of broken dishes said otherwise. But that wasn't the issue. The issue was, our problems weren't the kind that improved over time. They were the kind that festered in private before ending in a public display that would embarrass me and my future kids, assuming I ever had any.

She moved closer and practically purred, "And come on. You *know* you want it."

I'd returned my attention to the phone. "What?"

"*You* know." Her voice dripped with honey. "Makeup sex."

Yup. Subtle, all right.

I stopped scrolling and gave her a good, long look.

Now that she had my attention, she said, "Admit it. You still want me."

She was only half right. My dick said yes, but my brain said no. Sure, she was undeniably sexy, but I was done letting my lower brain make any decisions where Imogen was concerned.

We were done. Period.

Plus, there was something I needed to do, and it didn't involve dragging Imogen along for the ride.

One way or another, she had to go.

CHAPTER 5

Becka

I was hunkered down in my car, watching the condo though my driver's side window. I'd been watching it for a half-hour now, but saw nothing to be concerned about.

I tried to smile. *Maybe Nicky was gone. Hey, anything was possible, right?*

A low scoff escaped my lips. *As if I'd get so lucky.*

Lately luck had been thin on the ground, but I had only myself to blame. I mean, we make our own luck, right? And, assuming this was true, I'd been doing a sorry job of it.

Seriously, what on Earth had I been thinking?

I was still mulling that over when a tap on the passenger's side window made me jump in my seat. I whirled to look and stifled a gasp. It wasn't *him*, the guy I'd been watching for. It was the *other* him – Jack Ward.

I felt my eyebrows furrow. *What was he doing here?*

As I stared in open confusion, he pointed to the passenger's side door and said, "Open up."

I frowned. Even muffled through the glass, his words had sounded way too bossy for my liking. Unless I was mistaken, he'd just given me an order – and *not* a request.

I glanced around, taking in the quiet city street. *Where had he come from, anyway?* I had no idea. Beyond confused, I called through the glass. "Why?"

He eyed me through the car window. "Because if you don't, I'll have to get it myself."

I was still frowning. He *couldn't* get it. The car was locked – and for a good reason, too. *He* was out there, somewhere. And I *didn't* mean Jack Ward.

I took another glance around before returning my attention to the passenger's side door. Just as I did, it swung open, and Jack slid into the car, claiming the passenger's seat and shutting the door behind him.

I gave a confused shake of my head. "Wait. Wasn't it locked?"

"Not good enough," he said.

Okay, that made zero sense, but hey, what else was new? At least *now* he was wearing a shirt – a plain black T-shirt, as generic as you could get. And yet, on him, it didn't look generic at all.

The shirt looked…well, distracting, that's what.

I heard myself say, "What are you doing here?"

"The same as you."

I seriously doubted that. After all, *I* was watching for the psycho that was my new roommate – a roommate I'd met for the very first time only five days ago. I gave Jack a thin smile. "Which is…?"

He flicked his head toward the opposite side of the street. "Watching that condo."

I sat back in surprise. So he *did* know? But he couldn't know everything. As a test, I asked, "Watching for what?"

He gave me a hard look. "You tell me."

I didn't *want* to tell him. Cripes, I didn't want to tell anyone. Mostly, I wanted to crawl into a hole and hide.

I'd been so freaking stupid.

Stalling, I turned and looked once again toward the condo. The place was obnoxiously nice – one of six attached units located across from the waterfront city park. Probably it was *too* nice.

By this, I meant that it was well beyond my normal budget even for a rental. Even so, I'd gotten a heck of a deal – half-priced rent and free utilities.

Probably this should've been my first clue, huh?

I turned back to Jack and sighed. "Fine. You want the truth? I'm watching for my roommate."

"All right. So what's his name?"

Now *that* made me pause. "Wait. How do you know it's a guy?"

He gave a tight shrug. "Easy guess."

"How?" I asked.

He eyed me with apparent disdain. "Is that a serious question?"

"Definitely," I said. "For all you know, I could have a psycho *female* roommate. And *she'd* be worth avoiding too, right?"

His mouth tightened, and his gaze shifted past me toward the condo. He gave it a long, serious look.

As he did, I belatedly realized that by calling Nicky a psycho, I'd just revealed far more than I'd intended. Going for a distraction, I added, "I'm just saying, don't you think it's a bit sexist to assume it's a guy?"

With his gaze still on the condo, Jack replied, "Sexist to who? Seems to me I'm paying you a compliment."

If so, it had to be the most subtle compliment I'd ever received. "How so?"

"By assuming the psycho isn't you."

My jaw dropped. "What?"

"Or one of your female friends."

"Hey!" I said. "Girls can be psychos, too, you know." As soon as the words left my mouth, I wanted to take them back. After all, he'd just said basically the same thing. And more to the point, *why was I arguing against my own gender?* But I knew exactly why.

It was because of Jack. I found him nearly as unnerving as the guy I'd been avoiding for two days straight. And *that* guy was totally off his rocker.

Ignoring my protest, Jack asked, "When's the last time you saw him?"

"Who, my roommate?"

"Yeah. Him."

"Friday."

"Day or night?"

I almost shuddered at the memory. "Night."

"So it's been what? Forty-eight hours?"

"More or less."

I recalled the last time I'd seen Nicky. It had been just past midnight when I'd left my bedroom in search of something to drink, only to find Nicky naked in the kitchen – or rather, nearly naked if I wanted to count his open bathrobe, which just for the record, hid next to nothing.

Then again, Nicky had been – how to put this? – rather engorged at the time.

The worst part was, he'd acted like this wasn't a big deal. And when I'd informed him that it most certainly *was* a big deal and then told him flat-out that he needed to make sure he was decent before *ever* leaving his bedroom, he'd had the nerve to look offended.

On top of *that*, he'd refused to shut his robe.

Adding insult to injury, he'd called me, in his words, "a total downer" before offering up one of those sorry-not-sorry apologies and then leaving the kitchen with a jar of grape jelly.

For what?

I had no idea.

It's not like I'd asked.

Instead, I'd called Tara – the gal who'd rented me the place – and lodged an official complaint, not that it did a lick of good. Like Nicky, she'd acted like I was some kind of prude and suggested that I simply "chill out."

Of course, "chilling" would be a lot easier if I weren't missing two hundred dollars – money I'd tucked inside a book on my nightstand, until it mysteriously disappeared, that is.

The money. Not the book. Or the night stand.

Those were still there.

Fast forward to now. Even though I hadn't actually seen my roommate for nearly two days, I'd been hearing him plenty, making weird noises outside my bedroom door or talking way too loud on his cell phone.

The stupid thing was, Nicky was a decent-looking guy. If I'd passed him on the street, I might've found him appealing. But now, all I felt was revulsion – and yes, a tiny bit of fear.

It wasn't *only* that he was a creep – and probably a thief. He was apparently a *dangerous* thieving creep. I knew this because earlier today I'd overheard him on his cell phone, talking about his time in prison.

Maximum security – or at least that's what he'd said.

I didn't know for what, but I *did* know that I was done living with him. There were just a few tiny problems. For one thing, I had nowhere else to go. And for another, I'd already paid my rent in advance – three whole months for the entire summer break.

To my infinite shame, it hadn't even been my own money. It had come from my sister, which meant that it had come from her fiancé, Flynn Archer.

Okay, yes Flynn *was* a billionaire, which meant that he could surely afford it. But I *so* didn't want to be *that* person – the clingy relative who couldn't stand on her own two feet.

Plus, the way *I* saw it, he'd paid for more than enough already.

From the passenger's seat, Jack said, "So what's your plan?"

"I don't know," I admitted. "I'm still working on it."

"You said he's a psycho? What kind?"

A vision of the guy's erection flashed in my brain. I couldn't help but shudder. "You know. The creepy kind."

Jack's jaw clenched. "Tell me. Did he touch you?"

Heat flooded my face. "No. It wasn't like that. I just mean…" *How to put this?* "He's not shy about showing himself."

"So he flashed you."

"I guess." I bit my lip. "No, wait. That's not really fair." With a resigned sigh, I continued. "Basically, I came out of my bedroom, and he was in the kitchen. And he, uh, wasn't fully dressed."

"So he was naked."

My face was burning now. "Sort of. I mean, he was wearing a robe, but nothing else. And the robe was open, and he was, well...excited, I guess." Trying hard to be fair, I added, "Of course, he might've thought I was asleep."

"So?"

"So I just mean, that might explain why he wasn't careful."

"So this robe," Jack said. "Did he shut it after?"

"You mean after he saw me." I shook my head. "No. He didn't." In fact, he'd opened it *wider*, but that hardly seemed worth mentioning.

When Jack spoke again, his voice was eerily calm. "Anything else?"

"Well..." I hesitated. "He's been, um, moaning outside my bedroom door."

"Moaning," Jack repeated.

"Yeah. Like a ghost or maybe..." I forced a laugh. "...something more intimate."

Sometimes, when my imagination got the best of me, I envisioned Nicky pleasuring himself in the hall. But other times, I told myself that he was just messing with me as some sort of revenge for my reaction the other night.

Either way, this had become a total nightmare.

After a long pause, Jack said, "Anything else?"

"Uh, yeah. I think he's stealing from me." As Jack listened, I explained about the missing money – omitting the fact that I'd been storing the cash between the pages of Jack's latest best-seller.

Talk about ironic.

When I finished, Jack gave me a long, penetrating look. "What else?"

"What makes you think there *is* anything else?"

Jack studied my face. "Call it a hunch."

I hesitated. "All right. The thing is, he talks really loud on the phone, and sometimes, the things I overhear aren't so great."

"Like what?"

I tried to shrug it off. "Just stuff about his past, that's all."

My face was still burning, and my palms were sweaty. I hadn't meant to tell Jack anything at all. And yet, irritation aside, it had felt surprisingly comforting to tell someone what was going on.

I mean, who knows? He might have *some* idea of what I could do.

Turns out, he didn't.

And why? It was because for whatever reason, he decided that it wouldn't be *me* handling it.

CHAPTER 6

Becka

With his gaze still on the condo, Jack said, "Wait here."

I blinked. "What do you mean?"

"I mean, wait in the car."

"For what?"

"For me to have a talk with him."

I was staring now. "Who? Nicky?"

"If that's the name of your roommate." And with that, Jack reached for the door handle.

"Wait!"

Jack turned back to me and said, "For what?"

"Well, don't you think we should discuss this?"

"We already did."

"But why should *you* do anything?"

He gave me a hard look. "Better me than you."

If only that were true. "But it's not your problem," I said. "It's *my* problem." I lifted my chin. "And I'm sure I'll solve it just fine. I mean, it's really not that big of a deal."

He made no reply, but his look said it all. *You're so full of it.*

Yes. I was.

But having *him* deal with it seemed wrong on so many levels. For one thing, I barely knew him. Why would he go to any trouble on my account?

Was it because of his friendship with Flynn?

That had to be it.

Still, I hated the thought of him fighting my battles. In fact, I hated the thought of *anyone* fighting my battles. This wasn't his mess to clean up. It was mine.

And yet, I heard myself say, "I just mean…." I bit my lip. "What are you gonna do?"

"That depends," he said.

"On what?"

"What *he* does."

"But he could be dangerous," I warned.

Jack gave a low scoff. "Doubt it."

I gave him a serious look. "Yeah, well for your information, he was in prison." Even though we were alone, I lowered my voice. "Maximum security."

At this, Jack had the nerve to laugh. "Yeah, right."

He had a nice laugh, full and warm – and oddly comforting. Still, it annoyed the snot out of me. *Didn't he know? This was no laughing matter.* "What, you don't believe me?"

"Oh, I believe you," he said. "But *him?* Not a chance."

"So you think he's lying?" I gave Jack another serious look. "Well, for your information, he wasn't."

"And you know this, how?"

"Because when he said it, he wasn't even talking to me." I paused. "I just happened to overhear, that's all."

Jack gave me a dubious look. "Uh-huh."

"I did," I insisted. "But it wasn't my fault. He was talking *really* loud."

Jack gave another scoff. "Now *that*, I believe."

Comforting or not, his confidence grated on me. It was like he thought he knew more about Nicky than I did.

I felt compelled to point out the obvious. "But you've never even met him."

"True." Jack gave me the cockiest smile I'd ever seen. "*And* he's never met *me*."

Cocky or not, the smile did funny things to my stomach – annoying things that had nothing to do with the fact that I hadn't eaten all day. I asked, "What does *that* mean?"

Ignoring my question, he reached yet again for the door handle.

Again, I blurted out, "Wait!" When Jack stopped to look, I said, "You don't have to do this. You know that, right?"

He gave me a look. "You done?"

"No." I straightened in my seat. "Because I'm coming with you."

Based on his attitude so far, I half expected him to argue. But he didn't. Instead, he gave a slow nod and said, "Backup. I like it."

I felt my gaze narrow. "You're making fun of me, aren't you?"

"Pretty much." And with that, he opened his car door, leaving me to follow – or not.

By the time we reached the front door, I was a trembling, nervous wreck. As I pulled out my keys, I said, "Are you sure you want to do this?"

"Hell yeah. It'll be fun."

I stopped to stare up at him. "I'm serious."

"So am I."

I felt my brow wrinkle in confusion. The way it looked, he actually meant it. And suddenly, I didn't know who was crazier – my psycho roommate or the guy who was planning to – well, I didn't know what exactly.

But the way it looked, I was about to find out.

CHAPTER 7

Jack

The guy was playing her. I'd bet his life on it.

Why he was doing it, I didn't know. But I'd find out soon enough.

And then, I'd deal with it.

Next to me, Becka whispered, "I don't think he's home." We were standing in the condo's living room, a few paces away from the front door. It was the same door we'd used less than a minute ago after Becka had pulled out her key.

As if I'd need a key to get in.

Still, I'd stepped aside and let her go through the motions, figuring it was better to play along than to get her thinking.

As far as the roommate, she was right. The guy had left twenty minutes earlier, slipping out the back while Becka had been watching the front.

I'd seen him do it.

I'd also seen him hop into a silver sports car – one that had been parked along a neighboring street. The guy had driven off smiling like he'd just screwed the neighbor's cat and gotten away with it.

Asshole.

Still, the guy was no hardened criminal. I could tell that just by looking at him – skinny arms, tight pants, and eyes that saw nothing that wasn't directly in front of him.

He hadn't even known I'd been watching.

Dumb-ass.

I looked to Becka and said, "Let's make sure."

She glanced around before whispering, "What do you mean?"

I might've told her that whispering was a waste, but the truth was, it was cute as hell. *And so was she.*

Her eyes were green, and her lashes were long – the real deal, nothing fake about them. Her hair was brown with flecks of gold, and her body was tight and sweet with soft curves in all the right places.

As far as her personality, she was a stubborn pain in the ass who was obviously too impulsive for her own good.

Still, I might've liked her if I were inclined to like anyone, which I wasn't.

It didn't matter. She was strictly off-limits.

She was the little sister of Flynn's fiancée, which meant that in a roundabout way, she was Flynn's sister, too – or *would* be after the wedding.

Girls came and went. But a strong friendship, that was permanent – which meant I'd be smart to keep my hands and thoughts to myself. *No drama. No complications. No losing a friend when things went South.*

I flicked my head toward the rear of the house. "First we'll check his bedroom."

She glanced toward the farthest door on the right. "Do you really think we should?"

"Why not?"

"It just seems kind of risky." She bit her lip. "Like, what if he's sleeping?"

"Then I'll wake him up."

With a nervous smile, she said, "You're joking, right?"

"No joke," I said. "But if you want, you can wait here."

"But…" She hesitated. "I'm just saying, that's a little invasive, don't you think?"

I gave her a good, long look. "Compared to what?"

"What do you mean?"

I considered everything she'd told me in the car. "Is it more invasive than what he's been doing to you?" My voice was steady, but my thoughts weren't.

Yeah, Becka wasn't *my* sister, but the guy had stepped way out of line. And Flynn was out of town, which meant that it was up to me to make things right.

Becka sighed. "I get your point, but it's not like he actually touched me or anything. And even that thing in the kitchen, maybe it was just…I dunno…bad timing on my part."

Bad timing, my ass. I said, "And the noises?"

"Maybe he was just joking around." She glanced toward the guy's bedroom. "And who knows? Maybe I'm making too much of it."

"Or maybe the guy's an asshole."

"Yeah, but even if he is, there's no law against that, is there?"

No. There wasn't.

Good thing for me.

I smiled. "But we're *not* the law, are we?" As I said it, I began striding down the hallway.

She hustled to keep up. "But wait, I'm still not sure–"

"Don't worry. *I* am."

One twist of the knob, and the door was open. *No lock. No nothing.* The guy really *was* a dumb-ass. And disorganized, too. Silently, I scanned the cluttered space, taking in the discarded clothes, the empty beer bottles, and a single jar of grape jelly sitting on the night stand.

Now that was interesting.

From beside me, Becka said, "Yikes. No wonder he keeps it shut."

I was still scanning the room. "And he's been living here for how long?"

Becka paused as if thinking. "I'm not sure. I just met him like five days ago."

What the hell? I turned to study her face. "You serious?"

She drew back. "What's *that* look for?"

"You moved in with a guy you don't even know?"

"Hey!" she said. "It's not like I *knew* it was a guy."

My gaze locked on hers. "You're not making it better."

"I don't *need* to 'make it better'," she said. "And I don't want to be rude or anything, but this really is none of your business."

"You sure about that?"

At this, a slow blush crept up her cheeks. "Just because I accepted your help, that doesn't mean you can act like I'm stupid or something."

She was missing my point. "Did I *call* you stupid?"

"No. But you're acting like I am."

"Yeah, well, you said it, not me." The truth was, if she were *my* sister, I'd be giving her an earful. But I had no sisters, including her. So I kept my mouth shut and made a mental note to tell Flynn that he was slacking in the brother department.

Becka sighed. "All right, fine. You want the truth? I'm just subletting the place – or half of it, I guess – from this girl I met in psych class."

"And you've known *her* for how long?"

"At least a semester," she said.

"That long, huh?"

"Yeah, point taken," she said, not looking too happy about it. "But about the condo, she said there was this roommate named Nicky who was really..." Becka made air quotes. "...'fun' and 'friendly.'"

"Right." If the guy had been any friendlier, I'd be having some fun of my own, beating him senseless. "That's one way to put it."

"No kidding," she said. "But anyway, Tara – that's her name – swore up and down that Nicky and I would really hit it off."

If I had a sister, there's no way in hell I would've let such a thing happen. In the back of my mind, I had to wonder, where the hell was Flynn in all of this? He should've been doing a better job of looking out for her.

She was still explaining. "And by the time I realized that Nicky was short for Nicholas – and *not* Nicole – it was too late."

"Too late for what?" I asked.

"To get out of the deal."

Not the way I saw things. "It's never too late."

"Oh yeah?" She crossed her arms. "Well, it is if you've already paid."

"You mean the rent?"

She nodded. "Three whole months. In advance, too."

Again, I thought of Flynn. The guy was loaded. He could wipe his ass with the cost of the whole city block and never miss a dime. *Why was Becka worrying about the rent?*

"Wait here," I said, heading into the guy's bedroom.

From the open doorway, Becka said, "But wait, shouldn't I—"

"Keep an eye out? Yeah, good idea." I didn't need a lookout, but I didn't need her trailing after me either.

As I took a closer look around, I asked a few more questions. In reply, Becka explained that the girl who'd rented her the condo was off on some college internship in Chicago, which is why the place had been available for the summer.

I wasn't buying it.

As Becka watched from the open doorway, I rifled through the guy's dresser drawers and then searched through his closet – keeping half an eye on Becka as I worked. From the look on her face, she wasn't liking any of this.

Too bad. Sometimes things need doing. And this was one of those times.

I finished by looking under the guy's bed and then between his mattresses. From start to finish, the entire process took me less than ten minutes.

I was just shoving the top mattress back in place when Becka said, "This is so wrong."

Maybe. But it wasn't nearly as wrong as what he'd been doing to *her.* The way I saw it, the guy was getting off light. *So far.*

When I made no reply, she said, "Seriously, we should stop."

I moved away from the bed. "All right."

She blinked. "Really?"

"Sure." I headed toward the doorway. "Whatever you say."

Her eyes narrowed. "You're only saying that because you're done, aren't you?"

"You could say that."

"It figures." She was quiet for a long moment before asking, "So… did you find anything?"

During my search, I'd revealed nothing and offered up no commentary. Now I eyed Becka with reluctant amusement. "What happened to 'This is so wrong'?"

"Well…" She shrugged. "If *you* know, I should know too, right?"

"Maybe," I said. "But first, I need you to do something."

"What?"

"Move your car."

CHAPTER 8

Becka

An hour later, I was sitting in the condo's living room with Jack. The room was dark and quiet, leaving me feeling unsettled for reasons that had nothing to do with my creepy roommate – who still hadn't returned from who-knows-where.

I was perched on the edge of the couch while Jack occupied the easy-chair across from me. It was a funny choice, considering that there was nothing easy about him *or* his demeanor.

His gaze was hard, and his jaw was tight. Just before sitting down, he'd turned the chair so it faced the front door, which meant that I had all the time in the world to study his profile through the shadows.

This *should've* been boring. But it wasn't. His profile was very fine, just like the rest of him. His legs were long, and his muscular arms were so defined, I swear, I could see hints of their lines and ridges, even in the near darkness.

But all of that was just a distraction.

Not only was he *not* telling me anything I needed to know, he'd continued to scoff at my insistence that I could handle this on my own. The last time I'd mentioned it, he'd told me – and I quote – *"Sorry, not gonna happen."*

But he hadn't *sounded* sorry, not even when I'd suggested that all of this was taking way too long. Afterward, I'd gone on to remind him that he had someone waiting for him – a scantily clad someone, not that I'd mentioned *that* part.

But Jack wasn't budging. And he *still* wasn't telling me squat.

For what felt like the millionth time, I said, "So, are you gonna tell me what you found in his bedroom?"

"Yeah, but not now."

"Why not?" I asked.

"Plausible deniability."

"What?"

"If you're asked, you can say you don't know."

I made a sound of frustration. "If I'm asked by who?"

"Whoever."

"But you promised to tell me."

"Yeah. And I will."

"When?" I asked.

"When this is done."

"When *what's* done?"

"This."

Well that was informative.

Apparently, he was determined to keep me totally in the dark – *pun intended.* And, to make matters worse, I'd been trying to reach my sister for at least three hours now. But her phone kept going straight to voicemail.

After yet another unsuccessful try, I shoved my cell phone back into my pocket and said to Jack, "And you never *did* tell me where Flynn is."

His gaze was still on the door. "I know."

"Yeah. *I* know, too. Which is why I'm asking again. *Where* is he?"

Jack glanced at his watch before saying, "Seventeen minutes."

"What?"

"Ask me in seventeen minutes."

I didn't get it. "Why seventeen minutes?"

"Because that's when I'll tell you."

Great. More circular reasoning. My teeth were grinding now. "Just to make sure I understand, you're saying that in seventeen minutes, you'll tell me where Flynn is *and* why you couldn't tell me sooner?"

When his only reply was a silent nod, I muttered, "Fine, but just so you know, the clock's ticking."

He spared me half a glance. "Thanks for the warning."

He wasn't thankful. He was sarcastic. And stubborn. And way too mysterious for my liking.

Looking to make a point, I pulled out my cell phone yet again and announced, "I'm setting a timer."

He gave a slow nod. "Good idea."

Didn't he get it? I *wasn't* bluffing. I scrolled across the screen and set an alarm for exactly seventeen minutes. As I did, I said, "And you *do* realize, we're probably waiting around for nothing, right?"

When Jack made no reply, I persisted, "Seriously, we don't even know how long Nicky's been gone."

"Ninety minutes."

I blinked. "What?"

"Ninety minutes," he repeated. "That's how long he's been gone."

Stunned, I leaned forward on the couch. "Wait. How would you know?"

"I saw him leave."

My mouth fell open. *Seriously?*

With growing indignation, I studied his profile. The way it looked, he wasn't kidding. Through clenched teeth, I said, "What exactly do you mean?"

"I mean I saw him climb out the back window at seven forty-five."

Un-freaking-believable. "And you didn't think to tell me?"

He was still eyeballing the door. With a tight shrug, he replied, "Sure. I thought about it."

"But…?"

"But if you knew the guy was gone, you might've come in alone." He turned and gave me a serious look. "Unescorted."

Oh, so now I needed an escort?

To my own place?

I wasn't sure if I should be flattered or insulted. "So?"

"So that would've been a mistake. And you damn well know it."

Talk about arrogant.

Or obnoxiously chivalrous.

I just didn't know which.

Sometime within the past hour, I'd practically forgotten that he was Jack Ward, the author I'd been idolizing for years. *And why?* It was because he was so totally impossible.

Plus, he wasn't *acting* like a bigtime author. He was acting like, well, an obnoxious older brother, that's what.

I didn't have any brothers. I didn't even have a dad. My own had died when I'd been just a toddler. And his sorry replacement – a stepdad that made my creepy roommate look peachy in comparison – had been a total horror show.

To Jack's latest statement, I said yet again, "But for all we know he's not even coming back, at least not tonight."

Already, we'd been sitting here for a lot longer than I'd anticipated. When our vigil had started, it had still been light outside. Now, the only illumination in the condo came from a streetlight out front. And even *this* pathetic light was mostly obscured by the closed window blinds.

Probably I should've been thankful. If it weren't for that lone streetlight, we'd be sitting in total darkness.

And why? It was because Jack had absolutely refused to let me turn on even a single interior light.

Maybe I was stupid for listening to him, much less trusting him, but honestly, I didn't know what else to do. It's not like I had a better idea.

Still, the longer this went on, the more foolish I felt. Maybe I was making too much of Nicky's antics. After all, it's not like he'd assaulted me or anything.

Jack returned his attention to the door. "Don't worry. He'll be back."

At this, I had to scoff. "That's seven, you know."

"Seven what?"

"Seven times you've told me not to worry."

"You were counting?"

Going for a joke, I said, "Yeah, and I can spell, too."

His gaze shifted once again in my direction. From the look on his face, he didn't see the humor.

I cleared my throat. "I just mean, I can count *and* spell. Get it?"

He looked back to the door. "Don't worry. I got it."

Under my breath, I muttered, "Eight."

As far as the spelling thing, for some stupid reason, I couldn't let it go. "I mean, I probably don't spell as well as *you* do, since you're a bestselling author and all." I tried to laugh. "But hey, I can spell 'cat' with the best of them."

Cat? Good grief. Here I was three years into an English degree, and *this* was the best I could do?

He said, "I'll keep that in mind."

Damn it. I was making a total ass of myself. Even calling him "bestselling" – it was a massive understatement. He was, after all, Jack Ward – the guy who'd sold so many books, they could probably encircle the Earth several times over.

The guy was a billionaire, and not only from his books. According to my sister, he'd also made a fortune on all of the merchandise related to his novels – which featured a breathtaking blend of sword and sorcery along with old fashioned kings and castles.

His fictional world was brutal – but surprisingly just – in a head-lopping sort of way.

Maybe that explained it – his stubborn chivalry or whatever this was. I mean, he didn't *have* to be sitting here, dealing with a problem that wasn't even his own.

Still, he was making me just a little bit crazy.

Unable to stop myself, I said, "And just so you know, I can spell more than cat. Actually, I'm getting a degree in English lit."

In theory, anyway. I was twenty-four years old. I should've already graduated. But until just last year, I'd been attending only part-time, scratching out credits whenever I could.

Jack was silent for a long moment before saying, "Do me a favor."

I almost winced. *Oh, God.* He was going to tell me to shut up. All things considered, that probably wasn't such a terrible idea. *Still, how humiliating would that be?*

Bracing myself, I asked, "What kind of favor?"

"Find me a pencil."

I did a double-take. "What, why?"

"Just do it," he said. "Please."

"I'm not even sure I have one," I admitted. "Will a pen work?"

"No. But I need it now, okay?"

"For what?" I asked.

"When you find it, I'll show you."

Sure he would. "But what if I can't find one."

"Then look harder."

Beyond curious, I pushed myself off the couch and headed toward my bedroom. It was where I kept my notebook computer and other assorted supplies. If I had a pencil – which I highly doubted – that's where I'd find it.

As I left the living room, he said, "And remember, no lights, okay?"

I hadn't needed the reminder. Still, I couldn't help but think that he'd just given me an impossible task. Instead of finding a needle in a haystack, I'd be searching for a pencil in the darkness.

I never found it.

And why?

It was because I'd barely begun my search when I heard the unmistakable sound of the front door swinging open, followed by a quick slam and a sudden yelp of the human variety.

With a gasp, I whirled toward the sound. *What the hell?*

CHAPTER 9

Becka

I rushed from my bedroom only to stop in mid-motion at the sight of Jack holding Nicky by his throat. Nicky's back was pressed up against the front door while Jack held him in place, using one steady hand.

Nicky was sputtering something that I couldn't quite catch.

I dove for the nearest light switch and flicked on the lights as I called out, "What's going on?"

As my eyes adjusted to the light, Jack turned to me and asked, "You find the pencil?"

I was still blinking. "What?"

"The pencil," he said. "Did you find it?"

"No."

"Then keep looking."

I felt my gaze narrow. "You don't even need it, do you?"

His gaze shifted to Nicky. "Hey, you never know."

Okay, I didn't even want to speculate what he meant by that. *But forget the pencil.* I strode forward. "What are you doing, anyway?"

"Talking to your roommate."

If this was Jack's idea of a conversation, I hardly knew what to say. "You are not."

Against the door, Nicky was still babbling, which I was actually glad to hear. If nothing else, it meant that he was still breathing. *That was good, right?*

When Nicky saw me looking, he squeaked, "Call the police!"

Yeah, right.

It's not like I was glad to see him getting assaulted, but I wasn't that kind of person – the kind who'd accept help, only to stab the helper in the back the moment things got sticky.

And yet, this was a lot stickier than I'd ever envisioned.

I was still trying to come up with a decent response when Jack said, "Good idea."

I turned and gave Jack a questioning look. "It is?"

"Sure," he said. "I bet they'd love to see those vials in the bottom drawer."

I wasn't following. "What vials?"

Jack replied, "Ask your roommate."

I looked to Nicky. "What does he mean?"

Nicky gave a hard swallow. "Nothing."

With something that looked suspiciously like amusement, Jack said, "It didn't look like nothing to me. So tell me, who's Edna?"

Nicky made a sorry attempt at shaking his head. "What?"

"Edna Flake," Jack said. "The name on a prescription."

"She's, uh, my grandma."

"Nope. Try again."

"Hey!" Nicky sputtered. "I think I'd know my own grandma's name."

"Yeah?" Jack said. "And what about Marcus Jones? Or Jan Corben?"

Nicky tried – and failed – to look clueless. "What?"

"Or Maurice Brooks?" Jack said. "Is he your grandma, too?"

Nicky sucked in a ragged breath. "I don't know what you're talking about."

Oddly enough, *I* did. It wasn't hard to figure out that Nicky was collecting prescriptions and plenty of them. *But where on Earth was he getting them?*

Jack gave Nicky a cold smile. "Right."

Nicky turned accusing eyes in my direction. "What the fuck? You went through my stuff?"

Technically, I hadn't. But that was beside the point. "Even if I did," I said, "at least I didn't steal anything." *Unlike you.*

But I didn't say that last part, because even now, I couldn't be completely sure that Nicky was the one who'd robbed me. Still, he *was* my number-one suspect, which went a long way in explaining why my sympathy was running low.

I hated thieves, especially after my stepdad had robbed half the town with his shady dealings.

Jack spoke up. "Hey asshole. You're not talking to *her*. You're talking to *me*. Remember?"

As Nicky nodded, I stared stupidly from the sidelines. I wanted to say something to dial things down, but I didn't know what. For all of Jack's menace, he looked in absolute control, which only made him ten times more terrifying.

Again, I asked myself who *was* he, really? At that moment, I had no idea.

I edged closer to Jack and said, "Maybe you should let go – of his throat, I mean."

With a low scoff, he replied, "Yeah? Why's that?"

Wasn't it obvious? "Because it's hard for us to talk when you're choking him."

"If I were choking him," Jack said, "I'd have been done thirty seconds ago."

Yikes. "Okaaaaaay. But seriously, this *wasn't* what I had in mind."

Jack gave me a long, inscrutable look. "So, about that pencil—"

"Forget the pencil," I said. "I'm just saying, maybe we could dial it down a notch?" I gave him a desperate look. "Please?"

Nicky squeaked, "Yeah. Like what the hell, dude?"

Jack's gaze snapped in his direction. "So, tell me..." His voice hardened. "Are you gonna show us?"

Nicky stared in obvious confusion. "Show you what?"

Jack glanced down. "Your cock."

I stifled a gasp. "What?"

Jack didn't even look in my direction. Instead, he leaned a fraction closer to Nicky and said, "I hear you like that sort of thing. So, go ahead. Drop your pants. We'll wait."

I blurted out, "No!"

Jack turned to me in mock confusion. "No? You sure?"

"No," I repeated. "I mean, I don't want to see anything." *Cripes, I hadn't wanted to see it the first time.*

"Right," Jack said, turning once again to Nicky. "You catch that?"

Nicky nodded so hard, I was half-surprised he didn't choke *himself.*

But Jack still wasn't done. In a voice filled with menace, he told Nicky, "And let's get one thing straight, you're done hassling her. Got it?"

Again, Nicky nodded.

Still, Jack continued. "No calling her. No texting her. No saying 'hi' if you pass her on the street. She doesn't exist. And neither do I. You understand?"

After another frantic nod from Nicky, Jack finally let go. When he did, Nicky stumbled sideways with a long, unsteady breath and then bolted straight for his bedroom. Once inside, he slammed the door so hard, I swear, the whole condo shook.

As I stared after him, I asked, "What's he doing?"

"My guess?" Jack said. "Climbing out the back window."

I turned to face him. "What?"

"Wouldn't be the first time."

By now, I was nearly speechless.

For all the drama, nothing was solved, not really. Okay, sure, Nicky was suitably terrified and would probably avoid me from now on. But now, I had trouble of a different kind.

After that little scene at the door, I couldn't stay here another night. But I had to sleep *somewhere.* And there was no way on Earth I could leave my things unattended, not here, anyway.

Again, I asked myself, *What now?*

I was still trying to figure it out when Jack said, "Pack your stuff. We're leaving."

CHAPTER 10

Jack

She stared up at me. "We?"

Yes. We. Because I wasn't leaving until she did. "If you need boxes, let me know. I'll have some delivered."

"But..." She shook her head. "Who'd do that?"

"Do what?"

"Deliver boxes. I mean, nothing's open."

For the right price, everything was open. And whatever the price was, I'd pay it, not a problem. But she was wasting time.

I asked, "Do you need them or not?"

"No."

"Good. Then get packing."

She was frowning now. "Don't you think that's kind of bossy? I mean, I never said for sure that I'm moving."

Wrong.

She was moving, all right. Yeah, she wasn't *my* sister, but if I let her stay, and things went South, I'd be kicking myself later on.

I told her, "Well you're not staying. I can tell you that."

She glanced around, but still made no move. Earlier, she'd mentioned that she'd been living here for only a couple of weeks, which meant there was no need for a long goodbye.

I said, "Becka."

She jumped at the sound of her name. "What?"

"You're not packing."

"I know, because I'm thinking."

"So do both."

She sighed. "Just stop it, all right?"

"Stop what?"

"Stop badgering me. Listen, I'm not stupid. I know I can't stay. I'm just trying to figure out…" She blinked, and her eyes filled with tears. "…well, where I'm going next."

Shit.

The goal wasn't to make her cry. It was to get her moving. Deliberately, I softened my tone. "Listen, we'll go to Flynn's and work it out, all right?"

She gave a choked laugh. "Yeah, I'm sure your friend would just love that."

"If you mean Flynn, yeah, he would."

"I don't mean Flynn," she said. "I mean, your, um, girlfriend, I guess."

"She's not my girlfriend." *Or my friend – not after I'd sent her away with enough rudeness to keep her gone.*

Becka replied, "Yeah, but she's something. And I don't think she'll be any happier to see me now than she was the first time."

"It doesn't matter," I said. "She's gone." *Good thing, too.* But even if Imogen *weren't* gone, she wouldn't be getting a vote.

If I knew Flynn – and I did – he'd kick Imogen out on her world-famous ass before he'd ever let his fiancee's little sister go wanting.

Becka's eyebrows furrowed. "Seriously? Where'd she go?"

I didn't know. And I didn't care. All I knew was that I'd put her into the limo personally and watched it disappear down the dusty road. But hey, I was willing to speculate. "My guess? The airport."

"So you don't know for sure?"

I gave Becka a serious look. "The only thing *I* know is that you're not packing. You want some help?"

"From you?" She gave a shaky laugh. "I don't think so."

"Why not?"

She looked toward her bedroom. "No reason."

I looked in the same direction. Her bedroom door was open, but from this angle, I couldn't see inside.

Becka was hiding something. That much was obvious. What it was, I didn't know, and didn't have time to dwell on it. I made a show of looking at my watch. As I did, a loud beep sounded from Becka's pocket.

She reached into it and yanked out her cell phone. She glanced at the display and then turned the screen outward to face me. "Time's up."

I didn't bother looking. "Obviously."

"It's been seventeen minutes," she said. "You owe me answers, remember?"

I remembered. But we were wasting time. "Pack your stuff, and I'll tell you in the car."

"No," she said. "I don't think so."

I stared down at her. "What?"

"You promised to tell me now." She crossed her arms. "Where's Flynn?" Her voice rose. "And while we're at it, where's my sister?"

CHAPTER 11

Becka

From the look on Jack's face, he wasn't thrilled to be put on the spot. *But so what?* When *I* made a promise, I stuck to it. And I expected others to do the same.

Plus, I was getting more than a little worried. Something was definitely going on, and I was desperate to know what. I gave him a no-nonsense look. "Well?"

With a low curse, he said, "All right. Here's the condensed version. Flynn bought an island."

If so, that was news to me. "What?"

"An island," he said. "A piece of land surrounded by water."

Oh, for God's sake. "I *know* what an island is. I'm just surprised, that's all." But of course, it shouldn't have been terribly shocking. Flynn was a billionaire. Probably he could buy a bunch of islands if that's what he wanted.

"And," Jack said, "it's a surprise."

"For who?"

He gave me a look. "You wanna guess?"

"Oh. You mean for my sister?"

"Well, it wasn't for Imogen, if that's your other guess."

"Imogen?" *What did the floozy have to do with this?*

His jaw tightened. "You know, the girl you thought he was screwing."

I didn't appreciate his tone. "What was I supposed to think?"

"Not that."

"Oh come on!" I protested. "I go to Flynn's house, and I see a half-naked chick in the doorway, when my sister's out of town, no less. You've got to admit, it looked pretty bad."

"So you think he's a cheater."

I couldn't help but notice that Jack hadn't phrased it as a question. *So, who was assuming things now?* I coldly informed him, "I never said that."

"You didn't have to," he said. "Now answer the question."

"What question?"

Speaking very clearly, he said, "Do you think he's a cheater?"

Under his penetrating gaze, part of me wanted to wilt. But the other part? Well, *that* part was getting just a little bit ticked off.

"Just so you know," I said, "you didn't phrase it as a question."

Jack frowned. "What?"

"The first time you asked, you forgot the question mark." Lowering my voice, I did my best Jack Ward impression. "So you think he's a cheater." I gave him a stiff smile. "See, that's not a question. It's a statement. *And*, it just seems to me, as a writer you'd know the difference."

From look on his face, he wasn't amused. "Okay, so I'm *asking* now, do you think he's a cheater?"

Damn it. For reasons that I couldn't quite fathom, I didn't want to answer. Still, I grudgingly replied, "No."

Oddly enough, this was true. I didn't think very highly of movie stars in general, but Flynn was different. He was scarily tough and more reclusive than any person I'd ever met. And I *knew* beyond a doubt that he was crazy about my sister.

But didn't Jack get it? That was part of the reason I'd been so angry. I'd been so shocked, I could hardly think.

Jack made a forwarding motion with his hand. "But…?"

"But what?"

"But you still thought he was cheating."

When I made no reply, Jack said, "So, what were you gonna do? Call your sister? Get her all worked up for nothing?"

"Wait a minute," I said. "Was *that* why you wouldn't tell me anything? Because you thought I was going to cause some sort of trouble?"

"No," he said. "I *knew* you were gonna cause trouble."

Well, someone was overly sure of himself. "Oh yeah?" I said. "How?"

"By selling your sister a load of garbage."

"In case you didn't notice," I said, "I didn't 'sell' her anything. No. What *I* did was come up to the freaking door and demand some answers, which your 'non-girlfriend' refused to provide."

Jack's eyebrows furrowed, but he made no reply.

Undaunted, I continued. "Oh yeah. I asked her flat-out what she was doing there. And what does she tell me? She says that it's none of my business, even *after* I tell her who I am and who I'm looking for. I mean, seriously, she could've said, 'Oh hey, no need to worry. I'm here with Jack Ward. I'm screwing *him* and not your future brother-in-law.' But does she do that? *No.* What *she* does is act all sly and sneaky, like she's got something to hide."

At the mental image, my voice rose to a new crescendo. "Which, when you think about it, is pretty ironic, considering that she wasn't hiding anything, including her shaved pussy!"

As that final word echoed out between us, I stifled a gasp. *Crap.* I'd said way more than I'd originally planned, especially that last part.

Beyond embarrassed, I turned away, intending to march into my bedroom and get packing – not because I planned to leave with Jack Ward, but because I *had* to pack regardless of where I was going.

And *this*, in a roundabout way, was Jack's fault, too. I mean, yeah, my situation sucked, but now any chance of staying, even for one more night was completely out the window – just like my druggie roommate, assuming Jack was right.

As all of these thoughts swirled in my head, I stomped away, only to pause halfway to my bedroom when it suddenly struck me that I'd never received a full explanation.

I whirled back to face him and said, "Hah! I bet you think you think you're getting off the hook."

He was standing in the same spot, eyeing me with an expression that I couldn't quite decipher. "What hook?" he said.

With renewed determination, I marched back to him and said, "The explanation. You owe me the rest."

"The rest?"

"Yes. You said you'd tell me where Flynn was –"

"Which I did."

I gave him a stiff smile. "Just so know, you didn't actually. But hey, I can figure out for myself that he's probably at this so-called island."

"Which he is. Or will be shortly."

"Fine, whatever. But you never told me the other half."

"What other half?"

As if he didn't know. "You were going to tell me where Flynn was *and* why you couldn't tell me sooner." I made a vague waving motion with my hands. "Unless you were pulling that seventeen-minute thing out of thin air."

"Which I wasn't."

We'll see about that.

I gave him an expectant look and waited.

"All right," he finally said. "The reason I didn't tell you sooner was because they were still within cell reach."

I didn't get it. "What?"

"I knew the flight path," he said.

I *still* wasn't following. "So?"

"So I knew they'd be out of normal cell range at nine forty-five." He glanced at his watch. "Meaning now."

Huh?

I'd been trying to contact Anna for hours, but that was beside the point. I still didn't know what exactly he was getting at. "So?" I said yet again.

"So if you didn't know Flynn's destination, you couldn't tell it to your sister." He gave a tight shrug. "But now you *can't* blab, because she's out of range."

Blab? Seriously? I'd read all of Jack's books, multiple times. Nowhere in any of them did the word "blab" appear. And regardless of what he thought, I *wasn't* a blabber.

Through gritted teeth, I said, "So let me get this straight. You didn't tell me because you thought I'd ruin the surprise for my only sister?"

"You might've."

I was beyond insulted. "But why would I do that?"

He gave another shrug. "Got me."

As I glared up at him, I considered the ramifications of what I'd just learned. Originally, my sister had been planning to fly back here in just a couple of days, after getting our mom settled. But the way it sounded now, Flynn had surprised her in Wyoming and then had whisked her away to some private island.

But for how long?

Earlier at Flynn's place, Jack had implied that Flynn would be out of town for a month. *Did that apply to my sister, too?*

Regardless, this explained so much – why Jack had refused to say where Flynn was, why my sister hadn't known that Flynn *wasn't* here in town, *and* why she hadn't been answering her cell phone during the last few hours.

Obviously, she was on his private jet. And if I knew my sister, she would've turned off her cell phone just to be safe.

As these realizations hit home, I had to ask myself that same horrible question that I'd been asking all day.

Now what?

All along, I'd been counting on Anna returning soon, giving me the chance to crash with her for a few days, just until I figured out what to do.

Now, I was completely on my own, except for Jack Ward, of course, who was looking more irritated than ever.

At me?

It sure looked that way.

CHAPTER 12

Jack

I should've known.

From what I'd just heard, Imogen had stirred up more trouble than I'd realized. I recalled her standing in Flynn's entryway, pretending to be surprised that Becka was Anna's little sister.

Now, come to find out, she'd already known, courtesy of Becka herself.

I should've caught that. But I hadn't. And now I was dealing with the fallout.

And Flynn – what the hell?

For years, he'd been a miserable bastard – pissed off at the world and not bothering to hide it. Now his head was so far up his love-addled ass that he'd left his fiancee's little sister flailing in the wind.

And she *was* flailing. Make no mistake about that.

In the quiet condo, she glared up at me like *I* was the one who'd screwed her over.

Maybe I had.

I'd been a dick from the get-go, but that hadn't been my intention. The truth was, I wasn't big on trusting people, and I'd been determined to play it smart. This included not giving anyone the ammo to mess up Flynn's plans.

What a cluster.

But there was still time to fix it.

I looked to Anna and said, "How much of this stuff is yours?"

She glanced around the condo. "Not a lot."

"Good."

"Why is that good?"

"Quicker to pack."

"Yeah, about that…" She blinked long and hard. "Listen, you don't have to stick around, okay? Like I said, there's not much stuff, so…" She gave a loose shrug and didn't bother finishing the sentence.

It was a hint, or maybe a dismissal. Choosing to ignore it, I said, "Wait here. I'll pull my car into the driveway."

"But why?"

"So we can load it up. And your car too if it's needed."

She bit her lip. "But I just told you, you don't have to stick around. I mean, I'm sure it'll be fine." She tried for a smile. "I've got friends in the area, so…" Again, she didn't finish.

I knew why. *She was full of it.*

I gave her a serious look. "Yeah? And where are they?"

Her mouth tightened. "I *do* have them, you know."

"Right."

"Look, I can tell that you don't believe me, but I do have friends." She blinked a few more times before continuing. "It's just that, well, Vicky and Sarah are away at college, and Chelsie's doing this work-study thing in Japan. And you *know* that Anna's gone. So I'm a little short at the moment, that's all."

Again, she looked around. "And as far as anyone else, I'm not gonna show up on their doorstep with my suitcases. Or boxes, or whatever."

"Good," I said. "Because you don't have to. We'll go back to your sister's place. Like I said, we'll figure it out."

"But that place *isn't* my sister's. It's *Flynn's*. He's the one who owns it, not her."

"So?"

"So it's one thing if I'm staying with my sister, but don't you think it's kind of rude to move into Flynn's house when he's not even there? And it's not like I can call to ask him either."

"You don't need to ask," I said. "You're family, right?"

"Yeah." She rolled her eyes. "The leachy kind."

"Leachy how?"

"Actually, I don't *want* to be leachy. That's the whole point."

I wasn't following, but it didn't matter. "Trust me," I said. "I've known him longer than you."

"So?"

"So I'm telling you, it's not a problem."

"But you can't be sure."

She was wrong.

But hey, if she needed reassurance, I could do that, too. "I'll call him," I said. "Not a big deal."

"But I don't *want* you to call him."

"Why not?"

"Because I don't want Anna to worry *or* feel the need to rush home."

"So I'll tell Flynn to keep it just between us."

But already, she was shaking her head. "No way. I'm not gonna be the cause of secrets between them."

"You wouldn't be," I said. "*I* would."

"Yeah, but that's just a technicality. And besides, you couldn't call him anyway. Neither of us can, because like you said, they're out of cell range."

"Not with a satellite phone."

She hesitated. "You have one?"

I did, but that wasn't the issue. "I meant Flynn's satellite phone. I've got the number."

From the look on her face, she wasn't glad to hear it.

I asked, "What's the problem?"

"I already told you. I don't *want* you calling them." She glanced toward the front door. "Look, why don't you just leave, and I'll figure it out, okay?"

I didn't budge. "Sorry, that's not happening."

"But why not?"

I glanced toward her roommate's bedroom. "You've gotta ask?"

She turned and gave his door a long worried look before murmuring, "Yeah, but he's probably gone, like you said."

"You think he's gonna *stay* gone?"

Again she looked toward his bedroom door. "You never know." From the look on her face, she didn't believe this any more than I did.

"Listen," I said. "You don't have to decide now. But you *do* have to pack. We both know that, right?"

When she gave a reluctant nod, I said, "And you'll need some help loading it. So let's just start there, okay?"

When she gave another nod, I said, "You pack. I'll get my car. One step at a time, all right?"

When she made no reply, I took that as a yes. Good thing, too, because whether she realized it or not, I wasn't leaving without her.

CHAPTER 13

Becka

I was pretty sure he'd tricked me.

I was slumped in the passenger's seat of Jack's car – or rather the car he'd obviously borrowed from Flynn's garage. I'd seen the vehicle before. It was a dark sedan that Flynn rarely drove.

The city limits were long behind us, and we'd been traveling in silence for nearly twenty minutes now. Soon, we would reach Flynn's place. *And then what?*

As we turned down the final secluded road, I gave Jack a long sideways look. His posture was relaxed as he controlled the car with one hand draped casually over the steering wheel. Casual or not, he looked stupidly good, all lean and muscular, with an annoying degree of confidence.

But why *wouldn't* he be confident? He was rich and famous, and so insanely good-looking, it was a wonder I hadn't shown up earlier to find a *dozen* half-naked girls vying for his attention.

But of course *he'd* been half-naked too. In my mind, I could still see him standing there, shirtless, with his washboard abs and chiseled pecs. I felt my tongue dart out between my lips. *Nice shoulders, too.*

Damn it. This *wasn't* what I should be thinking of – or picturing in my mind. *Over and over.*

Going for a distraction, I broke the silence between us. "You really didn't have to do that, you know."

With his gaze still on the road, he replied, "Do what?"

I gave a nervous laugh. "Drag me out of there."

"Trust me. If I'd dragged you, you would've noticed."

I gave him another sideways glance. *Oh, yeah.* I would've definitely noticed, especially if he weren't wearing a shirt.

I gave myself a mental slap. *Oh, for God's sake.*
Enough already.

As far as the rest, technically Jack was right. He hadn't dragged me anywhere. No, what *he'd* done was prod me along one step at a time until I was sitting in the passenger's seat with all of my stuff loaded in the back.

He'd even talked me into riding in the same vehicle by promising to have someone deliver my own car to Flynn's place later on.

All in all, he'd been pretty darn crafty.

But who was I kidding? I'd *let* myself get prodded along because I didn't know what else to do. *Cripes, I still didn't know.*

As if reading my mind, Jack said, "What we'll do is crash at Flynn's for the night and figure it out in the morning, all right?"

He was being surprisingly nice, and I tried to smile. "Technically, *you* don't have to figure out anything. I'll be fine. But hey, thanks for the help."

He gave me a long sideways look, but said nothing.

I winced. "I guess I should've thanked you sooner, huh?"

He returned his gaze to the road. "That's not what I was thinking."

"Then what *were* you thinking?" I asked.

"Fuck."

The word made me jump in my seat. "Excuse me?"

"Sorry."

More confused than ever, I studied his face in profile. "So…" *What was I missing?* "You're sorry for swearing, or—"

"Yeah," he said. "And *that.*"

His gaze was still on the road, and I turned to look. Already, we were pulling up to Flynn's estate. But that wasn't the thing that made me pause. It was the sight of a long, dark limo idling outside the big iron gate.

I frowned in confusion. The limo was parallel parked, blocking the gate entirely. Until it moved, we'd have no way to get inside, not unless we abandoned the car.

I looked to Jack. "Were you expecting someone?"

"No." His voice hardened. "But I should've been."

CHAPTER 14

Jack

I knew damn well who was in that limo, and now I had to make a decision. *Stop? Or keep going?*

In the end, the call wasn't hard. *Running wasn't my style.* But the timing? *Yeah, it could've been better.*

By the time I pulled the car to a stop, Imogen was already climbing out of the limo's nearest back door. She was wearing the same lingerie getup as earlier, minus the coat that I'd draped over her exposed shoulders hours ago, when the limo had picked her up.

As I shifted the car into park, I glanced at the limo's license plate and gave a quiet scoff. *Same damn limo.*

Under the glare of my headlights, Imogen looked nearly naked, and I gave her a long, careful look.

Huh. Becka was right.

I *could* see Imogen's pussy. *Not shaved. Waxed.* Not that it mattered. The truth was, I preferred a more natural look, and this wasn't it.

I looked at Becka and said, "Wait here."

She gave the limo a worried glance. "But what are you gonna do? Like, do you need help or something?"

Help dealing with my ex?

No thanks.

I turned away. "No. I've got this. Don't worry."

I left the driver's seat and shut the car door behind me. As I did, Imogen stalked forward and said, "I knew it!"

I gave her a look. "You knew what?"

She pointed toward my passenger's seat. "I knew you and her had a thing."

If so, that made one of us.

But hey, I didn't owe Imogen an explanation. *We were over, period.* Hell, we'd been over for weeks now.

I passed her without comment and strode to the limo's driver's side door. I rapped on the glass, and when it slid down, I told the driver, "You need to move."

The driver was a doughy guy named Randy. He wore no nametag, but he didn't need one. I'd heard his name plenty of times already, thanks to a viral video that had been captured several months ago outside this very same gate.

More to the point, I'd met him in person earlier today when I'd told him to take Imogen wherever. *Anywhere but here.*

From the driver's seat, he gave me an apologetic smile. "Sorry."

I didn't need an apology. I needed him to get out of my way. "The limo," I said. "You need to move it. *Now.*"

He winced. "I, uh, can't."

He was wrong.

He could. And he would.

I leaned closer. "You wanna tell me why?"

Imogen sidled up to me and announced, "Because I *told* him to wait right here. *That's* why."

Without bothering to reply, I said to Randy, "You can wait all you want, *after* you let us through."

He cleared his throat. "Yeah, about that…" His gaze shifted to Imogen. "I, uh, don't have the key."

I looked to Imogen. "Give him the key."

She smiled. "What makes you think I have it?"

It wasn't hard to figure out. Still, I was a curious guy. I looked to Randy and asked, "How the hell did she get the key?"

From the sidelines, Imogen said, "Hey! You still don't know that I have it."

Oh, I knew.

Randy said, "We were sitting together up front. That's all." His face broke into a sudden grin. "Getting to know each other."

"Hey!" Imogen said yet again. "It wasn't the way *you're* making it sound!" She looked to me and said, "We were just visiting. That's all."

Right. Because Imogen just loved to visit with "the help," as she called them.

Randy spoke up. "See? That's what I said, too."

Imogen gave him an irritated look. "Yeah, but you made it sound way worse."

A funny thing about Imogen, when she got agitated, her high-dollar accent was shaky at best. It was shaky now and getting shakier with every passing word.

As if looking to prove the point, she told Randy, "I mean, it's not like I was blowing you or anything."

She could blow him *and* half of the town for all I cared. All I wanted was to get the limo out of my way.

I looked to Imogen and said, "Wait here."

"But—"

"I'll be right back." I turned away, heading toward the car I'd been driving. I strode to the passenger's side door and opened it up. As I did, Becka gave me a perplexed look.

I explained, "I just need to grab something out of the glove compartment."

Normally I wasn't one to explain myself, but hey, the storage was in her space, and the last thing I wanted was for her to bolt.

As she watched, I reached into the car and opened the glove compartment. Sure enough, there was a screwdriver buried under some paperwork. I pulled it out and slammed the compartment shut.

Becka frowned. "What do you need *that* for?"

"I'll be right back."

"Hey, you didn't answer my question."

"I'll tell you when I'm done."

"Done with what?" she asked.

I flicked my head toward the limo. "Getting them out of our way."

She gave the limo a worried glance. "You're not going to hurt them or anything, are you?"

If I was, I wouldn't need a screwdriver to do it. But that wasn't worth mentioning, so all I said was, "No." I shoved the screwdriver into my back pocket and turned away, shutting the passenger's side door behind me.

When I returned to the limo, Imogen and Randy were still arguing back and forth.

Imogen was saying, "I did *not* grab your crotch!"

From the driver's seat, Randy said, "Hey, I'm not complaining. I kind of liked it."

Imogen looked to me and explained, "I was just getting the key out of his pocket, that's all. He's reading way more into it."

Randy gave Imogen a perplexed look. "Hey, how come you're not English anymore?"

"Oh, screw you!" she said.

"I was just askin'…"

I moved between them and looked to Randy. "Get out."

He blinked. "What, why?"

"Because I'm gonna move it myself."

"The limo?" He frowned. "But you don't have the key."

Imogen grabbed my elbow. "Seriously, you saw where I was sitting when you drove up, right? I mean, I wasn't sitting up front. I was sitting in the back by myself. All alone."

Yeah. Her and the car key.

It didn't matter. I was only half-listening. "Good to know." I gave Randy a look. "Now, are you gonna get out or not?"

His eyebrows furrowed. "I don't think I should."

That's what he thought. "Why not?"

"Because the *last* time I got out at this gate, my limo got all smashed up."

Yeah. I'd seen the footage, along with a few million other people. But that was then. This was now. I replied, "Don't worry, I'm not gonna smash it." *Or at least, not most of it.*

Imogen looked to Randy and said, "He will, too. He smashes limos all the time."

If the guy believed *that*, he was more clueless than he looked. But it didn't matter. *He* wasn't my primary problem.

I turned and gave Imogen a look. "Your accent – he's right. It's slipping."

"Sorry, what?"

"Your English accent," I said. "It's getting sloppy."

She drew back. "Pardon?"

"You heard me."

With all the dignity of a duchess, she announced, "I don't know what you're implying, but I can assure you, I don't appreciate it."

Yeah. Welcome to the club.

I looked back to Randy. "You've got ten seconds."

"For what?"

"To get out, before I drag you out."

Imogen blurted, "Don't do it."

I didn't know who she was talking to – me or Randy. Either way, I *was* doing it, all right. "Five seconds."

Randy swallowed. "But—"

"Three."

That did the trick. Randy turned and scrambled into the passenger's seat before bolting out through the passenger's side door. He slammed the door shut behind him and stood a few feet away chewing on his bottom lip.

If I were a different kind of person, I might've felt guilty. But hey, the limo would be fine – or at least fixable. And in five minutes, Randy could reclaim his seat and sit here all night for all I cared.

It was a good plan – or at least good enough – until *she* ruined it.

And I didn't mean Imogen.

CHAPTER 15

Becka

What on Earth was going on?

I had no idea, but I didn't like the look on Randy's face as he scrambled out of the limo – on the wrong side, no less. Under the glare of our headlights, he looked worried and maybe even scared.

Until now, I hadn't even realized that Randy was the one driving. If I *had* known, I might've insisted on handling this myself regardless of what Jack said.

A few months earlier, I'd met Randy through my sister, who'd first met *him* when she'd been waitressing at the local waffle house. It's not like I'd call Randy a friend, but I liked him. He was nice and friendly – a lot friendlier than Jack Ward, that's for sure.

Without pausing to think, I pushed open my car door. Shutting it behind me, I strode toward them, calling out to Randy, "What's going on?"

But it wasn't Randy who answered. It was Imogen, who looked to me and yelled, "Go away! We don't want any."

I felt my jaw clench. *Any what?*

Whoop-ass? Because that's exactly what I felt like giving her.

By now, I'd had more than enough. I strode forward and sidled up to Randy, who was watching with obvious concern as Jack Ward yanked open the limo's driver's side door.

I called out to Jack, "Wait, what are you doing?"

"What does it look like?" he said, ducking into the limo.

Talk about a non-answer. I lunged forward and yanked open the passenger's side door. I lowered my head and looked inside just in time to see Jack settle himself into the driver's seat. He was holding the screwdriver in his right hand as if he were getting ready to attack the steering column.

"Wait!" I pointed to the screwdriver. "What are you gonna do with that?"

From behind me, Randy grumbled, "He's gonna ruin the limo, that's what."

I asked Jack, "Is that true?"

He replied, "You want this thing moved or not?"

"Of course I want it moved," I said, "but not if it ruins anything."

"Don't worry," he said. "It's fixable."

"But why not just ask for the keys? Or better yet, ask Randy to move it himself?" I gave Jack a hard look. "I know he would if you'd just ask nicely."

With cool deliberation, Jack lowered the screwdriver. With something like a smile, he said, "You wanna try that? Go ahead. I'll wait."

For some reason, his smile – as subtle as it was – was making me just a little bit nervous.

Obviously, he knew something that I didn't. But hey, I knew something, too, and I was perfectly willing to share it. "You know," I said, "sometimes politeness goes a long way in solving problems."

His eyebrows lifted. "Is that so?"

"Definitely. And if you wait, I'll prove it." With sudden inspiration, I said, "First, just get out of the car, okay?"

When he made no move, I said, "Please? I mean, it's hard for me to focus when I'm worried about you ruining something."

More to himself than to me, he said, "This should be good."

I wasn't sure what he meant by that, but it didn't matter. To my surprise, he actually listened to what I was saying and pushed open the driver's side door. A moment later, he was standing outside like the rest of us.

Randy and I were on the passenger's side, while Jack and Imogen were on the other. Forcing a sunny smile, I turned to Randy and said loud enough for everyone to hear, "Now, will you please do us a huge favor and move the limo?"

Randy frowned. "I can't."

My smile faltered. "But why not?"

"Because I don't have the key."

Now, I was the one frowning. "So, who does?"

From limo's other side, Imogen's voice rang out, loud and clear. "Looking for this?"

When I looked, she was holding out a car key in front of her, swinging it back and forth from its key fob.

Reluctantly, I looked to Jack. He said nothing, but his expression said it all.

I told you so.

My own words from just a few moments ago echoed in my brain. *"Sometimes politeness goes a long way in solving problems."*

Crap.

Still, I dug deep and forced another smile. I looked back to Imogen and replied, "Yes. As a matter of fact, I am. Would you *please* give that to Randy so he can move the limo?"

Now *she* was the one smiling. "No."

Double crap. Again, I looked to Jack. She was *his* non-girlfriend. *Shouldn't he be doing something?*

But then I remembered, he *had* been doing something. And I'd stopped him. But still, I couldn't quite regret it, or at least not *all* of it. After all, I still didn't want the limo damaged.

I looked back to Imogen and said, "Oh come on! If you don't give up the key, Jack will damage the limo. You don't want that, do you?"

"Why not?" she said with a sly look at Jack. "I think it's hot."

"What?" I shook my head. "Hot how?"

"Hot-wiring a car," she said. "It's sexy, don't you think?"

Embarrassingly, I did.

How messed up was that?

And yet, I didn't find it *so* sexy that I'd actually let it happen. I returned my attention to Jack. He looked more disturbed than flattered.

And yet, he made no move to retrieve the key.

Damn it. I knew exactly what he was doing. He was making me eat my own words, that's what.

With a sound of annoyance, I turned and stalked around the front of the limo. I bypassed Jack and stood facing Imogen. I held out my hand, palm up. "The key," I said. "I need it *now*."

From behind me, Jack said, "What, no 'please'?"

I whirled back to face him. "What?"

He grinned. "It's only polite, right?"

Damn it. The way it looked, he was actually enjoying this. *Jerk.* I looked back to Imogen and gritted out, "Please."

Her smile widened. "No."

I felt my eyebrows furrow. "Pretty please?"

Her eyes were glinting now. "Don't you mean with sugar on top?"

Oh, I'd give her sugar, all right. Still, through clenched teeth, I said, "Yes. Fine. With sugar on top."

Still, she made no move to hand over the key. "It doesn't count if you don't say it all at once."

Oh, for God's sake. Nearly choking on my words, I somehow managed to say, "Will you *pretty please*, with sugar on top, give me the key?"

"No." She gave a toss of her long, dark hair. "Sorry."

Sorry, my ass. She was enjoying this.

Well, I wasn't.

With a sound of irritation, I reached out, intending to snatch the key from her bony fingers. As I did, she jerked her hand upward, holding the key high above her head.

Dumbfounded, I stared up at the thing. *What now?*

She was still wearing those stupid heels, and I was in sneakers. But even footwear aside, she had at least five inches on me, which meant that the key was firmly out of my reach.

I turned to look at Jack. He was taller than her and then some.

I gave him a pleading look. "Well? Why don't *you* get it? I mean, it's right there." I jerked my thumb toward the key. "You can see it, right?"

His gaze shifted to the key. "I see it."

"So?"

"Hey, you have your approach. I have mine."

Obviously, his approach was to mangle Randy's limo. I wanted to scream. This whole thing was so incredibly stupid, like something straight out of grade school.

Already, I'd had a crappy day, and all of my worldly belongings were stuffed in one single car – a car that couldn't even get through the gate unless that limo moved out of the way.

Damn it.

Enough was enough.

CHAPTER 16

Becka

I turned and leapt for the key. Missing it by several inches, I collided with Imogen and tumbled forward of my own momentum, sending me and Imogen toppling into a nearby flower bed.

She screamed. I screamed. One thing led to another, and soon, she was on top of me, pressing my back into the begonias – or whatever they were.

It's not like I was a flower expert or anything.

At a sudden flash of light, both of us froze. I looked up to see Randy standing a few feet away holding out his cell phone like a camera.

I glared up at him. "What are you doing?"

He glanced away. "Nothing."

Imogen leapt up and whirled to face Randy. "I swear to God, if you took a picture—"

Jack's voice cut through the commotion. "You'll what?"

Like a total idiot, I was still lying in the flower bed. With a groan, I pushed myself up to a sitting position and looked from Imogen to Jack.

Jack was eying Imogen with a cold, steely gaze that would've made me shiver if it were directed at me.

As for Imogen, she was covered in bits of dirt and flower petals. She was missing both of her shoes, and her underpants were askew. Still, she thrust back her shoulders and announced, "If he took a photo, he'll be *very* sorry, that's what."

My gaze shifted to Randy. He was gazing down at his phone with bright eyes and a happy smile. Whatever emotion he was feeling, it *wasn't* sorrow.

Imogen barked out, "Hey! Limo driver!"

He looked up. "What?"

"You'd better delete that."

He blinked a few times before shoving his cell phone into his pocket. "Delete what?"

Part of me wanted the snicker. The other part was too busy wondering why my hair felt funny. When I reached back to smooth it, my hand came away covered with clumps of dirt and stray flower petals.

Well, this was just lovely.

As Imogen and Randy argued back and forth about the photo, I reluctantly looked to Jack.

He was eying me with thinly veiled amusement.

I said, "What's so funny?"

He shrugged. "Am I laughing?"

"No. But you want to. I can tell."

He flicked his head toward something a few feet behind me. "You wanna grab that?"

I turned to look, and spotted the key, lying in a patch of grass just beyond the flower bed. I lunged toward it and snatched it up quicker than you could say, *"Thanks for the help, buddy."*

I was still wallowing in dirt, but at least I had the thing I needed. When I looked back to Jack, he held out his hand, palm up as if waiting for me to give him the key.

But all I gave him was a cold look. "If you think I'm giving it to *you*, you're crazy." *No.* I was going to give it Randy, so he could simply move the limo and be done with this whole twisted scene – well, when he was done dealing with Imogen, that is.

Even now she was saying, "I *know* you took one."

He replied, "One what?"

"A photo, just like I said."

"A photo of what?"

"My ass! That's what."

When I looked back to Jack, his eyes filled with amusement as he nudged his hand closer. "Actually," he said, "I was gonna help you up."

Heat flooded my face. "Oh."

Technically, I didn't need any help, but it seemed incredibly rude to refuse, especially after snapping at him like that.

Reluctantly, I put my hand in his, and let him pull to my feet. His hand felt nice, and I gave a warm shiver as he asked in a surprisingly tender voice, "You okay?"

At this, Imogen turned to him and snapped, "I hope you're talking to *me*." She glared daggers in my direction. "After all, I was the one attacked, not her."

I gave a snort of derision. "Oh please. I didn't 'attack' you. I just lost my balance, that's all."

"Save it for the judge," she said.

I wasn't following. "What judge?"

"When I get back, I'm gonna sue your ass so hard, you'll be dead-broke."

That's what *she* thought. "Hah! I'm *already* dead-broke, so good luck with that." As the words echoed out in the night, it suddenly struck me that this was nothing to brag about.

Into the sudden silence, I said, "I'm just saying, it would be a waste to sue me." I cleared my throat and mumbled, "You can't get blood out of a turnip and all that."

Imogen shook her head. "A turnip? I'm not suing a turnip. I'm suing *you*." Her voice rose. *"Psycho!"*

My jaw dropped. *Psycho? Seriously?* I made a show of eying her up and down. "At least I wear clothes when I go outside." I gave her a stiff smile. "So who's the psycho now?"

"Oh, whatever." She turned away. "See you in court."

I was still searching for a snappy comeback when Jack told her, "No. You won't."

She smirked. "That's what *you* think."

Jack looked to Randy. "Let's say you did take a photo. Who was on top?"

With a sloppy grin, Randy looked to Imogen. "The one with no clothes on."

Well, that counted me out. I was wearing lots of clothes, especially compared to Imogen.

And now, she was sputtering, "What does that have to do with anything?"

"I'm just saying," Jack said, "it's gonna be hard to claim you were attacked if you were the one on top."

Imogen made a sound of protest. "But you saw what happened! She totally lunged for me."

As she spoke, it suddenly struck me that she sounded a whole lot different than how she'd sounded earlier, when I'd met her at Flynn's front door. I felt my brow wrinkle in confusion. "What happened to your accent?"

She whirled to face me. "What?"

"Weren't you supposed to be English or something?"

"Oh, screw you," she said. "I'm leaving." She looked wildly around. "Where the hell are my shoes?"

I pointed to the flower bed, where both shoes were still stuck in the dirt. She marched forward, swooped down, and grabbed one in each hand. And then, she turned to glare at Randy. "I hope you know, I'm calling your boss."

"Actually," he said, "I *am* the boss."

From the sidelines, I smiled with relief. "Really? Did you buy the limo company or something?"

He grinned back at me. "Yeah. I got me an investor." As he said it, he glanced toward Flynn's estate, and I recalled the drama outside this very same gate months ago.

It didn't take a rocket scientist to figure out exactly who his investor was – Flynn Archer, my sister's fiancé.

Well, that was good. Or at least *I* thought so.

As for Imogen, she looked less than thrilled as she stomped to the limo's nearest back door and said to Randy, "Well? Aren't you going to get this?"

"Get what?" he asked.

"The door." Under her breath, she added, "Idiot."

Randy gave her a hopeful smile. "You sure you don't want to ride up front?"

Turns out, she didn't.

By the time they left, I was feeling surprisingly chipper. Randy was fine. The limo was fine. And I was fine, well, except for the dirt, that is.

All in all, things hadn't turned out so bad.

As the limo disappeared down the dark, secluded road, I turned to Jack and said, "See? It all worked out just fine."

Slowly, he turned to look at me. He eyed me up and down, taking in my dirty clothes and messy hair. "You think so, huh?"

"Sure." I summoned up a smile. "Hey, I got the key back, didn't I?"

He never did answer. Instead, he led me back to the sedan, opened up the passenger's side door, and waited while I climbed inside and settled myself into the passenger's seat.

With an inscrutable look, he handed me the screwdriver and said, "You wanna put this back?"

As I took it from him, our fingers touched for the briefest instant, and I felt another warm shiver creep up my spine. He was so stupidly sexy, and I was, well, a mess, that's what.

But it didn't matter. Not only was he insanely out of my league, he was also just a little bit scary.

As I returned the screwdriver to the glove compartment, I heard myself say, "You know, you're nothing like I thought you'd be."

Standing beside the car, he gave me one of those looks, another long penetrating one that I couldn't quite decipher. "Yeah," he said. "And neither are you."

CHAPTER 17

Jack

I'd meant what I said. Anna's sister was nothing like I'd expected. As I drove down Flynn's driveway and hit the remote to shut the front gate behind us, I gave Becka a long sideways look.

She was sitting there, looking surprisingly happy in spite of everything that had just happened. Her face was smudged, and her hair was a tousled mess.

I frowned. She was so adorable, I could hardly stand it. I didn't know why or how. She wasn't my type. She was too nice, too impulsive, and too stubborn for her own good.

It was a lethal combination.

On top of that, she was practically Flynn's little sister. This meant that she was strictly hands-off – unless I wanted a big complication, which I didn't.

That was fine by me. Nice girls weren't my thing. It's not that I liked them nasty, but I wasn't looking for anything real. More to the point, I wasn't looking at all.

Given my plans, the next few months would be complicated enough without adding more trouble to the mix.

From the passenger's seat, Becka said, "Randy's nice. Don't you think?"

I felt my hands tighten around the wheel. "He's nice enough."

"What, you don't like him?"

I didn't like him *or* dislike him. I just found it odd that she was bringing him up. I looked to her and asked, "So, do you have a thing for him?"

I hadn't meant to ask. But now that I had, I *was* curious.

"What?" She turned in her seat to face me. "No. I mean, yeah he's a nice guy, but…" She shrugged. "He's just not my type, you know."

I *did* know. Becka was small and sweet, with a tight body and impish smile. As far as Randy, he wasn't nearly good enough – nice or not. Plus, there had to be at least ten years between them, maybe fifteen.

I said, "He's too old."

She gave it some thought. "Yeah, I guess."

"And not your type."

She paused. "Uh, yeah. That's what I said."

She had. Hadn't she?

Good. At least we agreed on *that.* I returned my gaze to the driveway. "Right."

She said, "I think he's in his thirties."

Funny, *I* was in my thirties – thirty-one, to be exact, which meant that I was also too old for her, not that it mattered. Still, it was something to remember. "So what are you?" I said. "Twenty?"

She gave a hard scoff. "No."

Obviously, I'd hit a nerve. "So…what? Younger?"

Now she laughed. "No. But I know why you'd think that."

I knew why, too. She looked too innocent by half. Still, I asked, "Oh yeah? Why?"

"Because I haven't yet graduated from college, so I can see why you'd think I'm a lot younger."

A lot younger?

While I was chewing on *that,* she added, "But I'm in my third year, so I'm not too far off – from getting my degree, I mean."

"Right. English lit."

"You remembered?"

I did. But that wasn't the point. "So, you never said. How old *are* you?"

"First, how old are *you*? Thirty-one, right?" She cleared her throat.

"I read it in your bio."

My bio. Some of it was true. Some of it wasn't. With a low scoff, I said, "Don't believe everything you read."

She hesitated. "So you're *not* thirty-one?'

"I am," I said. "But it still puts me in my thirties." Looking to drive the point home, I added, "Like Randy."

"Funny, you look younger. Not just younger than Randy. I mean, younger than thirty-one."

I got that a lot, especially when I spoke on college campuses. The truth was, I hadn't changed a lot over the last decade, except for my financials, that is.

I looked to Becka and said, "Your turn."

"Me? I'm twenty-four." She rolled her eyes. "Going on a hundred."

Not the way *I* saw it. She looked too sweet and too innocent. *Too damned tempting, too.*

But I declined to comment. We'd just reached the front of the house, and I pulled the car to a stop. "You wanna go in while I unload the stuff?"

She glanced toward the house. "Why would *you* unload it? I mean, it's *my* stuff."

I might be a dick, but I wasn't so big a dick that I'd let her do the heavy lifting while I sat on my ass. "Don't worry. I could use the workout."

She turned her head and gave me good, long look. As she did, her lips parted before she quickly shut them again. The motion, as subtle as it was, sent my thoughts drifting where they didn't belong.

This wasn't good.

It was time to toss some cold water on both of us – and fast.

CHAPTER 18

Becka

I was making a fool of myself. *I just knew it.* I reached up to touch the side of my face. *Was I drooling?* I *felt* like I was drooling.

But in my own defense, I could hardly help myself.

I was with my favorite author in the whole world, and he was so stupidly sexy. Ever since leaving my condo, he'd been surprisingly nice, too. *And,* he was giving me a look that suggested he didn't find me nearly as repulsive as I felt in my disheveled state.

I heard myself ask, "What are you thinking?"

His gaze – which had been amazingly warm – cooled several degrees as he replied, "I'm thinking you should go to your room, get some rest."

His words felt like a slap, although I couldn't quite figure out why. And then it hit me.

Oh, my God. I'd been molesting him with my eyes, hadn't I?

But it wasn't *all* my fault. He'd been looking at *me*, too.

Hadn't he?

Now his gaze was so cold, I almost shivered.

So much for that theory.

As I watched, Jack pulled the keys from the ignition and handed them over. "You get the door," he said. "I'll get the rest. You have the code, right?"

Clutching the keys, I glanced toward the front door. "The alarm code? Yeah, I have it."

"Good," he said. "I'll see you tomorrow."

Tomorrow? I wasn't quite following. "So, are you leaving or something?"

"No. But I've gotta make some calls."

"Oh. Well, that's good."

Was it?

I had no idea.

In reply, he gave the front door a pointed look as if to say, *"Off you go."*

If that wasn't a hint, I didn't know what was. So, with as much dignity as I could muster, I got out of the car and did what he suggested.

It really wasn't such a big deal. Or at least it *shouldn't* have been a big deal. But for some reason, I felt unsettled and confused – even more so the very next morning when I received the strangest phone call from my sister.

CHAPTER 19

Becka

On the phone, Anna was saying, "I heard where you're going. Are you sure that's such a great idea?"

I sat up in bed and rubbed at my sleepy eyes. I'd just been awakened by the ringing of my cell phone – a call from an unknown number.

I wouldn't have answered at all if not for the faint hope of the caller being my sister.

But now that she *had* called, I was having a hard time understanding what she was getting at. As I tried to gather my wits, I asked, "So, are you calling from Flynn's satellite phone?"

"Yeah, but forget that," she said. "I need to know if it's true."

"If what's true?"

"Oh come on," she said. "I heard it from Flynn, so you might as well tell me."

I frowned. "Tell you what?"

"That you're going on Jack's book tour."

Huh? I shook my head. "I am?"

"Yeah. As his intern or something?"

I was so stunned, I didn't know what to say. "And you heard this from Flynn? When?"

"Just now," she said. "Jack told *him,* and he told *me*. So I'm asking *you*. What's going on?"

Good question.

My head was swimming, and I was barely awake. Stalling for time, I said, "Hey, first, tell me something."

"What?"

"Where are you?"

"You don't know?"

I *thought* I knew, but I couldn't risk ruining the surprise. Forcing a laugh, I said, "Just tell me."

"An island. But Flynn said you already knew." A smile crept into her voice. "Our own private island. Can you believe it?"

I could, but only because I'd heard it just yesterday. Still, it *was* pretty amazing. I let out a shaky breath. "Wow."

"Yeah, no kidding. Get this. He says it's an anniversary present."

"But wait, you're not even married."

"I meant the anniversary of..." She hesitated. "...well, when we first said we loved each other."

Obviously, there was a lot she wasn't saying. But I knew what she meant. I could practically hear her blushing through the phone. "Wow," I said yet again. "That's some anniversary present."

In a dreamy voice, she replied, "Yeah, well, he's like that, you know."

I almost scoffed out loud. He hadn't *always* been like that. In fact, he'd been a total prick when he'd first hired my sister for a secret job that was best forgotten.

Speaking of mysterious jobs, I still had no idea what she'd been getting at. I *wasn't* Jack's intern. I wasn't his anything.

But something was definitely going on, and I needed to find out – preferably *before* continuing this conversation.

I said, "Hey, I just woke up. Can I call you back in a bit?"

"But wait," she said. "You never answered my question."

No kidding.

The truth was, I had questions of my own, and zero answers to give. Still, I refused to make her worry.

In the breeziest tone I could muster, I said, "Everything's great. I just need to shower, that's all. If I call this number in a half-hour, will you answer?"

"Yeah. Of course, but—"

"Great," I chirped. "I'll call you back, okay?" And with that, I ended the call.

I didn't shower, but I *did* brush my teeth and freshen up before stomping down the stairs in search of you-know-who.

I found him at the kitchen table, drinking coffee and scribbling in a black notebook, using a pencil, not a pen.

So he'd actually found a pencil?

Well, goodie for him.

When I marched up to the table, he didn't even look up.

I cleared my throat.

He *still* didn't look.

With a loud sigh, I finally said, "Hey, do you have something to tell me?"

Without pausing in his scribbling, he replied, "Not now."

"What?"

"Not now," he repeated.

"But why not?"

"Because I'm in the middle of something."

"Oh yeah?" My jaw clenched. "Me, too." In fact, I was in the middle of wondering what my sister knew that *I* didn't.

But from Jack, I received nothing but silence, except for the sounds of his pencil scratching at the paper.

I moved closer. "Don't you want to know what *I'm* in the middle of?"

"No."

"Why not?"

"Because if I stop now, I'll lose it."

"Lose what?"

"My train of thought."

Big whoop. My train had derailed like fifteen minutes ago with that surprise phone call. *I needed information, pronto.*

I crossed my arms and gave him a hard stare until he finally looked up. As he did, I swear, my heart skipped a beat.

In the pale morning light, his eyes were so blue, they took my breath away. My mouth opened, but my mind went stupidly vacant.

He was wearing black running pants and a gray sleeveless shirt. His hair was rumpled, and his biceps bulged, like he'd just finished doing a hundred pushups and who-knows-what-else.

After a long, awkward silence, he set down his pencil and asked, "You done?"

Heat flooded my face. *Done what? Staring?*

Crap. I was doing it again, wasn't I?

I wasn't normally like this – all star-struck and mindless. But in my own defense, I'd gotten only a few hours of sleep and was still reeling from yesterday's events, not to mention my sister's odd phone call.

"No," I told him. "In fact, I haven't yet begun."

"Obviously."

"Well?" I said. "Do you – or do you not – have something to tell me?"

"That depends," he said. "Are you gonna listen?"

"I'm listening now, aren't I?"

Without breaking eye-contact, he shoved aside his notebook and said something that I should've seen coming. "Tomorrow, you're starting a new job." He frowned. "Working for me."

I was staring again, but now for a totally different reason. "Is that so?"

With no trace of shame, he replied, "Yeah. It is."

"And what *supposedly* will I be doing?"

"Administration."

Well that was suitably vague. "Of what?"

"My book tour."

With growing indignation, I said, "So let me get this straight. You think I'll be what? Traveling with you?"

"I don't *think*," he said. "I *know*."

God, what a total ass. "In case you haven't noticed," I said, "I didn't apply for any job."

He didn't even flinch. "Wrong."

"No. *You're* wrong," I said. "Because I think I'd remember."

"Remember what? Applying for an internship?"

My mouth opened, but once again, words utterly failed. This time, it wasn't because of Jack's amazing eyes. In truth, I *had* applied for an internship.

But that had nothing to do with Jack. *Did it?*

At the local university, I'd been one of countless students to apply for a work-study internship as part of the English lit program. If I'd gotten such an internship – which I hadn't – it would've been a dream come true, especially if it came with an actual paycheck.

But those were few and far between, not that it mattered. The deadline had come and gone without an offer of any kind, paid *or* unpaid. I hadn't even gotten an interview.

I knew why. It all came down to Professor Greenberg, who ran the program. He liked me well enough, but my status as a part-time student *hadn't* been a mark in my favor.

Plus, there was the little matter of my stepfather embezzling half the town. The truth was, mine wasn't a name that inspired confidence regardless of my own credentials.

But none of that mattered, not really. Timing-wise, that ship had already sailed.

I gave Jack a sarcastic smile. "In case you didn't know, the deadline was in March."

"So?"

"So that was two months ago."

"Yeah, well." He shrugged. "It was extended."

Now *that* made me pause. "It was? When?"

He glanced at his watch. "An hour ago."

My brow wrinkled in confusion. That *couldn't* be right. It was barely eight o'clock in the morning. "But I don't get it," I said. "How would *you* know if the deadline was extended?"

"I made some calls."

"To who?"

"Whoever it took."

I recalled what he'd said last night, something about making a few phone calls. *Were those the calls he'd been talking about?*

I studied his face. "So, did they extend the deadline for everyone?"

"No."

I felt my gaze narrow. "All right. What *exactly* aren't you telling me?"

CHAPTER 20

Jack

It was a loaded question.

The truth was, there was a lot I wasn't telling her. For one thing, late last night, her roommate had been busted for selling pharmaceuticals out of his car.

The bust wasn't my doing, but I wasn't sad to hear about it. I was, however, pissed at Flynn for not doing a better job of checking out Becka's living situation.

I might've told him so, too, if not for the fact that I'd promised Becka – in so many words, anyway – that I wouldn't do anything to worry her sister.

In spite of what Becka might think, I wasn't one to go back on my word – *or* drop the ball when it came to protecting the people I cared about.

Yeah, maybe she wasn't mine to protect. But she was Flynn's future sister, which made her mine, too, in the same roundabout way. As such, there was no way in hell that I was leaving town without making sure that she wasn't headed for trouble.

There was only one hitch. I was leaving tomorrow, which meant that Becka was coming with me, whether she realized it or not.

In reply to her question, all I said was, "Check your email."

"Why?"

"Because it's got all the details."

She hesitated. "So, you sent me an email?"

"Not from me," I said. "From your professor."

What I *didn't* tell her was that I knew exactly what the email contained, because I'd drafted most of the wording myself.

Becka would receive a generous salary, along with class credit by serving as my temporary assistant for the summer semester – fall, too, if she decided to stay on.

It was a compelling offer – plenty of money, but not so much that she'd be suspicious. There was no way she'd turn it down – not if she was smart.

After she stalked off to check her email, I figured it was a done deal. But then, twenty minutes later, she was back, looking like she wanted to chew me up and spit me out.

She sputtered, "You bribed him? Seriously?"

I was still working at the table. "Who? Your professor?"

"Yeah. Professor Greenberg. So, did you?"

"If you're asking if I paid him off, the answer's no."

"I don't mean with money," she said. "I meant with that lecture."

Every once in a while, I lectured at college campuses – usually Ivy League or something nearly as pricey. None of these had been my idea. Rather, they'd been favors for some bigwig or another as part of the publishing or movie deals.

But this one? For once, the idea was all mine.

And why?

It was because Professor Numnuts had gone squeamish at the idea of setting up an internship two months past the deadline.

Even as he'd kissed my ass up and down, he'd told me that it was never done, apologizing repeatedly while making noises about the college administrators being "real sticklers for the rules."

In reply, I'd told *him* that this was the exception – and then sweetened the deal to make it happen. The thing is, I would've bribed him with a fat check if that's what it took.

For me, it would've been better. Money, I had in spades. But time? Not so much.

Still, I knew what I was doing. For Becka's sake, this was the best way to go – sealing the deal *without* raising red flags that would haunt her down the road.

But now, from the look on her face, she wasn't seeing it.

I asked, "What's the problem?"

"I don't want any special treatment."

"Good," I said. "Because you're not gonna get it. It's hard work. And your boss is a dick."

Her eyes narrowed. "You mean you?"

"Well, you're not working for someone else."

"I'm just saying, I feel kind of funny that I didn't get it on my own."

"Don't," I said. "The truth is, I had a sudden vacancy."

"Oh come on! You did not."

"You wanna bet?"

"Yes." Her chin lifted. "As a matter of fact, I do."

In case she didn't get it, I informed her, "That was a rhetorical question."

"So what?" she said. "I'm *still* willing to bet." She gave me a thin smile. "So…you have proof of this 'vacancy'?"

I did. But she wouldn't like it. Still, I leaned back in my chair and said, "Let's say I do. Are you gonna accept the gig and be done with it?"

"Maybe."

"That's no answer," I said. "Say yes, or you don't get the proof."

She stiffened. "All right, fine. Yes."

I reached into my pocket and pulled out my cell phone.

As I did, Becka gave me a wary look. Ignoring the look, I pulled up my last voicemail and hit play. I handed Becka the phone without further comment.

And then, I waited.

CHAPTER 21

Becka

His phone felt warm in my suddenly cold fingers. Whoever the caller was, she was crying. Through choked sobs, she said, "Listen, Mister Ward, I'm sorry, okay? I didn't realize that it was such a big secret."

I frowned. *A secret? What secret?*

With a loud sniffle, she continued. "And she claimed she had a big surprise, something *really* good. She promised over and over again that you'd be delighted to see her."

As I listened, I tried to think. *Her?*

Who on Earth was she talking about?

Imogen?

More to the point, who was the caller? *His last assistant?*

It sure sounded that way.

If so, this didn't bode well.

None of it did.

I gave Jack a horrified look as my fingers tightened around his phone. By now, his eyes had grown so cold that my fingers felt nearly warm in comparison.

He held my gaze as I continued listening to the woman sob and eventually begin repeating herself.

The whole thing was beyond awful. Cripes, I didn't even *know* the woman, and I felt like crying along with her.

As for Jack, he looked like he'd be fine with using her teardrops to wash his boots.

Between sobs, she was still going. "Just please, give me another chance, okay? I'll do better. I won't tell anyone anything, just like the agreement says. I'm sorry. Really, *really* sorry."

By now, I was sorry, too.

Not only was the call beyond depressing, I felt dirty and disgusting for eavesdropping on someone else's misery.

Finally, the message ended with the promise that she'd be waiting by the phone, just in case he changed his mind.

In the sudden silence that followed, I didn't move a muscle. With the phone still pressed to my ear, I stared at the guy who'd been so nice – *and* so horrible, depending on the situation.

Finally, I heard myself say, "I'm not sure I want to work for you."

"Yeah? Well, too bad," he said. "A deal's a deal."

My hand dropped to my side, and his phone clattered to the floor. On instinct, I crouched down to swoop it up, mumbling, "Sorry."

"Don't be," he said. "That's yours."

I was still crouched on the floor. With the phone once again in my hand, I looked up. "What?"

"That's my business phone," he said. "From now on, it's *your* problem, not mine."

I stood. "But wait a minute. I never accepted the job."

His eyebrows lifted. "You sure about that?"

"Oh come on," I said. "You're not talking about that stupid bet, are you?"

But from the look on his face, that's exactly what he was thinking. He replied, "What do *you* think?"

Why lie? "I think you're horrible."

"Good."

I shook my head. "Why is that good?"

"Because we're not friends. I'm your boss."

What a crock. Even at the burger place, I'd been friends with my supervisor. Then again, *she'd* been a nice person – and not just *some* of the time either.

To Jack, I replied, "Not yet, you're not. I haven't signed anything."

"Yeah. But you will."

"Oh yeah?" I scoffed. "And why's that?"

"Because it's a good opportunity, and you know it." He gave me a tight smile. "And, like I said, I've got the opening."

If this were remotely funny – which it wasn't – I might've laughed in his face. "Yeah, but only because you just fired someone. The caller, the one who was crying – that was your assistant, right?"

"Not anymore."

I considered the events of the last twenty-four hours and tried to put them into context. "That call? It was about Imogen, wasn't it?"

"So that's your theory, huh?"

"Of course it is. I mean, it seems pretty obvious."

"All right. Let's hear it."

"Hear what?" I asked.

"Your theory."

I wanted to tell him to shove it. And yet, I *was* curious to know if my hunch was correct. "All right," I said. "Your assistant told Imogen that you were here, at Flynn's place. But you didn't want Imogen to know. And it made you angry."

"Not angry," he said. "Careful. There's a difference."

"Oh, please," I scoffed. "And you must *still* be angry if you can listen to someone cry like that and not care one single bit."

"*I* wasn't the one listening. You were."

I was glaring now. "Was that a joke? If so, it *wasn't* funny."

As usual, he looked completely unashamed. "Eh, says you."

"I'm serious," I said. "How can you not care?"

His gaze met mine. "I care."

"Oh stop it. You do not."

"I care," he continued, "that she didn't follow clear instructions."

Talk about unreasonable. "But Imogen must've lied to her."

He shrugged. "So?"

"So that's hardly your assistant's fault."

"My *ex*-assistant," he said.

I studied his face. I had to be missing something. In fact, I'd bet my life on it. "There's more to this story, isn't there?"

"If there is," he said, "*you're* not gonna hear it."

"Oh, well that's nice." I was still clutching the phone. Placing it firmly on the table in front of him, I said, "Before this conversation goes any further, I need to ask you something, and I want you to be honest."

When he made no reply, I asked the question, anyway. "Her firing – it didn't have anything to do with me, did it?"

He looked at me for a long, penetrating moment. "What are you asking?" he said. "Did I fire *her* so there'd be an opening for *you*?"

I blinked. "What? No. That's not what I'm asking at all." Beyond offended, I said, "You must think I'm pretty full of myself."

"Trust me. That's not what I'm thinking."

By now, I knew better than to ask him what he *was* thinking. Instead, I returned to the topic at hand. "What I mean is, well, yesterday, I know that things with Imogen got kind of tense. And if I'm being totally honest, I might've added to the tension—"

Now he looked almost amused. "Might've?"

"Fine," I said. "Point taken. But what I'm asking is… was *that* reason you fired your assistant? Because of all the drama from yesterday?" I winced. "Drama that *I* caused, I mean."

Abruptly, he stood. "No."

Compared to my long question, his answer seemed woefully short.

Plus, now that he was standing, I felt even smaller in comparison. As I craned my neck to stare up at him, I wondered yet again, *who was this guy?*

I definitely needed to know. Fortunately, I had someone I could ask.

My sister. I still hadn't called her back, but I was planning to, ASAP.

Already, I was making a list of questions and stacking them like cordwood in my head. By now, the stack was so big, my head literally ached.

I was tossing yet another question onto the pile when Jack said,

"The jet leaves tomorrow morning."

I shook my head. "What?"

"And we leave for the airport at nine. Be ready."

"But wait," I said for what felt like the millionth time. "I already told you, I haven't accepted."

"And I already told *you*, don't worry, you will." As he said it, he picked up the cell phone and returned it to his pocket. And then, he turned and walked away, leaving me standing alone in Flynn's kitchen.

Almost in a trance, I moved toward the table and claimed the seat that Jack had just vacated. And then, I heard myself sigh. *Damn it.* He was right, yet again.

I would be accepting.

Cripes, I'd be stupid not to. The pay was amazing, and more importantly, I needed the college credits.

If I played my cards right and doubled up on some other classes, this might enable me to graduate a whole semester earlier than I'd planned.

That was the upside.

But the downside was a lot more complicated. Thanks to that godawful phone message, not to mention Jack's heartless attitude, I knew for a fact that the job would be no picnic.

Just a couple of days later, I was proven terribly right – but *not* for the reasons I'd been anticipating.

CHAPTER 22

Becka

"I'm really sorry," I said for the third time. "But I'm not lying. You can't go in."

The brunette frowned. "But why not?" She was tall and leggy, just like her companion – an equally attractive blonde who was standing by her side. They were both dressed in skin-tight sparkly tank tops – one red and one purple – along with identical black miniskirts and high strappy sandals.

The skirts were so short, I just prayed that neither one of them bent over any time soon, especially considering the number of guys who were ogling them from the sidelines.

As for myself, I was wearing a long navy skirt, my favorite white chiffon blouse, and low navy pumps. Compared to the girls in front of me, I felt positively frumpy.

"Because," I told her, "it's a private lounge. And Mister Ward is, um, lounging."

This was only half true. The lounge wasn't open to the public, but he wasn't quite lounging. He was scribbling in his black notebook again, using that same pencil – now marred with bite marks along the top.

The last time I'd seen him, just five minutes earlier, he'd been doing more stabbing than scribbling, as if the pencil were his weapon of choice and the notebook had done something to personally offend him.

From what I could tell, he was *not* in a good mood.

We were at a hotel and convention center in downtown Atlanta.

The publisher had scheduled Jack to appear here for the next three days as part of a giant comic book expo.

At first glance, the event had seemed a strange venue for a book signing, given the fact that Jack wrote sprawling epics with no pictures whatsoever.

But then, I saw the full program. The expo also featured a few stars from the movies that had been adapted from his books – so I guess I could see the connection.

What I *couldn't* see was why the door to the V.I.P. lounge wasn't being guarded. There'd been a security guard earlier, when we'd arrived maybe a half-hour ago.

Where on Earth was the guard now? I glanced around, but saw no sign of him.

As for the lounge itself, it was strictly off-limits to regular attendees. Inside the lounge were a few of the aforementioned movie stars, along with other famous writers and artists – none of whom I knew personally.

The lounge also contained its share of lowly assistants, me included. At the moment, I wasn't quite sure what I was supposed to be doing, but I *did* know there'd be hell to pay if I moved aside and admitted the girls into Jack's private sanctuary.

After all, I didn't want it to be *me* sobbing on the phone the next time around.

The brunette gave me a desperate smile. "But we can help."

I wasn't following. "Help with what?"

Her smile turned sly. "Well, you said he's lounging, right? We can help him do that. You know, relax." She looked to her companion and said, "Isn't that right, Darbie?"

The blonde named Darbie gave an enthusiastic nod. "Oh sure," she gushed. "We're great at that." She licked her glossy upper lip and said, "We know *all* the tricks."

I had no doubt of *that.*

I was still trying to come up with a decent response when the brunette said, "So, how come *you're* allowed inside?"

I hesitated. *Should I tell them? Or not?*

I hadn't mentioned who I worked for. A few minutes earlier, I'd simply had the unfortunate timing to be coming *out* just as they were preparing to sneak *in.*

When I'd politely informed them that the lounge wasn't open to the public, they'd asked for Jack personally and suggested that I go find him. When I'd refused as nicely as I could, they'd renewed their efforts to be let inside.

That *wasn't* going to happen.

And why? *It was because I knew better. That's why.*

One thing about Jack, he was the most anti-social person I'd ever met. He was quiet and brooding, like a secret agent who'd failed on his last mission and was plotting some sort of dastardly revenge.

Stalling, I turned and gave the door behind me a long, worried look. *Why, oh why, had I chosen this particular moment to dash out for a cup of coffee?*

As far as I could tell, the door wasn't even locked.

The sound of throat-clearing made me turn once again toward the girls. As I did, the brunette gave me the squinty-eye and said, "I think I know what's going on here."

I was glad *somebody* did. "Oh yeah? What?"

"You want him all for yourself."

Huh? Her statement was beyond insane. And besides, Jack wasn't the *only* celebrity in the lounge. For all *she* knew, I could be working for any one of them.

Or, I could be working for the convention center. The point is, she was assuming far too much.

I forced a laugh. "Don't be ridiculous."

Her gaze zoomed in on the oversized paperback that I held in my hand. She pointed. "So what's that?"

I glanced down. It was a copy of "Swordplay," Jack's first bestseller. It was the book that had made him a household name, not just here in the U.S., but also globally.

I'd purchased the book years ago. It was a special edition, published before the movies had even come out. Unlike recent editions, *my* book had the original cover, which made it a collector's item, at least the way *I* saw it.

But I hadn't brought along the book as a trophy. I'd brought it to help kill time during flights and what-not. And, with Jack being so unsociable, it was a good thing I had.

I replied, "It's a book, obviously."

"It's not just *a* book," she said. "It's *his* book. You got it signed, didn't you?"

Actually, I hadn't. But the fangirl part of me was seriously tempted. Probably I would've asked for his signature already, if only Jack weren't acting so ominous lately.

I said, "No I didn't."

The two girls exchanged a look. This time, it was the blonde – aka Darbie – who spoke up. "Oh yeah? Prove it."

I glanced down at the book. "Like, what? You want me to *show* you that it's not signed?"

"You bet your ass I do." Darbie held out her hand, palm up. "Now fork it over."

I drew back. The book was mine, and I had no intention of giving it up. Plus, her attitude hardly inspired trust. So instead, I lifted the book between us and rifled its opening pages. Forcing a smile, I said, "See? No signature here."

"I don't believe you," she said and then – what the hell? – made a mad grab for the book. Her hands closed around the upper half, and she gave the entire book a hard yank.

I refused to let go. "Stop that!" Now *I* was holding on with both hands, too.

Darbie gave another tug. "No!"

I tugged back. "You can't have it!"

"Oh yeah?" she said with another tug. "Then you can't either!"

I tugged again. "But it's my book!"

"Says you!"

By now, the guys on the outskirts had sidled closer to watch the commotion. Some of them were dressed in medieval costumes, obviously inspired by Jack's books – or the related movies.

As far as the specifics, I didn't know. And I didn't care. All *I* knew was that the book was mine, and I *wasn't* letting go.

From the sidelines, a big burly guy, dressed normally in jeans and a T-shirt, called out, "I've got ten tucks on the blonde."

Talk about insulting.

As I gave another tug, I called back, "Oh, shut up!"

"Hey, no need to get offended," he said. "I'm just saying, she's putting a lot more oomph into it."

I'll give you oomph, I thought.

Still, the guy wasn't lying. Darbie was tugging her little heart out and making some sort of low growling noise as she did it.

As for the brunette, she was edging around the both of us, heading casually toward the V.I.P. door.

Without letting go of my book, I yelled, "You *know* you can't go in there!"

She laughed. "Oh yeah? And who's gonna stop me? *You?*"

Shit. They were tag-teaming me. I just knew it. With a low growl of my own, I looked back to Darbie and gave one massive tug.

That did it. Suddenly, the book was free.

I stumbled backward of my own momentum and caught my balance just in time to see the brunette make a mad dash toward the forbidden door.

Damn it.

In a sudden burst of inspiration, I turned and smacked the side of her hip with the oversized book, sending her toppling sideways in the other direction.

As she fell, she made a wild lunge for my blouse and held on tight. With a little yelp, I tumbled forward as a horrible ripping noise tore through the sudden silence.

Together, we both hit the floor – with me on top and the brunette underneath. She pushed. *I* pushed. There might've been a slap or two, and soon, we were wrestling side-by-side on the hard tile floor.

I was pretty sure my blouse was ruined.

But that wasn't the thing that filled me with sudden horror. It was the sound of Darbie calling out from the sidelines, "Oh, my God. It's *him*. Jack Ward!"

CHAPTER 23

Becka

I froze. So did the brunette.

Oh, no.

In that brief, horrible moment, I couldn't help but wonder if there was a chance – *any* chance at all – that if I could somehow hide my face, Jack might not realize that it was me sprawled across the floor.

I mean, stranger things have happened right?

But of course, that was just desperation talking. So instead, I slowly turned my head toward the door of the private lounge, only to see Jack along with a few other V.I.P.s standing just outside the now-open doorway.

The people around him were watching with expressions ranging from confusion to raw delight.

But not Jack. He didn't look confused *or* delighted. *No.* He looked royally pissed off in his own silent sort of way. *And oh yeah. He definitely knew that it was me.*

Our eyes locked, and his jaw tightened.

I was just wondering if I should give him a little wave or something when a sudden push toppled me from my side onto my back. It was the brunette, who'd leapt up, and with a squeal of excitement, scurried toward Jack as I shakily got to my feet.

Her effort was a total waste. Wordlessly, Jack sidestepped around her and made a bee-line straight for me. As he moved, I glanced nervously around, wondering just how many people had seen that little skirmish.

The answer came in an instant.

A lot.

That's how many.

Jack was wearing a dark sports coat. Without breaking stride, he yanked it off and then draped it over my shoulders the moment he reached me.

As he did, I looked down, only to realize that the front of my blouse was wide open.

Well, that wasn't good.

On the upside, I was wearing a camisole underneath – not that Jack seemed to notice the distinction.

He yanked the jacket shut over my torso and *held* it shut with one steady hand, even though my arms weren't even in the sleeves.

And then, he turned to the crowd. "Show's over," he said just before turning me toward the open doorway and propelling me forward like I was some sort of ship to be steered in the night.

I dug in my heels. "Wait. My book – where is it?" I looked around. Near the front of the crowd, I spotted Darbie standing with both hands hidden behind her back.

I felt my gaze narrow. I knew exactly what she was hiding. I called out to her, "You took it, didn't you?"

She smiled. "I don't know what you mean."

Oh, yes, she did. That was much was obvious, not that I could do anything about it now. Already, I'd caused far too much commotion for one day.

So with a sigh, I muttered "Forget it," and then let Jack guide me into the private lounge, where I could look forward to a nice scolding and maybe a good kick to the curb as far my employment situation went.

But as it turned out, my expectations were only half correct.

CHAPTER 24

Jack

Becka was something else, all right.

When we entered the lounge, the place broke into raucous applause. Ignoring them, I kept going, steering Becka toward a private powder room off to the side.

I had an arm wrapped around her torso as I held the jacket shut with one hand. Yeah, I'd seen the thing she was wearing underneath her blouse, but that didn't mean I liked the idea of strangers seeing more than they should – like the outline of a nipple or the sweetness of her curves.

But I'd seen.

The camisole – or whatever it was called – was thin and lacy, and did a sorry-ass job of hiding things that only a lover should see.

I wasn't her lover. And I planned to keep it that way.

But hell if I'd let strangers ogle her in the meantime.

When we entered the powder room, I shut the door behind us and released my grip on the jacket. I asked, "What the hell was that about?"

She turned to face me. When our gazes locked, she winced. "Actually, it's kind of a long story."

It couldn't have been *that* long. She'd been gone for less than fifteen minutes.

I didn't get it. *How could someone so small cause that big of a ruckus in that short of a time?*

I told her, "Then you'd better get started."

She bit her lip. "Well, you see, they wanted to come into the room—"

"What room?"

"The lounge."

I made a forwarding motion with my hand. "And…?"

"And I knew you wouldn't want them to."

I gave her a hard look. "So? It's not *my* lounge."

She drew back, and the jacket opened maybe an inch or two, enough to make me want to look down.

I didn't. *Much.*

She replied, "Well, yeah. But they were looking for you personally, and acting a little psycho about it, too."

My eyebrows lifted. "Is that so?"

She squinted up at me. "I know what you're thinking."

I doubted that. I was thinking the same thing I'd been thinking for the past two days. *And it wasn't good.*

Bringing Anna's little sister along on this tour had been a mistake – and not because trouble seemed to follow her wherever she went. It was because I liked her company *and* the way she looked.

Too much.

And there was nothing sisterly about it.

When I said nothing in reply, she said, "You're thinking that *I'm* the psycho. Aren't you?"

No. I wasn't.

I'd lived an interesting life and had seen *real* psychos up close and personal. Becka was an angel compared to them.

I cut to the chase. "You know that wasn't your job, right?"

"What wasn't?"

My shoulders tightened as I considered the potential danger she'd put herself in. "Guarding the door."

"I wasn't 'guarding' it," she said. "I mean, yeah, I ended up *sort of* guarding it. But really, I'd just gone out to grab a cup of coffee." She tried for a smile. "I asked you if you wanted one. Remember?"

I crossed my arms. "I remember."

But that wasn't the *only* thing I remembered. When we'd arrived at the lounge not too long ago, there *had* been a guard at the door. My jaw clenched. *Where the hell was he?*

I felt a cold rage building deep inside me. Becka, misguided though she was, had felt compelled to do his job, because *he'd* been slacking.

This wasn't over. Not for me. And not for him.

Becka was still explaining. "And I knew you'd be angry if I just let them waltz in."

Hell, I was angry now, no waltzing needed. "Let's get one thing straight," I said. "Guarding the door, *any* door – that's *not* your job."

"Yeah. I know. You already said that."

"Then I'm saying again. If you run into trouble, you get *me*, okay?"

She sighed. "But that's exactly my point. They *wanted* me to get you. But I knew that's not what you wanted."

"So?"

"So isn't it obvious?" She fluttered her hands, making the jacket open another inch.

I almost groaned out loud.

Oblivious to what she was doing to me, she continued, "Seriously, look at it from my point of view. Your last assistant – whose name I don't even know by the way –"

"Audrey."

"Fine. Audrey. Anyway, *she* got fired because she let Imogen get past her."

"That's different."

"It is not," she said. "Look, maybe Audrey wasn't 'guarding the door' personally, but she was guarding your privacy, right? And then, when she failed, you got all mad and fired her with no warning."

"And you know this, how?"

"I heard the phone message, remember?"

"I meant about the warning."

"I know the sound of surprise when I hear it." Her mouth tightened. "Well, between all the sobbing, that is."

On some of this, Becka was right. Audrey *had* been surprised. She'd been with me for nearly two years, and had been an adequate assistant until this past week. But then, she'd messed up – and more than Becka realized.

I told her, "Surprised or not, she had to go."

Becka frowned. "Can I ask you a question?"

"What?"

"It's not really professional," she warned.

"Are you gonna ask it or not?"

"Well, I'm just curious...You weren't dating her or anything, were you?"

I stiffened. "I don't 'date' my employees."

Becka persisted, "But she seemed really upset, like it was more than losing her job. Were you two friends or something?"

"No. And we're talking about *you*. Not her."

From the look on Becka's face, she wasn't thrilled with the reminder. "So, I guess you might as well tell me..." She winced. "Am I fired?"

A smart man would've said yes, not because of the recent commotion, but because she was making me feel things, dangerous things that were best avoided.

It made no sense. She wasn't even my type. And, as far as I could tell, she had no idea what she was doing to me, even now.

Her face was flushed, and her lips were full. Her hair was a tousled, sexy mess, like she'd just been rolling around in the sheets.

My sheets.

My bed.

My mistake. For a moment there, I'd almost forgotten who I was dealing with.

So far, I'd been smart enough to keep my distance, but she'd been haunting my thoughts far too often. *This wasn't good.*

"Well?" she said.

I shook my head. "What?"

She frowned. "Oh, God. I *am* fired, aren't I?"

I studied her face. "I thought you didn't *want* the job."

"Yeah, but now that I'm actually here..." She shrugged, making the jacket open another fraction.

I didn't look, but my imagination saw plenty.

Enough was enough.

I told her, "No. But wait here, all right?"

Her face broke into a smile. "So I'm *not* fired?"

I didn't smile back. "You *will* be if you leave this room."

Her smile faltered. "Why?"

"Because I'm gonna get you a shirt."

She looked down and stifled a gasp. Using both hands, she yanked the jacket shut and mumbled, "Oh. Right."

No. Wrong. That's what my thoughts were. *Very, very wrong.*

When she looked up, she said, "But you don't need to get me a shirt. I'll just get one myself. Our hotel room is what? A ten-minute walk?"

Our room.

I liked the way that sounded. And I hated my own reaction to it. My shoulders felt stiff, and they weren't the only thing.

I said, "*Your* hotel room. Not mine. And *not* ours."

"Oh. Right." She gave a shaky laugh. "That was just a slip, honest. Of course I *know* we're not in the same room. Jeez. Who do you think I am, anyway?"

I shook my head. I knew who she was. *And* what she was.

Pure trouble.

CHAPTER 25

Becka

The powder room wasn't terribly large, but I was still pacing back and forth.

And why? It was because if I stood still for even an instant, I was pretty sure that I'd try to drown myself in the sink.

What on Earth was wrong with me? I'd just made a total ass of myself, *repeatedly*.

The incident with those girls was bad enough, but then afterward with Jack, I'd gotten way too personal with my questions.

And had I stopped there?

No. Not me.

As icing on the cake, I'd apparently flashed him my goodies and *then* made an accidental innuendo about our sleeping arrangements.

Our hotel room?

Seriously?

Talk about a Freudian slip.

I stopped pacing and squared my shoulders. *No more.*

From now on, I decided, I was going to turn over a new leaf. *No more drooling over him. No more inappropriate questions. And for God's sake, no more fighting with his fans.*

I glanced down. *And oh yeah. No more flashing him.* That was a big no-no. But in my own defense, I hadn't realized my camisole was so transparent.

As I yanked the borrowed jacket tighter around my torso, I said a silent prayer that no one in the crowd had taken pictures – or heaven forbid video – of me in my semi-topless state.

Jack was beyond famous. But *I* wasn't.

And I didn't *want* to be, especially for *that.*

I was still making a mental list of things I needed to improve on when my cell phone rang in the pocket of my skirt. I recognized the ring and felt a surge of relief.

It was my sister. And from her regular cell phone, too.

Finally.

I fumbled for the phone and answered right away. "Anna? Where are you?"

"Miami. Where are you?"

"Atlanta."

She groaned. "So you took the job? After I warned you not to?"

I wasn't following. My sister and I had only talked once during the past few days, and even *that* conversation had been very brief.

I said, "You warned me? When?"

"On the phone, Monday morning."

"You didn't warn me," I said. "You just asked if it was such a great idea."

"Yeah. That's a warning. And you were supposed to call me back, remember?"

"Hey, I tried." *Repeatedly.*

"You did not. I waited for like an hour."

I cringed. "Sorry, I got distracted. But I *did* call, just a little later than I planned. Why didn't you answer?"

Anna sighed. "It wasn't me. It was the satellite phone. I accidentally dropped it."

"Oh, so it broke?"

"More like it drowned," she said with a rueful laugh. "Don't ask. Anyway, that's why we're in Miami – to get a new one, or rather, *two* new ones, since Flynn wants me to have my own."

I snickered. "Probably so you don't drown *his* anymore."

"Maybe. But tell me…" She lowered her voice. "Jack's not with you now, is he?"

"No. He's out getting me a shirt."

"What, why?"

"Because mine got ripped."

"How?"

Probably I'd said too much already. "Oh, the usual way."

In a tight voice, she said, "There *is* no usual way."

"All right, fine," I said. "There was this little altercation with these two girls, but it was nothing, so don't worry."

"But—"

"Forget that," I said. "Jack should be back any minute." In reality, he *should've* been back a while ago. But that wasn't worth mentioning, so I cut to the chase. "Why would you warn me not to work for him?" I tried to laugh. "Don't tell me he's a serial killer or something."

But my sister *wasn't* laughing. "If he were, I'd be flying up there to get you myself."

Knowing my sister, she probably would. Still, I didn't get why she was so concerned. "Okay, so what's wrong with him?"

"Nothing's *wrong* with him," she said. "But he's *really* secretive."

"Yeah. No kidding." On our way to Atlanta, I'd spent nearly three hours alone with him on his private jet, and he hadn't said more than a dozen words to me the whole time.

In cheerier news, he'd looked *very* good doing it.

On the phone, my sister was saying, "I think he might've been a spy or something. Or maybe he still is."

Now I couldn't help but laugh. Normally my sister was one of the most sensible people I knew. This was *not* one of those times. "Oh, stop it."

"I'm not kidding," she said. "He broke into Flynn's house."

I stopped laughing. "Really? So he stole stuff?"

"No. It was more like a game."

"What kind of game?"

"Well…Flynn has this amazing security system. *No one* can get past it." After a dramatic pause, she added, "Except for Jack. I saw it myself."

I envisioned Flynn's estate. Even the yard was practically a fortress. "So he got past the gate?"

"Not just the gate," she said. "The house, too, meaning the *inside*."

I tried to think. "Well, maybe Flynn gave him a key. After all, you gave *me* one."

"That's not it," she said. "Trust me. Jack has nothing – no remote to the gate, no key to the house, and no alarm code either."

"Are you sure?"

"Positive. Flynn told me so himself."

"So…Is Jack *still* breaking in?"

"No. Not since the engagement, anyway."

"I can see why," I said. "He probably doesn't want to scare the pants off you."

"Yeah, but it's still kind of scary. Like, how does he do that?"

Good question. "Did you ask Flynn?"

"Sure."

"And what'd he say?"

"All he said was, 'Jack's an interesting guy.'"

No kidding. "But you didn't ask for details?"

"Sure," she said yet again.

"But…?"

"Flynn said they weren't *his* secrets to share and asked me to leave it at that."

"And you did?"

"Of course. It's only fair. It's not like I tell Flynn everything about *you*. I mean, you like *your* privacy, too, right?"

Damn it. As usual, my sister was way too reasonable for my own good. I muttered, "I guess."

And now I was seriously torn. Part of me wanted to beg Anna to learn everything she could. But on the other part realized the request would only make her worry.

This was the last thing I wanted. "Well, his secrets can't be *that* bad," I said, "or he wouldn't be friends with Flynn."

"Yeah, but Flynn can handle himself. He was in juvie, remember?"

Of course I remembered. Flynn was a poor kid who'd had some hard knocks – much harder than he deserved, thanks to my stupid stepdad.

Still, I replied, "Yeah, but what does that have to do with anything?"

"I'm just saying, if there's trouble, Flynn could handle it."

"And *I* couldn't?" I made a scoffing sound. "For your information, I totally kicked a girl's ass today."

"What?" she said. "*Please* tell me you're joking."

"All right, fine. I *guess* I'm joking." This was surprisingly true. At best, I'd come out even. Still, I tried to look on the bright side. "But she didn't kick mine either."

My sister was quiet for a long moment before saying, "Well…I *guess* that's good."

I smiled. *Yes. It was.* "But back to Jack," I said. "What are you saying? You don't like him?"

"That's not it," she said. "I *do* like him, a lot, actually."

"But…?"

"But I don't really know him. And even that book tour – it doesn't make any sense."

"What do you mean?"

"Well, for one thing, Jack's never done any book-signings, until now."

"So?"

"So, what's changed?"

"Maybe he just never had the time."

"Maybe," she grudgingly admitted. "But did you check out the list of cities? They're all over the place. It makes no sense at all."

I knew what she meant. Over the next few months, we'd be bouncing all over the country in no predictable pattern. Most of the cities I didn't even recognize, so yes, it *did* seem a bit strange.

But to Anna, all I said was, "Well, he's got a private jet, so maybe he doesn't *need* to make sure the cities are close together." I paused to think. "I mean, it's not like we're traveling by bus."

"Yeah, but the cities on their own don't make any sense either. Do you know, one of them has a population of only five-thousand people? It doesn't even have a book store. He's doing the signing at the local library."

"So?"

"So why would he even go there?"

"Maybe he likes small towns. Or libraries. I don't know."

"I like those places, too," she said. "But Jack hates publicity."

"So?" I said yet again. "Maybe that's why he picked small towns." I smiled. "Less publicity. See?"

"But they're not *all* small."

"Well maybe he likes a mix." And now, I just had to ask, "And why were you looking at the cities, anyway?"

"Because I was worried about you." She sighed. "I wasn't lying. I like Jack, truly. I'm just saying he's kind of scary."

Did I really need to say it? "So is your fiancé."

"He is not." She cleared her throat. "And besides, that's different."

Not the way I saw it. I loved my sister. Really, I did. But sometimes she forgot that I wasn't a kid anymore.

It was sad and funny at the same time. If our mom had only worried half as much, our lives would've been a whole lot easier.

Looking to put Anna's mind at ease, I said, "Well, we're in Atlanta now. And this event *totally* makes sense. It's part of a huge expo."

"Yeah, I guess." She perked up. "But you know what you should do?"

"What?"

"Forget the tour. Come to the island with us."

"But I can't just quit," I said. "That would be awful rude, don't you think?" In truth, I was surprised she'd even suggest it. Usually, my sister was polite to a fault.

But on the phone, she was saying, "Not as rude as you'd think. According to Flynn, Jack was planning for a solo trip, anyway."

My jaw dropped. "What? With no assistant or anything?"

"Exactly."

"But how could he do that?"

"I don't know," she said. "Probably he'd just have the local people handle it, like librarians and what-not."

I frowned. *So my job was what? A pity thing?*

This *wasn't* what I wanted to hear.

And my sister *still* wasn't giving up. "And as far as the island, there's a wonderful house with lots of room, and a guest bungalow, too. You could stay for the whole summer."

Now I didn't know what to say.

When I made no reply, she said, "You *do* know, Flynn thinks of you as a sister, right?"

"I know." I smiled through my distress. "He feels like family to me, too."

"And I'm just saying, if you want to take the summer off, you wouldn't need to worry about anything."

It was an old debate, one we'd been having for months. But I didn't want to be that person – someone who couldn't stand on her own two feet.

I asked, "Will I be getting college credit, too?"

She hesitated. "I don't know. I mean, maybe we could—"

"It was a joke," I said.

"Oh." She paused. "But my offer was serious. Will you at least think about it?"

I didn't *have* to think. "Thanks, but no."

"Why not?"

"Because of my internship. It'll be good experience." And, I silently vowed, I was going to earn every penny – while proving to Jack that my position *wasn't* superfluous.

My sister was still trying to convince me when a knock sounded at the powder room door. I turned and called out, "Who is it?"

"Jack," he said. "I've got the shirt."

Into the phone I whispered, "I've gotta go. But trust me, everything's fine."

"But wait," she said. "First, let me give you the number to my new phone."

"Just text it to me, okay? Now sorry, but I've *really* gotta go." And with that, I ended the call and shoved my cell phone back into my pocket.

Clutching the borrowed jacket tight around my torso, I opened the powder room door. When I did, Jack thrust a colorful wad of clothing vaguely in my direction.

With my free hand, I took it and shook out its folds. "What's this?"

"A shirt, like I said."

I frowned down at the thing. "Are you sure?"

"I'm sure enough," he said. "The signing starts in five minutes. You gonna be ready?"

I was still looking at the shirt. I didn't want to complain, but it really *was* hideous. It was like a checkerboard had gotten drunk and fathered a love child with a medieval clown.

Yikes.

When I gave Jack a perplexed look, he said, "Hey, it is what is." His gaze dipped to my torso. "And I don't trust the jacket."

I didn't either. But that wasn't the point. More confused than annoyed, I said, "But I gave you the key to my room."

"So?"

"So I had lots of shirts in the closet. And I guess I'm a little curious why didn't you just grab one of *those*."

"Because I didn't have time."

How was that possible? He'd been gone for forty minutes. My hotel room was only a ten-minute walk away. There and back would've taken him twenty minutes with another twenty to spare.

I stared up at him. "So, did you stop off for coffee or something?"

"No." His voice hardened. "Now are you gonna get dressed or not?"

Still, I hesitated. *Maybe this was some sort of test?*

Or maybe a punishment?

I frowned. *A Shirt of Shame?*

Given Jack's personality, I could almost see it.

But if he wanted to watch me cringe and shudder – well more than I had already– he was in for a rude awakening, because I refused to give him the satisfaction.

So instead I summoned up a cheerful smile. "Sure. I'd just love to put it on, as soon as you leave."

He was gone before I'd barely finished the sentence – like the mere thought of my flesh made him want to run for the hills.

Well that wasn't humiliating or anything.

Unfortunately, my humiliation was far from over.

CHAPTER 26

Becka

The book signing started out surprisingly well.

After a brief introduction by one of the event's organizers, I leapt into action, guided by a list of instructions provided by the publishing company.

It was a good thing I had them, too, considering that Jack had given me nearly no direction at all. *No.* All *he'd* said was, "Remember, it's not your job to keep the peace."

It's not like I'd needed the warning. The crowd, even as big as it was, looked peaceful enough. They'd even formed an official line in front of the table where Jack would be signing his books.

Sure, the line was obscenely long, but I saw no reason to worry. The process was nice and simple. Someone would come up with a book – or sometimes multiple books – and I'd greet that person while Jack finished up with the previous person.

In short, he manned the table while I manned the line. *Easy-peasy.*

I had to admit, Jack was a lot friendlier than I might've expected – not to *me*, of course, but to his fans.

But his fans were nice, too. In fact, some of them were a little *too* nice. By the end of the first hour, Jack had been propositioned three times already – once by someone old enough to be his grandmother and twice by girls younger than me.

And then, there were the guys. The way it looked, they practically worshipped him, treating him like some sort of rock star or something.

I was watching Jack sign a paperback for a guy named Maurice when the next guy in line – someone who'd given his name as Bradley

– asked, "So, who are *you* supposed to be?"

"Me? I'm Jack Ward's assistant." With a sheepish smile, I added, "Well during the tour, anyway."

The guy frowned. "No. I meant your costume. Are you like a clown or something?"

I looked down. Okay, my shirt *did* have a certain clownish quality, but it's not like I was wearing floppy red shoes. "Nope. I'm just wearing plain ol' regular clothes."

His frown deepened. "You sure?"

I considered my shirt. "Um…Maybe?"

He eyed my outfit up and down. "Nah. I don't think so."

"Well, my *skirt's* regular." I pointed to my feet. "And so are my shoes."

The guy studied my outfit for another long moment, and eventually gave a slow nod. "Ohhhh, I get it." With a sudden grin, he announced, "You're a half-clown hybrid, like in *Circus House 3*."

I froze.

Circus House?

Three?

I had no idea what that was. *A video game? A movie? A comic book?* But the guy looked so pleased with himself that I didn't have the heart to pop his proverbial balloon.

I smiled. "Boy, that's a really good guess." *I think.*

"So I was right?" His grin widened. "I knew it!"

Well, that made one of us. But hey, if he was happy, I was happy.

As the book signing continued, I took at least *some* comfort from the fact that my outfit wasn't nearly as outlandish as some others, even if it did generate more commentary than I liked.

But why fight it, right?

I was just getting into a nice, steady groove when, at the back of the line, I spotted trouble times two.

It was the two girls from earlier.

When they saw me looking, the blonde gave a fluttery little wave and lifted an oversized paperback high enough for me to see.

I felt my gaze narrow. It was *my* book.

I was sure of it.

With growing concern, I turned and gave Jack a sideways glance. From his spot at the table, he was signing a new hardcover of "Swordplay" for a cute older lady name Marie.

If Jack noticed the dynamic duo, he gave no sign.

Was that good? Or bad?

Heck if *I* knew.

As for the line itself, I still managed to keep it going. As I did, I watched with growing unease as the girls moved ever closer to the front. By the time they finally reached me, I was simmering with anger and agitation.

The blonde gave me a sunny smile. "Hi."

I didn't smile back. "Hi."

She held up the paperback. "I'm here to get my book signed."

My jaw clenched. "*Your* book?"

She gave a toss of her golden hair. "It's mine now."

Next to her, the brunette snickered.

Now here's where things got sticky. I wasn't stupid. I knew they were goading me. But I'd be foolish to take the bait.

Even so, I had to forcibly remind myself that the paperback was probably replaceable, especially with the money that I was earning from Jack.

Plus, I was here in a professional capacity. *I could be professional, right?*

Stiffening my resolve, I forced a smile and held out my hand toward the book. "Great. And your name's Darbie, right?"

She clutched the book tighter. "Heeeeey, how do *you* know?"

Wasn't it obvious? "Because I heard it earlier."

"Oh," she said with a little frown. "I *guess* that's okay."

Fine. Whatever. Again, I reached for the book.

Again, she made no move to relinquish it. Instead, she eyed me with obvious suspicion as she said, "I'm not sure I should."

Yeah, I knew the feeling. Through clenched teeth, I said, "What, you're worried someone will steal it?"

She gave a hard nod. "Exactly."

"Sorry, but that's the process," I said. *"You* hand me the book. *I* open it to the right page, and then I tell Jack Ward your name so he can sign it."

Her gaze shifted to Jack, and her eyes brightened. Reluctantly, I turned to look. He was still occupied with the guy in front of her – a teenager who was wearing a metallic shirt designed to look like chain mail.

When I looked back to Darbie, she informed me with a smirk, "I'll hand it to him myself, thank you very much."

Yeah, well, you're not welcome. Still, I gritted out, "Terrific. I'll let him know."

Next to her, the blouse-ripping brunette chimed in, "You bet your ass, you will." Leaning closer, she practically hissed, "And you should've told us that you worked for him."

I smiled. "And you should've told me you were a psycho."

I stifled a gasp. *Damn it.*

I hadn't meant to say that.

Now both of them were glaring, which was pretty rich considering that one of them was holding stolen merchandise.

My merchandise, to be exact.

The blonde said, "If anyone's a psycho, it's you." She glanced down at my chest, and her tone grew snotty. "Nice shirt, by the way."

Instantly, heat rose to my face. *Ah yes. The Shirt of Shame.*

Still, I summoned up the brightest smile I could muster. "Thank you. Jack Ward gave it to me."

She blinked. Again, her gaze shifted to Jack. "Really?"

I looked toward the table and felt my blush deepen. The teenager was long gone. But Jack was still there. And he *didn't* look happy as his gaze shifted from me to the girls.

Great. On top of everything else, I'd been caught flat-footed.

Going for a recovery, I hustled toward him with the two girls on my heels. As I closed the distance, I told Jack, "This is Darbie. And *apparently*, she's going to hand you the book herself."

The blonde gave him a winning smile. "That's Darbie with two e's."

Huh? I tried to think. *Darbee? Derbie? Something else?*

I looked to Darbie and suggested, "Maybe you should spell it on an index card? You know, so there's no mistake?"

As I spoke, I reached for the stack of blank index cards, helpfully provided by the event organizers. I was still in mid-reach when Jack's voice cut in, saying, "No need. I've got this."

I drew back my hand. "Oh. Okay." And with that, I turned and left the table to greet the next person in line – an older guy holding a hardcover book in each hand.

As I made a note of the new guy's name, I was overly conscious of the sounds emanating from the table behind me. Even now, Jack was saying, "So, Darbie, huh?"

"Right," she said. "And remember—"

"Two e's. Got it."

Darbie giggled. "If you want, you can write down my phone number, too, like below your signature or something."

Her phone number? *Inside the book?*

Under my breath, I said, "A fat lot of good *that'll* do."

The guy in front of me frowned. "Excuse me?"

I summoned up a smile. "Nothing. Sorry."

Still, I couldn't help but marvel at the ridiculousness of Darbie's request. After all, if Jack wrote down *her* phone number inside the actual book – a book that she was obviously planning to keep – how on Earth would Jack know which number to call?

Bye-bye phone number.

And here, I thought *I* was the one not thinking straight.

Then again, Jack *did* have that effect on people.

And now, Darbie was saying, "And write something really nice too. Pretty please?"

I muttered, "You forgot the sugar on top."

The guy in front of me said, "Sugar? What sugar?"

"Sorry," I said. "Bad joke."

"But I love jokes." His face broke into a wide grin. "Go ahead. Hit me with one."

I froze like a clown in headlights. I loved jokes, too. But suddenly, I couldn't recall a single one.

From behind me, Darbie gave another giggle. "Oh, please. I am *not* a trouble-maker, honest."

The brunette chimed in, "But look here, Darbie. He wrote that you're his *favorite* trouble-maker. That's good, right?" Her voice grew husky as she added, apparently to Jack, "Just so you know, we sometimes cause trouble together."

From the tone of her voice, it was pretty obvious what kind of trouble she meant.

Naked trouble.

Times two.

Or times three, if I counted Jack.

Against my better judgment, I turned to look. Jack was still writing in the book while the girls ogled his pen like it was their new favorite sex toy.

The blonde gushed, "I just *love* the way you do it, saving my name for last. It's like you're building suspense or something."

As I gave a mental eye-roll, she pointed to something on the signature page. "And I see *your* name right there at the bottom." She leaned in close, offering up a nice view of her cleavage. "Your signature's so sexy, too, all big and bold like that."

Oh, for God's sake.

I'd been a fan of Jack for years. And even *I* wouldn't drool over his signature.

Much.

From behind me, the guy waiting in line said, "Hey, have you heard the one about the talking dog?"

I jumped at the sound of his voice. "Um…" I turned to face him and summoned up an encouraging smile. "No, actually. But I'd love to hear it."

I wasn't even lying. At the moment, a distraction – *any* distraction – would be a very good thing.

"Sorry, but I was hoping you could tell *me*." He chuckled. "I only caught the tail end."

"Oh." Now I hardly knew what to say. "Gosh, that's too bad."

He frowned. "But that *was* the joke. Get it? Tail end? Because dogs have tails?"

"Ohhhhh." I forced a laugh. "Yeah. I haven't heard that one before."

And yet, from the table behind me, I was hearing plenty.

"But wait," Darbie was saying. "My name – I think you made a tiny little mistake."

I gave a derisive snort. *What, not enough e's?*

At the table, Jack told her, "No mistake here."

"See, but, actually…" Darbie lowered her voice to nearly a whisper. "That's not my name."

Jack said, "Sorry, no do-overs."

Again, I turned to look. Darbie had retrieved the paperback and was studying its opening pages. She looked up, and her eyebrows furrowed. "But *I'm* not Becka."

CHAPTER 27

Jack

Right. She *wasn't* Becka.

Unlike Anna's little sister, Darbie – however the hell she spelled it – was a star-fucker if I'd ever met one. And that went double if I included her friend.

I said, "And your point is…?"

She turned the signature page outward so I could see it. "It's the wrong name." She smiled like she wasn't getting the hint. "Mine's Darbie, with two e's, remember?"

I didn't smile back. "Want to know what I remember?"

"What?'

"You giving my assistant a hard time."

Darbie's smile faded. "But she was totally rude to us."

Next to her, the brunette added, "Yeah. And she's a total psycho."

My gaze shifted to Becka. She was talking to the next guy in line, but I'd be a fool to think she wasn't listening.

I looked back to Darbie. "Maybe," I said. "But she's *my* psycho, so take your party somewhere else." I looked toward the paperback I'd just signed. "And leave the book."

"But it's mine!" Darbie protested.

I knew better. "You sure about that?"

She lifted her chin. "Well, it's mine *now*."

"We'll see."

"What does *that* mean?" Darbie asked.

"It means it's time for you to go."

"Fine," she said. "But I'm still taking the book."

I shrugged. "Suit yourself." Signed or not, the book was replaceable. *Or retrievable.* I still couldn't decide which.

Later.

I sent the duo on their way, looking decidedly less happy than when they'd arrived.

Good.

I wasn't happy myself.

Becka was proving to be a problem in more ways than one. And like most problems, I'd find a way to fix it, one way or another.

Until then, I'd be smart to keep my distance.

It was a good plan – nice and neat. The plan lasted for less than twelve hours before things got surprisingly messy.

And I had only myself to blame.

CHAPTER 28

Becka

Ten hours later, I was still stewing. Not only had Jack practically called me a psycho, he'd neglected to retrieve my book. Instead, he'd simply let those two girls waltz out of the conference room, as if they *weren't* taking something that didn't belong to them.

I hated thieves.

My stepdad had been the biggest thief I'd ever met. Oh sure, he wasn't a criminal of the smash-and-grab variety, but he'd still managed to chalk up an impressive array of financial crimes, many that harmed people in our own community.

So yes, I realized that a signed paperback wasn't such a huge deal in the big scheme of things.

And yet, it still grated. The fact that Jack had actually held the book in his hands, signed it to *my* name, and then let those girls carry if off anyway, well, it was making a little crazy.

Not psycho.

Just crazy. There *was* a difference.

Unfortunately, this same craziness made it nearly impossible for me to sleep that night, even in spite of my posh hotel room and comfy mattress.

At nearly 3 a.m., I gave up entirely. I crawled out of bed, got dressed, and left my room. I wandered down to the lobby with a different paperback – one *not* written by Jack Ward – in hopes that a change of scenery might help me relax.

I found a nice cozy chair behind a big potted plant and tried to focus on my book – a new one that I'd purchased in the hotel gift shop for just such an emergency.

The effort was a total waste. I couldn't focus at all. My thoughts kept returning to Jack, wondering what exactly he was up to.

Other than the actual book-signing, I'd barely seen him, unless I wanted to count our tense discussion in the powder room.

Either he hated my company, or he was the least sociable person I'd ever met.

As my thoughts swirled, and my attention wavered, I happened to look up just in time to see something that made me stop and stare.

It was Jack Ward, striding in through the hotel's main entrance. His clothes were dark, and his hair was rumpled. He was *almost* smiling.

He looked, well, satisfied, like he'd just gotten lucky.

I froze. *Oh.*

Given the fact that it was nearly four in the morning, it wasn't hard to guess what he'd been doing *or* what kind of "luck" he'd had. At the realization, I slumped deeper in my chair – not out of disappointment, but rather because I didn't want to be seen watching him.

Yes. That *had* to be it.

But then, in mid-slump, I spotted something that made me sit up with a sudden jolt.

He was carrying a book – and not just any book. It was an oversized paperback that looked all too familiar.

How on Earth did he get it?

I stared in total confusion as a whole slew of possibilities slithered across my brain. Very few of them were nice. Some of them were downright nasty. All of them made me feel just a little bit nauseous.

I was still staring when Jack suddenly stopped moving. Slowly, his head turned in my direction, and our gazes locked.

His smile, faint as it was, disappeared entirely as he eyed me across the nearly empty lobby.

I didn't flinch, and I didn't look away. Instead I waited, nearly certain that he would simply walk over and return the book.

Except he didn't.

Instead, he looked forward once again and resumed his original path toward the elevators.

No hello. No wave. No nothing.

Unable to stop myself, I stood and began stalking toward him.

Yes, he was my boss, but I still wanted answers.

And I wanted them *now.*

CHAPTER 29

Becka

By the time I reached him, the nearest elevator was already open, and he was striding into it. I rushed in behind him and watched in awkward silence as he hit the buttons for two floors – seventeen and eighteen.

Eighteen was mine, so I could only assume that seventeen was his.

As the elevator doors slid shut, leaving the two of us alone in the confined space, I looked to him and said, "Well?"

He didn't even glance in my direction. Instead, he kept his gaze straight ahead, facing the elevator doors instead of me. In a tight voice, he replied, "Well what?"

"Oh come on. You know what. Listen, I know you're not big on wasting time, so why don't you just tell me?"

With slow deliberation, he finally turned to face me. "If you've got a question, you're gonna have to be more specific."

"All right." I pointed to the paperback. "Is that my book?"

He made no move to hand it over. "No comment."

It was easy to guess what *that* meant. "So how'd you get it?"

His gaze hardened, and the silence stretched out. As the elevator climbed, my heart sank. I could just imagine how he'd come into contact with the book, along with the person who'd swiped it from me.

I said, "I'm just curious, that's all."

"Yeah? Well I'm not paying you to be curious."

I almost flinched. His words stung, even more so because they were technically true. And if he were an ordinary boss – as opposed to a family friend who'd practically dragged me here against my original wishes – I might've simply let it go.

I might've even apologized for being so intrusive.

But I'd been on-edge ever since the book signing, and his secrecy wasn't helping. It's not like I expected to hang out with him or anything. But it *was* strange that I was supposedly his assistant, and yet had no idea where he went or what he did when we weren't together.

I still had that cell phone, the one he'd given me at Flynn's place a few hours after I'd listened to that tearful message. But no one ever called. And even that one godawful message had been wiped clean, along with any contact information.

The whole thing was beyond strange.

Under his steady gaze, I started to squirm. Unable to stop myself, I finally looked away. As I did, my gaze landed on the elevator buttons, and I felt myself frown.

The numbers went all the way up to seventy. I wasn't the most experienced traveler in the world, but even *I* knew that billionaires didn't stay on the lower floors.

No, they stayed at the very top in penthouse suites with private balconies and room to spread out.

If Jack were anyone else, I might've wondered if he was afraid of heights – *or* if he was trying to save a buck.

But I'd seen his demeanor during the fight that had carried us here. He'd been as cool as a cucumber, even on takeoff and through enough turbulence to make me uneasy. And, as far as the whole penny-pinching idea, it was beyond ridiculous. We'd flown here on his private jet, for God's sake.

As these thoughts bounced around in my sleep-deprived brain, I realized that I hadn't yet responded to his last statement.

I'm not paying you to be curious.

Who knows? Maybe he didn't expect an answer. Either way, I wouldn't learn anything by staring like a coward at a bunch of numbered buttons.

Reluctantly, I looked back to Jack, only to see that he was still hammering me with those ice blue eyes of his, as if he could freeze me on sight.

He was wrong.

I wasn't freezing. I was melting with embarrassment.

By now, I knew exactly how he'd obtained that book, and for some stupid reason, it irritated me more than it should.

Obviously, he'd given in to Darbie's charms, which had been on clear display earlier.

I didn't want to believe it, but it was the only explanation that made sense. After all, no one returned smiling at four in the morning from simply retrieving a book.

Plus, if he'd gotten the book a different way, like if he'd just found it on the sidewalk or something, he'd surely tell me.

Right?

But instead, he was acting like I'd just caught him in mid hump.

I muttered, "Never mind. Forget it."

"Done."

And with that, he turned away just in time for the ding that announced our arrival on the seventeenth floor. When the elevator doors slid open, he strode out, taking my book with him.

Fine.

I didn't want it, anyway.

All I wanted was a shower, if only to wash away the unpleasantness of our encounter, along with all of those visions of Jack Ward encountering Darbie, and maybe even her friend, in the most intimate of ways.

Forget the book.

And forget *him*, too.

Except it wasn't that easy.

CHAPTER 30

Becka

On the phone, Anna was saying, "So, you think he had sex with them?"

"Maybe not both of them," I said. "But probably *one* of them at least."

"Oh come on. You don't know that."

"Not for sure," I admitted. "But it's the only thing that makes sense. I mean, why else would've he acted so strange?"

"Aside from you lying in wait?"

I frowned. *What, like a spider?*

I didn't get it. Just yesterday, she'd warned me away from this job – and from Jack Ward in particular. Now she was singing a totally different tune.

Given my current mood, the tune felt wrong and off-key. "I wasn't 'lying in wait,'" I told her. "I was reading in the lobby. Big difference."

"Look, I get it," she said. "But did you ever think of just letting him walk on by?"

"Oh, please. I couldn't, even if I wanted to. You *did* hear the part where he spotted me, right?"

"Yeah. And I *also* heard the part where you followed him into the elevator and got all nosy with him."

Nosy? Seriously? I made a sound of annoyance. "Whose side are you on, anyway?"

Her voice softened. "Yours. You know that."

It was eight o'clock in the morning, just four hours after that scene in the elevator. I was tired and cranky – and with good reason.

Sleep had proved nearly impossible – just like my boss, and now my sister, too.

This was *not* going to be a good day.

And now Anna was saying, "He's a really private person. You knew that going in."

"So?"

"So you made your own bed by accepting the offer. And now that you've *made* the bed, you might as well sleep in it. Or just quit. But you can't exactly stay and expect *him* to change."

Bed? Sleep? What a joke. I hadn't slept. Instead, I'd spent most of the night tossing and turning with agitation.

And the single time I *had* drifted off, I'd seen him in my dreams. He'd been holding my book in one hand while he pleasured Darbie with the other.

Stupidly, obscenely, Darbie was wearing that hideous multi-colored shirt, the one he'd given me as a replacement for my ripped blouse. Even worse, the Darbie in my dream wore nothing else – well, except for big red floppy shoes.

Talk about messed up.

At this rate, I might never sleep again.

When I said nothing in reply, my sister said, "And you still don't know for sure what he was doing."

"Last night? Oh come on. You can't be serious."

"But I am," she said. "Maybe he couldn't sleep. Maybe he went out for a walk. Maybe he just got up really early."

I recalled his tousled hair and satisfied smile.

No one looked like that in the morning unless they'd had a really good night.

I glanced at the nearby mirror, and frowned. *I* didn't have a good night. That much was obvious from the dark circles and red-rimmed eyes.

Damn it. I needed to pull myself together – and fast. In just a couple of hours, I'd be seeing him again. Today it wasn't a book-signing, but rather some sort of speech, followed by a Q&A with audience members.

According to the publisher's instructions, I'd be holding a microphone and going from person to person as they asked whatever.

Too bad *I* couldn't be in the audience. *I'd have some questions, all right.*

"Listen," my sister said, "there's something I need to tell you, but it's sort of a secret."

I perked up. "Oh yeah? What?"

"You remember when I mentioned the book tour, right? How the cities made no sense?"

"Yeah, so?"

"And the only one that *did* make sense was the event in Atlanta, where you are now?"

"Right."

"Well, the thing is…" She hesitated. "I just discovered something, and I'm feeling a little guilty."

"What is it?" I asked.

"Did you know, Jack wasn't originally scheduled to do that event?"

"Really?"

"Really," she said. "He was a substitute for someone else. And the thing is, the only reason *Jack's* doing the Atlanta thing at all is because the *other* person had something he wanted to do instead, and asked Jack for a favor – a *big* favor, considering how reclusive Jack is."

It wasn't hard to figure out who she meant. "You're talking about Flynn, aren't you?"

"Uh, yeah."

Suddenly, her change in attitude made total sense. My sister – heaven help her – was way too nice for her own good.

As I listened, she went on to tell me that Jack had agreed to do this event as a favor for Flynn because it fell during the week of Flynn and Anna's one-year anniversary as a couple. Apparently, Flynn had been determined to spend the full week alone with Anna, away from prying eyes.

And Jack had stepped in to make that possible.

I had to admit, it *was* pretty nice.

Anna finished by suggesting that I try to make amends, if only to ensure that I didn't have a miserable summer.

Of course, she was right, even if it *wasn't* what I'd wanted to hear.

When the call ended, I sank back onto the bed and tried to think. Jack was such a mess of crazy contradictions, with so many sides to his personality, I hardly knew what to think.

But then, I brightened.

Today was that Q&A. I'd be there the whole time. Surely, I'd learn *something* useful – maybe some new details about his private life or some insight into what made him tick.

Turns out, I was wrong. In the end, I learned nearly nothing – except that he was really good at dodging questions.

CHAPTER 31

Jack

The center stage wasn't my thing. Now don't get me wrong. I was grateful to my fans and not just for the money. But I didn't enjoy the spotlight – and enjoyed lying even less.

Everyone had a history. As for mine, there was the real version and the one written by the publisher's P.R. people.

Those histories didn't match.

That was fine by me. The less people knew, the better. But that didn't mean I enjoyed standing on a stage, shoveling shit to people who deserved more honesty than I could give them.

As Becka handed the microphone to a gray-haired woman in a flowered dress, I smiled to put the stranger at ease. She'd been waiting with her hand raised for a while now as Becka went from person to person, trying to give everyone a fair shot.

I had to admit, Becka was doing a good job of it, too. She had a way of putting people at ease, making them smile through their nerves. I'd seen it yesterday at the book-signing and more so today as she dealt with a crowd of people all wanting the same thing at the same time.

She was better at this than I'd expected. *Smarter, too.*

This would've been a good thing, if only I hadn't counted on the opposite – meaning someone who saw only what they were meant to see.

But that wasn't Becka. She was too curious, and noticed far too much.

Across the crowded auditorium, the woman in the flowered dress turned toward the stage and clutched the microphone tighter. "I was wondering... " She gave a nervous giggle. "Do you write your own sex scenes?"

The crowd laughed, and I smiled. *No need for me to be a dick about it.*

Okay, my books had sex. Not a lot, but enough to keep it real – and to balance the brutality of the other parts. The truth was, my characters were more likely to lose their heads than their hearts – and I didn't mean metaphorically.

With my smile in place, I replied, "I write it all, the good *and* the bad."

She was still holding the microphone. "If you ask me, it's all good." Her eyes brightened. "Especially *those* scenes."

My gaze drifted to Becka, whose cheeks had just gone rosy.

She was a blusher, all right.

I liked it.

And I hated it.

The truth was, I was more attracted to her than I should be, even if she *was* a pain in the ass.

When the laughter died away, I thanked the woman for the compliment and waited for the next question. And then, the one after that, and so on.

Most of the questions were fairly basic. *Where do I get my ideas? How do I name my characters? What's the back story of this character or that?*

These were the easy questions.

But others, they were more complicated.

My books – I could talk about just fine. But when it came to the topic of myself, I said as little as I could without being a prick. The questions continued hard and fast as Becka hustled from person to person.

Where did I call home? A cabin in the mountains.

Except the cabin was more like a fortress. And it was large enough to host a small army.

Favorite color? Black.

Not because it made me happy, but because it was best for melting into the shadows.

Favorite reading material? Non-fiction.

Not because I didn't enjoy a good story, but because information equaled power, which could be used for good *or* bad. And then, there were the murky spots in the middle, where people did good things for bad reasons, or vice versa.

Favorite food? Burgers.

Nothing more to that. Just hey, I liked a good burger as much as the next guy.

By the time the session ended, I was ready to move on. And hey, the audience seemed happy enough.

But Becka? She saw more than she should, and I had no doubt that soon, she'd be asking more questions of her own.

I wasn't wrong.

CHAPTER 32

Becka

Talk about frustrating. I'd just spent over two hours listening to Jack talk – first during his introductory remarks, and then during the Q&A session that followed.

During his actual speech, which had lasted barely thirty minutes, I'd been watching and waiting, thinking that I might finally get some clues into what made him tick.

I hadn't.

Mostly he'd talked about his characters and the process of getting his books made into movies. The audience had been utterly enthralled. But me? I'd been waiting for the good stuff, meaning clues as to who he *really* was.

No clues came – or at least no clues that told me anything I didn't already know.

Seriously, didn't this guy ever talk about himself?

Apparently not.

But if he thought he was fooling anyone with all of those non-answers, he was crazier than I was. And just for the record, I was feeling pretty darn crazy.

Other than a tense hello, we hadn't said more than two words to each other before his public appearance. And, in spite of my lingering curiosity, I hadn't mentioned the stolen paperback or the fact that he hadn't returned it.

As for Jack, he hadn't mentioned the fact that I'd been – in my sister's words – rather nosy last night.

By mutual agreement, we were apparently pretending that last night had never happened.

There was just one tiny problem. *I wasn't feeling all that agreeable.* Even worse, I'd come to realize that my sister was right. I *had* been rather intrusive, which meant that I owed him an apology whether I felt like it or not.

As Jack left the stage to thunderous applause, I stood near the main door, thanking people as they filed out, chatting and laughing like they'd actually enjoyed themselves.

As they did, I tried to put myself in their positions. A week ago, I would've been thrilled, too.

But now, I was mostly unsatisfied. This was Jack's last appearance in Atlanta. Tomorrow morning, we'd be flying out to our new destination – some mid-sized town in Eastern Tennessee.

When the auditorium finally emptied, I turned and strode toward the private area behind the stage. By the time I reached it, Jack was already heading out, leaving through a rear exit.

I called out to his receding back, "Wait."

He stopped and turned around, giving me a look that wasn't exactly welcoming.

I hustled forward and asked, "Is there anything else I should be doing?"

"Yeah," he said. "Enjoying yourself."

"What?"

"Do whatever," he said. "You're off the clock." Again, he turned to go, without so much as a goodbye.

Probably I should've just let him leave. But like a moth to the flame, I fluttered forward, drawn by a sudden urge to put all of this unpleasantness behind us.

"Wait," I said for the second time.

Once again, he stopped and turned around, looking even less enthused than he had the first time.

I cleared my throat. "Listen, about last night, I'm sorry, okay? I didn't mean to be rude."

"Forget it," he said. "Anything else?"

The question was way too tempting. Against my better judgment, I said, "Well, since you asked…"

In the back of my mind, I *knew* I should stop. *But I didn't. I couldn't.* Bracing myself, I said, "I *am* still a little curious. How'd you get that book?" I forced a laugh. "Did you find it on the sidewalk or something?"

His mouth tightened. "No."

So much for that theory.

"Uh, yeah," I stammered. "I didn't think so."

His gaze hardened. "So what *did* you think?"

At his sharp tone, I almost flinched. "Nothing."

"Wrong answer."

"What, why?"

"Because you're lying."

"You don't know that."

"I do," he said. "So go ahead. Just say it."

I wasn't following. "Say what?"

"What you're thinking."

Yeah, right. "You're not serious."

"Wrong again." He made a forwarding motion with his hand. "So go on. Tell me your theory."

"You mean about the book? And how you got it back?" My stomach knotted, and my spine grew twitchy. I *so* didn't want to say. But he *had* asked, so I took a deep breath and just tossed it out there. "Well, if I had to guess, I'd say that you probably, um, charmed her out of it."

His gaze darkened, and the knot in my stomach grew. From the look on his face, he wouldn't know charm if it bit him on the ass.

In a tight voice, he replied, "Yeah? How?"

"What do you mean how?"

"Do you mean I said pretty words and made her blush?" His gaze dipped to my lips, and something in his expression changed. "Like you."

Absently, I reached up to touch my face. It felt warm. *Too warm.* Suddenly distracted, I murmured, "I'm not sure Darbie's the blushing type."

"So, you wanna know if I fucked her? Is that it?"

I drew back. *Talk about cutting to the chase.* I wasn't sure what was more shocking – his language or his bluntness.

I stammered, "Well, I wouldn't have put it that way, but yes, it *would* make sense. At the book-signing, she, uh, made it pretty clear that she was yours for the taking."

"Yeah? And how about me?"

"What do you mean?"

"Did *I* make it clear that *I* was interested?"

"No," I grudgingly admitted. "But people change their minds all the time."

His gaze sharpened. "Do they?"

"Yes, actually." I was living proof of that, because right now I was wishing that I'd been smart enough to leave with everyone else.

But I hadn't.

And now that I'd started this, I felt compelled to finish it.

In a fit of pique, I said, "I don't know why you're acting so funny. It's not like you murdered her to get it." I made a scoffing sound. "Or did you?"

He looked for a long moment before saying in a dangerously quiet voice, "You might want to make up your mind."

"On what?"

"Your theory," he said. "So tell me. Did I fuck her? Or kill her?"

His words were so cold, I stifled a shiver. But if he thought he could scare me off with *that* attitude, he had another thing coming.

And besides, two could play at this game.

I forced a smile. "Hey, why not both?"

He stared down at me. And for the briefest moment, he looked almost ready to laugh. But he didn't. Instead, he simply asked, "In what order?"

"What?"

"In this scenario of yours, did I fuck her, then kill her?" His mouth tightened. "Or the opposite?"

It took me a moment to realize what he was really saying. And then, when I caught the gist of it, I did the dumbest thing imaginable.

I laughed.

It wasn't a big laugh, more like a secret laugh, like when someone farts in the library. But I couldn't help it. His question was so sick and twisted, and yet so stupidly funny.

Right. Because necrophilia was everybody's idea of a jolly good time.

My hands flew to my mouth, and I stared up at him in total horror – not because of his statement, but rather because I fully realized that I was acting like a total idiot. *Again.*

Should I apologize?

Probably not.

I had to face facts. There was no way on Earth he'd take me seriously *now*, not with me acting like a crazy person.

And besides, I never had the chance to apologize anyway, because once again, he was heading out the door.

This time, I didn't try to stop him.

Regardless, I decided, it was time to turn over a new leaf, even if my curiosity *was* killing me – even more so the very next day, when the mystery of the book only deepened.

CHAPTER 33

Becka

I was in the hotel lobby waiting for Jack when a snippy female voice from somewhere behind me called out, "Have you found your book yet?"

Crap. I recognized the voice.

I turned to look. Sure enough, there she was – Darbie, along with the same brunette as before. They were striding toward me, wheeling fashionable suitcases behind them.

Darbie looked beyond satisfied, and maybe a little smug.

So Jack *hadn't* killed her. *Go figure.*

It was a joke, obviously, even if I didn't feel like laughing. *And why?* It was because I was all too aware that Jack had probably done the *other* thing while retrieving the book – a book which he *still* hadn't returned, by the way.

Jerk.

And that went double for the dynamic duo, who'd just stopped directly in front of me. From what I could tell, they were checking out of this very same hotel.

As far as Darbie's question, I wasn't quite sure how to answer. Obviously, she'd relinquished the book. *But did she realize that Jack hadn't bothered to return it to me?*

If not, I *so* didn't want to be the one to enlighten her. *After all, how humiliating was that?*

Looking to reveal as little as possible, I stiffly replied, "Yeah. I saw it. So I guess you deserve a thanks."

From me?

I honestly didn't know. On top of *that*, I had no idea what *she* knew either. All in all, I was at a serious disadvantage.

Darbie and her friend exchanged a look. With an odd little smile, the brunette asked, "Are you being sarcastic?"

I felt my eyebrows furrow. *Was I?*

"No," I murmured. "I don't think so."

At this, both of them laughed like I'd just said something funny. Through her laughter, Darbie said, "What, you don't know?"

All *I* knew was that my timing sucked. As part of my vow to be a better employee, I'd come down to the lobby fifteen minutes early so I'd be waiting when Jack arrived to leave for the airport.

Apparently, that had been a terrible mistake. Probably I should've waited in my room, or maybe even out on the sidewalk – anywhere the two girls *weren't*.

With a sigh, I turned away, leaving them to think whatever they wanted.

But when I did, they sidled up beside me, suitcases and all.

I had no suitcases, not with me, anyway. A half-hour earlier, a bell hop had come up to my room and retrieved my luggage for delivery to the limo, telling me that Jack Ward had ordered the service personally.

The guy wouldn't even accept a tip, telling me that this, too, had been taken care of by Jack.

All in all, it was surprisingly thoughtful.

Who knows? Maybe I wasn't the only one trying to turn over a new leaf. Still, this whole leaf-turning business would've been a whole lot easier if only the girls had simply ignored me and kept on walking.

But they hadn't. And now, they were sidling even closer, as if they were determined to make me feel as uncomfortable as possible.

It was working, too. Still, I refused to run off like a coward.

As I stood in stubborn silence, the brunette turned to the blonde and said in an overly conversational tone, "Hey Darbie, by any chance, do you have some reading material that I could borrow?"

"Why yes," Darbie replied. "I have a bestseller right here in my carry-on."

Oh, for God's sake. They sounded like bad actresses in a late-night infomercial. I could practically see them appearing on my TV. *"Say Darbie, do you have a disgusting social disease? Well, I have just the cream to take care of it..."*

I rolled my eyes. *Give me a break.*

And now Darbie was saying, "The author signed it personally, you know."

Her point was obvious. Apparently, Jack had given Darbie a new book as a replacement for mine. And he'd signed it, too.

I gave a silent scoff. *Big whoop.*

Still, I had to wonder, if Jack had been willing to give them a signed book, why on Earth hadn't he simply done it at the book-signing? I mean, he'd had a whole stack of brand-new copies underneath his table for just such an emergency.

And then it hit me. Probably he'd wanted an official reason to meet up with the girls later on, away from prying eyes, including my own.

I frowned. *What a total faker.* To think, he'd actually made a pretty good show of giving them the brush-off.

And me? Like a total idiot, I'd fallen for his act.

Talk about stupid.

It didn't help when Darbie crouched down and reached into the outside pocket of her carry-on. She retrieved an oversized paperback and gave it a little wave. "Oh look!" she said. "I have it right here."

As I stared at the thing, I felt my brow wrinkle in confusion. The book *wasn't* new. *Far from it.* In fact, it looked exactly like mine, right down to the original cover and all of those tell-tale creases along the spine.

My stomach sank. *Oh, no.*

With growing mortification, I recalled that tense scene in the elevator, along with our argument after the Q&A. That book he'd been carrying – it *hadn't* been mine.

And this meant what, exactly? That Jack *hadn't* seen Darbie again?

Shit.

No wonder he'd been so angry. Forget killing her, or even the *other* thing. The way it looked now, he hadn't seen her at all.

I might've been thrilled at the discovery, if only I didn't feel like throwing up. *Or strangling someone, maybe even myself.*

And now Darbie was saying in mock sympathy. "Oh no. Someone looks unhappy."

Yes. Because I was.

I was *very* unhappy, not because of their little show, but because I'd made an ass of myself, *repeatedly*, over that stupid book. And now, I wanted to crawl into a hole and hide.

Not from the girls.

From Jack.

I gave Darby an annoyed look. "I don't get it," I said. "Why would you even *want* that book, anyway?"

With feigned innocence, she replied, "What do you mean?"

"It's not even signed to you. So why would you want it?"

She smiled. "Better me than you. And besides, I can write in my own name later on."

Seriously?

And yet, in some twisted way, I could actually see it. There was just one detail missing. With a bitter scoff, I said, "And the two e's – where do they go anyway?"

She frowned. "What e's?"

"The ones in your name." *Dumb-ass.*

She smirked. "That's none of your business." And with that, she tossed the paperback to her friend, who with a smirk of her own, opened it up to the title page.

But soon her smirk faded. She turned a few more pages before looking up in apparent confusion.

Darbie asked, "What's wrong?"

With a little frown, the brunette replied, "The signature. It's gone."

Darbie gave a snort of disbelief. "Oh, stop it. It is not." Darbie reached over, yanked the book out of her friend's grip, and began leafing through the pages. Soon *she* was frowning, too.

From this angle, I couldn't see the book's interior, but I *could* see their confusion as plain as day.

The brunette sidled closer to Darbie and said, "Do you think he used disappearing ink or something?"

In unison, they both looked to me.

I shook my head. "Don't ask *me*. I have no idea."

And I didn't.

But boy, did I ever want to find out.

CHAPTER 34

Becka

As we headed to the airport, I gave Jack yet another sideways glance. He was engrossed in his cell phone, saying nothing as the limo driver navigated the busy morning traffic.

Recalling my vow to no longer pester him with questions, I hadn't asked about the book – although heaven knows I wanted to.

Earlier at the hotel, by the time Jack had arrived in the lobby, the two girls had already stomped off, looking confused and irritated.

I could definitely relate.

I still had no idea why the paperback in Darbie's possession no longer contained Jack's signature. Recalling the brunette's theory, I almost rolled my eyes. Disappearing ink? *Please.* I wasn't buying *that* for a minute.

No. Obviously the book had been switched out for another copy.

But when?

During the actual signing?

No. I'd been there. I surely would've seen. Plus, Darbie would've noticed *that* right away.

This led to my next theory. Maybe Jack had switched out the books sometime afterward. *But how?*

And then, there was the dumbest theory of all. Maybe Darbie and her friend had gotten a second paperback and were just messing with me.

But that wasn't believable either. For one thing, the book's cover was several years outdated, which meant that an identical book wouldn't be easy to find – not unless they robbed a library or found a copy in some used book store.

On top of that, I'd seen their reactions to the unsigned book. They'd been just as surprised as I was.

This meant it was definitely Jack's doing.

As these thoughts churned in my brain, I gave Jack yet another glance, only to freeze in mid-motion when I realized that he was no longer looking at his phone.

He was looking at *me*.

It wasn't just a glance either. He was giving me one of those penetrating looks, like he was trying to puzzle something out.

Now *that* was hilarious. If anyone needed to solve a mystery, it was me.

Maybe the script called for me to glance away, embarrassed that I'd dared to look in his direction. *But forget that.* If *he* looked, *I* could look, too.

I gave him a stiff smile and kept on looking, staring straight into his eyes as he stared into mine.

It felt like a game or a challenge. And since *he'd* started it, I was determined to finish it.

I kept on looking. And so did he.

But then something happened.

His gaze changed, morphing from curiosity to interest. And then, for the briefest instant, he looked almost fascinated.

With me?

Now *that* was an eye-roller for sure.

Still, I felt my cheeks grow warm and my mouth go dry. If this were a movie, we might inexplicably fall into each other's arms and lock lips, like we'd been swept away in the moment.

But this *wasn't* a movie.

And he was my boss, not my boyfriend. Plus, Jack Ward wasn't the type to be swept away by anything. I knew *that* just as surely as I knew that he was the most fascinating person I'd ever met.

From reading his books, I had some decent guesses on the way he thought. He valued justice over mercy, family over strangers, and a glorious death over a lifetime of cowardice.

Maybe that's why I enjoyed his books so much, just like I enjoyed looking at him now. His hair was blond and thick. His jaw was square in the classic style. His lips were full, and his eyes were so blue, I was swimming in them.

Or maybe I was drowning, because soon I had to remind myself to breathe at all.

What was wrong with me, anyway?

What had started as a game was feeling like something else entirely. What, I didn't even know.

I heard myself say, "You're not gonna win, you know."

His gaze didn't waver. "Win what?"

"The staring contest." I gave him a sunny smile. "I can do this all day."

And I could. In truth, it would be stupidly easy, considering how attractive he was. It was no punishment to stare at him, that's for sure.

At my bold claim, his lips curved into the hint of a smile. "No you can't."

Hah! That's what *he* thought. Not bothering to hide my confidence, I replied. "Oh yeah? Why not?"

"Because we're here."

"What?" I looked around, but had no idea what he meant. All *I* saw was traffic and plenty of it. And it's not like the limo was slowing down. If anything, it was speeding up.

I turned back to Jack and asked, "What do you mean?"

He leaned back in his seat. "I win."

My jaw dropped. "What?"

Looking way too satisfied, he said, "You looked away first."

"But that's cheating!" I protested.

"Wrong," he said. "It's strategy."

"Oh yeah?" I felt my gaze narrow. "Well, I'll remember that the next time."

He smiled. "Good."

No. It wasn't good. It was terrible, because his smile sent a swarm of butterflies straight to my stomach.

Even worse, they refused to fly away, even on his private jet, when Jack turned the tables by asking some questions of his own.

CHAPTER 35

Jack

There's a saying, *No good deed goes unpunished.*

This trip was proof enough.

I'd begun with the noble intention of looking out for Flynn's future sister. But now? Let's just say, I was feeling less noble every time I saw her.

And, as far as my intentions, they were getting murkier by the minute.

In the limo, I'd wanted to kiss her. Hell, I'd wanted to do more than kiss her. *She made me smile.*

And I didn't like it.

Smiles led to attachment, which led to complications. And forget the fact that she was related to Flynn in a roundabout way.

Whether she realized it or not, I'd smiled more with her than I had with anyone over the last few years. Even so, I'd been working hard not to show it, if only to keep her at a distance.

It wasn't working.

This meant it was time to take a different approach.

We were fifteen minutes into the flight, and she'd surprised the hell out of me by not asking about Darbie's unsigned book.

Oh yeah, I'd caught that scene in the lobby, when Darbie and What's-her-name had been waving that book in Becka's face.

I hadn't liked it.

And I'd liked it even less when I realized what would happen afterward. I'd be hit with an avalanche of questions from Becka.

But that didn't happen.

Instead, she'd kept quiet, even while the questions played across her face. She hadn't asked them, but she *had* been thinking them.

At the condo, I hadn't pegged her as a thinker. But now, the more time I spent with her, the more I realized that her wheels were always turning – probing, speculating, watching.

She was different. And she'd captured my interest.

Still, she saw far more than she should. It was dangerous – just like my thoughts in the limo, when I'd been looking into her eyes and liking what I saw.

As far as questions, it was time to turn the tables. I looked to her and said, "So, an English lit degree, huh?"

She jumped in her seat, as if she were surprised that I'd spoken at all. With a trembling laugh, she replied, "Who, me?"

The jet seated ten, but there was just the two of us, sitting across from each other in the passenger area.

I made a show of looking around. "You see anyone else?"

She pointed toward the front of the plane. "The pilots?"

I didn't turn to look. "No."

"It was a joke," she said.

"Yeah. I got it."

She frowned. "Well, it couldn't have been too good if you didn't laugh."

I leaned back in my seat. "I'm laughing on the inside."

"Oh please," she said. "You are not."

She was right. *I wasn't.* The purpose of this conversation wasn't to yuck it up. It was to get Becka out of my system, verbally, that is.

The plan was to get her talking. The truth was, conversation was always a deal-breaker when it came to getting serious. Hell, an hour's worth of conversation with Imogen had been more than enough for me to know that we'd be going nowhere fast.

To Becka, I repeated the gist of my question. "So why English lit?"

She gave me an odd look. "Are you asking for real?"

"Sure. Why wouldn't I?"

"Well..." She hesitated. "I guess because you haven't been terribly chatty, so I'm wondering what's up."

I had to give her credit. She was good at cutting to the chase.

I liked that. *Not a good sign.*

I replied, "Hey, it's a two-hour flight."

"So?"

"So, you want to sit in silence?"

She gave it some thought. "I don't mind silence."

Huh. Me neither.

Still, it didn't fit with what I'd seen so far. "You seem talkative enough."

"Well maybe I'm a nervous talker."

"Meaning?"

She gave an embarrassed laugh. "Well, when I get nervous, I ramble sometimes. But normally, I'm not a huge talker, unless I know someone really well." She smiled. "Like my sister."

Shit.

I was the same way.

I tried again. "You realize you never answered the question, right?"

"About why English lit?" She paused to think. "Well for starters, I like the language, especially the old stuff."

"Old stuff?"

"You know, the classics."

Again – me, too.

I asked, "Like what?"

"Almost anything," she said. "I like the way they talked back then. It was so beautiful."

"It wasn't *all* beautiful," I said.

"Yeah. But even the ugliness was beautiful in its own way. Like take 'Macbeth.' It was so ghastly, but the language was so profound." She leaned forward. "And the brutality of it all. It really makes you think."

"You *do* realize they all die in the end, right?"

"They don't *all* die," she said. "And besides, I like happy stuff, too."

My lips twitched with the sudden urge to smile. "Well, that rules out my books."

"Hah!" she said. "Yours are happy."

I gave her a look. "Is that so?"

"Definitely." She grinned. "Like when Lord Brisbane was eaten by his own pigs, it was glorious."

My lips were still twitching. "Technically they weren't *his* pigs."

"Right," she said. "Because he stole them from that poor farmer. But they *were* his when they ate him." She paused, and her smile faded. "But I was kind of hoping they'd eat his wife, too."

I couldn't help it. I smiled. "Yeah? Why the wife?"

"Oh, you know," she said. "Because she conspired with that magistrate to steal her cousin's inheritance." Becka's voice hardened. "I *hate* corruption, especially when it hurts regular people."

Huh. Me, too. "Like the pig farmer."

"Exactly."

I just had to ask, "And what about pigs?"

She paused. "Well, I *do* like bacon."

Oh yeah. Me, too.

But that was a given.

Into my silence, she said, "You know what I think?"

"What?"

"I think it's nice when bad people get what's coming to them."

I felt my fingers clench. *Me, too.*

And the way *I* saw it, if they didn't get it by chance, there were ways to help that process along. But this, like many things, was better left unmentioned.

I said, "So you know a lot of bad people, do you?"

"No." She hesitated. "Well, maybe just one."

Her stepfather, obviously.

I knew more of her history than she realized. Still, I asked, "Does that include your roommate?"

"Okay, make that two people."

"And Tara, the girl who rented you the place – what about *her*?"

"All right." She bit her lip. "Two and a half then."

"Why the half?" I asked.

"Because," she said with a laugh, "if you keep going, I'll be up to a dozen. And that's just too depressing to consider."

Funny. She didn't look depressed.

And now I was only more intrigued. "A dozen, huh? Who?"

"Nobody in particular," she said. "I'm just saying, you find bad people wherever you go." She brightened. "But good people, too. Like Anna."

I'd met Anna and couldn't disagree.

Still, the conversation wasn't living up to my expectations. The more she talked, the more I *wanted* her to talk – *and*, the more *I* wanted to say in return.

The plan was backfiring, and I was just thinking of cutting my losses when she said, "How about you? Why'd you become a writer?"

"Better than working construction."

It was also better than following in my father's footsteps. He didn't create things. He destroyed them. Or stole them. But the topic of my father was strictly off-limits.

Becka said, "Oh come on. I answered *your* question."

"Yeah. And I answered yours, too."

"What? The construction thing?" She rolled her eyes. "Oh, please. That doesn't count."

"Why not?"

"Because it was a total non-answer, the kind you give when you really don't want to say." She studied my face. "You do that a lot, you know."

I *did* know. But that was the point. "Hey, it wasn't a lie."

"Yeah, but it wasn't the whole truth either."

When I made no reply, she said, "All right, fine. But speaking of questions, I have one that's related to my job."

"All right. Go ahead."

"It's about your last assistant," she said. "Was she supposed to come along on the tour?"

I gave it some thought and settled on the simplest answer. "No. She was fired, remember?"

"Oh, stop it," Becka said. "That's not what I meant, and you know it. Let's say she *hadn't* been fired. Would she be here right now?"

It was a dangerous question, and I considered several answers before settling on, "If you mean, was she going to support the tour, the answer's yes."

"Oh." Something in Becka's shoulders eased. "Well, that's good." But then her gaze narrowed. "Wait a minute. How many stops?"

"What do you mean?"

"I mean, there are like a hundred stops on the book tour. Was she planning to attend all of them?"

I didn't like the question. Still, I wasn't going to lie. "No."

"All right. So how many?"

I didn't want to say. But she *had* asked, which meant she probably knew the answer already. "One."

Becka's face fell. "You mean Atlanta, the one we just finished?"

I nodded. "That's it."

"Seriously? So I'm not even needed?"

Something in my chest tightened. "That's not what I said."

"But if you were planning on a solo trip—"

"I was. But not anymore."

"Why not?"

It was a good question. And I had no good answers, or at least none I was willing to admit. But there *was* something I could say, and it was the honest truth. "I like the way you deal with fans."

She gave me a dubious look. "Even Darbie?"

"Forget Darbie."

"After all the drama? I'm not sure I can. Can you? I mean, Darbie and I didn't exactly hit it off."

I put on my confused face. "Derbie who?"

Becka gave me an odd look. "Don't you mean Darbie?"

"Hell no." I shrugged. "Gotta put that extra 'e' somewhere, right?"

Becka laughed, filling the jet with an emotion that I hadn't felt in a long time – happiness. And that's when I knew, she was even more trouble than I'd thought.

This wasn't good.

Her eyes filled with mischief as she said, "And speaking of 'Derbie', I *know* you did something funny with that book." Her chin lifted. "But I'm *not* going to ask."

I didn't believe it. And from the look in Becka's eyes, neither did she. I said, "Is that so?"

"Definitely." She paused. "Okay, maybe." Again, she hesitated. "But just tell me one thing. Do you think I'll ever see it again?"

"What, your book?"

"Yeah."

Again, I couldn't help but smile. "Maybe."

CHAPTER 36

Becka

It was more than a maybe.

I found the book fifteen minutes after checking into the new hotel. The book was tucked into the outside pocket of my carry-on, exactly where Darbie had pulled out *her* copy in Atlanta.

I yanked out the book and stared at it for a long moment, not daring to look inside. *Not yet.* Instead, I focused on the book's exterior, noting the classic image on the cover and the spine creased with repeated use.

I studied the book long and hard before coming to an unsettling conclusion. On the outside, it looked exactly like the one Darbie had been waving in my face. Or more accurately, Darbie's book had looked exactly like mine.

This couldn't be an accident.

Finally I took a deep breath, opened the book, and peered inside. Right there on the title page was the inscription from Jack, written in bold blue ink. Until now, I hadn't had the chance to read it for myself, even if I *had* gotten hints from listening to Darbie's commentary at the book-signing.

Now in the quiet hotel room, I read it out loud. "To Becka – a trouble-maker of the highest order."

I smiled. *Highest order, huh?* That phrase was used frequently in Jack's books, usually by some cleric or nobleman looking to make a point. With a little laugh, I pulled the book closer and studied Jack's signature, all bold and wonderful on the bottom of the page.

Suddenly I was feeling a little misty. Somehow, Jack had not only retrieved my book, he'd given Darbie a taste of her own medicine – all without causing a giant spectacle like *I* had.

The whole thing was kind of scary – but absolutely glorious in its own way.

Clutching the book more tightly now, I glanced toward the door of my hotel room. *Should I track him down and thank him?*

The answer came in an instant. *No.*

In the hotel's lobby, he'd made it perfectly clear that I wouldn't be seeing him again until noon tomorrow, when we'd be leaving for the actual book-signing.

With a sigh, I glanced at the clock on the night stand. The time was 1:05 in the afternoon, which meant that I had the whole day to do nothing at all.

I spent it obsessing over Jack, wondering what he was doing, and how he'd managed to pull of such a crazy switch.

Again, I asked myself, *who was this guy, anyway?*

And what made him tick?

In search of clues, I pulled out my little notebook computer, the one my sister had gotten me for my last birthday. I scoured the internet in hopes of discovering something that I didn't already know.

Instead, I found the same kind of stories I always found – articles about his string of best-sellers, his impressive net worth, and his reclusive nature.

Reclusive or not, there were at least *some* articles linking him to various love interests – a software developer in California, a violinist in New York, and of course, Imogen from who-knows-where.

During my research, I also discovered that Imogen had an interesting habit of dropping his name on social media whenever she could, even now when they were apparently broken up – not that she was sharing *that* little factoid.

During the past week, she'd even posted a series of photos of herself at Flynn's place, including several taken out on his back patio.

She'd been showing off the same undergarments that she'd been wearing when I'd first spotted her in Flynn's front doorway.

In person, the undergarments had hidden nearly nothing. But in the patio photos, she was perfectly posed to hide her juiciest bits behind potted plants, strategically placed flowers, or even her own hair.

I had to admit, she'd done a masterful job of making the photos sexy *without* being technically obscene.

Still, looking at her spectacular body and beautiful face, I couldn't help but feel rather ordinary in comparison, especially when I came across several photos of her and Jack together at some movie premiere in L.A.

They made a stunning couple, even if Jack wasn't smiling.

This got me thinking, and I retraced my Web pages, looking at picture after picture.

Funny, he wasn't smiling in any of them.

And yet, he *did* smile with me. *Well, sometimes that is.*

Holed up in my hotel room, I spent an obscenely long time jumping from article to article, until I came across the strangest thing. Way down on some obscure Web forum, an unknown guy was insisting that during the Atlanta convention, he'd sold half a jester costume to – yup, you guessed it – Jack Ward.

I rolled my eyes at the ridiculousness of it all, until a sudden realization made me gasp out loud.

The shirt – the one he'd given me to replace my ripped blouse. It had been absolutely hideous – some twisted checker-board thing with purple patches and a funny collar.

The Shirt of Shame.

It was something I'd never forget, especially because I'd endured quite a bit of commentary while wearing it.

At the time, I'd figured it was some sort of joke, or more likely a punishment for all the trouble I'd caused with Darbie and her friend.

Now, I wasn't so sure.

Tomorrow, I decided, I'd simply ask him.

Oh sure, he might not answer, but it was worth a try, right?

CHAPTER 37

Becka

I looked to Jack and said, "I saw the strangest news item yesterday."

We were in the rental car, driving to the book-signing. Jack was behind the wheel, navigating the quiet country road while I drove myself crazy in the passenger's seat.

Crazy with curiosity, that is.

In fact, I was stewing in it.

With his gaze trained on the road, Jack replied, "Oh yeah?"

"Yeah," I said, and then waited. When he said nothing more, I asked, "Don't you want to know what?"

"Probably not." He gave me a sideways glance. "But you're gonna tell me regardless."

I tried for a scoff. "You don't know that."

The corners of his mouth lifted. "Yeah I do."

With a sound of frustration, I turned once again to face the front. *Fine. If he didn't want to know, I wasn't going to tell him.* In fact, I wasn't going to say anything at all, not unless he spoke first.

Already, I'd thanked him for the book, so really there was nothing I *had* to say, assuming the rest of the drive would remain wordless.

My silence lasted for less than a mile before I heard myself ask, "So, were the hotels in Redville booked or something?"

"No."

I felt my brow wrinkle in confusion. *I didn't get it.* The book-signing – scheduled at a local book store in a neighboring town – was an hour away from our hotel.

I asked, "So, why are we staying so far away?"

"What, you don't like the drive?"

Actually, the drive was lovely. The road was smooth, and the traffic was light. Around us, the country was green with rolling hills. Plus, I was sitting with Jack Ward, the most interesting person I'd ever met.

In the big scheme of things, I had nothing to complain about. "That's not it," I said. "I'm just curious, that's all."

"You? No kidding?"

He looked so darned sure of himself – and so insanely sexy – that I wanted to toss something at him. *Like my panties.* But that would be entirely unprofessional, so I contented myself with saying, "I know you're teasing me."

"Good."

"Why is that good?"

"It saves me the trouble of explaining."

"Explaining what?" I said. "That you're giving me a hard time? I can figure *that* out for myself."

"Obviously."

"And you never answered the question. Why aren't you staying in Redville? You know, where the signing is?"

"You mean why aren't *we* staying in Redville?"

"Yeah. Fine. Whatever. I'm just wondering. Are you hiding from your fans or something?"

"Something like that."

Great. Another non-answer.

Okay, yes, I *had* vowed to stop pestering him with questions. But the way *I* saw it, this could be classified under "making conversation" – like asking about the weather or someone's favorite sports team.

Looking to make a point, I said, "I hear the weather's nice in Redville."

His gaze shifted briefly in my direction, but he said nothing in response.

"See?" I said. "I'm just making conversation. You know, for the road."

At this, he looked almost ready to smile. "What happened to you being comfortable with silence?"

For some stupid reason, I wanted to laugh. "Is that a hint?"

He gave me another glance before saying, "No."

This wasn't the answer I'd been expecting, and for a moment, I almost didn't know what to say.

In the end, it was Jack who broke the silence. "All right. Tell me what you saw."

"Where?"

"The news item," he said.

"Oh. That." Funny, I'd been thinking about it nearly nonstop since yesterday. And yet, sitting here with Jack, it was like my brain had suddenly stopped working.

Still, I rallied to the cause. "See, the thing is, I read on some forum that you purchased *half* a jester costume in Atlanta."

"On a forum?" he said. "That's not news. It's gossip."

"But that's irrelevant," I said. "Did you, or did you not, buy half a costume?"

He appeared to give it some thought. Finally, he replied, "No."

I studied his profile. He was lying. I was almost certain of it. *But did I really want to call him on it?*

Yes. I did.

But how?

I was still trying to come up with a tactful way of telling him that he was full of crap when he said, "I bought the whole thing."

I did a double-take. "What?"

"The costume," he said. "I only *took* half, but I bought it all. Seemed kind of rude to cheat the guy."

"What?" I repeated like a total idiot.

"Yeah," he said. "I took the shirt, but left the pants."

Forget the pants. I sat back in the seat. "I knew it!"

"Knew what?"

"When you gave me that shirt to wear, I *knew* that thing wasn't normal."

In the driver's seat, Jack looked entirely unrepentant. "Got that right."

I made a sound of frustration. "Do you realize, I wore that thing for hours? Do you know how many people teased me about it?"

"An exact number?" he said. "No."

"Forget the number," I said. "I'm just saying, there were a lot."

"Not surprising," he said. "The thing was ugly as hell." He paused. "Nice colors, though."

As I stared at his profile, I had the distinct impression that he was teasing me yet again. "I don't get it," I said. "Why on Earth would you do that?"

Before he could even to think to answer, I held up a hand. "And *don't* say it was because I needed a shirt. I *know* I needed a shirt. I'm just saying, why didn't you simply go to the hotel room and get one of mine like I suggested?"

"Because I didn't have the time."

"You did, too," I said. "You were gone like forty minutes."

"So?"

"So our room was only ten minutes away."

At this, he turned his head a gave me a long, inscrutable look.

A smart person would've reminded him to watch the road. But I wasn't *feeling* smart. And, at something in his eyes, a surge of heat crept up my face and then dipped lower. *Way lower.* And I *didn't* mean to my toes.

By the time Jack looked away, I was nearly breathless. "What was *that* look for?"

"It wasn't *our* room," he said. "It was yours."

I almost cringed. *Had I seriously said it again?*

Into my silence, he added, "You had your own room."

As if I needed the reminder. "Right. I mean, I know."

"And I had mine."

"Yeah, I remember. On the seventeenth floor."

"Right."

By now, I was so flustered, I didn't even *try* to stop myself from asking, "And, why were you staying on that floor, anyway?"

"Why not?"

"Well…" I wasn't quite sure how to put this. "Normally people with your, um, financial means, stay higher. Are you afraid of heights or something?"

He gave a low scoff. "You realize, seventeen will kill you the same as seventy."

"Exactly," I said. "So why weren't you staying on a higher floor?"

At this, he turned and gave me another look, this one more serious than the last. "That's a funny question."

"It is not," I said. "It's a perfectly reasonable question."

Returning his attention to the road, he said, "Maybe I like options."

"What kind of options?"

"Like using the stairs."

From the passenger's seat, I gave him a good, long look. *What was he saying?* That he actually *preferred* taking the stairs? As opposed to an elevator?

If so, why? *For privacy? Or as some sort of workout regimen?*

From the looks of him, seventeen floors would be nothing. Cripes, *seventy* might be nothing for someone in *that* great of shape.

I asked, "You mean for the exercise?" It seemed unlikely. The Atlanta hotel had boasted a world-class workout facility. *Unless – maybe that's where the privacy came in?*

He replied, "You could say that."

It felt like yet another non-answer, but I didn't want to push the issue, not when I was dying to ask something more pressing. "Back to the shirt," I said, "I still don't understand. Why didn't you have time to go to the hotel room?" I cleared my throat. "Meaning *my* hotel room, not yours."

And certainly not ours, as interesting as that sounded.

He said, "I was busy."

"Doing what?"

"Trust me, you don't want to know."

Probably that was the worst thing he could've said. Because now, I *really* wanted to know, even more so than before.

I said, "I do, too."

Jack shook his head. "You just *think* you do."

I wasn't buying it. "You realize that if you *don't* tell me, I'll just think it's something way worse than whatever it is."

"I doubt it."

"So what does *that* mean?" I asked. "That it was really bad?"

"All right, if you really wanna know," he said, "ask me after the signing."

"Why *after* the signing?"

"Because we're almost there."

This wasn't quite true. We were still fifteen minutes away at least. But hey, I'd waited *this* long, right? What was a few more hours in the big scheme of things?

I just hoped the wait would be worth it.

CHAPTER 38

Becka

In Redville, the book store was ridiculously easy to find. *And why?* It was because there was a huge line of people circled around the block.

From the passenger's seat, I spotted them from several blocks away, which made it even more surprising when Jack drove past the book store and kept going.

"Wait," I said, turning in my seat. "Aren't you going to stop?"

"Not here," he said. "We'll park out back."

I didn't see how that was possible, considering that the line went literally around the whole block. But soon, I saw what he meant.

He took a left and eventually drove into a parking garage three blocks over. Technically, yes, it *was* behind the book store, but it wasn't *so* close that he'd be mobbed the moment he left the vehicle.

He pulled into the garage and claimed a spot on the lower level, parking between a long white van and a big red pickup. I watched as he backed into the spot rather than pulling in front-first.

When he finished, I looked to him and said, "Lemme guess. You're hiding out *and* planning for a quick getaway. Is that it?"

In the driver's seat, he cut the engine and turned to look at me, almost as if the question was actually interesting, which of course it wasn't. After a long moment, he replied in a carefully neutral tone, "Something like that."

Confused by his reaction, I asked, "Is something wrong?"

"No." He glanced at the dashboard clock. "You ready?"

I nodded. "Oh yeah. Definitely."

But as it turned out, I was entirely unprepared for the commotion his appearance caused. Back in Atlanta, the whole convention center had been crowded with eager fans, but that was somehow different.

There, with thousands of attendees and a surprising number of celebrities, the mayhem had seemed almost normal. But here, on a regular everyday street, the excitement Jack generated was entirely surreal.

In spite of his efforts to keep a low profile, he barely made it into the store's back entrance without getting completely mobbed.

Still, I had to give him credit. He was a good sport – better than I might've expected, considering how private he was in general.

The signing was scheduled to last for three hours. But five hours later, there was still a line. Plus, two local news channels had turned up, desperate for interviews.

According to the publisher's instructions, part of my job was to act as a liaison between Jack and the people wanting his attention. This included all of the reporters who were eager for some of Jack's time.

All this to say, between the fans, the media, and even the owner of the book store, I was kept busy and then some – but not *so* busy that I forgot Jack's promise.

After the signing, I would *finally* be getting some answers.

But the funny thing was, Jack was right.

In the end, I probably *was* better off not knowing.

CHAPTER 39

Becka

By the time we pulled out of the parking garage, I was a hungry, exhausted mess.

I hadn't eaten since breakfast, and already it was past eight o'clock. Still, if given the choice between food or information, I knew exactly what I'd pick.

Information. I was starving for it.

As Jack turned onto the city street that would take us out of town, I said, "Time's up. You promised to tell me, remember?"

He kept his gaze on the road. "I remember."

"Well?" I said. "That's your cue, you know."

"I know." And yet, he still said nothing.

I remained silent, determined to wait him out. And for once, it actually paid off.

"All right," he finally said. "Here's the deal. You remember that fight you got into?"

Embarrassingly, I'd gotten into two fights since I'd met him – one with Imogen and one with Darbie's friend. With a nervous laugh, I asked, "Which one?"

With no trace of humor, he said, "You know which one."

Of course I did. After all, we were talking about that godawful shirt, which had nothing to do with Imogen.

"Yeah," I said. "I was making a joke." Quickly I added, "And just so you know, I don't normally do that."

"Do what? Joke?" A hint of humor crept into his voice. "Or fight?"

As if he didn't know. "You know exactly what I mean. I'm just saying, it's not like I intended to fight with either one of them. And they weren't *really* fights anyway."

Jack gave me a sideways glance, but said nothing.

"They weren't," I insisted. "They both just kind of happened. And technically, the thing with Imogen wasn't a fight at all. Mostly, I fell on her, which hardly counts since it was sort of an accident."

Was I rambling?

Probably.

But I knew why. Something in his demeanor was making me nervous, and I was getting the distinct impression that whatever he was about to tell me, it was worse than I might've imagined.

He was silent for nearly two whole blocks. But then, at the next red light, Jack turned and gave me a serious look. "The thing is, your undershirt, it didn't hide much."

Heat flooded my face. "You mean my camisole? Uh, yeah. I know. But I wasn't counting on anyone seeing it."

"Then you counted wrong."

I almost winced. I really *had* made a giant spectacle of myself, even if that hadn't been my intention. "Then I guess I owe you an apology, huh?"

"Forget that."

As if I could. And now, adding to my embarrassment was the fact that I hadn't apologized sooner. If he were a normal boss, I might've apologized up and down by now. But the truth was, he didn't feel like a boss at all.

He felt like something else. I just didn't know what.

Regardless, I needed to say it. "Just for the record, I really *am* sorry. I should've told you sooner. And honestly, it's not the kind of thing–"

"Stop."

I bit my lip. "Stop what? Apologizing?"

"Stop all of it." His gaze locked on mine. "I'm trying to tell you–"

"I *know* what you're trying to tell me."

As my face burned and my palms grew sweaty, I forced myself to say it so he didn't have to. "I know people got glimpses or whatever of my, um, chest, I guess. And I know that's not terrific. But honestly, it could've been *so* much worse, so in a way, I should be relieved."

In the driver's seat, Jack turned forward once again. I followed his gaze and was surprised to see that the light had just turned green.

Already, the cars ahead of us were moving again.

As our own car moved forward, I asked, "How'd you know it was green? You weren't even watching."

"Yeah I was."

"But you didn't *look* like you were watching."

"Peripheral vision," he explained.

"Oh." I was pretty sure that everyone had it, but not to *that* extent. This, like so many other things, was something to remember. *The guy missed absolutely nothing.*

And yet, he still hadn't answered my question. "So, about that ugly shirt," I persisted, "what was it? Some sort of reprimand, like a 'Shirt of Shame' or something?"

"That's what you think?"

"Actually, I don't know what to think, because you still haven't explained why you didn't just grab a shirt from my hotel room." I tried to smile. "I even gave you the key, remember?"

"I remember."

I still had no idea what I was missing. "But…?"

"Listen," he said. "A minute ago, you said it could've been worse, right?"

"Right."

"And it was."

I studied his face in profile. "So you're saying that it *was* worse?" Bracing myself, I asked, "How?"

"Pictures," he said. "Some video, too."

I felt the color drain from my face. "What?"

"You heard me."

"So you're telling me that someone took pictures of me looking…

what? Obscene?"

"Not just pictures," he reminded me. "Videos, too."

As if I needed the reminder. Still, this didn't make any sense. Jack was a world-famous celebrity. I was his assistant. We'd been at a very public place. If those pictures had gotten out, I surely would 've seen them *somewhere* by now. *Right?*

I shook my head. "But I never saw anything."

"Yeah." He frowned. "But *I* did."

Now I was absolutely horrified. "So *you* saw the pictures? How?"

He gave something like a shrug. "Buying them mostly."

"What?" I sputtered. "From who?"

"From whoever took them."

"How?"

"The usual way," he said. "I offered money. They accepted. Done deal."

Reluctantly, I asked, "How much money?"

"Not a lot."

I bit my lip. "Do you mean, not a lot for *you*? Or not a lot for a normal person?"

"Forget it," he said. "It doesn't matter."

"It does too," I said. "I should pay you back."

"If you want to pay me back," he said, "be more careful."

Finally I understood why he hadn't told me on the way to the signing. With the way I felt *now*, I might've hidden in the car until I pulled myself together. And who knows how long *that* might've taken.

Still, I had to ask, "Were you *ever* planning to tell me?"

"No."

"But why not?"

"Because it's handled."

I considered everything he'd told me so far. "But you never explained. The photos, how could you buy them?"

"The easy way. With cash."

"Forget the cash," I said. "I just mean, they were probably on someone's phone, right? So how exactly does that work?"

"Simple," he said. "Forward the pictures and delete the originals."

My stomach clenched. "Forward the pictures to who?"

He was quiet for a long moment before saying, "Me."

Oh, God. Now I *really* wanted to crawl into a hole and hide. "So you have obscene pictures of me? Seriously?"

"I wouldn't call them obscene."

"You would, too," I said. "In fact, I'm pretty sure you just did."

"No. *You* called them obscene. Not me."

"But you didn't argue."

When his only answer was a tight shrug, I said, "Do you still have them?"

"I might."

Talk about humiliating. "But why would you keep them? Don't you think that's a little intrusive?"

Already, the small downtown area was firmly in the rear-view mirror. In the sky, the sun was creeping ever closer to the horizon. Soon it would be dark.

Good.

All the better to hide my embarrassment.

"These photos," I said, "where are they now? On your phone?"

"If you mean the phone I was carrying at the time, the answer's yes."

I already knew he had multiple phones. But that wasn't the point. "But why keep them?" I asked. "Shouldn't you just delete them or something?"

"No."

Great. So now I was embarrassed *and* annoyed. "But why not?"

"Because," he said, "if any of those pictures come out, I'll want to know who cheated me."

"Why?"

"So I can deal with it."

"How?" I asked. "You mean by suing them or something?"

His tone grew a shade darker. "Something like that."

At something in his voice, I stifled a shiver. I had a funny feeling that however he resolved it, the law *wouldn't* be involved. Or maybe that was just my imagination talking.

Regardless, the whole thing was beyond unsettling. And now, for the sake of my own sanity, I had to say it. "Show me."

CHAPTER 40

Jack

Show her?

Not a good idea. This conversation had gone too far already.

It was becoming a habit, and not a good one. When it came to Becka, I said too much. I did too much. I thought too much.

Shit. I *looked* too much.

The truth was, I'd seen those photos more times than were decent, considering that I'd acquired them for *her* benefit, not mine. The first time I'd looked, it had been for a good reason – to buy the images and make sure they didn't get out in public.

But looking a second time? Or a third? In private? It was something only a cad would do.

But it hadn't started out that way.

In the passenger's seat, she said, "I'm serious. I want to see them."

"Why?" I asked.

"Because I want to know how bad they are."

"Don't worry. They're not."

"But that can't be true," she protested. "You wouldn't have bought them if they were just fine."

They were fine, all right – too fine for the public to see, even if Becka was too reckless for her own good.

But that was part of the appeal. I'd been buttoned up so tightly for so long that her exuberance was like a magnet to my soul – making me feel things I hadn't in a long while.

When I made no reply, she said, "I deserve to see them." In her seat, she turned to face me. "In fact, I want to buy them off you. I'll just pay what you paid."

She couldn't afford it. And, I wasn't about to give them up – not because I'd looked one time too many, but because that would defeat the purpose of my storing them in the first place.

"You can't," I said.

"But why not?"

"I already told you. If they get out, I'll need to pay someone a visit."

"Honestly, you don't need to do that."

That's what she thought. "Hell if I don't."

"But even if that happened," she said, "you wouldn't need the pictures, would you?"

She was missing the point. "I would if wanted to match the picture with the taker."

"You know what I think?"

"What?"

"I think you don't *want* to give them up."

She was right. I didn't. But this wasn't exactly news. "I know. I told you as much."

"And honestly, I think you *like* looking at them."

It was an accusation – and true, which made me feel like a giant shit-heel. But already, I'd promised myself that I wouldn't be looking again – not unless someone welched on the deal.

And in *that* case, she'd have bigger problems than me refusing to hand over the files.

When I didn't deny it, she said, "What are you doing with them, anyway?"

"What do you mean?"

"I mean, do you pull them out and laugh?"

I didn't get it. "Why would I laugh?"

"Why does anyone laugh?" she said. "Because they're funny."

My jaw clenched. *They weren't funny to me.* "*That's* what you think?"

"Well, that must be it," she said. "Or you'd put them on a memory stick or something and let *me* hold onto them."

Some might agree with her logic. *But me? I wasn't a trusting guy.* I knew all too well that memory sticks could disappear the same as anything else, especially with a little help.

I said, "And you think they're safe on a stick?"

"Safer than with you," she said. "Because at least then I'd know that no one would be looking at them."

"I promise," I said, "I'm not gonna look." I meant it, too. I was done with that. Yeah, I *wanted* another look. *Who wouldn't?* But looking without her say-so made me feel like a total dick.

And, speaking of dicks, it didn't help that the brain down below liked the images nearly as much as I did. She was sweet and sexy, like the mythical girl next door, except if *she* were my neighbor, I'd be looking to move even closer.

My fingers tightened around the steering wheel. *What the hell?*

I was supposed to be acting like a big brother, not some pervert at the window. Still, the thought of *anyone* getting their hands on those images, well, I didn't like it.

With a hard scoff, she said, "I mean, I know I'm not exactly Imogen."

Imogen? I wasn't following. "What?"

"I'm just saying, I've seen *her* pictures, like the ones she took at Flynn's place."

"So?"

"So I'm just saying I know you wouldn't need photos of *me* to get your kicks."

I turned to look. "You're kidding, right?"

"No." Her cheeks were red, and her mouth was tight. "But I'm just saying, I get it."

"Get what?"

"*You* know. There's that saying, why go out for burgers when you've got steak at home." She frowned. "Anyway, you get the gist."

I did. And I didn't like it. I told her, "I like burgers."

She rolled her eyes. "Yeah. I know. I heard at the signing. But I'm just saying, I realize you get steak all the time, so—"

"So what?" I said. "You ever think that *you're* the steak?"

With an awkward laugh, she said, "Actually, I'm not even sure I'm a burger." She glanced around. "And speaking of which, I'm starving. Would you mind hitting a drive-through on the way back?"

"Screw that," I said.

She stiffened. "Why?"

"Because I'm taking you out."

I hadn't meant to say it. But now that it was out there, I realized how much I wanted it, to spend some time with her outside of this so-called book tour.

She replied, "You don't have to do that."

"What, you're not hungry?"

"That's not what I meant," she said. "I just know that you probably feel obligated or something. And you're not, honest. A drive-through is fine."

Up ahead, on our right, was a bait and tackle store, closed for the night. I pulled into the parking lot and cut the engine.

And then, I turned to face her. "You're nuts, you know that?"

"Yeah, I know," she said. "You're *making* me nuts. So really it's your fault just as much as mine."

"Oh yeah?" I said. "You ever stop to think that you're making *me* nuts, too?"

"Why?" she said. "Because I'm such an awful employee?"

"First off, you're not. And second, I'm not talking about your work."

"So what *are* you talking about?"

"You." My gaze locked on hers. "And you wanna know why?"

"Why?"

"Because you're steak *and* burger. And apple pie, too, while we're at it."

"Oh shut up," she scoffed. "I am not."

Now it was my turn to scoff. "Wanna bet?"

She sighed. "Look, I'm just saying it's all relative. I know I've got my good points, and it's not like I think I'm ugly or anything. It's just that I know, well, compared to what you're *used* to looking at, it's not like you'd be jerking off to *my* stupid pictures."

As the words echoed out between us, her hands flew to her mouth. "Oh, my God," she groaned. "I don't believe I just said that."

Neither did I.

But the truth was, her words hit harder than she knew. I hadn't jerked off to the pictures, but let's just say those images weren't far from my mind during my shower this morning. *And last night, too.*

And now, she was sinking lower in her seat. She squeezed her eyes shut and said, "I just realized something."

"What?"

"Remember before today's book-signing, when you told me that I didn't want to know?"

"I remember."

"I should've listened." She opened her eyes and turned to face me. "As a matter of fact, can we just forget this conversation ever happened?"

"No."

"But why not?"

"Because you've got it all wrong."

"I've got *what* all wrong?"

"Hang on," I said. "I'll show you."

CHAPTER 41

Becka

At first, I wasn't quite sure what he meant. But then he reached into his pocket and pulled out his cell phone.

Now I wanted to groan all over again. "So I was right? You've got the photos *on* you?"

"Just for now," he said. "Until I transfer them for safe-keeping."

"To where?" I asked.

"Forget that," he said, scrolling across the screen. "I want you to see what *I* see."

Part of me wanted to bolt from the car. The other part realized that the sooner I got this over with, the better. After all, they couldn't be nearly as bad as I imagined.

Could they?

Reluctantly, I held out my hand. But he didn't drop the phone into it. Instead, he leaned sideways toward me and held out the phone in front of us, so we could both see the screen at the same time.

At the first image, I didn't know whether to laugh or cry. I was lying on my back, with the brunette sprawled out beside me. My hair was wild, and my face was flushed. My skirt was hiked a lot higher than I'd realized at the time.

As far as the skirt itself, its position wasn't so much indecent as suggestive, like with another inch or two, I'd be flashing my panties – or worse – for everyone to see.

But the true horror lied in my shirt – or lack thereof. Yes, I *was* wearing it, but the buttons were gone, and the blouse was wide open.

The camisole underneath was thin, skin-tight, and lacy, which had been the whole idea, considering that it had been serving double-duty as a bra.

Regardless, it was *not* meant for public viewing – obviously. Through the lace of its sheer fabric, the outlines of my nipples were embarrassingly easy to see, even more so, considering that they were clearly erect, straining against the thin fabric.

I heard myself mumble, "Stupid temperature."

When Jack made no reply, I felt the need to explain. "It was really cold in there. I mean, you probably didn't notice because you're a guy. But it truly *was* freezing."

Still, he said nothing.

Fearing the worst, I slowly turned my gaze in his direction. He was still looking at the photo, and something in his expression made my nipples harden all over again.

This time, it *wasn't* because of the cold.

His gaze lingered on the image. "You wanna know what I see?"

Now *that* was a loaded question. I looked back to the image and tried to laugh. "I don't know. An idiot?"

"No." When he spoke again, his voice was nearly a caress. "That's not what *I'm* seeing." As he said it, he turned his head and looked straight in my direction.

Fearful of making a fool of myself, I kept my gaze on the photo. Still, from the corner of my eye, I could just barely tell that he was still looking – not at the image, but at me.

And even if I couldn't *see* him, I swear, I would've felt his gaze, burning into my skin, making it grow warm and tingly – and not just on my face.

Into my silence, he said, "What *I* see is the girl who's been keeping me up at night."

What? I turned to look. Our gazes locked, and his lips parted. *Mine, too.* I felt my tongue brush against my teeth as I studied his face. He looked nearly enthralled, and I was suddenly finding it hard to breathe.

I'd been keeping him up at night? *Seriously?*

After a hard swallow, I asked, "Why?"

His gaze flicked briefly to the nearby image. "You've gotta ask?"

"Oh, please," I said with an embarrassed laugh. "You can find photos a lot more suggestive than this."

"I know," he said. "But they wouldn't be of you."

Again, I swallowed. "Me?"

"I wasn't lying," he said. "You *are* a trouble-maker, you know." His voice was smooth and silky in the quiet car. "Of the highest order."

Woah.

He couldn't mean it, or at least not the way he made it sound *now.* Probably I was imagining things.

I tried to smile. "Yeah. But I'm trying to do better." Forcing a laugh, I added, "I mean, no more fighting with fans, I promise."

"Don't."

I blinked. "Don't what?"

"Don't pretend you don't know what I mean."

"I wasn't pretending," I said. "I just don't want to read too much into this." I looked again to the photo. "Like, you're probably just being nice or something."

He lowered the phone, setting it face-down between us. "If you think I'm being nice, you've got the wrong guy."

Once again, I turned to face him. "What do you mean?"

"I mean, if I were being nice, I'd keep my thoughts to myself."

I considered the hours we'd spent together so far. Most of the time, he'd been reclusive, distant, and impossible to figure out. I heard myself say, "You're good at that, you know."

"With you?" he said with a scoff. "Not as good as I should be."

"Why do you say that?" I asked.

"I'm supposed to be looking out for you, not taking advantage."

Taking advantage? It was such an old-fashioned concept. This shouldn't have been a surprise, considering that his books dealt with things long-forgotten – chivalry, justice, honor, and so much more.

I leaned closer to him and asked in a breathless whisper, "How do you know it's not *me* taking advantage of you?"

He gave me a wry smile. "Trust me. I know."

"But I'm serious," I said. "Look at you. You're rich and famous. Everyone wants you."

His eyed filled with mischief. "Everyone, huh?"

I drank in the sight of him. *Oh, yeah.* Somehow, I managed to say, "You know what I mean."

"I don't want 'everyone,'" he said. "You want the truth?"

Utterly entranced, I felt myself nod.

"That's not my style."

I wasn't following. "What's not your style? You mean like quickies with fans?"

That look in his eye was still there. Very slowly and deliberately, he said, "I don't do quickies."

Oh, wow. My pulse quickened. I *really* liked the way he'd just said that. And I actually believed him, too. Still, I was curious. "And what about the fan part?"

"Starfuckers?" he said. "Not my thing."

This, I also believed. During the book tour, I'd seen the way women looked at him – *and* the way they propositioned him. Sometimes they were subtle, hinting that they'd love to show him around, *personally*. Other times, they weren't so subtle, whispering things in his ear that I could only imagine.

It was funny in a way. I was a huge fan of his work, and I'd done my share of drooling over him. But I never would've jumped in bed with a total stranger regardless of who they were or what they did.

But now, I simply had to know. "So crazed fans, huh? Am I in that category?"

"You?" Slowly, and without breaking eye-contact, he shook his head. "You're in a category all your own."

CHAPTER 42

Jack

I wasn't just a cad. I was a bastard – because when her lips parted, and she leaned closer, I didn't stop myself.

Instead, I pulled her close and kissed her like I meant it.

And I did mean it. Somehow, she'd managed to burrow under my skin, itching and scratching, tempting and teasing, warming and willing, whether she realized it or not.

I was done trying to hide it.

Her lips were sweet and warm. Her body was small and tight. Her sounds, light and muffled, were music to my ears. My cock was so hard, I wanted to take her right here and now.

Still, I wasn't so big of a bastard that I wouldn't give her the chance to rethink it.

Me? I'd been thinking of her all day, watching as she worked the line of people – smiling and talking like she knew them personally.

She had a good heart and a contagious smile. She had a way of making people feel comfortable, whether they were eight or eighty. *No pretense. No games. No pretending to be something she wasn't.*

She was a real girl in the real world – and yet, so different from anyone I'd ever met, especially lately.

And I loved the way she looked. Her ass – it had looked so sweet in that little black skirt, the one she was still wearing. I wanted to yank it up around her waist and explore her body like I'd been doing in my thoughts.

And then, I wanted to make her mine.

But not here. And not without giving her some time to catch her breath.

I pulled back and said, "You realize what you're doing, right?"

"What do you mean?"

"I'm your boss. And your brother's best friend."

Her skin was rosy, and her voice was breathless when she said, "I don't have a brother."

"You know who I mean – Flynn. And your sister. They might not like it."

"I don't care," she said. "Do you?"

"No." *I meant it, too.*

But I *should* care. I'd started out caring. There was a code when it came to these things. Those codes – they were there for a reason, to keep people from devolving into animals, from taking what they wanted just because they could.

And I *did* want her – even if that hadn't been part of the plan.

Her chin lifted. "And besides, they don't have to know."

They'd know. Of this, I was certain.

Becka – she wasn't good at hiding things. She was too honest, too straight-forward, and too likely to jump first and think later.

I wanted her, and not just for the night. But there was something I *didn't* want – her waking up to regret it in the light of day.

And what the hell? Was I supposed to take her here in the car? Or not much better, to some local hotel, where I'd fuck her silly without so much as a dinner together first?

I was an asshole for even considering it.

I said, "Just think about it."

She frowned. "Think about what?"

"What you want." I smiled. "For dinner."

CHAPTER 43

Becka

I didn't want dinner. I wanted him. I asked, "Are you giving me the brush-off?"

He shook his head. "No. I'm giving you time to think."

I didn't need time. I didn't even *want* time. By now, I wanted him so badly, I didn't even care that I hadn't eaten since breakfast. *Who needed food when a fantasy was yours for the taking?*

Not me, that's for sure.

But Jack was insistent, so in the end, I told him to pick a restaurant, and I'd be happy with whatever.

Still, I had to give him credit. He picked exactly what I might've picked for myself – a cozy local place with an amazing mountain view.

As the hostess led us to a candlelit table by the window, I looked to Jack and smiled. He smiled back, making my heart flutter and my knees go weak.

Wow.

No wonder he didn't smile very often. His smile was dangerous, like an airborne opiate. And I was feeling intoxicated already.

One glass of wine later, and I was a total goner. We spent the first part of dinner talking about our favorite books, and I was glad to discover that we had similar tastes.

It was the same when it came to movies and just about everything else. Actually, it was pretty uncanny, and I was just in the middle of telling him so when I suddenly realized something.

I felt my gaze narrow. "Hey, you know what?"

"What?"

"You're the *real* trouble-maker here."

"How so?"

"You never *did* tell me the whole story of that ugly shirt."

He grinned. "Didn't I?"

Oh, God. He looked so sexy. And now, there was something in his smile that was just a little bit wicked.

But I refused to be distracted. "No. You didn't. Or at least, I'm sure you didn't tell me *all* of it."

Without breaking eye contact, Jack took a slow drink of his wine. When he finished, he said, "You don't miss a thing, do you?"

If only that were true. Still, I smiled. "You're one to talk. It's like you have eyes on the back of your head."

"Me? Nah."

I persisted. "But about the shirt thing, you *are* planning to tell me, right?"

"I might," he said with a gleam in his eye.

"And start from the beginning," I said, "meaning when you first left the powder room to get me a shirt. What happened after?"

"All right," he said. "So when I go out, most of the crowd's still there. And I see a couple of guys checking out each other's phones." His tone darkened. "And it wasn't hard to guess what they were looking at."

It wasn't hard for me to guess either. Still, there was at least one bright spot, or at least it sure sounded like it. "So there were just two of them?"

"At first glance," he said. "But then I pull the security footage—"

I blinked. "What?"

"Video from the convention center cameras."

"That's what I *thought* you meant," I said. "But how would you be able to get it?"

"The footage?" He shrugged. "It was digital and routed through an outside connection."

"So?"

"So it's not hard to get if you know where to look."

"Oh, please," I said. "I don't believe that for one minute."

He leaned back in his chair. "It's true."

I studied his face. He looked absolutely serious. But there was a catch. There *had* to be.

And then it hit me. "Do you mean it's not hard for everyone?" I paused. "Or not hard for you?"

His lips twitched. "No comment."

"I knew it!" I said. "So tell me, does the convention center *know* that you looked at the footage?"

"Probably not."

I studied his face. There was still something that he wasn't telling me. I said, "But…?"

"But if they tried to pull it up, yeah, they'd know that *someone* was in there."

"Why do you say that?"

"Because a few minutes are missing."

It wasn't hard to guess which footage he meant. "Do you mean the footage of me?"

"Exactly."

"So you erased it?"

"Erased, deleted – either way, it's gone."

I stared across the table. "And you didn't even have their permission?"

He gave a low scoff. "Permission takes time."

"And how about the deleting?" I said. "Does that take time, too?"

"Not as much as you'd think."

I was flabbergasted. "But you did *all* of that just to delete it?"

"It wasn't just the deleting," he said. "I needed to see who was watching you with their phones out."

Ohhhhh. Right. Finally, I knew what he meant. Obviously, he'd looked at the footage so he could see exactly who was taking pictures or video.

Jack continued. "And once I knew who they were, the rest was easy."

Not to me, it wasn't. "So what'd you do next?"

"What else? Track them down."

"Seriously?"

"It wasn't hard," he claimed yet again. "They were still at the convention center."

"And then…?"

"So then I go up, say hi, and buy the photos. Piece of cake."

He made it sound oh-so easy. But I knew it wasn't. *It couldn't be.*

"So then what?" I said. "You just hand them some cash, and they send you the images? Is that what you're saying?"

"More or less."

"Oh come on," I said. "It can't be that simple. Like what if someone doesn't want to sell?"

"Then I talk them into it."

"But how?"

"It depends on the person. With some people, you ask nicely." He reached out and took a sip of his drink. "With others, you might have to get creative."

"Creative how?" I asked.

"Don't worry," he said, returning his glass to the table. "It wasn't necessary."

I wasn't quite sure I believed him. But then again, the *entire* thing beggared belief. I considered everything he'd done from beginning to end. "So you did *all* of this in forty minutes?"

"Thirty-five," he said, "including firing the guard."

"What guard?"

"The security guard," he said. "I found him whacking off in the men's room."

My jaw dropped. "*Please* tell me you're joking."

"I could say it," he said, "but it wouldn't be true."

"So he *really* was?" I shook my head. "But wait, how could *you* fire him? He doesn't even work for you."

"It doesn't matter," he said. "The guy's gone."

Desperately, I wanted to know more. *And* I wanted to forget everything I knew. *Talk about mental whiplash.*

Trying to focus, I said, "Okay, so you did *all* of these things? In *thirty-five* minutes? Seriously?"

Jack nodded. "Plus five minutes to get the shirt. So there you go. There's your forty."

Stunned, I sat back in my seat. *What could I say to that?*

I hardly knew.

Still, there was something he hadn't yet explained. "So about that shirt," I said. "I don't want to sound ungrateful, but why'd you pick *that* one?" I tried to smile. "Be honest. You *wanted* to make me look ridiculous."

Again, he leaned back in his chair. "Right...The Shirt of Shame." He gave a slow nod. "I might have to use that in a book."

I couldn't tell if he was joking or not, but knowing his plots, I could almost see it. Still, I *had* to know. "So was it?" I made little air quotes. "A Shirt of Shame?"

"No," he said. "It was a shirt of convenience."

"What do you mean?"

"By then, I'm running low on time, and there's this vendor going by, late to set up. And he's selling costumes for participants or whoever."

I almost laughed. "And I suppose he was selling *only* ridiculous costumes? There was nothing cute or fun?"

"Hey, *I* thought the jester one was fun."

"Fun for you," I accused with a laugh. "Not for me."

"Hey, it was the only two-piece costume he had. The rest were one-piece only."

"So?"

"So I was supposed to bring you a shirt, not a whole outfit."

"What kind of outfit?" I said. "Give me an example."

"My favorite? A serving wench." His gaze dipped briefly to my torso, and he smiled. "Low cut. Not good for the signing though."

I almost snickered. "Oh, really?"

His tone grew speculative. "But if you wanted to wear that in private…" He finished with a shrug and let his look speak for itself.

Holy hell. He was definitely flirting with me. And he wasn't being subtle about it either. Beyond flattered, I just had to ask, "What's gotten into you, anyway?"

"The truth? I'm tired of fighting it."

"Fighting what?"

"You don't know?"

"No. Actually, I don't," I admitted. "Honestly, I wasn't even sure you liked me."

He gave me a wicked smile. "Me neither."

"I'm serious," I said. "You were so cool and distant. Do you realize, this is the first time we've even eaten together?"

"Not true," he said. "We had pastries on the plane, remember?"

"That doesn't count."

"I know," he said. "But we're here now, aren't we?"

I smiled. "Yes. We are."

"Speaking of which," he said, "there's something I need to say."

"What?"

"We can't do this. You know that, right?"

CHAPTER 44

Becka

I wasn't quite sure what he meant. From across the table, I said, "Sorry, I'm not following."

"This trip," he said. "It was a mistake."

And just like that, all of the warm, fuzzy feelings went straight out the window. I asked, "What do you mean?"

"I mean, I saw the warning signs. I should've paid attention."

"Warning signs?" I shook my head. "What warning signs?"

"Like your roommate," he said. "I wanted to kill him."

I frowned. At that moment, I could hardly recall my roommate's name. "So?" I tried to laugh. "I can't say I blame you."

But Jack wasn't laughing. Unlike me, he wasn't even trying to. "Yeah, but I blame myself."

"For what?" I asked. "The way you treated him?"

"Hell no."

"Then what?"

Slowly, Jack reached out and smoothed a stray lock of hair from my face. His touch was electric, and I couldn't stop myself from leaning into it.

In a low voice, he said, "I don't want you as an employee."

His words were a caress, and I smiled in spite of the earlier tension. "What does *that* mean?"

"It means I want to see you, but not like this." He pulled back and said, "You shouldn't be here."

Suddenly, I was no longer smiling. "Here? At the restaurant? Or on the book tour?"

"The tour."

I was staring now. "So what are you saying? You're firing me?"

"Don't worry," he said. "I'll pay you for the full thing, make sure you get college credit, too."

What was this? A dismissal? I gave him an expectant look. "But...?"

"But you should fly home. Or better yet, go see your sister. I'm betting she'd love to see you."

What the hell?

So not only was he firing me, he was sending me away?

I didn't believe it.

Beyond confused, I asked, "What's gotten into you, anyway?"

"Nothing." His gaze didn't waver. "I'm being smart."

"No you're not," I said. "Because if you were, you wouldn't be sending me all these mixed messages."

"I know," he said. "But trust me, it's better this way."

"For who?"

His voice was very quiet. "You."

What a load of crap.

I recalled our conversation in the car, and suddenly it all made sense. With a bitter laugh, I said, "Oh, I get it."

He studied my face. "No. You don't."

"Oh yeah? How do you know?"

"Because I can tell."

I rolled my eyes. "Oh, so you're a mind-reader now?"

"No. But I can read your face."

"Great." I gave him a stiff smile. "So what am I thinking?"

"You're thinking I don't want you here."

"That's no mystery," I said. "You just told me that yourself."

"No." His jaw tightened. "What I *told* you was that it would be smarter if you left. That's not the same."

"Oh, give me a break," I said. "What, you think I forgot what you said in the car?"

"Sorry, but you're gonna have to be more specific."

I lowered my voice. "You said 'starfuckers' weren't your thing. Is that what you think I am?"

"You?" He frowned. "No."

"Oh, please," I said. "You don't have to be nice about it." I made a show of looking around, taking in the candle-lit tables and romantic view. "What was this? Some sort of test? To see if I'd swoon if you turned on the charm?"

He stiffened. "What are you getting at?"

"You know exactly what I'm getting at," I said. "You ran a fun little test, and I failed. So now you're giving me the boot."

He looked at me like I'd lost my mind. "That's what you think?"

I lifted my chin. "Well the timing can't be a coincidence."

With a low scoff, he said, "In case you didn't notice, I could've fucked you in the car."

I sucked in a breath. "What?"

"Shit." His eyes filled with regret. "I shouldn't have said that."

I forced a smile. "Why not? We're being honest, right?"

"Listen…" He shoved a hand through his hair. "Let's start over, okay?"

"From when?" I tried to think. "The beginning of the book tour?"

"No." His voice softened. "The beginning of dinner."

Dinner. The food had been delicious, and the company had been amazing.

Until now.

Now I was wishing that I hadn't eaten a thing, because it suddenly wasn't sitting so great. I pushed back my chair and stood. "Forget it. Dinner's over."

And with that, I turned and marched out of the restaurant, refusing to look back.

CHAPTER 45

Jack

Fuck.

Noble intentions. Of those, I had plenty. But making them work? It wasn't so easy.

I yanked out my wallet and pulled out a wad of cash. I tossed it onto the table and headed for the door, only to be stopped mid-way by our server, who wanted to make sure that nothing was wrong.

Something was wrong all right. But it had nothing to do with the food or the service. Trying not to be a dick about it, I assured her that everything had been great and kept on going.

Still, the delay had cost me.

By the time I caught up with Becka, she was halfway to the car. I strode up behind her and said, "Becka, wait."

When she didn't stop, I moved forward and reached for her elbow.

Without turning back, she yanked free of my grip and kept going. Short of tackling her in the parking lot, there wasn't much I could do, except hit the keyless entry to make sure she had someplace to go.

She made straight for the car and yanked open the passenger's side door. Wordlessly, she climbed inside, slamming the car door shut behind her.

As for myself, I strode around the opposite side and claimed the driver's seat. By the time I shut the car door behind me, Becka was buckled up and ready to go.

Not so fast.

I turned to her and said, "You're not getting what I'm saying."

"Sure I am."

"No. You're not." Deliberately I softened my tone. "My fault, not yours."

"Sure, whatever." She pointed to the steering wheel. "So, are we swinging by the hotel?" Her mouth tightened. "Or, are you just taking me straight to the airport?"

I could. It would be easy enough. The jet was fueled and ready. But I didn't want her to go, not like this.

Still, I had to know, "Is that what you want?"

"Yes." Her shoulders sagged. "And no."

"I know the feeling."

She whirled in her seat to face me. "No you don't. You have no idea how I feel." She sighed. "Look, I'm really thankful for what you did, I mean as far as the pictures and everything else. Truly, I am. But do you realize, you've been treating me like a pariah for most of the trip?"

She was wrong. She was no pariah. But she *was* other things – a temptation, a distraction, a complication. She was the thing that kept me up at night, and the person who made me smile when I was supposed to be getting serious.

And she noticed far more than she should.

I replied, "It wasn't my intention."

"It was, too," she said. "You practically admitted it, remember? You told me flat-out that you didn't want to encourage me, or however you put it."

Wrong again. "No. What I said was, I didn't want to encourage myself."

"Well it must be nice to have that kind of luxury."

"Meaning?"

"Meaning you avoid me for days, then turn on the charm for like two whole hours, and then all of sudden, you announce that you're sending me away." She shook her head. "I don't get it. I'd *never* do that to you. I'd never do that to anyone."

I believed her. But that didn't change a thing. "You would if you were me."

"And why's that?"

"Maybe I'm looking out for you."

"Do you realize, you've been 'looking out for me' ever since we met?" She made a sound of frustration. "Has it ever occurred to you that I don't need looking out for?"

"No."

"Why not?"

"Because it's not true. We *all* need that."

"Oh, really?" Her tone grew sarcastic. "Do *you?*"

"I'm different."

"Yeah, no kidding."

"And," I said, "if you think I'm *not* gonna look out for you, you're crazy."

"Well, I may be crazy," she said, "but I still don't want to be treated like a child."

From the driver's seat, I gave her a good, long look. *She was no child. Far from it.*

Her lips were full, and her curves were sweet. And her eyes – brown with flecks of gold – made me want to yank her into my arms and prove to her how terribly wrong she was.

But this wouldn't be doing her any favors. So instead, I replied, "I'm not treating you like a child. I'm treating you like something else."

"Oh yeah? What's that?"

"Someone worthy of protection." I leaned toward her. "You think I act this way with everyone?"

"I don't know. Do you?"

"No."

"So why me?" she asked. "Is it because of the Flynn connection?"

"It started out that way."

"And now?"

"Now?" I said. "It's complicated. And believe me. I *do* want to see you." I paused. "But *after* the tour."

She frowned. "Why after?"

"Because you're too smart for your own good."

"Oh, so now you're flattering me?"

"If I wanted to flatter you, I can think of better ways."

"Like what?"

"You really wanna know?"

She gave a tight shrug. "Sure, why not?"

"All right," I said. "But remember, you asked."

CHAPTER 46

Becka

As I stared at him from the passenger's seat, I was dying to hear what he'd actually say. *Pathetic, I know.*

Who knows, maybe he wouldn't say anything. Maybe this was all one senseless game, where he got off on seeing me dance to his twisted tune.

He was good at that.

But this time, I was ready.

I gave him a no-nonsense look. *Go ahead. Bring it on, Smart Guy.*

Finally, he said, "You know what? Screw flattery. I'm gonna tell you the truth."

"Oh yeah? What's that?"

He frowned. "You make me happy."

I studied his face. "Yeah, I can tell."

"I'm not happy *now*," he clarified.

"Why not?"

"Because the timing sucks."

It sounded like an excuse, a brush-off, a way to make me leave without hurting my feelings. As far as flattery, it was seriously lacking. I looked away, eyeing the parking lot ahead. "So, are you done?"

"Not by a longshot." His voice softened. "Becka, look at me."

I turned to look. And when I did, my pulse quickened. His eyes were so vividly blue and filled with an emotion that I couldn't quite decipher.

Longing?

Frustration?

Something more?

And already, I was falling under his spell. I wanted to say something, but I didn't know what.

Softly, he asked, "You wanna know what I did last night?"

"What?"

"I thought of *you*." He paused. "And I don't mean for a few minutes, or for an hour. I mean, I thought of you all night."

The petty part of me wanted to throw his claim back at him, to tell him that thoughts were cheap, just like his oh-so pretty words.

But I couldn't, and now I was more curious than ever. "So let me get this straight," I said. "You sat in your hotel room *all* night, thinking of me? That's what you expect me to believe?"

"Something like that."

"See? That's exactly what I mean. Why is a simple yes or no so hard for you?"

"Because things *aren't* that simple."

"All right. Enlighten me. What part of the statement was true? And what part *wasn't*?"

"Okay… I *was* thinking of you."

"But what? You weren't there all night?"

He frowned. "See? *That's* the problem."

"*What's* the problem?"

"You've got this way of cutting to the chase, asking things you shouldn't. And I don't want to lie, even by omission."

Already, my wheels were turning. If he wasn't in his hotel room all night, what did that mean?

Was he out with someone else? It sure sounded that way.

I just had to ask, "So, where were you?"

"Not where you think."

"How do you even know what I'm thinking?"

"It's written all over your face," he said. "So let me save you the trouble of asking. I was alone."

I felt annoyingly relieved, but even more curious. "Doing what?"

In what felt like a change of subject, he said, "I need a favor."

"What?"

"Stay," he said. "Not as my assistant. And not as a family friend. But as my guest."

"But I don't get it," I said. "Inside the restaurant, you told me you wanted me to leave."

"That's not what I said. I said you *should* leave. But trust me, that's not what I want."

"You *do* know that's another mixed, message, right?"

"I do," he said. "And you haven't heard the full favor."

"Okay, so what is it?"

"Stay," he repeated. "But stop asking questions, all right?" He paused. "And you might see things. I need you to ignore them, pretend you *don't* see."

It was one of the oddest requests I'd ever received.

And now I didn't know what to say. As I considered his request, I studied his face long and hard.

A few years earlier, I'd gone through this whole paranormal romance phase, where most of my reading list consisted of stories where the guy had a secret life as some mythical creature or another.

For some reason, his request made me recall all of those stories. With a shaky laugh, I asked, "So what are you? A vampire or a werewolf?"

"Neither," he said. "I'm just a guy."

Now *that* was a joke. He wasn't just a guy. He was a billionaire, a world-famous author, and the sexiest person I'd ever seen.

And, as if this weren't fantastical enough, he was also looking at me like *I* was the interesting one.

What he was asking, it was no favor – other than the one condition I'd *never* agree to.

I said, "So let me get this straight. If you come back with lipstick on your collar, I'm supposed to pretend that I don't see it?"

"If you see lipstick on my collar," he said, "it'll be yours." Slowly, he shook his head. "There's no one else. And there won't be. I promise."

Desperately, I wanted to say yes. But it felt like I was giving in way too easily. Plus there was the fact that I actually enjoyed working on the book tour.

I liked meeting his fans, and I liked going places with him. And I hated the idea of getting money or credit for something that I wasn't doing.

With sudden inspiration, I said, "If I say yes, do I get a favor, too?"

"Name it," he said.

"All right. I want to keep working."

"That's no favor," he said. "Name something else."

"What are you saying? You won't let me do my job?"

"I'm saying, that's a favor for *me*, not for you."

I wasn't quite sure I agreed. But I didn't want to be too hasty either. I said, "Then maybe you'll owe me *two* favors."

"Done."

A reluctant smile tugged at my lips. "But you don't even know what I'm gonna ask."

"It doesn't matter," he said. "Ask it, and it's yours."

It was an odd thing to consider, because Jack was one of the few people in the entire world who could probably deliver just about anything.

But at the moment, I didn't want just anything. *I wanted him.*

Now *that* would be a favor.

Still, his claim from earlier echoed in my brain. *"I could've fucked you in the car."*

How humiliating was that? It didn't help that it was true.

Even *more* humiliating, I still wanted him, even now. And yes, we *were* sitting in a car.

I gave the back seat a quick glance, enjoying the mental image that popped into my head just before I gave myself a mental slap.

Forget the car. We had not just one, but two, perfectly good hotel rooms waiting and ready.

Good grief.

Maybe I *was* a starfucker, chasing after someone for *what* he was, not *who* he was. It was a sobering thought and scarily appropriate, considering that I knew very little about Jack Ward – meaning the guy, not the author.

And yet I'd been embarrassingly eager to jump into his arms – or worse, his back seat – just because he'd expressed a smidgen of interest.

That wasn't me. And, in spite of my eagerness, I realized just how foolish I'd been.

After a long moment, I said what needed saying. "All right. Here's my favor." I bit my lip. "But it's a toughie."

His gaze met mine. "I think I can handle it."

Oh, God. Even now, he looked so annoyingly sexy that for the briefest instant, I almost blurted out my *original* favor – which involved a whole lot of nakedness regardless of the location.

But instead, I stiffened my resolve and said the thing I'd been dreading. "I think we should pretend that today didn't happen."

I braced myself, wondering what he'd say. *Would he be angry? Upset? Disappointed at all?*

Apparently not.

With a shrug, he replied, "Done."

I should've been relieved. But stupidly I wasn't. "Don't you want to know why?"

"Hey, it's *your* favor. You don't need to explain."

Oh, but I did. "It's just that, well, it seems like we went from zero to sixty in just a few hours, and–"

"It's all right," he said. "Like I said, you don't owe me an explanation." And with that, he turned away, fired up the engine, and backed out of the lot.

As I'd done so many times before, I studied his face in profile, wondering what exactly was going through his head.

I didn't bother asking. *And why?* It was because I fully realized it would be for nothing. He was Jack Ward, the king of non-answers.

When his profile offered zero clues, I finally turned and slumped deeper in the seat.

Who knows? Maybe he was glad that I'd come to my senses.

As for myself, I felt oddly unsatisfied, especially when it became painfully clear that he still expected me to live up to *my* end of the bargain.

CHAPTER 47

Jack

She was a bullet to my heart, and I should've been relieved. Dodging the bullet had been easy, thanks to her sudden bout of sanity. But forgetting the taste of her lips and what might've been – now *that* was hard.

It didn't get any easier over the next few weeks as we both pretended that nothing had happened between us.

She was a good employee, and I was a decent boss.

This might've been enough, if not for the fact that I couldn't stop thinking about her.

Her sweet lips, her tight body, and her inquisitive mind – these were the things that haunted my nights, even as I prowled through the places on my list.

It was just past three in the morning in downtown Indianapolis, and I was returning from one such place when I spotted her in the hotel lobby, sitting with her head buried in a book.

I stopped in my tracks. *What the hell?*

She looked too sweet and too vulnerable, curled up on the lobby's sofa like she was sitting in the safety of her own living room.

I didn't like it.

The lobby was empty, and the security was a joke.

Shit, she didn't even realize that some guy was ogling her from afar. Okay, so the guy was me, but the point was still valid.

I strode forward and didn't stop until I reached her side. In a quiet voice, I asked, "What are you doing?"

She looked up. "Reading. What are you doing?"

"Forget *me*," I said. "You realize you're alone down here?"

"I'm not alone," she said, glancing toward the front desk.

I turned to look. The desk was empty. I looked back to her and said, "You sure about that?"

"Well, maybe they're not there *now*," she said. But they *were* there when I came down. And I'm sure they'll be back any minute."

Obviously, she meant the front desk clerk, whoever *that* was tonight. But it didn't matter. Becka was missing the point.

I asked, "What's wrong with your room?"

"Nothing."

"You realize it's past three, right?"

"Yeah, so?"

"So don't you think you'd be better off up there?"

She was wearing white cropped pants and a little yellow t-shirt. The shirt wasn't obscene, but it clung to her curves and revealed just enough down the front to make me want to see more.

Still, I kept my gaze where it belonged as I waited for Becka's reply.

Abruptly, she shut her book and stood to face me. "What about *you*?"

"What about me?" I asked.

"Don't you think *you'd* be better off up there, too?" As the words left her mouth, she gave a little wince. "I mean *your* room, of course. Not mine."

And now she was blushing.

It annoyed the piss out of me, because she looked so beautiful doing it. Her cheeks were flushed, and her lips were full and pink.

The thought of joining her in the hotel room might've made me groan out loud if I were a different kind of guy – meaning the type who *hadn't* made self-control a top priority.

I told her, "Don't worry. I know what you meant."

"Good," she said. "So you get the point."

"Which is…?"

"I'm just saying that *I* was right here reading in the lobby, while *you* were out of the building entirely. So it just seems to me that you're in no position to judge – or to lecture me, for that matter."

"Except I'm your boss, remember?"

"Not now, you're not." Her chin lifted. "You said I was done for the night." She gave me a tight smile. "Remember?"

I remembered, all right. That conversation had occurred nearly eight hours ago, and it had taken all of my willpower to say goodbye after dinner.

Lately, we'd been doing that far too often – having dinner, meeting up for breakfast, or talking for hours during those long car rides and private flights.

The truth was, I couldn't get enough of her. And I wasn't blind. The feeling was obviously mutual – which made it harder than hell to keep things casual while we both pretended there was nothing there.

But there was.

I could see it in her eyes and feel it in my own. *She wanted me. I wanted her.* And neither one of us was thrilled to pretend otherwise.

But when I gave my word, I didn't look for loopholes. *No.* I kept that word and stuck to it – even if it *was* killing me.

And seeing her like this, alone in the middle of the night, let's just say it wasn't helping. *She shouldn't be out here.*

I said, "If you want, I'll get you a suite."

"Why?"

"So you can read up there."

With a perplexed look, she asked, "Do *you* have a suite?"

"No." It was true. For reasons of my own, I was staying on the fourth floor. *No suites there.* As for Becka, she was staying on the eighth. I knew exactly where her room was, even if she couldn't say the same in return.

Her eyebrows furrowed as she looked me up and down, taking in my black pants and dark jacket. From the look on her face, she wasn't liking what she saw.

Good.

Temptation aside, the less interested she was, the better. And more to the point, I was dressed this way for a reason, and it *wasn't* to draw attention – not from her or anyone else.

When she finished with her impromptu inspection, she said, "Just so you know, you're not fooling anyone."

I didn't know what she meant. But it didn't matter. I was fooling plenty of people, including her.

I replied, "Is that so?"

"Sure." She lowered her voice to just a whisper. "So tell me. Who were you sleeping with *tonight?*"

CHAPTER 48

Becka

I shouldn't have said it.

I knew this just as surely as I knew that Jack *wasn't* pleased. I could see it in the set of his shoulders and the look in his eyes – cold and wary, as if sizing me up.

In a tight voice, he replied, "What?"

On instinct, I took a step backward and nearly tumbled ass-first onto the same sofa that I'd been occupying for the last three hours.

It wasn't even my own balance that saved me. It was Jack's hand, reaching out to steady me just in time.

Without releasing my arm, he said, "You remember the deal, right?"

I swallowed. "What deal?"

"No questions."

A low scoff escaped my lips. He had an awful lot of nerve, reminding me of that stupid agreement when that whole conversation had become null and void.

I told him, "That doesn't count." And with that, I yanked my arm out of his grip.

He gave me a good, long look. "Yeah? Why not?"

"Because we agreed to forget that day entirely, remember?"

"Your idea," he said. "Not mine."

"Well, it's not like you argued about it." *I mean, seriously, wasn't there a middle ground in there somewhere?*

His gaze darkened. "I told you I'd give you any favor you wanted. And I did. So if you're unhappy, look in the mirror."

I felt my brow wrinkle in sudden confusion. From the look on his face, I wasn't the only one who'd been frustrated with that hopeless bargain.

Oh sure, it had been the smart thing to do, and I *shouldn't* be regretting it, especially now, when he'd been out doing who-knows-what.

Still, the last few weeks hadn't been easy.

After that mind-blowing kiss, not to mention all of the things he'd said in the car, it had been nearly impossible for me to act like nothing had happened. In fact, I was pretty sure that I'd been doing a sorry job of it.

But Jack? Until now, I'd seen no sign whatsoever that he recalled that day at all, even if we *had* been spending far too much time together.

But didn't he get it? That was part of the problem. The more time I spent with him, the less I liked how this was going.

Stupid or not, I wanted more.

In reply to his statement, I said, "Maybe *you* should look in the mirror. You ever think of that?"

"No."

"Why not?"

Something in his gaze softened. "Because it's not me I want to look at."

I blinked. "What do you mean?"

His gaze dipped to my lips. "I think you know."

Under any other circumstance, I might've gone all weak-kneed and silly. And maybe I had, just a little. But there was no way on Earth that I was *ever* going to show it.

I looked away. "Even if I *do* know, so what?"

His voice, softer now, reclaimed my attention. "Becka."

"What?"

"I wasn't doing what you think."

It shouldn't have mattered. Still, relief coursed through me, and I tried for a joke. "Don't you mean *who* I think?"

"And who's that?"

"Actually, I don't know," I admitted. "I'm just really confused, that's all."

"Don't be. Like I said, I was alone."

He hadn't put it *quite* that way the first time. But I knew what he was getting at. And now, I hardly knew what to say. As I stared up at him, I finally managed to ask, "So, what *were* you doing?"

"Nothing like that." The corners of his mouth lifted. "Even if you *are* cute when you're jealous."

My jaw dropped. *Talk about cocky.* "I wasn't jealous."

He smiled. "Yeah you were."

I refused to smile back, even if I *was* seriously tempted. "Well, *you're* awful sure of yourself."

"Yeah. And you wanna know why?"

Wordlessly, I nodded.

"Because if it were me, I'd wanna kill him."

My heart skipped a beat. *Was he implying what I thought he was implying?* After a long, awkward moment, I asked, "Who?"

"Whoever you were with." He gave a slow shake of his head. "Even if I have no right."

That last part made me pause. I knew exactly what he was getting at. *I* had no right to be jealous either. We weren't even a thing.

So, what was this? Some sort of trick? With renewed suspicion, I felt my gaze narrow. "Are you trying to distract me? Like, from asking questions, I mean?"

His gaze locked on mine. "If I wanted to distract you, I could think of better ways than this."

Woah.

Me, too.

In fact, I'd been thinking of potential distractions all day. And now, I just had to ask, "How?"

"I think you know."

Did I ever. In fact, I was feeling a little distracted already. I glanced toward the elevators and felt myself swallow.

I'd only come down to the lobby because I couldn't sleep. By now, I should've been used to it. Sleep had proven nearly impossible for weeks now. Oh sure, I *tried* to sleep. But I almost always ended up tossing and turning – or worse, fantasizing about my enigmatic boss.

He was a mystery that I wanted to solve, a puzzle that I wanted to piece together, and a fantasy that I was having a hard time resisting.

Perversely, the last few weeks had only fueled my interest – knowing that my fantasy could've been a reality, if only I hadn't played it so annoyingly safe.

As these thoughts swirled in my head, I stared up into his amazing eyes. They were so vividly blue and filled with obvious interest that I couldn't help but wonder if this was all part of a dream.

Maybe I *was* sleeping.

But if so, I didn't want to wake up.

As I tried to catch my breath, I said, "Just tell me something, all right?"

"What?"

"*Wherever* you were tonight..." I bit my lip. "You're *sure* it didn't involve anyone else? I mean romantically?"

"I'm sure. And you wanna know why?"

"Why?"

"Because there's only one girl I want, and she asks far too many questions."

My mouth opened, but the only sound that came out was a half sigh, half whimper. Beyond embarrassed, I clamped my lips shut and looked away.

And of course, my gaze landed directly on those elevators.

I studied them long and hard. A short walk, followed by a simple press of a button, and we could be on our way upward to a nice hotel room with a massive bed, perfect for getting tangled in the sheets.

Naked.

Together.

It was so very tempting – *and so very wrong.*

I still knew so little about him.

But holy hell, did I want to learn more.

CHAPTER 49

Jack

As I studied her profile, I could practically hear the wheels turning. *She was thinking again.*

She was dangerous. Not like me. But that didn't make her presence on the tour any less of a problem.

In the beginning, I'd had her pegged for something else – someone who'd support the tour with blinders on, seeing only what I wanted her to see – the cold-hearted writer with a nice, cushy life.

But I wasn't that guy. Not anymore.

And she wasn't that girl.

Together, we were something else.

And I didn't want her thinking at all. Not now.

As she studied the bank of elevators, she chewed on her bottom lip. Her eyes were bright, and her cheeks were pink with the remnants of her blush.

If I wanted, I could deepen that blush – not with words, but with actions. Once upstairs, I could make her forget her questions, forget her curiosity, or hell, even forget her own name.

For now.

But when morning came, I knew precisely what would happen. The questions would return, along with my need for privacy – for her sake *and* mine.

If I were smart, I'd keep my distance. If I were even smarter, I'd send her packing, maybe find something else for her to do – something nice, safe, and far away.

I had some research that needed doing – some castle thing in

Romania for an upcoming book. I could send her there within hours, and we'd both sleep easier from now on.

The thought was like a dagger to my heart.

Fuck that.

I wanted her. She wanted me. And I wanted to pull her close, not push her away. I moved toward her. "Becka."

She turned to look. "What?"

"That deal we made?"

"Yeah?"

"If you want to rip it up, say the word."

Her breath caught. "Actually, I didn't write it down. Did you?"

"No."

"But wait..." She hesitated. "Do you mean the deal where we agreed to forget that day? Or the *first* deal, where I was supposed to stay on as your guest and *not* ask any questions?"

"You pick," I said. "Name the deal, and it's yours."

"But why do *I* have to choose?"

"Because I gave you my word."

"So?"

"So if the choice were mine, you wouldn't be going upstairs alone."

Her lips parted. "Oh." Again, she looked toward the elevators. And then she looked to me. When our gazed locked, a soft sound escaped her lips. The sound went straight to my groin.

I lowered my head and whispered in her ear. "Your choice."

When she replied, it was more like a breath than a statement. "I choose *you.*"

With a smile, I pulled back to look at her face. "Yeah?"

She nodded. "That deal we made? I've been hating it for weeks."

I wasn't gonna lie. "Me, too." And with this, I reached for her hand. I turned it upward and lowered my head to kiss her palm. Her skin was smooth and warm and smelled like honey.

If we weren't in a public place, I would've left a trail of kisses from her palm to her shoulder – and then, to her lips.

But that wasn't me. When it came to something I wanted, *really* wanted, I didn't share – visually or otherwise. And there was no way on Earth that I'd be sharing her blushes or sounds with anyone else, not even the cameras that monitored the lobby.

So instead, I pulled back and said, "Wait here."

"For what?" she asked.

"I'm gonna get a room."

"But we already have a room." She gave a trembling laugh. "We have two, actually."

"Not good enough."

She frowned in confusion. "For what?"

I smiled. "You."

CHAPTER 50

Becka

In the doorway to the suite, I stopped and caught my breath. The room I'd been staying in on the lower floor was perfectly lovely. *But this? It couldn't compare.*

I looked to Jack and said, "You realize, you didn't have to do this, right?"

"Do what?" he asked, making a move to flick on the lights.

I spoke up. "Actually, would you mind waiting? I mean, there's lots of light coming in from outside, so maybe we can hold off a minute?" I was feeling just a lit bit shy and mesmerized by the view.

Without comment, Jack abandoned the light switch and moved closer. "You were saying?"

Already I was feeling almost too rattled to think. "I was just saying, you didn't have to get a whole new room."

As I said it, I glanced around. This wasn't a room. It was a suite on the very top floor. And even in the dim light, it was beyond spectacular. The décor was welcoming and plush, the windows were floor-to-ceiling, and off to the side was a room that could only be the bedroom.

Silently, I moved toward the main window. Through the pristine glass, I swear I could see for miles.

In front of me, the lights from nearby buildings shone like little squares in the night. But beyond that? I could see countless streetlights and traffic lights, all laid out before me in long, straight rows.

Given the late hour, the streets were nearly empty. From this far above, the scene looked like something out of a movie – the kind where humanity's gone, but the technology remains.

I couldn't help but smile at the wonder of it all. When Jack joined me at the window, I said, "I just realized something."

"What?'"

"I've never been up this high." With a nervous laugh, I added, "Not counting when we're flying of course. Then, we're *a lot* higher." I gave him a sideways glance. "But I guess you knew that already, huh? I mean, you're on the same airplane, right." I hesitated. "Or is it a jet? A jet's still an airplane, isn't it?"

Damn it. I was rambling again. I hadn't meant to, but my nerves were getting the best of me. I wanted him so badly I could taste it. And yet, I'd be lying if I didn't admit, even to myself, that I wasn't quite sure how to go about this.

I gave Jack a tentative smile. "I bet you don't want to talk about airplanes, huh?"

He smiled back. "I'm game if you are."

He didn't mean it.

He couldn't.

With an embarrassed laugh, I said, "I should take you up on that, if only to prove a point."

He asked, "And what point is that?"

"To always be honest."

With an easy smile, he replied, "You think I wasn't?"

"Not really," I said. "But I don't blame you. I mean we didn't come up here for a conversation, right." I blew out a shaky breath. "Especially about planes. And you paid extra for this room, so…"

"Becka."

I swallowed. "What?"

"We have all night."

"Not really," I said. "I mean, it's almost four in the morning."

"It doesn't matter," he said. "If you want, we can just talk."

I studied his face. In the darkened room, I couldn't see his expression as clearly as I might've on a sunlit day. But he *did* look sincere.

Still, I wasn't stupid. I knew full well that no guy on Earth would spring for an extra hotel room in the middle of the night, only to be told, *"Let's just talk."*

Besides, I was long past the talking phase. I'd been thinking about this – about *him* – for so very long that if I chickened out now, I'd be kicking myself forever.

There was just one stupid problem. I wasn't quite sure where to start. I bit my lip. "I don't know if I mentioned this, but I, uh, don't really do this a lot."

Quickly, I added, "I'm not a virgin or anything, but the whole one-night-stand thing. I guess I sort of skipped that phase in college. Or in high school. Or whenever people do that."

Oh yeah. I was definitely rambling.

And probably, he was wondering what the hell he'd been thinking, bringing me up here, only to listen to me babble on and on.

Enough was enough. Deliberately, I shrugged off my purse and set it carefully on the nearby side table.

I looked to Jack and said, "Well, I guess we should probably head to the bedroom, huh?"

CHAPTER 51

Jack

She was so sexy, I could hardly stand it.

Watching her mind whirl and her body tense, it was all I could do not to toss her over my shoulder and carry her straight to the place she'd just mentioned. *The bedroom.*

Once there, I could toss her onto the bed and take her hard and fast. *I could make sure that she liked it, too.* But this was our very first time. And I knew there was something else she'd like more.

I gave her a long, lingering look, drinking in the sight of her. Her lips were parted, and her eyes were bright.

She wanted this just as much as I did. And given how much I wanted her, that was saying something. Still, if I had *my* way, she'd soon be wanting it ten times as much.

I flicked my head toward the nearby sofa. "First, let's sit a minute."

She gave the sofa a puzzled glance. "Oh. Okay."

In her white cropped pants and little yellow T-shirt, she looked too sweet and too innocent by half. And the look suited her, because judging from her demeanor, she wasn't quite sure how to begin.

That was fine by me.

I knew enough for the both of us.

As she settled herself onto the sofa, I made my way to the stocked mini bar and opened up the small fridge under the counter. I pulled out a miniature bottle of wine and gave it a quick look. It was a cabernet, and the brand was nothing special.

But that didn't matter. Becka was no snob, and when it came to wine, it was all the same to me. And besides, I wasn't thirsty.

I pulled out two wine glasses and emptied the bottle into them. I returned to the sofa and handed Becka a glass.

As she took it, she frowned. "But you gave me like twice as much as you gave yourself."

"So?"

"So I feel a little guilty, like I'm cheating you or something."

"Don't worry," I said. "There's plenty more where that came from."

"Are you sure?'

"Trust me. If I want another bottle, I know where to get it."

"Oh." She gave me a tentative smile. "Well that's good."

The truth was, I wasn't in the mood for wine or any other drink. I was in the mood for her.

But no one liked drinking alone, and I'd poured the wine to help her relax, not to give her something else to think about.

As she took her first sip, I took a drink of my own, mostly for show. Afterward, I set my glass on the side table and said, "You *are* a trouble-maker, you know that?"

She laughed. "Oh, am I now?"

"You know it."

"And why is that?"

I gave her a long, appreciative look. "Because you've been distracting the hell out of me."

Her lips twitched like she wanted to smile. "When?"

"Always."

"Oh, stop it," she laughed.

"You think I'm lying?"

"Well…" She took another drink, this one longer than the first. When she finished, she said, "If you're not lying, you're at least exaggerating."

"I don't lie," I said. "And it's no exaggeration."

She gave me a dubious look. "Is that so?"

"It is," I said. "You wanna hear a secret?"

"Sure."

"When I'm signing those books and catch sight of you, it makes it hard for me to remember people's names."

And now she was laughing again. "Oh come on."

"No lie." I lowered my voice. "You wanna know what I was thinking today?"

"Sure. If you want to tell me."

"All right. You remember what you were wearing?"

She paused to think. "A black skirt and a pink top?"

"Right," I said. "That top? It had a lot of buttons, little pearl things right down the front."

She took another sip of her wine. "Yeah, I guess it did."

"I was thinking…" I leaned closer. "…how much I'd enjoy popping those buttons, one by one."

Her breath caught. "You were not."

"I was," I said. "In my mind, I was doing it nice and slow, so you could feel every pop, and the cool air creeping in."

"Oh." She gave a hard swallow. "Really?"

I glanced down to her chest. "That book store…it was colder than you liked."

"Yeah." Her chest was rising and falling now with every breath. "A little."

"So tell me," I said. "Were your nipples hard? They looked hard."

She gave another swallow. "Did they?" Her breaths were coming faster now.

Good. I wanted her breathless and quivering. "So…were they?"

"Actually, I don't know. But …" She gave a little shiver. "They're kind of hard now."

My tone grew teasing. "Are they?"

"I *think* they are. I mean, they *feel* like they are."

And now she was blushing again. Even in the dim light, the flush of her cheeks was deep and alluring, and I leaned slowly toward her. In a low voice, I offered, "If you want, I'll check."

She sucked in a breath. "Oh. Yeah. You definitely should. For research purposes. I know that writing and research – it goes hand in hand, right?"

I knew where *my* hands wanted to be. And now I smiled. Even when she was so adorably flustered, she had a certain way about her. She was warm and funny, and so sexy, she took my breath away.

I reached out with the back of my index finger and stroked her nipple through her shirt. Her back arched, and she made a little sound.

At the sound and sight of her, I almost groaned out loud.

She wanted more. And so did I.

But I was on a mission.

I was going to make her crave it – crave *me* and everything I wanted to do to her – until her mind shut off and her body took over.

With the back of my finger, I stroked her again, barely skimming the hardened nob. When she made that same sound, I felt like I'd bust out of my pants.

Breathlessly, she asked, "Isn't it kind of hard to tell through the shirt?"

I smiled. "Maybe."

"Oh, it is," she breathed. "I'm sure of it."

If that wasn't a hint, I didn't know what was.

But first, there was something I'd been wanting to do for far too long. Her wine was nearly gone now. I reached for her glass and pulled it gently from her fingers.

I set it on the coffee table next to mine and turned once again to face her. I pulled her close and kissed her long and hard, enjoying the feel of her tongue and the taste of her lips.

When she gave a muffled moan against me, I wanted to take her right then and there.

Not yet, I reminded myself.

Instead, I deepened the kiss and reached under the hem of her shirt, savoring the feel of her smooth stomach as I slid my hand deliberately upward, heading toward her breasts.

Her bra – thin and lacy – was the kind that fastened in front. It was a good thing, too, because my fingers were already there. With one practiced motion, I popped the clip and felt the lacy fabric fall aside.

Finally.

Her shirt was still on, but the bra was no longer between us. Slowly, deliberately, I cupped her breast upward, loving the weight of it in my hand and the soft sounds she made against my lips.

When my fingers found her nipple, she arched her back as if begging for more. She was so responsive, so perfect, and so genuine, that in the back of my mind, I couldn't help but wonder where she'd been my whole life.

I didn't know. But she was here now, and that's all that mattered.

I pulled back and said, "Do you know how many times I've thought of this?"

In a near-whisper, she replied, "It can't be more than *I* have."

"Wanna bet?"

She shook her head. "No way."

"Why not?" I teased.

"Because there's something else I want more. *A lot more.*"

"Oh yeah? What's that?"

"You."

I grinned. "I know."

She laughed. "Hey!"

"And guess what?"

"What?"

"You're gonna get it." And with that, I dove forward and gathered her up in my arms. It wasn't what I'd been planning to do, but it felt so right that I didn't even try to stop myself.

She was warm and willing, and I'd been craving her for weeks. I felt younger than I had in forever as I threw her over my shoulder and turned toward the bedroom.

She was still laughing. "Hey, that's not fair!"

I kept on going. "Why not?"

"I don't know," she laughed. "It just isn't."

"Nice try," I said and propelled us through the open doorway of the bedroom. With a few long strides, I reached the side of the bed and tossed to her onto it. She landed in a laughing heap, and I reached for her ankles.

I yanked her downward, enjoying her mock protest as she squealed, "But I'm still wearing my shoes!"

"Not for long," I said and yanked them off one by one.

I tossed them aside, and reached for the button of her pants. My fingers worked fast, and soon the pants were unbuttoned, unzipped, and ready to go. I pulled back and reached for the bottom hem of each pantleg. With both hands, I gave a hard yank and tossed the pants aside.

And then, I took a nice, long look.

Her panties were small and lacy. Her hips were rising and falling. And when I looked to her face, her eyes were warm, and her lips were parted.

I swear I fell in love right then and there – or maybe I'd loved her for a while now, and hadn't been willing to believe it. Either way, it was a new sensation, and it shook me to the core.

Until tonight, I'd barely kissed her. But she'd brought something new into my life, something that I hadn't known was missing.

And now, I was going to make her mine.

I lowered my head and kissed her pelvis, loving the feel of her warm skin through the lacy fabric.

Breathlessly, she said, "You know, you should get undressed, too." She made a move to sit up. "Wait, let me do it."

"Not yet."

"Why not?"

"Because I'm not done."

"With what?"

"This." I gave her panties a gentle tug, lowering them just an inch or two, enough for me to kiss her right where she wanted, even if she hadn't said so.

When she fell back with a soft moan, I smiled against her skin. She was wet and sweet, and warm under my mouth – and I'd only just begun.

I took her clit into my mouth and sucked it lightly at first, and then harder, loving the sounds she made as I kept going. I pulled back and let my tongue dance across her hardened nub until she was a quivering, moaning mess.

Oh yeah. She wasn't thinking *now.*

She was feeling.

And so was I.

It was a new sensation, and I let myself get lost to everything except the taste of her, the sound of her, and the feel of her.

When I stroked her opening with my finger and then slid it slowly inside, the walls of her body closed around me, warm and tight, and so damn welcoming.

If she felt this tight *now,* I could just imagine how she'd feel later, when I fully claimed her. At the mere thought of it, my heart pulsed, and my erection throbbed.

Again, I reminded myself, *not yet.*

From the bed, she breathed, "I want you. We should get you undressed and–"

I added a second finger to the first, loving the movement of her hips and the sounds she made, even as she said in mock protest, "I think that's cheating."

I lifted my head only long enough to smile up at her. "I know."

And then, I lowered my head once again, letting my mouth and fingers do the talking until Becka became wordless herself, except for her soft moans and whimpers as she ran her fingers through my hair and writhed on the bed.

Soon, she shuddered so hard against me that I thought *I'd* climax too from the sound and feel of her.

But I wasn't done, and neither was she. Soon, we were both naked in the sheets, ready, willing, and so eager we were trembling. When I slid my length into her depths for the very first time, it felt like I'd died and gone to heaven.

She was so slick, and so tight, I had to ask, "Are you all right?"

She nodded against me. "Oh yeah. More than all right. I'm wonderful."

Yes. She was.

Finally, I let myself go, driving into her sweet warmth until the sheets were tangled, and we were warm and damp from the heat of our bodies and the motions of our hips.

We climaxed at nearly the same time, almost like it was planned, or more likely, like we were custom-made only for each other.

It sure as hell felt that way.

As the few precious hours slipped away, we kissed and talked, and held each other tight until I felt like I'd known Becka forever.

I wasn't one to believe in past lives or soul mates. But if I were, I knew exactly what I'd believe.

She was made for me. And I was made for her.

When she fell asleep in my arms, I drifted off myself, satisfied like I'd never been before.

And we might've stayed like that forever, if only I hadn't forgotten to do one simple thing – send one quick message to the guy who'd be pissed as hell if he knew what I'd just done.

CHAPTER 52

Jack

I woke to the sound of buzzing from somewhere on the floor. *My phone.*

Shit.

Becka was curled naked in my arms, and I had no intention of dislodging her. Ignoring the phone, I cradled her close and savored the feel of her naked skin against mine.

Last night – it had been more than sex. It had been a real connection – precious and rare, especially in *my* world. I was a loner by nature *and* by necessity. But Becka – somehow she'd burrowed her way past all of that.

And I liked it.

No. I loved it.

Screw the phone. *Screw everything.*

It was a good plan until the phone buzzed again. I didn't want to wake her, so as gently as I could, I pulled away and fumbled beside the bed until the phone, still vibrating, was within my grip.

When I saw the display, I frowned. *Bad timing.* And that was an understatement.

I hit "ignore" and climbed out of bed. With the phone still in my hand, I made my way into the bathroom and shut the door behind me. The phone buzzed again within thirty seconds. *No surprise there.*

I answered with a curt, "What?"

On the other end of phone, Flynn said, "What's going on?"

I looked toward the bed. Through the bathroom wall, I couldn't see it. But the image was clear in my mind. His future little sister was lying naked in the sheets.

Flynn didn't know.

Of this, I was certain. I replied, "You tell me. You're the one who called." Under my breath, I added, "Three fucking times."

"Yeah? Well maybe if you'd answer, I wouldn't keep dialing. You were supposed to check in at six, remember?"

I did. But there was a reason I hadn't. And the reason was lying naked in the next room.

Flynn and I had a system. He was my backup, the guy I'd call if things went South. *They never did. Not yet.*

Still, as part of my routine, I texted him on a schedule that I provided in advance. If he didn't get a text, that meant I was in trouble, which meant that it was time for Plan B.

And now I was being a dick about it.

I didn't want to be.

I thought of Becka in the next room. She was naked and sweet. The sooner I finished with Flynn, the sooner I could return. Envisioning her in my arms, I explained, "Sorry, I got tied up."

"Fuck."

"What?"

"Just tell me."

I frowned. "Tell you what?"

"First, where the hell is she?"

I didn't ask who he meant. It would've been an insult to his intelligence and mine. I replied, "In the hotel."

It wasn't a lie. But the full truth? It was better left unsaid, at least for now.

"Whose room?" Flynn's voice hardened. "Hers? Or yours?"

It was a dangerous question.

We had a code, and I'd broken it. I wasn't sorry, even if I should've been. Still, I wasn't going to mess things up for Becka if she didn't want her sister to know.

Technically the hotel room wasn't hers *or* mine. It was *ours*. And I liked it that way. I replied, "Don't ask."

He groaned. "Fuck."

I didn't bother telling him that he was repeating himself. In fact, I didn't bother saying anything at all. *Really, what could I say?*

On the phone, he gave a hard scoff. "So I was right? Dude, what the hell?"

Dude? It sounded funny, but I wasn't laughing. "It's not what you think."

"Oh yeah? So you didn't fuck her?"

My grip tightened on the phone. I didn't like that word, not in this context. "No." I paused. "Not the way you make it sound."

"Call it whatever you want," he said, "I'll take that as a yes."

I *could* deny it, but why bother? And now I was curious. "How'd you know?"

"When you said you were tied up, you were fucking smiling. I could hear it."

Shit. I didn't remember smiling, but his answer made sense. Becka had that effect on me. She made me smile when I shouldn't, like when I was talking to a justifiably pissed-off friend.

I made a mental note. *From now on, watch the voice.*

But first, it was time for damage-control. "Listen, this stays between us, all right?"

"So I'm supposed to lie to Anna? *That's* what you're telling me?"

"No. I'm saying keep quiet until you hear otherwise. This doesn't have to be a problem."

He was silent for a beat before saying, "Anna was worried about that, you know."

According to Becka, Anna worried too much. Whether that was true or not, I couldn't say for certain. But I *did* know that some things had definitely slipped through the cracks.

I told Flynn, "Yeah, well maybe Anna should've spent the time worrying about something else."

"Meaning?"

"Tell me, you ever meet her roommate?"

He paused as if thinking. "You mean Tara?"

"No. Some pill-popping loser. A guy named Nick."

Flynn was silent for another long moment. And when he spoke, he didn't sound happy. "You're joking, right?"

"No joke. So let me throw it back at you. Dude, what the hell?"

"Is that supposed to be funny?"

"No. It's supposed to make you think. Did you realize, she was worried about money?"

"Becka?" He sounded surprised. "No."

"Yeah." My jaw clenched. "So, what the hell were you doing?"

"You know what?" His voice rose. "For someone who fucked my fiance's little sister, you might want to lay off the lectures."

"Why?" I said. "Because I'm wrong? Or because you were doing a sorry job of looking out for her?"

I hadn't meant to say it. But now that it was out there, I was determined to get to the bottom of this. I asked, "Just what the hell were you doing, anyway?"

"Not enough." He gave a low curse. "Obviously."

From his end of the phone, I heard Anna's voice somewhere in the background. I couldn't make out what she was saying, but the voice alone was a grim reminder that things had become more complicated than I'd intended.

Abruptly, Flynn said, "Thanks, asshole." And with that, he hung up.

He was angry.

This wasn't a surprise.

I didn't blame him. But I was angry, too. I'd meant what I'd told him. When it came to Becka, he'd fallen short.

And if I were the kind of guy to keep score, I might've told him that none of this would've happened – including my sleeping with her – if only he'd done a better job of looking out for Becka on his own.

After all, that was the reason I'd brought her along in the first place.

But even as the thought crossed my mind, I realized the stupidity of my logic. If Flynn had done a better job, Becka wouldn't be here with me right now.

And I *wanted* her with me.

As far as Flynn and Anna and everything else, well, I'd deal with that later. Now I had a warm bed and someone to get back to – someone who enchanted me in ways I hadn't thought possible.

Maybe I'd wake her. Or maybe I wouldn't. Either way, I wanted her back in my arms.

It was a nice thought. But it didn't happen. And why? It was because when I opened the bathroom door, I came face-to-face with Becka, looking decidedly less happy than she had last night.

CHAPTER 53

Becka

I glared up at him, wondering what on Earth was going on. He was still naked. *Not me.* On my way to the bathroom door, I'd grabbed the top sheet and wrapped it around me like a blanket.

But I still felt naked, and not in a good way.

I asked, "Who were you talking to?"

I knew the answer, but I still wanted to hear what he'd say. *Would he lie to me? Or dodge the question entirely?* He was good at that, as I'd seen so many times already.

He replied, "I think you know."

"What makes you say that?" I asked.

"It's written all over your face."

Great. As usual, I was an open book. But Jack? *He* wasn't an open book. He was the most complicated person I'd ever met. And he had more secrets than I cared to consider.

But his cell phone conversation? That *hadn't* been a secret.

I hadn't meant to eavesdrop, but his voice had carried through the bathroom door, waking me from a blissful slumber. And, after I'd realized exactly who he was talking to, I couldn't simply lie in bed waiting for the damage to be done.

And there *had* been damage, which meant that I had some serious fixing to do.

All that aside, I couldn't help but feel at least some embarrassment at being caught lurking outside the bathroom door. I explained, "I was just about to knock."

"You sure?"

"Of course I'm sure."

"But why knock when you can listen in?"

It sounded like an accusation, and I didn't like it. "So you don't believe me?"

He shrugged. "It's just a question."

Well, that was rich. I had questions, too – not that he was big on answering them. But that was an issue for another time.

I said, "Regardless of what you might think, I *was* going to knock. And I'll tell you why." I gave him a serious look. "I don't appreciate what you told him."

His expression softened. "Listen, he guessed on his own, okay?"

I made a sound of frustration. "I don't mean about us sleeping together."

That made him pause. "So you don't care that they know?"

"Okay, yes. I care. I mean, if nothing else, that's not the way I would've liked for them to find out. But you're missing the point."

"Which is…?"

"Why were you giving Flynn such a hard time?"

"Because he had it coming."

I recalled Jack's accusations, the things he'd said to my future brother-in-law. I hadn't enjoyed hearing them, especially because they weren't true. "In case you didn't realize it," I said, "Flynn and Anna have given me a ton of help, a lot more than I ever wanted."

In front of me, Jack looked less than convinced. "Is that so?"

"Yes. Definitely." I met his gaze head-on. "Do you know, Flynn paid for my last year of college? And he's offered to pay for the upcoming year, too."

From the look on Jack's face, he wasn't impressed. "So?"

"So that's a big deal."

"Not to Flynn."

I knew what Jack meant. Flynn was absolutely loaded. But Jack was missing the point. "It's a big deal to me," I said. "It totally changed my life. Do you know, he even paid for a dorm room?"

Before then, I'd been living off-campus and commuting. I wouldn't have minded if not for the fact that my car was unreliable, and driving an hour each way was no picnic, especially when it snowed, which it did quite often in Northern Michigan.

But Jack's expression still didn't waver. "Yeah? So why weren't you living in it?"

"The dorm?" I gave a loose shrug. "Because I was older than almost everyone else. And I didn't really fit in."

At the memory of it all, I sighed. "It was weird and awkward. Plus, everyone there knew about Flynn and my sister, and it made everything kind of strange. Everyone kept asking to meet him, and I guess I wanted to be a little more anonymous, that's all."

As I fumbled for the words to explain, I became increasingly aware that Jack was still naked.

With growing embarrassment, I looked down, skipping his pelvis entirely. At his knees, I did a double-take.

Last night, the suite had been mostly dark. But now, in the morning light, I saw something that I hadn't noticed before – deep, jagged scars running from his ankles to his knees.

On both legs, too.

Weird.

It took me a moment to realize that I'd stopped talking.

And so had he.

When I looked up, he frowned.

For a long moment, he said nothing, and neither did I.

Finally, it was Jack who broke the silence. "Go on. Finish what you were saying."

But now, I was almost too distracted to think. *The scars – what were they from?* They weren't burns. They were cuts. Or at least, I *thought* they were cuts. *But from what?*

Absently, I replied, "About the dorm thing? Actually I was done."

Was this true? I couldn't say for certain. In fact, I was half-afraid that I'd stopped talking in mid-sentence.

Desperately I wanted to ask about the scars, but it seemed unbearably rude, especially now in mid-argument.

Into my silence, Jack said, "I fell through a window."

I blinked. "What?"

"A window," he said. "I fell through it." He glanced down. "I was wearing shorts. Cut my legs to hell. But it's not a big deal. Do you want breakfast?"

I did. But not this instant. I asked, "How old were you?"

"Maybe ten."

I tried to envision it. "But how exactly do you fall through a window?"

He gave me a rueful smile. "It's not as hard as you think."

I wasn't buying *that* for one minute. "Where was this?"

"Does it matter?" he said. "A window's a window, right?"

I recalled Jack's official bio. He'd grown up in a series of foster homes. No specifics were ever mentioned. That wasn't a good sign. *What on Earth had happened to him?*

Jack's voice interrupted my thoughts. "Don't."

"Don't what?"

"Don't think about it. Like I said, it's wasn't a big deal." As he spoke, he set his cell phone on the bathroom countertop. "So, how about breakfast?"

I glanced toward the phone. Distracted or not, I was still angry about that call. "But we're not done talking."

"About what?"

"The thing with Flynn."

"Don't worry. He can handle it."

"I know," I said. "But he shouldn't have to. You seriously need to apologize."

"All right. I'm sorry."

I rolled my eyes. "Not to me. To Flynn."

He shook his head. "Forget it."

"But you were awful," I said. "And he's done so much for me. It's not right. *Or* fair."

"Yeah? Well life isn't fair." He gave a tight shrug. "Ask Flynn. He'll tell you."

It felt like a dig. Flynn and my sister had a history. The early part hadn't been so great. And yes, some things *had* been particularly unfair, especially to Flynn.

I asked, "Are you talking about that thing in high school?"

"No. I'm talking about *now*. What I said to Flynn, I meant every word." He gave a low scoff. "And a bullshit apology isn't gonna change a thing."

"You never know," I said. "It might."

"Not if I don't mean it."

Obviously, Jack still wasn't getting it. I tried again. "Do you realize, they try to pay for everything?"

Jack looked less than impressed. "Trust me. They can afford it."

"You mean *Flynn* can afford it."

He shrugged. "Same difference."

"Not yet," I said. "They're not even married."

"But they will be."

"Yeah, I know. But that's not even the issue. I don't want to be *that* relative – the one who can't stand on her own two feet. Do you want the truth? I wouldn't have taken any help at all, except for the fact that Anna was so excited for me."

"Good."

"No. It's *not* good. And do you want to hear what Flynn said?"

"What?"

"That I wouldn't need to worry about anything from now on."

"Good," Jack repeated.

"But don't you see? It doesn't work that way. Like what if I make a mistake? What am I supposed to do? Ask them for more money? That's not me. And it's not just about the money either. A couple of months ago, I ran into a problem on a date, and do you know what Flynn did?"

"What?"

"He almost kicked the guy's ass."

Jack looked at me for long moment before saying in an eerily calm voice, "Oh yeah? For what?"

From the look in Jack's eyes, I was almost afraid to say. I offered up the briefest explanation possible. "The guy just got a little aggressive, that's all."

"Yeah? And what's the guy's name?"

"If you think I'm gonna say, you're crazy."

"Why?"

"Because you've got that same look Flynn got after he learned what happened."

"Which was…?"

"Not as much as you'd think."

When Jack's only reply was a long, silent look, I sighed. "All right fine. The guy got handsy when I wasn't interested. And then, when I left in a hurry, I forgot my purse, which wouldn't have been *so* bad, except that the guy refused to give it back."

Jack's gaze darkened. "Is that so?"

"Yes. But I'm sure he would've eventually. I think he was just giving me a hard time. But anyway, that night, I mention it to Anna, and *she* mentions it to Flynn, and the next thing I know, Flynn's knocking on the guy's door."

"So, you were there?"

"Sort of," I said. "I was visiting with a friend in the same apartment complex."

"And then what?"

"So the guy gets one look at Flynn, and practically throws my purse out into the hallway."

Jack gave a slow nod. "Smart guy."

"Yeah, a real genius. Anyway, like I said, it wasn't such a huge deal. I'm just saying, Flynn has *really* been there for me." I gave an embarrassed laugh. "Even more than I ever wanted. And Anna, too. So

I think it's pretty awful what you said to him."

And with that, I clamped my lips shut and waited for a response.

Finally, Jack said, "All right. How about this? An apology for breakfast."

"You mean like a trade?"

"If that's what you want to call it."

I felt the hint of a smile. "So I actually convinced you?"

"You might say that."

"So, what did it?" I asked. "Was it because he showed up on that guy's doorstep?"

"Hey, it didn't hurt."

I wasn't sure what that meant. But I wasn't one to look a gift-apology in the mouth, so instead, I pointed to his cell phone. "So, will you apologize now? I mean, *before* breakfast?"

He gave me a wry smile. "What, you wanna listen in?"

"Maybe," I admitted.

"All right." And then, looking a lot more reasonable than I might've expected, he grabbed his cell phone and tapped at the screen. He turned it to face me, where I saw Flynn's name as the contact before Jack put the cell phone to his ear.

After a few beats, he said into the phone. "Hey, sorry I was a dick. You were right. I was wrong." And then, with a significant look in my direction, he added, "The way I hear it, you did your best." He flashed me a cocky grin. "But me? I'm gonna do better."

CHAPTER 54

Becka

Over breakfast, I said, "You never told me. What did he say?"

"Who?"

"Flynn. After you apologized, how did he respond?"

We were freshly showered and sitting on opposite sides of a cozy booth in a local pancake house within walking distance of the hotel. Sunlight filtered in through the nearby window, making Jack's golden hair shine like a halo over his gorgeous face.

But he was no angel. Of this, I was certain.

In reply to my question, he said, "Nothing important."

"Well, he must've said *something.*"

Jack's eyes filled with mischief. "Nope."

"What do you mean?"

"I mean," he said, reaching for his coffee cup, "I was talking to his voice mail."

"What?" I sputtered. "Why didn't you just tell me?"

"Because I wanted breakfast."

"But what does that have to do with anything?"

He took a casual drink of his coffee. "You might've said it didn't count."

"The apology? Why wouldn't it count?"

"Because he wasn't there to hear it."

Some might say that Jack had a point. But his claim had a serious flaw, and I couldn't help but smile. "Just admit it. Breakfast had nothing to do with it."

He speared a piece of pancake off his plate. "Why do you say that?"

The restaurant was crowded and noisy with the clatter of dishes and the sounds of people talking. Still, I lowered my voice to say, "Because you weren't so eager to get down here, that's why."

He grinned. "Yeah? Well neither were you." He popped the bite of pancake into his mouth and winked. "Don't blame *me* if you're more tempting than breakfast."

I wanted to giggle. And, I wanted to toss something at his head, like maybe a napkin or possibly my panties.

He was quite literally the sexiest person I'd ever met. And he was flirting like crazy.

I'd never seen him like this, playful and happy.

I was happy, too. I loved spending time with him, in public *and* in private. Even now, my toes were tingling from our pre-breakfast distraction.

"Speaking of temptations," I said, "do you know how frustrating it is not to pummel you with questions?"

He arched an eyebrow. "You can't be *too* frustrated."

"Why do you say that?"

"Because you haven't stopped asking them."

"But that's not true," I protested. "You might not believe it, but I've been doing a pretty good job of keeping them to myself."

"You're right." He grinned. "I don't believe it."

I resisted the urge to roll my eyes. "Oh, stop it." I recalled our original deal, the one where I agreed to stay on as his guest under that "no-questions" clause.

I said, "Can I ask you something? It's about our deal."

"What about it?"

"Surely it doesn't mean that I can't ask you *any* questions." My face grew warm as I considered the events of the past day. "I mean, that would be a little unnatural, don't you think?"

He leaned back in the booth. "So what is this?" he said, looking surprisingly intrigued. "A renegotiation?"

"It's just a clarification, that's all. Like, let's say I wanted to ask you about the weather. Are you saying that I can't?"

He smiled. "What's with you and the weather?"

"It's just something people talk about, that's all."

His gaze met mine. "I think we both know the weather isn't the issue."

"See?" I said. "That's my whole point."

"Is it?"

"Definitely." And then, before he could say anything in response, I added, "Like, you never did tell me why you stay on the lower floors."

"Sure I did." He shrugged. "I like the stairs."

Maybe that was true. Maybe it wasn't. Still, I had to say, "But I've never seen you take them."

His lips twitched. "If you want, we'll take them after breakfast."

"But you're missing the point." I tried again. "Like, do you stay on the lower floors so you're harder to find?" I leaned forward to whisper, "So you can stay incognito?"

He glanced around. "I'm *already* incognito."

This wasn't quite true. Around us, more than a few people kept glancing in his direction – the women in particular. But of course, they might've been ogling him for reasons unrelated to his celebrity status.

After all, he *was* quite the specimen.

With a laugh, I said, "No offense. But I think you're wrong."

"Am I?"

"Definitely," I said yet again. "Everywhere we go, people stare at you. And I think most of them know who you are, too."

"Maybe," he said. "But they're never sure. That's the nice thing about being a writer. Now take Flynn, that guy's screwed."

I knew what he meant. Flynn had actually starred in the movies, which meant that his face was plastered everywhere. When Flynn had first moved back to our hometown, he'd caused a stir wherever he went.

Sometimes, he still did.

To Jack, I said, "You mean because everyone recognizes him?"

"Right," he said. "But me? I can fly under the radar."

I gave it some thought and decided that his logic made sense. At the book signings, he was absolutely mobbed. But away from all of that, he had a surprising amount of freedom and privacy.

Still, I had to say, "Yeah, but *I* recognized you right away, meaning when I first saw you at Flynn's house."

His tone grew teasing. "Did you now?"

"Oh come on," I laughed. "You know I did."

"Maybe. But you already knew that Flynn and I were friends. And you saw me in a place that made sense. But let's say you passed me on the street, you probably wouldn't've made the connection."

He was wrong. I would've recognized him anywhere.

But then, at a sudden realization, I sat up straighter in the booth. "So *that's* why you don't stay in the same cities as your book-signings. You're hoping that people won't recognize you." I smiled. "Am I right?"

"It's one reason," he said.

"So, what are the other reasons?"

"Do I *need* other reasons?"

"No. But with the way you phrased it, I just figured there had to be more."

From across the table, he gave me a long, speculative look. "You don't miss a thing, do you?"

He'd said something similar before. But it wasn't true. I missed plenty. And the longer I got to know him, the more I realized that he had more secrets than I knew.

And he *wasn't* fond of sharing them.

CHAPTER 55

Jack

We were in some hotel in Arizona when she said, "Hey, can I ask you something?"

We were naked in a king-size bed, and I pulled her close. As I nuzzled her hair, I asked, "Can I stop you?"

"Probably not," she said with a laugh. But then her laughter faded. "Those scars on your legs, you remember how you said you fell through a window?"

I stiffened. "I remember."

She pulled back and gave me a worried frown. "You weren't pushed or anything, were you?"

"No. Why do you ask?"

"Because I care about you. And you were so young."

"Ten?" I might've laughed if it were funny. "It's not *that* young." Or it least it hadn't been for me.

But Becka wasn't done. "I just mean...I know you were in a bunch of foster homes."

"Forget it."

"Why?"

I didn't want to lie, not to *her*. "Because it's not true."

"What?" She gave me a perplexed look. "Are you sure?"

"I think I'd know."

"I know. I just meant..." She paused. "Why does your bio say that if it's not true?"

There was the long answer, and then there was the short answer. I went for the short one. "Because my dad's a dick."

"So?"

"So if I give his name, they'll go looking for him. And it's better if they don't."

"So wait…you *weren't* an orphan?"

"I'm an orphan *now*."

"What do you mean?"

"My mom, she died when I was a baby. And my dad…" I made a sound of disgust. "He's dead too, except he's still walking around."

"Where?"

"No place you'd want to visit."

"But how can he be dead if he's still alive?"

"He's dead to *me*," I said. "End of story."

"So you don't want to talk about it?"

"No." I put some more distance between us. "So drop it, all right?"

Her mouth tightened. "All right. If that's what you want." And with that, she yanked up the covers and turned to face the other way.

Shit. I was being a dick. I didn't want to be, but even if I *wanted* to bare my soul, now wasn't the time.

And, I wasn't used to this.

Silence – it was an old habit, ingrained so deep it had become second-nature. Almost no one really knew me, or hell, even who I was. It was better this way.

Until now. Or more accurately, until Becka.

Until her, keeping my distance had been easy.

Not anymore.

Already, she'd burrowed too deep under my skin, making me reconsider everything I thought I knew.

And now I'd hurt her.

Not for the first time either.

I gave a silent curse. If she stuck around, there was plenty more where *that* came from.

A smarter guy – hell, a *nicer* guy – would end this now and be done with it. Some might say I'd be doing her a favor.

Screw that.

What I wanted was *her*. I liked the way she made me feel. And I wanted to spoil her like she deserved to be spoiled.

If she thought her sister had done too much for her, she hadn't seen anything yet. When it came to resources, I had plenty. We could build a life, a *phenomenal* life. But first, I needed to get through this tour.

As we lay in silence, I thought of everything my money could buy – houses, cars, travel, whatever. I could give her the world on a silver platter.

But I couldn't give her myself, not fully, and not yet.

Still, there was something I *could* do. I reached out to caress her shoulder. "Listen, I don't mean to be an ass, okay?"

Slowly, she turned in the bed to face me. "Oh yeah?" she said. "And I don't mean to thump you on the forehead."

I wasn't following. "What?"

A split-second later, she reached up and flicked my forehead with her index finger. "See?" she said with a laugh. "Total accident."

"I'll give you an accident," I said and pulled her back into my arms. And right there, tangled in the covers, I kissed away her questions along with my own concerns, which were growing by the day.

If I were smart, I'd send her straight to her sister, where she wouldn't be tainted by anything I did on my own. And yet, like an asshole, I did nothing of the sort.

Already, we'd extended her internship for another semester, and she'd registered for a couple of additional classes – distance learning, where she could earn the credits without setting foot on campus.

As the weeks turned into months, we traveled back and forth across the country, hitting city after city on my list – small cities, medium cities, and even a few larger ones on the way.

Becka didn't realize it, but I'd planned this trip personally, choosing each city for a specific reason.

But there was something I hadn't planned on – falling for a girl who noticed far too much.

CHAPTER 56

Jack

From the passenger's seat, she said, "Hey, what happened to your notebook?"

We were driving from our current hotel to the next stop on the tour. The drive would take an hour each way, and I was feeling relaxed and easy behind the wheel.

I replied, "What notebook?"

"Oh come on," she said. "You know which one. It's that black notebook you used to carry with you sometimes. Did you lose it?"

I hadn't. The truth was, I still had it with me. And I still made notes in it. I just didn't see the upside of pulling it out where Becka could see.

I said, "It's around somewhere. Why do you ask?"

"Because we were just talking about your next novel." She paused. "Do you know, when I first started, I was convinced that you had writer's block or something?"

"Oh yeah? Why's that?"

"Because you always had that notebook, and you'd be scribbling and stabbing at the pages, like the notebook had wronged you somehow."

I shrugged. "Maybe the notebook had it coming." I'd meant it as a joke, but there was more truth to the statement than she knew.

Undaunted, she continued. "I used to think you were making notes about your plot or outline or whatever. But now I think it's something totally different."

It was. But it *wasn't* something I wanted to discuss. Still, I kept my tone neutral. "Oh yeah? Why?"

"Because whenever we're pondering your next book, and you want to make a note of something, you pull out your phone, not the notebook. So I'm thinking that probably the notebook's for something else."

She was right.

I asked, "Like what?"

"You tell *me*," she said with a laugh. "So…what *were* you scribbling in there? Notes about the tour?"

I gave it some thought before saying, "Yeah. To-do lists mostly."

"Oh." She hesitated. "Probably I should've guessed that, huh?"

She practically had.

I didn't get it. For all Becka knew, I hadn't touched the notebook in weeks.

This wasn't the case, but I *had* been careful. And now I was curious. "What made you think of it?"

"The notebook?" she said. "I just realized that I hadn't seen it in a while, which was odd, because it seemed so important at first."

It still was. As I drove along the rural highway, I studied Becka from the corner of my eye. Even now, her wheels were still turning.

I'd met a lot of girls over the years. Some were book smart. Some were street smart. But none of them were like Becka, who had plenty of both – and made a habit of saying exactly what she thought.

And yet, when I'd first met her, I'd had her pegged as a different kind of person, someone who went through life with blinders on – someone with a lot of heart, but not a lot going on upstairs.

Almost from the start, she'd proved me wrong.

I liked it.

But it was still a problem.

Silently I compared the Becka I'd seen at her condo to the Becka sitting in my passenger's seat. They were the same girl. *And they weren't.*

That earlier version had been wearing blinders so big it was a wonder she saw anything at all.

"Here's a question," I said. "All these things you notice – why didn't you do that with your roommate?"

"What do you mean?"

"There was plenty to see. The dilated pupils, the sweaty skin, the pharmacy in his bedroom. And you didn't notice?"

"Maybe I didn't want to get close enough to notice."

Recalling the guy's behavior, I felt my fingers flex around the steering wheel. "But you noticed his dick. He made damn sure of that."

She hesitated. "Just what are you getting at?"

"Your safety," I said. "The guy's a druggie and a pervert. And you were still living there? Why?"

"Well, I'm not living there *now*."

"Obviously." I softened my tone. "I'm just asking why."

"You mean, why I didn't move?"

"That, and why you didn't see the trouble straight-off."

"I saw," she said. "I just needed time to come up with a plan, that's all. And besides, I wasn't dealing with *him*, not at first. I was dealing with Tara, the girl who rented me the place."

I still wasn't buying it. "Even with Tara, you missed more than you saw. So I'm curious why."

"Wait a minute..." Becka turned sideways in her seat to face me. With a smile, she said, "Does this mean that *you're* the one with questions for a change?"

"You could say that."

"Hmmm." Her tone grew speculative. "If I were smart, I'd whip out a no-questions clause and make you suffer."

I knew what she was getting at. "Like *you've* been suffering?"

"Exactly."

I turned my head and gave her a long, lingering glance. "You weren't suffering last night."

"I was, too," she said. "My stomach is still sore."

I frowned. "What happened? Are you all right?"

"Oh sure, *I'm* fine," she said. "But my abs? With all that convulsing, they're...well, let's just say they got a super good workout." She snickered. "So really *I'm* the victim here."

"Oh yeah?" I was grinning now. With feigned innocence, I asked,

"Convulsing from what?"

"Oh, shut up," she laughed. "You know what."

I did. Last night, we'd been up until nearly dawn. I couldn't get enough of her. And vice-versa.

I'd never been with anyone so responsive. She was sweet and sexy and up for just about anything.

I loved making her climax. And I was damn good at it, too.

"Is that a complaint?" I teased. "Because I could ease off a little…"

"No," she blurted. And then, she cleared her throat. "I just mean, well…" She laughed. "You know what? This conversation has gone way off track."

It had. *But in a good way.*

I wasn't used to it – the laughter, the teasing, the way she made me smile even when we disagreed. For me, it was a new sensation. *I loved it.*

But that didn't satisfy my curiosity. "So, are you gonna answer the question?"

With mock confusion, she replied, "There was a question?"

"You know there was." Still I repeated the gist of it. "With the roommate, why didn't you see the trouble sooner?"

"So you really want to know?"

"If I didn't, I wouldn't be asking."

Again, her tone grew speculative. "If I tell you, will you tell *me* a secret in return?"

Now *that* got my attention. "So it's a secret, huh?"

"Maybe not a secret." She paused. "More like a theory."

"Go ahead. I'm all ears."

"Oh yeah?" she teased. "I know that feeling."

"How about this?" I said. "You tell me this theory of yours, and I'll tell you something in return."

"Like what?"

"Something nobody else knows."

That made her pause. "No kidding?"

"No kidding."

And I knew just the thing I'd tell her.

CHAPTER 57

Becka

It was an intriguing offer. From the passenger's seat, I studied his face in profile. "So it's a secret?"

"You could say that."

"What is it?" I asked.

He smiled. "You first."

I loved his smile. I recalled how rare those had been in the beginning. Some days they were *still* rare. *Not today.*

And now I didn't want to ruin it by dwelling on things that I couldn't change. "Actually, I'm not sure we should talk about it."

"Why not?" he asked.

"Because it's such a nice day, and I'll probably get all morbid. Nobody wants that, right?"

"Morbid how?"

"Oh, you know. Depressing." Still, I forced a smile. "So actually, maybe we should just talk about the weather or something."

The whole weather topic had become a longstanding joke. I waited for him to laugh, or at least smile.

But he didn't. "Forget the weather," he said. "Tell me what you're thinking."

"It's just the answer to your question – as to why I didn't notice the stuff with my roommate. I guess I have a theory, but it's kind of disturbing." I almost winced. "To be honest, I'm not even sure you'd want to hear it."

"And *I'm* sure I do."

Still, I hesitated.

In a quiet voice, he said, "Tell me."

"All right." I bit my lip. "But remember, you asked for it."

"Duly noted."

With growing dread, I said, "Okay, you remember that my dad died when I was little, right?"

"Right."

"And my mom got remarried, pretty soon, actually. The guy's name was Gordon, and he was kind of a creeper."

In the driver's seat, something in Jack's posture changed, becoming more rigid, or at the very least, less relaxed. Still, his voice remained eerily calm as he said, "Is that so?"

"Yeah. The way he looked at my sister, it was *really* weird." At the recollection, I stifled a shudder. "Maybe I didn't realize it at first, but later on, when I hit junior high and became more aware of things, I started to notice that he looked at Anna *all* the time."

Now I *did* shudder. "It was like he wanted to eat her alive or something. And it's the *'or something'* that was the real problem."

"So he was attracted to her. That's what you're saying?"

I gave a snort of disgust. "That's putting it nicely. But anyway, yes, he was attracted to her, maybe even obsessed with her. It made our house *really* stressful, especially for Anna."

"I can imagine. And what about *you*?"

"It was different. I mean, I was three years younger than Anna." I tried to laugh. "I still am, actually. But I just mean, it wasn't the same."

"How so?"

"Well, the thing is…" I couldn't help but cringe. "…I hadn't yet 'blossomed', as Gordon liked to put it."

Under his breath, Jack said, "What the fuck?"

"Yeah. No kidding. But anyway, once I was old enough to realize that he was drooling over Anna, it was worse for both of us, especially her." At the memory, my stomach clenched, but not in a good way. "And not just because she had to deal with Gordon. She was dealing with *me*, too."

"What do you mean?"

"I mean, she started to notice that I was noticing." I sighed. "And it made everything so much worse."

"Worse how?"

"She was really embarrassed. And even *more* worried." In a quieter voice, I added, "Not just about herself. About *me*."

"I can see why," Jack said, giving me a sideways glance. "So I've gotta ask—"

"Don't." I cleared my throat. "I just mean, no, Gordan never had that kind of interest in me." I looked heavenward. "Thank God." Desperately I tried to look on the bright side. "And even with Anna, nothing ever happened."

"You sure about that?"

"Yes. Absolutely." I tried for a shrug. "Who knows, maybe he just liked to look. But trust me, I know. He *never* touched her."

"Because Anna told you?"

"That's part of it," I said. "But even if she *hadn't* told me, I still would've known. My stepdad? He kept getting crabbier all the time, like he was living with a warm cherry pie he couldn't eat." Again, I cringed. "That sounded awful, didn't it?"

"The situation? Yeah. But your wording? No. I get what you mean."

"Yeah, well, he's in prison now anyway – financial crimes and what-not. That's why Mom finally moved back to Wyoming."

Forcing some cheer into my voice, I explained, "Her best friend from high school just got divorced, and apparently they're going to conquer the world."

Jack's jaw tightened. "Is that so?"

I hesitated. "Is something wrong? I mean, other than the obvious?"

"It seems to me, she was no kind of mom."

"Yeah, well…" I shrugged. "She had her good points, too, I guess."

From the look on Jack's face, he wasn't buying it.

Still, I was beyond eager to end this already. I finished by saying,

"Anyway, all that to say, Anna had a pretty rough time of it, but as long as I acted like everything was normal, she seemed to feel better."

"And how about *you*?"

I smiled. "If *she* felt better, *I* felt better."

Jack was quiet for a long moment before saying, "I get what you mean."

"So I guess the lesson is, if you can't do anything anyway, sometimes it's better to suck it up and pretend you're *not* seeing what you're seeing, if only so the people you love don't feel so bad." And now, I just had to ask, "Does that make me a coward?"

Jack didn't hesitate. "No."

I wasn't quite sure I believed him, but it was still nice to hear. "Well …thanks." I blew out a long, shaky breath. "See? I *told* you I'd get all morbid."

And now I was desperate to end on a high note. Going for a joke, I said, "And now that all I'm all grown up, if Gordon ever gets out, I'm pretty sure I'll have to kill him."

It wasn't the first time I'd said such a thing. And it probably wouldn't be the last. But it was the only time I'd said this to Jack.

I waited for him to laugh, or at least smile. *But he didn't.* Instead, after a long, terrible silence, he said, "No, you won't."

"Oh yeah? Why not?"

"Because I'll get him first." He paused as if thinking. "Or maybe second."

"Sorry, what?"

"I'm just saying, Flynn's local, so…" With a loose shrug, he let the sentence trail off.

I wasn't sure if he was joking or not, but for some stupid reason, it made me feel just a little bit better.

Now I almost smiled for real. "What are you saying? I'm third in line? Behind you *and* Flynn? That's not fair."

"Fair's for pussies."

"Oh come on," I said. "You don't really believe that. I've read your books, remember? You're big into justice."

He didn't deny it, and his tone grew speculative. "True."

"See?"

"Of course," he said, as if thinking out loud, "if the guy were a character in one of my books, he wouldn't die an easy death. Something like that? Could be stretched out for weeks." He gave a slow nod. "Maybe months."

I stared from the passenger's seat. I didn't know whether to laugh or shudder, because in that moment, I wasn't quite sure if he was joking. I heard myself say, "And here I thought *I'd* be the morbid one."

With a glance in my direction, Jack said, "You wanna know what I think?"

"What?"

"I think I owe you a secret."

I bit my lip. "I hope yours is better than mine."

"We'll see."

"So...?" I prompted. "What is it?"

"Hang on," he said.

"For what?"

"I'm gonna pull over."

It was a rural two-lane highway, which meant there was no need to wait for the next exit. *Thank God.* By now, I was dying to hear what he'd say.

As the car slowed, I admitted, "I can't decide if this is a good sign or a bad sign. I mean, if you have to stop the car..." A nervous laugh escaped my lips. "This isn't where you tell me that I'm going to be walking, is it?"

"Hey, if you're walking, *I'm* walking." As I watched, he pulled the car off to the shoulder and turned in his seat to face me. "The secret," he said, "it's a two-parter."

I gave him the squinty-eye. "But I *do* get both parts, right?"

"Hell yeah." His gaze met mine. "Part one. I've never been in love."

I blinked. "Not ever?"

"Not ever."

My breath hitched. "Oh." It didn't sound like a warning. It sounded like something else. I held my breath and waited.

He leaned closer. "Until now."

And just like that, the gloom was gone. My pulse quickened as I said, "Really?"

"Really."

"So…Is that part two?"

He smiled. "What, you think I'm a pussy?"

I shook my head. "What do you mean."

"You think I'm not gonna say it?"

By now I could hardly breathe. "Say what?"

He leaned closer until our lips were nearly touching. "I love you, Becka."

It was *exactly* what I wanted to hear. Maybe in the back of my mind, I'd known his feelings already. But to hear him come out and say it – it felt like something out of a dream.

And now I couldn't stop smiling. "I love you, too."

He grinned. "I know."

"Hey!"

His smile faded as his gaze met mine. "I should've said it sooner."

I snickered. "I know."

And with that, I leaned forward and pressed my lips to his. I might've done more if not for the seatbelt holding me back – and yes, the presence of other cars rumbling past.

Still, I laced my fingers around the back of his neck and kissed him with everything I had, even as I gave my wrist a little pinch, just to make sure it wasn't a dream.

Happily, it wasn't – even if the very next week, I was dealing with a total nightmare.

That nightmare had a name.

Imogen St. James.

CHAPTER 58

Becka

I stared across the crowded book store. *Was that who I thought it was?*

She was tall with long dark hair and a figure to die for. She was wearing a form-fitting black dress, high black heels, and huge sparkling earrings.

She looked like visiting royalty or the trophy wife of a rich oligarch. But she wasn't either one of those things. She was Jack's ex-girlfriend and yes, a world-famous model.

But even if she weren't famous, she'd stand out like a princess on a pitcher's mound.

The store was located in a working-class suburb in Northern Ohio. According to the local news, the town had seen better days. But that hadn't stopped the bookstore from attracting an impressive crowd to the signing.

Already, Jack had been signing books for nearly two hours. During those hours, the crowd had grown bigger, not smaller. By now, the line of people waiting snaked all the way through the store, taking up several aisles and half of the attached coffee shop.

As for the store's employees, they were too busy manning the coffee bar and cash registers to help with crowd control. That was fine by me. With only a few exceptions, everyone in line had been really nice. *And patient, too.*

Would Imogen be patient?

I somehow doubted it.

As I stared across the distance, I murmured, "What's she doing here?"

The guy at the front of the line said, "Excuse me?"

I turned to look. "Sorry, what?"

"You said something. Were you talking to me?"

I gave him an apologetic smile. "No. Sorry. It was nothing." As I spoke, my gaze drifted back to Imogen as she wandered to a display table stacked impressively high with thick hard-cover books.

The stack had been even higher when we'd shown up. The books were written by Jack, and they were selling hot and heavy.

Reluctantly, I turned to look at Jack, who was signing a stack of books for a trio of teenagers and their mom. If he noticed Imogen, he gave no sign.

Still, if I were a betting person, I'd put up a decent chunk of money that Jack had spotted Imogen long before I had. During our months of traveling, I'd seen firsthand that Jack saw *everything*.

Only a week had passed since we'd exchanged those three magical words, and I'd been walking with my head in the clouds ever since.

Over the course of the book tour, a lot had changed – not just during the past week, but also during the past few months.

As far as hotels, Jack was no longer staying on the lower floors. Instead, he was staying in the nicest – and yes, highest – suites they had available. And I was staying with him.

The suites weren't necessary, and I told him so, repeatedly. But Jack had insisted, and I had to admit, it *was* really nice.

To keep up appearances – Jack's idea, not mine – he'd continued getting me hotel rooms of my own. I never used them, and neither did Jack, who cradled me close every night – or through *most* of the nights, anyway.

But that was an issue for another time.

Now, I was too busy staring at his ex. *Should I say something?*

Do something?

Or should I play it cool and pretend to not notice her?

I was still trying to figure it out when the guy at the front of the line said, "So, I can go, right?"

I blinked. "Sorry, what?"

He pointed toward Jack. "His table's free, so…"

"Oh. Yes. Of course. Sorry."

God, how many times had I said that already?

Too many – not because I minded apologizing, but rather because I shouldn't be messing up *this* badly. Normally I did a pretty good job of keeping the line flowing. But the sight of Imogen had thrown me seriously off my game.

It was time to get back on track – and quickly, too. Plastering a bright smile onto my face, I escorted the guy to Jack's table and announced, "This is Blake."

The guy frowned. "You mean Blain."

I winced. "Sorry," I told him yet again. "I'm not normally this dense, I promise."

When I looked to Jack, he pushed back his chair and stood. He looked to Blain and said, "Hang on. We'll be back in a minute."

And with that, Jack hustled me toward the private storage room, where we'd been keeping our stuff. When we reached it, he shut the door behind us and said, "If you want her to leave, say the word."

"Who? Imogen?"

He smiled. "Unless there's someone else you want me to kick out."

Something about his smile made me feel warm and wonderful all over. "Would you really do that?"

"Hell yeah."

Now I couldn't help but laugh. "But what about the negative publicity? I mean, that would look pretty bad, don't you think?"

Jack shrugged. "Don't know, don't care."

"But wait," I said, "*I'm* supposed to be the one shuffling people around. And *you're* supposed to be famous and charming."

"Forget fame," he said, pulling me close. "And if you want, I'll charm you right here."

I stifled a giggle. "Actually, I'd rather be 'charmed' without a hundred people outside the door, thank you very much."

He grinned. "You're welcome." His grin faded as he glanced toward the door. "So, do you want me to get rid of her?"

I gave it some thought. It was so incredibly tempting. Still, I shook my head. "No, but thanks, seriously." I gave him my sunniest smile. "I'm sure it'll be fine."

But guess what?

It wasn't.

CHAPTER 59

Becka

True to Jack's word, we were back within a minute. At the table, I gave Blain yet another apologetic smile. "Should I say it again?"

"Say what again?" he asked.

"I'm *really* sorry – for the delay, I mean." I looked to Jack and said, "Anyway, this is Blain, and I'll leave you to it."

And with that, I hustled back to the front of the line, where a couple of teenage girls were clutching paperbacks and grinning at Jack with starstruck eyes.

I could totally see why. Every once in a while, I almost forgot how famous he was. He didn't act famous when we were together. He acted like, well, my dream guy, that's what.

As for his ex-girlfriend, I'd completely lost sight of her. Nervously I glanced around but saw no sign that she'd ever been here at all.

Had she simply left? It seemed unlikely, but hey, anything was possible, right?

Wrong.

Just when I'd decided that I'd dodged a huge bullet, I caught sight of Imogen moving through the crowd, heading straight for Jack.

Her smile was smug, and her hips were swinging. She looked like she was strutting along a fashion catwalk rather than through a crowded book store.

Unsure what to do, I whirled around to catch Jack's reaction.

There was none.

As I watched, he finished signing Blain's book and handed it back like everything was fine.

I whirled back toward Imogen and stifled a curse. Already, she was just a few paces away from where I stood.

Without pausing to think, I lunged toward her and stopped directly in her path, causing her to halt in mid-stride. I planted my feet wide apart and gave her a no-nonsense look. "Excuse me, but where do you think you're going?"

In that English accent of hers, she replied, "Where do you think?"

"Sorry, but he's working."

Her lips pursed. "So am I."

Oh, please. "Doing what?"

"Publicity, not that it's any of *your* concern." And with that, she made a move to sidestep around me.

Nice try, Psycho. I sidestepped to block her path. "I told you, he's busy."

She smirked. "We'll see about that."

I glared up at her. "Yes. We will."

Before she had time to answer, I heard Jack's voice, cool and steady, directly behind me, saying, "You need to leave."

Imogen frowned. "You don't mean *me*, do you?"

"Sure I do," he said. "So beat it."

At this, I couldn't help but cringe. Although I appreciated the fact that he wasn't slobbering all over her, I hated the idea of this scene playing out in public – with me in the middle, no less.

Plus, I'd meant what I'd told Jack in the storage room. This was *my* responsibility, not his. I turned to him and insisted, "It's okay. I can handle this, really."

From the look on his face, he didn't agree. "One," he said, "it's not okay. And two…" His gaze flicked to Imogen. "She's my problem, not yours."

From behind me, Imogen gave a little huff. "Hey! I'm nobody's *problem.*"

I almost scoffed out loud. *Oh, she was a problem, all right.*

And of course, everyone was staring, not that I could blame them.

Cripes, I'd be staring, too, if only I weren't co-starring in this little drama.

I gave Jack a pleading look. "Seriously, will you *please* let me do my job?"

His mouth tightened, but he made no reply.

Before he could change his mind, I turned back to Imogen and said, "If you're here for the signing, you'll have to wait in line like everyone else."

Okay, I knew darn well that she wasn't here for the signing, but I was looking to make a point.

From the look on Imogen's face, she'd gotten it loud and clear.

And she *wasn't* happy.

Taking her sweet time, she looked me up and down before saying, "And who are *you*?"

As if she didn't know. After all, this wasn't the first time we'd met.

I replied, "If you want to know, you'll have to wait in line, just like I said."

"Why?" Her lips formed a sneer. "I'm not here to see *you*."

"Good," I said. "Because I'm not either." I froze. *What?* Even to my own ears, that made absolutely no sense.

 I was still trying to come up with something a whole lot smarter to say when Jack's voice cut across the short distance. "Forget it. She's leaving." His voice hardened. *"Now."*

Imogen looked past me, toward Jack. In a low hiss, she replied, "You'd like that, wouldn't you?"

Jack said, "You know it."

She was glaring now. "Has anyone told you, you're a stone-cold bastard?"

"Hell yeah," he said. "I hear it all the time."

Not from me, he didn't, because it wasn't true. But that was hardly the point. I turned and gave him a pleading look. "Seriously, I've got this, okay?"

From behind me, Imogen said, "Oh, stay out of this. Nobody asked *you."*

Once again, I whirled to face her. "Yeah? And nobody asked *you* to show up today." I extended my arm and pointed to the rear of the line. "There's the line. Get in, or get out."

This was her cue to leave. But she didn't. Instead, she gave a loud sigh. "All right. Fine. I *guess* I'll wait."

I blinked. Now *that* was unexpected. *Was she joking?* I felt my eyebrows furrow. She didn't *look* like she was joking.

I turned to Jack and whispered, "Do you think she's serious?"

From behind me, Imogen said, "I *never* joke about lines."

Huh. Go figure. Apparently, she was calling my bluff.

Even so, it beggared belief. The line was at least three hours long. And this latest delay hadn't helped.

How would this go, anyway? *Would she stand around for three hours, glaring at me while I tried to do my job?*

But of course, I reminded myself, this wasn't about *me* at all.

This was about Jack.

When I turned to look at him, he said, "Say the word, and she's gone."

The offer was so incredibly tempting. But I could only imagine how this would play out.

Would Imogen go peacefully?

Not likely.

I envisioned Jack hustling her to the door, or worse, dragging her out while she screamed and hollered. She might even cry.

Talk about a shit-storm.

I could practically see the headlines now. None of them were good, for Jack in particular.

That settled it. As much as I appreciated his offer, there was no way on Earth I could take him up on it. "No," I told him. "I'll handle this, just like I said."

He frowned. "Becka—"

"Please?" I gave him a desperate look. "I mean, this *is* my job, right?"

From behind me, Imogen muttered, "Don't you mean *blow-job*?"

I whirled to look. "What?"

Again, she eyed me up and down, making it painfully clear that she *wasn't* impressed. And then with a mean little smile, she said, "Oh, honey. I know exactly what you're here for."

Well, that was nice.

I gave Jack a nervous glance. His eyes were hard, and his mouth was tight. He looked like he was two seconds away from tossing her out on her ass.

I summoned up a smile. "All righty then." I made a little shooing motion toward the table where Jack had been signing books. "I guess it's time to get the show back on the road, huh?"

Actually, it was long overdue.

Even though the three of us had been talking for less than five minutes, it felt like forever, especially considering that we had an embarrassingly large audience.

Even worse, Jack *still* wasn't moving.

With renewed desperation, I looked back to Imogen. She wasn't moving either.

Well *someone* had to move. I looked back to Jack said, "How about this? *I'll* sign the books. And *you* can handle the crowd."

From behind me, Imogen gave a snort of derision. "Who'd want *your* signature."

I whirled to face her. "No one. That's my point."

And then, I whirled back to Jack. "Please, I'm begging you. Let me handle it, okay?" In a low whisper, I added, "I mean, if you don't, I'm going to get a complex or something. You don't want that, do you?"

His jaw clenched. "All right. You want it? You got it." And with that, he turned and strode back to the table.

I should've been happy. But I wasn't, especially when Imogen turned and started heading toward the line.

To the front.

Not the back.

Damn it.

I scrambled after her. "What are you doing?"

Without breaking stride, she tossed me a confident smile. "Getting in line, of course. That *is* the protocol, right?"

My fingers clenched. *Oh, I'd give her protocol, all right.*

At the front of the line, the two teenage girls were still waiting politely. I called out to them, "Go ahead. He's ready."

I didn't need to tell them twice. Already, they were hustling forward like they'd just won the line lottery.

As far as their names, I had every confidence that Jack could handle the logistics just fine. As for myself, I had a different problem entirely.

I watched with growing concern as Imogen claimed the spot where the two girls had just been standing. Immediately a chorus of complaints broke out behind her.

The loudest came from the next person in line – an older lady in a postal carrier uniform. She looked to Imogen and said, "What the hell are you doing?"

I spoke up. "Nothing. She's moving to the back."

Imogen said, "No, I'm not." She gave the woman a dismissive look. "Don't you know who I am?"

"I don't care if you're Princess Buttercup," the woman said. "I was here first."

Imogen smiled. "Yes. But I was here better." She threw back her shoulders and announced. "I'm a V.I.P."

From somewhere in the back, a deep male voice hollered out, "You mean S.O.B.!"

I frowned. *S.O.B.? As in son-of-a-bitch?*

Weird. I'd never heard a woman called that before.

Imogen turned and glowered at the crowd. "Who said that?"

A woman's voice called out, "I did!"

"You did not!" Imogen yelled back.

"Well, I am now!" the woman hollered.

Yikes. As much as I agreed with the sentiment, I didn't like the way this was going.

In the calmest voice I could muster, I called out to no one in particular, "Don't worry. Everything's under control."

This wasn't exactly true. Imogen's face flushed a deep red as she turned to glare at me. "Aren't you going to do something?"

"Yeah. I just did."

"I meant something better."

I scoffed, "Like what?"

She made a little fluttering motion with her hands. "Oh, I don't know. Kick them out or something."

I almost laughed in her face. "If anyone's getting kicked out, it's you."

Imogen gave another huff. "We'll see about that."

Yes. We would.

When Jack finished with the teenagers, I motioned the postal carrier forward. I didn't even bother getting her name, because my primary concern was keeping the line moving – *without* causing a riot.

Unfortunately, just as the woman moved toward the table, Imogen did, too. They jostled for position until the postal carrier gave Imogen an elbow to the side and kept on moving.

With a grunt, Imogen staggered sideways like she'd been hit by a linebacker. When she caught her balance, she turned accusing eyes on me. "Did you fuckin' see that?" she said in a voice that was all American. "I was totally assaulted."

I threw up my hands. "Sorry, no one cares. And what happened to your accent?"

She froze. "Pardon?"

"Nice try," I said. "And as far as the line, you might as well give it up. You're *not* going next."

The guy behind her said, "Got that right."

True to his word, he hustled forward even before Jack had finished with the postal carrier. Imogen glared daggers at the guy before saying in a voice that was all duchess, "Well, I never!"

If this were remotely funny, I might've laughed. *Did people actually say that in real life?*

I had no idea.

I just knew that this *wasn't* going well. I snuck a quick glance at Jack. Judging from his expression, we were in total agreement.

CHAPTER 60

Jack

It was a shit-show if I ever saw one. And there she was in the middle of it – the girl I loved, even if she *was* a magnet for trouble.

Screw it.

She could beg all she wanted. This *wasn't* happening. I pushed back my chair and stood. A few strides later, I was at the front of the line.

I looked to Imogen and said, "You're leaving."

Her lips formed a familiar pout. "Oh, so *now* I have your attention?"

"Yeah. For twenty seconds." I glanced toward the main entrance. "Ten if you hustle."

With a jerk of her chin, she replied, "I'm not 'hustling' anywhere."

Becka edged her way between us and gave me a tense smile. "How about this? I'll just escort her out. Easy-peasy."

From behind her, Imogen muttered, "God, you are such a yokel."

Becka whirled around to face her. "Yeah. And *you're* a big faker. So I guess we're even."

Imogen looked ready to snap. "What?"

Becka rolled her eyes. "Oh, please." And then, in the worst English accent I'd ever heard, she continued by saying, "Oh, look at me. I'm all fancy and English. Oh, do bring me some tea, and a..." She paused as if thinking. "Crumpet?" She turned and gave me a questioning look.

I shrugged. "Hell if *I* know."

We both looked to Imogen.

She said nothing.

Becka made a forwarding motion with her hand. "Go on. Tell us."

Imogen drew back. "Pardon?"

"Well, surely you know," Becka persisted. "What's a crumpet?"

A guy near the front of the line said, "It's a donut."

"It is not," a female voice said. "It's a pastry."

"Yeah," the guy said. "Donut, pastry – same thing."

"You're so full of it," the woman said. "I'm telling you, it's more like a croissant."

A third voice, female and older, chimed in, "No, it's a muffin."

The first woman snapped, "If it's a muffin, they'd just call it a muffin."

"Yeah, but it's an *English* muffin," the older woman said. "Except they only toast it on one side."

The donut guy said, "Oh come on! That's not even a pastry."

The older woman replied, "I never said that it was."

The first woman said, "It isn't? Are you sure? Muffins are pastries, right?"

They were still debating it when Imogen turned and yelled out to the crowd. "You know what? You're *all* idiots!"

Next to her, Becka gave a snort of derision. "At least we know what a crumpet is."

Imogen whirled to face her. "You do not!"

"Well…" Becka said. "We do *now*." From the line, there was a chorus of agreement.

Imogen turned once again to the crowd. "Yeah, and so do I. Big whoop!"

The donut guy spoke up. "Hey, how come you're not English no more?"

"Oh, shut up!" Imogen yelled. "How come *you're* still an idiot?"

Enough was enough. As the guy returned an insult of his own, I moved forward and reached for Imogen's elbow. "Time to go."

She yanked it away and announced, "And I suppose *you're* going to make me?"

Shit.

From the gleam in her eyes, this was exactly what she wanted – a nice public spectacle for her social media followers. Apparently, I'd be playing the role of Bad Guy.

I didn't give two shits about her followers – *or* the bad publicity. But the concern in Becka's eyes made me pause.

Not for long.

One way or another, Imogen *was* leaving.

With a slow smile, I lowered my head until my lips nearly brushed her ear. In a casual whisper, I said, "Oh, I don't know, Rachel. I think you're gonna head out on your own."

She gave a hard swallow. "What?"

"Or should I call you Ms. Krepke?"

With a gasp, she pulled back. Our eyes locked, and she swallowed again. Her surprise was obvious, but she shouldn't have been.

Her accent was sloppy, and her back story was paper thin. On the internet, or hell, even on TV, she did a fine enough job. But here, in a crowd of hostiles, she was way out of her league.

I flicked my head toward the entrance. "You've got ten seconds."

"Fine," she said. "If that's what you want." And with that, she turned on her heel and stalked toward the entrance.

Silently, the others watched her go.

When she pushed open the door and walked through it, a cheer erupted from the crowd. At the sound, Imogen whirled back and flipped all of us the double bird before turning and stomping away for good.

When I looked to Becka, she gave me a tentative smile. "You know," she said, "that didn't turn out half as bad as I feared."

What could I say to that? Hell, I produced words for a living. But Becka – she left me tongue-tied and wordless, even when I should've been ranting.

And now I couldn't help it. I smiled back.

Talk about messed up.

And if I knew Imogen, this *wasn't* over.

CHAPTER 61

Becka

From the car's passenger's seat, I stared at the image on my cell phone. "A trollop?"

From behind the wheel, Jack said, "What?"

I didn't know whether to laugh or cry. "A trollop – that's what she called me."

Even worse, Imogen had done this on her infamous social media account, which meant that a few hundred thousand people were now under the impression that I was a boyfriend-stealing ho-bag.

Jack frowned. "When?"

I checked the time of the post. "A couple of hours ago."

Until now, I'd been utterly oblivious. The book signing had ended only fifteen minutes earlier, and we were on our way to the airport.

I'd just powered up my cell phone, only to discover that I had at least a dozen voicemails and a whole slew of texts.

In one of those texts, a friend had included a link to the original post, where Imogen had shared a photo of me, obviously taken sometime during the book-signing.

The photo's caption read, *"Becka the Trollop."*

Underneath the photo, Imogen had gone on to announce to the whole world that I'd run off with *her* guy. She'd even included my last name.

How very helpful.

I sighed. *Yup. That was me. Becka Burke, Trollop Extraordinaire.*

Stupidly, I couldn't help but wish that I'd spent more time on my hair and makeup. It's not like I looked terrible in the photo or anything, but given the photo's description, I couldn't help but feel that my appearance was just a tad disappointing – to me in particular.

Seriously, shouldn't trollops be glamorous?

Scrolling through the comments, I saw links to other news articles. I clicked on a random link and saw an image of Jack and Imogen at a charity thing in New York.

In the photo, Imogen was clinging to him and smiling for the camera. As for Jack, he was neither smiling *nor* clinging. He *didn't* look happy.

Earlier today, Imogen had called him a stone-cold bastard. In the picture, he actually looked the part.

When I glanced in his direction, he had that *same* look. *Yikes.*

I asked, "Is something wrong?"

He glanced toward my phone. "You've gotta ask?"

I tried to look on the bright side. "Yeah, well, it could always be worse."

When he made no reply, I lowered the phone and said, "But it *does* make me wonder…were the two of you serious?"

He shook his head. "Not even close."

I *was* glad to hear it. Still, I *was* curious. "Did *she* know that?"

"She should've," he said. "Trust me. I never gave her reasons to think otherwise. But forget Imogen. We need to talk."

I tensed. *That sounded ominous.*

Bracing myself, I asked, "About what?"

"The next time trouble breaks out – and I don't care what it is – you're not gonna argue with me, okay?"

"But—"

"And," he continued, "I'm not gonna give in. So don't waste your time begging. It's not gonna work. Not again."

My face grew warm as I recalled that yes, I *had* actually begged for him to let me handle today's commotion. Still, I couldn't quite regret it. After all, I'd only been doing my job.

"But why should *you* handle it," I said. "You're the one signing the books."

"Yeah? And you're the girl I love." He gave me a serious look. "So give it up – unless you want me to hire someone else."

My jaw dropped. "Are you seriously threatening to fire me?"

"If you're not more careful?" he said. "Hell yeah."

Talk about offensive. Working hard to keep my cool, I said, "I thought we were past all of that."

"Past what?"

"You threatening to send me packing."

"You can't have it both ways. You know that, right?"

"Just what are you getting at?"

"Ask yourself this," he said. "Would you have pulled that stunt if I was a regular boss?"

"A stunt?" I said. "What stunt?'

"Looking at me with those pretty eyes of yours and asking for something stupid."

"Stupid?" I sputtered. "Did you *seriously* just call me that?"

"Not you," he clarified. "But your idea to handle it alone? Yeah, that was stupid." He shook his head. "And me? I was dumber for listening."

I muttered, "Well, at least we were both stupid."

When he made no reply, I said, "But I was doing it for *you*."

From the look on his face, this *wasn't* welcome news. "That doesn't make it better."

"Well, it should."

"Not the way I see it."

I made a sound of frustration. "But I really *did* want to do my job."

"Tell me. You ever see a crowd get ugly?"

"Yeah," I scoffed, "a few hours ago."

"That was nothing."

"Well, if it was truly nothing," I said, "I don't see why you're all worked up."

"And *I* don't know why you're fighting me on this."

By now, I wanted to scream. "Because I love you, that's why."

"Yeah?" he shot back. "Well I love you, too."

He sounded so pissed off saying it, that I fought a sudden urge to laugh.

I glared at his profile for like thirty whole seconds before a snicker escaped my lips. And when it did, Jack's mouth twitched in a reluctant smile.

At the sight of it, something eased in my heart. "Don't you get it?" I said. "I want to look out for *you*, too."

"Yeah? And you wanna know what *I* want?"

"What?"

"You." He paused. "But from now on, *I'm* handling security. Got it?"

CHAPTER 62

Jack

I meant what I said. I wanted her in every possible way.

During the past few months, she'd claimed a piece of my heart that I hadn't realized was there.

Still, it was a problem.

Nearly every day, I considered sending her elsewhere until the book tour was over. And nearly every day, I rejected the idea as too sorry to consider.

She'd take it personally. And I'd never be able to explain. So we rocked along, going from city to city, with a few unspoken changes after that scene with Imogen.

It was a rainy night in Vermont, and I was sitting alone in the living area of our hotel suite when Becka wandered out of the bedroom looking sleepy and anxious. When she spotted me on the sofa, she smiled. "Oh, there you are."

She was bundled up in a fluffy white robe, the kind the hotel provided as a courtesy. She looked cute as hell, and I smiled back. "And there *you* are."

Her smile faded as she glanced around. "So, where were you?"

"When?"

"Maybe a half-hour ago," she said. "I woke up, and you were gone."

Shit.

With an easy shrug, I replied, "Well I'm here now."

She gave a little frown. "So, where'd you go?"

I pointed to the mini bar, with its assortment of glasses and bottled beverages. "I went for ice."

"Yeah, so did I." She bit her lip. "Around midnight, remember?"

No. I didn't. That was three hours ago, but it made sense. When I'd grabbed the ice bucket, it *hadn't* been empty. Sure, I'd topped it off, but apparently, I was getting sloppy.

Not a good sign.

She added, "I filled it when you were on the phone with Flynn." As she spoke, her gaze strayed once again to the bucket. "Are you sure we needed any?"

"Hey, we can always use more, right?"

She chewed on her bottom lip for a long, silent moment before saying, "Yeah. I mean, ice is good." She looked back to me, and her frown deepened.

I wasn't dressed for bed. But hey, it's not like I'd go out for ice in my boxers, so I figured I was okay.

But then she asked a second time, "So where'd you go?"

"I just told you."

She gave me a long, careful look. "So, it was raining in the hallway?"

Fuck.

I resisted the urge to reach up and check my hair. I didn't need to. It wasn't soaked, but it *was* damp. I'd noticed that in the bathroom mirror.

I was *definitely* getting sloppy. It wasn't like me. But the truth was, Becka was one hell of a distraction – far more than I'd apparently realized.

With an easy smile, I replied, "Hey, I took the long way."

She didn't smile back. "Right."

I tried again. "And I got some fresh air."

So far, I hadn't lied to her. I *had* gotten ice. And I *had* gotten fresh air. But I'd also gotten a list of phone calls and some very interesting documents.

After a long pause, she said, "You do that a lot, you know."

"I do what?"

"Disappear in the middle of the night."

Her words hit like a hammer. Until now, she hadn't said a thing. And because of this, I'd had every reason to think I was okay. The truth was, more times than not, I remained with Becka all through the night. And on the nights I *did* leave, I might be gone for only an hour, maybe two.

Every time I'd left, she'd been asleep. And she'd never said a word.

Until now.

I was still processing this when she added, "The first time I noticed was in Seattle."

Seattle?

What the hell?

That was what, months ago?

Now I wasn't sure how to play it. In the back of my mind, I'd always figured that I'd have some warning. Like maybe she'd notice one time and ask me about it on the spot – at which point I'd go to Plan B.

But nowhere in my plans, did she remain quiet for months and spring it on me by surprise.

Just how many times had she noticed?

And why hadn't she said anything until now?

I shook my head. "Seattle? You serious?"

"Well, I'm not kidding." She crossed her arms. "And I *know* you know what I'm talking about. I can tell by the look on your face."

That, too, was sloppy on my part. Normally, hiding my feelings wasn't a problem. But with Becka, it was just one more thing that was different.

With a low curse, I stood and moved toward her. "There's no one else, if that's what you're thinking."

"Good. But it's not. I mean, that's not what I'm worried about."

I stopped to study her face. From the look in her eyes, she meant it. And now I had to know, "So what's your theory?"

She made a scoffing sound. "Well that's rich."

"Meaning?"

"Meaning that instead of giving me a straight answer, you're tossing out a question of your own. Does that sound fair to you?"

I met her gaze. "No."

She said, "But...?"

Now I was seriously off my game. "But you're right. There's no one else."

"But that's not even the question," she said. "I already told you, I believe you."

I searched her face for clues. "But why?"

"Why do I believe you?" She shrugged. "Call me stupid, but I don't see you as a cheater." Her eyes filled with tears. "And maybe I believe you *too* much when you say you love me."

Her tears cut me to the bone. "You should, because it's true."

"But you don't trust me."

I moved toward her. "That's not it."

And it wasn't. During the past few months, I'd come to realize that Becka wasn't a gossip. In some ways, she was nearly as private as I was.

After Imogen's social media tirade, Becka had been the subject of intense media scrutiny. At nearly every book signing afterward, she'd been confronted by at least one reporter, sometimes two or three.

On top of that, she always got plenty of questions from people waiting in line. I'd heard them with my own ears.

Are you and Jack really a couple?

What's he like in private?

Is it true you that met at Flynn Archer's place?

Through all of this, Becka never revealed anything – not to the media or to the crowds. Instead, she deflected their questions with jokes and good humor.

I saw no trace of that humor now.

In front of me, she said, "And, as long we're laying it out there, I saw that blonde again at the book signing."

At today's signing, there'd been at least twenty blondes, thirty if I counted the guys. I asked, "Which one?"

Ignoring the question, she said, "And that burly guy with the baseball cap. I saw *him* again, too."

Something in my chest tightened as I realized what she was getting at. In a carefully neutral tone, I asked, "Anyone else?"

"The tall guy with glasses. He wasn't there *today*, but I've seen him like a dozen times."

I was stunned. "And you never said anything?"

"No. But I'm saying it now."

"Why?"

"I don't know." She sighed. "I guess I was waiting for you to tell me. It just seems like you would've opened up by now."

We were standing within arm's reach. I wanted to gather her close and kiss away her concerns. But from the look on her face, that wouldn't do the trick.

Not this time.

So I simply said, "I'm not lying to you."

"You are by omission," she said. "Like even now, why aren't you telling me who those people are?"

"Because you already know."

Her mouth tightened. "Oh, do I?"

"Sure. Go ahead and tell me."

"No," she snapped. "For once, *you* tell *me*." Her tone grew desperate. "Please?"

"All right. They're security."

"I knew it," she muttered.

"See?"

"See what?"

I tried for a smile. "You already knew, just like I said."

"Still, it would've been nice to hear it from you."

"And you did."

"When?" she scoffed. "Just now? Are you serious?"

"I meant in Ohio," I said, "when I told you I'd handle security." I searched her face. "You remember, right?"

"I guess." Her shoulders slumped. "But you never told me that you'd be hiring people. *And*, you never mentioned when you actually did it."

"Yeah. And I shouldn't have to."

She stiffened. "Why not?"

"Because I'm running the tour, not you."

"I know. But that's not the point."

"And," I continued, "because they're under cover."

"So?"

"So it's better if you're not friendly." I looked into her eyes, willing her to understand. "And come on, you know how you are."

"And how's that?"

"You're a nice person. And I mean that as a compliment."

"I'm not *that* nice," she said.

"You're wrong," I said. "You *are*." I shook my head. "Nicer than I deserve."

"Even if I believed that – which I don't – what does my so-called 'niceness' have to do with anything?"

"I'm just saying, if you knew they worked for me, you'd feel bad not saying 'hi.'"

"So what?" she said. "I feel bad *now*. Seriously, you should've told me."

"Maybe," I admitted. "But I didn't want you to worry. Or feel funny about it."

"Oh come on," she said. "*You* knew about them. Did *you* feel funny?"

"No. But I'm a different kind person."

She scoffed, "No kidding."

"I just wanted you safe," I explained.

"What are you saying? You did this for me?"

"For both of us."

She grimaced. "So, do you want credit or something?"

"Fuck credit," I said. "I want you to be happy."

"Safe *and* happy?" She shook her head. "Tell me, do I look happy *now?*"

I gave her a look. "You really expect me to answer that?"

Ignoring my question, she said, "And how are they getting from place to place?"

"The same way as everyone does. By plane, car, whatever."

"And you're paying for all of that?"

"Well they're not doing it for free. And I don't expect them to."

"But why don't you just have them fly along with us?"

"Aside from privacy?"

"Yes," she gritted out. "Aside from that."

"All right. Because if they're seen with us, it defeats the purpose. Don't you think?"

"Actually, I don't know what to think," she said. "Which reminds me, you never did say. *Where were you tonight?*"

Fuck.

I didn't want to do it. But unless I wanted to send her away, I had no choice. "You remember that clause?"

She shook her head. "What clause?"

"The no-questions clause."

In front of me, she grew very still. "You're not seriously suggesting—"

"Yeah. I am."

At this, she looked like she wanted to strangle me. I knew the feeling. Hell, I felt like strangling myself.

She glared up at me for a long moment, and I half expected her to pack her stuff right then and there. But she didn't. Instead, she asked in a carefully controlled voice, "This clause of yours, does it ever expire?"

I nodded. "Next month."

"At the end of the tour? That's what you're saying?"

"Pretty much."

"Well, that's nice," she said.

Carefully, I reached for her hands. "Becka, listen..." But as my hands closed around hers, I didn't know what to say. Obviously, she was upset. And I hated that. But I'd rather upset her a million times than put her in any danger.

Finally, I said, "I'd never do anything to hurt you. You know that, right?"

She blinked away tears. "But don't you get it? You're hurting me now."

"Not as bad as I could."

"What does *that* mean?"

"I just mean..." *Shit.* I didn't want to say it. But now I had no choice. "If it's a problem, maybe we should catch up after the tour. I mean, hey, it's only more three weeks."

Her eyebrows furrowed. "What?"

"It's not what I want," I clarified. "But if it's what *you* want, I get it." I stared into her eyes. "I love you. You know that, right?"

After a long moment, she gave a silent nod.

"So do me a favor. Please?" I gave her hands a squeeze. "No more questions."

"But—"

"Not 'til the tour's over, okay?"

What I *didn't* say was that if something went wrong along the way, she'd be glad that she'd been kept in the dark.

In front of me, she blew out a long, trembling breath. "I must be an idiot."

Something in my shoulders eased. "So that's a yes?"

Finally, she gave another nod.

At this, I gathered her into my arms. "No," I said into her hair. "You're the girl I love. And trust me. The tour will be done before you know it."

No truer words were ever spoken – because just four days later, it became painfully clear that she wouldn't make it to the end.

CHAPTER 63

Becka

It was 3:24 a.m., and I was alone in our hotel suite – or more specifically, alone in our king-size bed.

Only a few days had passed since our argument, and things were still way too tense between us. Oh sure, we'd been working hard to go through the motions, but still the tension lingered like a bad case of the flu.

Jack was wary, and I was impatient. Even now, I couldn't decide if confronting him had been a mistake.

Maybe I should've stuck with my original plan – to wait it out, believing for some stupid reason that he'd eventually tell me everything on his own.

But he hadn't. Not even *after* I'd confronted him.

And now he was gone.

Again.

We were in a different hotel in a different city. But the dynamic was all too familiar. Now, lying in the darkness, I couldn't help but wonder if I'd made a mistake by agreeing to that whole no-questions clause.

Was I a sap?

Maybe.

And yet, I *did* believe him when he claimed there was nobody but me. And crazy or not, I honestly couldn't see him doing anything terribly immoral.

In spite of all the secrets, I'd come to feel like I truly knew him. He was big into codes of conduct, old-fashioned honor, and everything associated with those things. And I loved him all the more for it.

Still, in a perverse sort of way, this only made his disappearances more unsettling.

What was he doing, anyway?

As I stared up at the darkened ceiling, the question haunted me to the point of distraction. Finally, I couldn't take it another minute.

I got up, got dressed, and grabbed my newest paperback. I considered going down to the lobby, and immediately rejected *that* idea. After all, the last thing we needed now was something else to argue about it.

And then, I remembered something. I had my *own* hotel room – not that I was staying in it. Still, it was someplace to go, if only to clear my thoughts.

Did it work?

No.

Because the moment I opened the hotel room door, I realized my mistake. *The room was already occupied.*

By him?

It sure looked that way.

As the door swung silently shut behind me, I stopped to stare. The lights were already on. And right there on the bed were the same dark clothes I'd seen Jack wearing on several other occasions. They were wrinkled and worn, like he'd just taken them off.

Silently, I glanced around, trying to put everything into context. The bathroom door was shut, and the shower was running.

I could hear it, even if I couldn't see it.

Was Jack in there? He *had* to be.

And surely, he was alone. *Right?*

Like someone in a trance, I moved toward the bathroom door, only to pause halfway when I spotted his black notebook, along with a large manila folder, sitting on the nearby night stand.

By now, I was beyond curious – so curious, in fact, that I did the unthinkable. I picked up the notebook and leafed quickly through it.

On its tattered pages, I saw names and cities, along with notations that made no sense at all. Words like "private network" and "open secret" jumped out from the random scribbles of names, dates, and who-knows-what-else. Without any real context, I had no idea what any of this meant.

With trembling fingers, I set aside the notebook and reached for the folder. Unable to stop myself, I opened it and looked inside. What I saw there made gasp out loud.

Just then, the sound of the shower suddenly became louder. I turned to look and felt the blood drain from my face.

The bathroom door was now wide open. Standing in the open doorway was Jack, wearing only his boxers and a deep, ominous frown.

I was still holding the folder. And now I didn't know what to say.

On so many levels, this *wasn't* good.

CHAPTER 64

Becka

From the bathroom doorway, he said, "So, did you get a good look?" His eyes were cold, and his mouth was tight. He was obviously angry.

But so what? I was angry, too.

With a hard scoff, I tossed the folder back onto the night stand. When it hit, a few of the pictures slid halfway out, revealing an older man with a much younger woman.

As far as her exact age, I couldn't say for sure. She might've been the same age as me, or possibly even younger.

Either way, the guy was several times her age and girth. Both of them were naked and going at it, doggie style, in what appeared to be an upscale hotel room.

I glanced around. *Was it this hotel room?*

No. It couldn't be.

Could it?

I looked to Jack and said, "Did you take those?"

He frowned. "You think I did?"

"I don't know what to think," I said. "None of this makes any sense."

He gave me a hard look. "What are you doing here?"

Wasn't it obvious? "It's *my* room."

"Which you weren't staying in."

My chin lifted. "Yeah, so?"

"So who gave you a key?"

Obviously, he didn't mean a physical key, but rather one of the key cards assigned by the hotel.

I replied, "It was on the nightstand."

He looked toward the nearby nightstand, where those awful pictures were on partial display.

I looked, too. At the sight of the images, I felt like throwing up. It wasn't that I thought sex was ugly or anything. But to have naked pictures of another couple in mid-thrust, well, it was more than a little disturbing, especially considering the differences in their ages and appearance.

I yanked my gaze from the photos and looked back to Jack. "I meant the nightstand in *your* room."

His jaw clenched. "You mean *our* room."

I knew what he meant. And if I were feeling any less distressed, I might have admitted that he was right. But I *was* distressed and tired of being reasonable at all. "No. I mean *your* room, just like I said."

"Your bags are up *there*. Not here."

"So what?" I threw up my hands. "And why are you putting *me* on the spot, anyway? You're the one who's running around doing Lord-knows-what." My voice rose. "Seriously, what *are* you doing here, anyway?"

In a deadly calm voice, he replied, "I might ask the same of you."

As if he didn't know. "I woke up and you were gone." I crossed my arms and waited for his response.

None came.

I tried again. "And I couldn't fall back asleep."

"So?"

With a sigh, I pulled the paperback out of my purse. I gave it a little wave and said, "So I was going to read until I got sleepy."

He barely glanced at the book. "We have a suite."

Now it was *my* turn to say it. "So?"

"So what's wrong with reading up there?"

"Maybe I needed a change of scenery." I made a scoffing sound. "And obviously, hanging out in the lobby isn't an option." Under my breath, I added, "At least according to *some* people."

He didn't look thrilled with the reminder. "And that's a problem?"

"Yes. Sort of." I paused, and my shoulders sagged. I was angry, but I didn't want to be unfair. "All right, I guess not. I mean, I see your point about safety. But don't you get it? That's why I came down here instead. I thought this room would be empty."

From the look on Jack's face, he wasn't buying it. "Right."

"What, you don't believe me?"

"Should I?"

And just like that, I was playing defense yet again. *I didn't like it.* "Hey, *I'm* not the one skulking around at night."

He gave a low scoff. "You sure about that?"

"Of course I'm sure. Unlike *you*, I haven't left the hotel."

"But you left our room."

I stared up at him. "You say that like I'm some sort of prisoner."

He stiffened. "Is that how you feel?"

"No. Of course not." *It was true.* But once again, he was missing the point. "And this *isn't* about me." I extended my arm and pointed to the photos. "Who *are* those people? And why do you have pictures of them?"

"No questions. Remember?"

I forced a laugh. Even to my own ears, it sounded wrong – half-crazed and devoid of any real humor. "How could I forget?" My head was swimming, and my thoughts were a mess. I blurted out, "And do you realize, I don't even know where you live?"

As I said it, it occurred to me how disturbing this was. For months, we'd been spending nearly every day together. *Nights, too.*

And we'd talked. *A lot.*

By now, I knew how he felt about politics, the world in general, chivalry, honor, pop culture, and everything in-between. *But about his own life?* I knew very little, because Jack seldom talked about it.

In contrast, I'd shared countless details about my own life.

And now I couldn't help but wonder at the imbalance. Maybe he'd only encouraged me to ramble on about myself because it spared him the trouble of doing the same.

He said, "It's a cabin in the mountains, as you damn well know."

Oh, please. Because his bio said so?

I crossed my arms. "Do I?"

"If you want," he said, "I'll fly you there tomorrow."

Silently, I considered his offer – *and* the way he'd phrased it.

Me.

Not us.

I asked, "Would you be coming, too?"

"Sure." He paused. "*After* the tour."

At this point, I wasn't even sure I believed him. *But what did it matter?* If we had so little trust between us, I'd be a fool to even consider it.

Again, I glanced toward the pictures. "And I suppose you're not going to tell me why you have those?"

In reply, he said nothing.

Into his silence, I added, "Or who those people are."

Still no response.

"Or," I persisted, "how you came to have those photos at all."

When he *still* said nothing, I gave a snort of derision. "You know what? Forget it." I glanced toward the hotel room door. "Now will you please get out of my room?"

He wasn't even dressed. But hey, that could be solved easily enough. When he made no move, I marched to the bed and grabbed his clothes. I wadded them up and gave them a hard toss in his direction.

He caught them with one hand and said, "Forget it."

"Forget what?"

"I'm not leaving."

"Why not?" I said. "It's *my* room."

Okay, yes, he was the one paying for it. But that expense was part of the book tour. And in spite of our relationship, I *had* been doing the job I'd been hired to do.

He said, "If you want to be alone, take the suite."

The suite was three times the size and several times nicer. Maybe I *should* take the suite, if only prove a point.

But what that point was, I hardly knew. And besides, the thought of returning to that bed, the one we'd been sharing, well, it was more than I could stomach.

I replied, "I can't. That's *your* room. Not mine."

"No. It's *our* room. Remember?"

"It doesn't matter," I said. "I'm not going back there."

He stared at me. I stared at him. In the background, the shower was still running. The frugal part of me wanted to march in and turn it off.

The less-than-frugal part wanted to set fire to the whole room and laugh while it burned.

Maybe I'd start with the photos.

Yeah, right. I didn't even have a lighter. And besides, as crazy as I felt, I'd never take things that far.

In the end, I simply said, "All right. If you won't leave, I'll just get a room of my own."

Good thing I'd brought my purse.

I clutched it tighter and turned away, only to stop when he said, "Becka, wait."

I stopped and turned around. "For what?"

For a long moment, he said nothing as he stared across the short distance. From the look on his face, he wasn't any happier than I was.

And that was saying something.

Still, like a total sap, I felt a twinge of hope. Maybe he'd *finally* tell me what was going on.

But he didn't.

Instead he said something that made me want to scream. "Go to the front desk. By the time you get there, they'll know where to put you."

CHAPTER 65

Becka

True to Jack's word, the nice lady at the front desk was expecting me when I arrived. With a mouthful of apologies, she informed me that a "lovely room" was available, but that she'd need another fifteen minutes to get me settled.

Settled? I wasn't even sure what that meant. But I was in no mood to argue. Already I'd argued more than enough for one single night. *Or should I say for one single morning?*

It was, after all, shockingly close to sunrise.

So instead I pulled out my paperback and sank into the nearest armchair. I opened the book in front of me, but couldn't bring myself to read more than a page or two.

I was seething with anger and confusion. Some of this was directed at Jack, and even more of this was directed at myself.

When I considered all of the foolish decisions I'd made ever since meeting him, it made me feel so incredibly stupid.

From the first moment I'd laid eyes on him, I'd been too star-struck to think straight. And then, after getting to know him better, my fan-girl fascination had morphed into real feelings.

Now in hindsight, I realized that I'd been so blinded by my own emotions that I hadn't stopped to consider the terrible possibility that our relationship might be mostly one-sided, even in spite of his pretty words.

I didn't *want* to think this. I didn't want to think *any* of this. And yet the dark thoughts kept coming.

Maybe I was just his bed-buddy, someone to enjoy while he was on the road. Maybe this was the reason he'd been so tight-lipped about himself. Maybe he hadn't planned on me sticking around past the actual book tour.

I couldn't quite believe any of this, which only made me feel like a bigger fool. Maybe I was the biggest idiot on the planet, because even now, I still loved him – and believed that he loved me, too.

What a mess.

Fifteen minutes later, I was still drowning in uncertainty, even as the elevator carried me upward to my new room – a suite located just a few doors away from the suite I'd been sharing with Jack.

But it wasn't until I opened the suite's door that the odd fifteen-minute delay finally made sense. On a stand near the bed were my suitcases, presumably containing all of my things.

I should've been happy. And yet happiness eluded me in spite of the fact that Jack had apparently also delivered all of my toiletries to the new bathroom.

Or maybe someone else had.

Either way, the result was the same. I was officially alone with my stuff.

Goodie for me.

By the time I got undressed and climbed into bed, I had a raging headache and a serious case of the blues.

I felt like I should've handled things better, but for the life of me, I couldn't figure out how. And if the situation didn't miraculously improve, I simply *couldn't* stay on the tour.

After all, going back to our previous boss-employee relationship was completely out of the question. Even if Jack could pretend that nothing had happened between us, I knew that *I* most certainly couldn't.

And yet, I still waffled. *Should I stay? Or should I go?*

But it wasn't until breakfast the next morning that I realized the futility of trying to decide at all. *And why?* It was because apparently, while I'd been asleep, a certain someone had made the decision on my behalf.

And I didn't like it.

CHAPTER 66

Jack

As Becka glared at me from across the table, I asked, "Who says you're being fired?"

"You. Just now."

"No. What I said was, I'm sending you out on assignment. Big difference."

"Oh, please," she said. "It is not. You're sending me away." Her mouth tightened. "You might as well fire me and be done with it."

I leaned back in the booth. "You realize what you just said, right?"

"What?"

With a wry smile, I explained, "You admitted you're not being fired, *and* that you know it."

Becka didn't smile back. But then again, I hadn't expected her to. "Oh, stop it," she said. "Now you're just splitting hairs."

I considered all of the people I'd fired over the years. There hadn't been a lot, but each and every one of them had known damn well what was going on.

A few cried. Some got angry. None of them had ever doubted they were being shown the door.

To Becka I said, "Trust me. If I were firing you, you'd know."

"Do you want to hear something funny?" she said. "I almost quit last night. And this morning, too."

"But you didn't."

"Right. And you wanna know why?"

I *did,* more than she realized – and more than I was willing to show at the moment. With a casual shrug, I said, "Sure, why not?"

Her eyes filled with tears. "I don't even know. I *should've* quit. I still should."

I wanted to pull her close and kiss away her sadness and frustration. But that would be a mistake, for her in particular. She was my drug, my muse, the only person who made me smile – *really* smile.

But I'd rip out my own heart before I'd put her at risk, which is why she had to go – the farther away the better.

And sooner rather than later.

It was time to dial it up a notch. I told her, "You can't quit."

"Why not?"

"Because if you do, I'll give you a shitty evaluation."

Her jaw dropped. "What?"

"The college credit," I said. "Your grade depends on what I say."

She looked at me like I was the biggest piece of shit on the planet. "Are you seriously threatening me?"

I put on my best poker face. "It's not a threat if it's true."

"What?" she sputtered.

"Look, if you quit with no notice, what am I supposed to say? Am I supposed to tell your professor that you finished the gig when you didn't?"

She frowned. "But the summer semester's already over."

"Yeah so?"

"So you gave me a glowing review. I earned that. And you know it."

"Yeah, but like you said, the summer's over."

"So?"

"New semester, new grade, which means, if you want *another* good review, you'll get on that plane."

"You can't be serious." She looked like she wanted to slap me. And I couldn't say I blamed her. But sometimes things needed doing. And this was one of those times.

When I said nothing in response, she gave a slow shake of her head. "I swear, I don't even know you right now."

Good. And if things went South, she could tell everyone what a dick I was – *without* needing to lie.

With a tight shrug, I replied, "Yeah, well, things happen. But I'm still not gonna lie to your professor."

"Oh, so *now* you care about ethics?"

I cared.

I never stopped caring.

But some ethics were murkier than others. And right now, I'd do just about anything to get her on that jet.

We were wasting time.

I said, "You've got a passport, right?" I knew the answer, but I wanted to get her thinking in the right direction – to the future, not to the past.

She slumped deeper in the booth. "I guess."

There was no guessing involved. A few months ago, Flynn had made sure that both sisters had passports at the ready, just in case.

He'd been thinking of family vacations. But me, I was in a different mode. It was time to seal the deal and be done with it – *before* I changed my mind.

Across from me, she was saying, "But I don't even have it on me – the passport, I mean."

I glanced at my watch. "You will when you get there."

"Where?"

"The airport. The jet's fueled and waiting. And so is your passport."

"But how'd *that* happen. What'd you do? Have someone go to Michigan to get it?" Her voice rose. "How long have you been planning this, anyway?"

Four hours and ten minutes. But I didn't say it, because she didn't need to know. In fact, the less she knew the better.

The truth was, I hadn't slept. *And* I'd been busy since our encounter last night. *But I hadn't been only one.*

"Cheer up," I said. "There's a surprise waiting for you at the airport."

Looking anything but cheerful, she said, "What kind of surprise?"

"Let's just say you're not going alone."

CHAPTER 67

Becka

Turns out, the surprise was my sister. I should've been happy to see her. But at the moment, I felt bluer than ever, even as she greeted me with a big smile and a fierce hug at the small private airport.

After a long moment, she pulled back to say, "So, Romania, huh?"

"Supposedly," I muttered. The so-called assignment involved me traveling through Romania for three whole weeks, researching the country's most famous castles.

At breakfast, Jack had claimed that he was planning to use the research in his next book – *and* that he needed the research right away.

I wasn't buying it. And why? *It was because I wasn't stupid, that's why.*

If this were such a priority, he surely would've mentioned it earlier than this morning. But he hadn't, which told me exactly one thing. *He'd simply wanted me gone.*

And, as if this weren't bad enough, he'd somehow managed to drag my sister along for the ride – without consulting me at all.

I loved her company. *Really I did.* But the thought of her being pulled away on such short notice made me feel guilty and awkward, not to mention severely annoyed with a certain someone.

If Jack wanted to get bossy with *me* that was one thing. He was, after all, technically my boss. But Anna? She didn't deserve the disruption, even if she *was* being a terrific sport about it.

In front of me, she was still smiling. "I just love castles, don't you?"

Anna was cheerful by nature. *Me, too, normally.* But even for Anna, this was a bit much.

It wasn't even nine o'clock in the morning, and if my calculations were correct, she'd just flown at least two hours to get here.

Doing the math, this meant she'd left Michigan sometime around seven on incredibly short notice. And that didn't even account for time to pack or travel to the airport.

How could she be so cheerful?

With yet another smile, she reached into her purse and pulled out a familiar blue passport. She gave it a little flutter and said, "Look what I've got."

Obviously, the passport was mine. I frowned. "Well that's convenient."

Her smile faltered. "Is something wrong?"

I gave her a long, sullen look. Her dark, glossy hair was pulled back into a loose ponytail, and she was dressed in casual but expensive clothes.

These days everything she owned was expensive, thanks to Flynn's insistence on spoiling her like crazy whether she wanted him to or not.

In reply to her question, all I said was, "Don't ask."

By now, her smile was long gone. "You're not disappointed to see me, are you?"

My shoulders slumped. *Great.* Now I was ruining *her* day, too. "No. Of course not. I'm just in a bad mood." I gave her an apologetic smile. "I'm really sorry, okay?"

She smiled back. "You can tell me all about it on the plane." She reached out and squeezed my hand. "You'll feel better in no time, I promise."

Fat chance.

Still, I tried to be a better sport about it, even when I discovered that we'd be taking *Flynn's* jet to Romania, further fueling my guilt. *How much was this trip costing him, anyway?*

It was one thing if Jack wanted to spend a fortune to send me away. But there was no need to get my sister and her fiancé involved.

I considered everything that Anna and Flynn had done for me already – the tuition, the dorm, the little notebook computer, and countless other things along the way.

They all added up. Cripes, even my passport – *that* had been paid for by Flynn, too, at his insistence.

It was all so incredibly nice.

So why did I feel so crappy?

But I knew why. It was because I'd been shuffled off with nearly no notice, just like Jack's *last* assistant. At the memory of that godawful phone message, I felt my jaw clench and my fists tighten.

She'd been crying.

Today I'd been crying, too. Oh sure, I hadn't cried in front of him. But I'd cried plenty in the limo as it carried me to the airport.

The similarities between my situation and hers were impossible to ignore. And almost before I knew it, I'd already asked my sister to wait while I made a private phone call to you-know-who.

Even if he didn't answer, he was going to get an earful, and *not* later on from Romania.

Instead, he'd be hearing from me now.

CHAPTER 68

Becka

When Jack answered the call, I was actually kind of surprised. After the events of this morning, I'd been nearly certain that he'd simply avoid talking to me at all.

He was, after all, annoyingly good at that.

And now, I almost didn't know what to say. Stupidly, I murmured, "I thought I'd get your voicemail."

"Well you didn't," he said. "How's Romania?"

I felt my brow wrinkle in confusion. He couldn't be serious. I'd left the hotel only forty minutes ago. "Was that a joke?"

"Judging from your tone," he said, "I'm guessing not."

Tears pricked at my eyes. Even though he was being a total ass, it felt embarrassingly good to hear his voice. Still, I *had* called for a reason. "I've got a question."

"You?" He sounded almost amused. "No kidding?"

I wasn't in the mood to be teased. "It's about your last assistant."

"What about her?"

"There's something I need to know." Bracing myself, I asked, "Were you two sleeping together?"

He was quiet for a long moment before saying, "You already asked that."

"Yeah, but that was months ago."

"And what? You think you're gonna get a different answer?"

"I just want the truth," I said.

"And I already gave it to you. Where'd this come from?"

"Isn't it obvious?" I said. "You got rid of her on *really* short notice." Something squeezed at my heart. "Just like me. And she was crying."

Just like me.

But I didn't say it. Instead, I waited for Jack's reply.

He said, "Except she was fired. You weren't."

Oh sure, maybe he hadn't fired me outright, but he *was* sending me to a different country. Probably he'd *wanted* to fire me, but hadn't *only* because of the Flynn connection.

"So why *didn't* you?" I said. "Is it because I'm Anna's sister?"

"No."

I waited for him to elaborate. And when he didn't, I sighed. "All right, fine. About your last assistant, you never did tell me. Why was she fired?"

"You *know* why," he said. "My location was confidential. And she released it."

"Yeah, but only to your girlfriend."

"*Ex*-girlfriend," he clarified. "And trust me. My instructions were crystal clear."

"So?"

"So she didn't follow them."

God, what a hard-ass. "Yeah, but that's such a tiny mistake. And the way it sounded in that voicemail, she really *did* think she was doing you a favor."

"Maybe. Maybe not," he said. "She still needed to go."

"So let me get this straight," I said. "She makes one little mistake, and you send her away just like that?"

Was I projecting?

Probably.

But suddenly it seemed very important to know. Into his stubborn silence, I added, "It just feels like I'm missing something, that's all."

"All right," he said. "You want the truth? She took a bribe."

I blinked. *Seriously?* "What do you mean?"

"I mean," he said, "Imogen paid her a thousand bucks for information on where I was."

Woah. "And she accepted it?"

"She didn't decline it. I can tell you that."

"But how do you know?" I asked.

"Because she did a sorry job of covering her tracks."

"Oh." Now I didn't know what else to say.

On the phone, Jack gave a low scoff. "Satisfied?"

Was I? Maybe a little. Still, I had to ask, "Why didn't you tell me sooner?"

"Because you didn't need to know."

"But—"

"And," he said, "I didn't know you. Not yet."

On this, he was right. At the time, we'd known each other for less than a day. So of course he wouldn't be sharing such personal details. Still I *was* curious. "But why didn't you tell me later on, after we knew each other better?"

"Because you didn't ask."

Logical or not, this was probably the worst thing he could've said. "Yeah," I replied. "And you wanna know why? It's because you hated me asking questions."

"And yet it never stopped you."

I started to object, but then stopped myself. *He was right. Sort of.* In the end, I could only say, "Well, I didn't ask nearly as many as I wanted."

"And I answered more than I should've." An edge crept into his voice. "So let's call it even."

That was easy for him to say. He held all the cards. And now, I wasn't even sure that I'd ever see him again. Did I *want* to see him again?

My heart said yes, but my brain said no.

I was still dwelling on this unsettling question when he said, "On the trip, don't forget to take notes."

And with that, he hung up.

Well, that was nice.

CHAPTER 69

Becka

I stared at my sister. "Do you want to say that again?"

She bit her lip. "From the look on your face, I'm not sure I should."

When my only reply was a sullen look, Anna persisted. "I'm just saying, maybe he had a perfectly good reason for sending you here."

Hearing her say this the *first* time had been bad enough. But hearing it a second time? It was maddening to the core.

We'd just landed in Romania and were on our way to our first hotel, courtesy of a town car that had been waiting at the airport.

I wasn't even sure who arranged it – Flynn or Jack. And honestly, I was almost afraid to ask.

Even by private jet, the flight had been too long and way too turbulent, just like my own emotions. During the twelve hours we'd spent in the air, I'd resisted the urge to tell my sister everything that had happened during the past week.

And why? It was because I *still* wasn't quite sure what was going on and hated the thought of worrying her for nothing. Already, I was worried enough for the both of us.

So in the end, I decided to hold off until I did some research – not only into castles, but into Jack's activities during the past several months.

In the meantime, I vowed, I'd try to be a better sport.

During the latest leg of our flight, I'd vowed this at least a dozen times, only to break that vow repeatedly by sulking like a petulant child.

No more.

If there was one thing I'd learned from growing up in a dysfunctional home, it was that bad moods were contagious. Already I'd contaminated Anna more than enough with my sorry attitude.

I needed to do better, starting now. In reply to her last statement, I summoned up a smile. "Maybe you're right. Either way, there's nothing we can do about it now, huh?"

But soon, my smile faltered. "I probably should've asked this hours ago, but how did *you* get suckered into this?"

"I wasn't 'suckered'," she said. "I wanted to come."

"Why?"

She laughed. "Because I missed you. Is that so hard to believe?"

Given my current mood, I couldn't imagine *anyone* missing me.

Still, I appreciated the sentiment. "I missed you, too." And I meant it. Even though my time with Jack had been amazing, I'd be lying if I didn't admit that I'd been longing to spend more time with Anna.

And now I smiled for real. "Thanks for coming along, seriously."

"Don't thank *me*," she said. "It was Flynn's idea."

"More like *Jack's* idea." I tried to laugh. "I'm pretty sure you're my baby-sitter."

She grinned. "It wouldn't be the first time."

This much was true. But that was a long time ago, and I wasn't a kid anymore. I didn't need a babysitter even if selfishly, it was really nice to have Anna along.

I said, "Hey, can I ask you something? How much do you know about Jack?"

She laughed. "Not much as *you* do."

I wasn't so sure. After all, she was engaged to someone who'd known Jack for a lot longer than I had. "How about Flynn? What does *he* know?"

"More than he's saying, that's for sure."

I perked up. "Really? What makes you say that?"

"All right, get this," she said. "On the way to the airport, Flynn asked me to keep him updated on how you're doing."

I smiled. "Awwww—"

"Daily." As she said it, she gave me a significant look. "Gee, I wonder who *that's* for."

Something squeezed at my heart. "So you think the updates are really for Jack?"

"Definitely," she said. "Not that Flynn doesn't care about you. I'm just saying, he was *very* specific."

"Yeah, but even if your theory's right, does it really matter? I mean, it's probably just a pity thing." *Or, he wanted to make sure that I didn't "blab."*

"Oh, please," she said. "According to Flynn, Jack's crazy about you."

"Seriously?"

Anna nodded.

With a trembling laugh, I said, "And you just thought to mention this?"

"Oh come on," she said. "You knew it already. Why would you need *me* to tell you?"

"Maybe I knew it *then*," I said. "But I don't know anything *now*. Even about those daily updates, if Jack *really* wanted to know how I was doing, why wouldn't he just talk to me himself? Or ask *me* to give him updates?"

"I don't know," Anna said. "But I'm sure he's thinking about you."

That was Anna, the eternal optimist. But me? I wasn't so sure. Regardless, I was definitely thinking about *him*.

In fact, I thought about Jack non-stop, even as I toured the castles on my list. I was taking plenty of notes, too. But all of this was during the day.

Meanwhile, every night, I was doing *other* research, which in the end, proved to be even *more* interesting.

CHAPTER 70

Becka

My jaw dropped as I stared at the image on my computer screen. It was a mug shot of a heavy-set man in his sixties.

I'd seen the guy before.

I was absolutely certain. Oh sure, in *this* picture, he was wearing clothes, and his sex-partner was nowhere in sight. But it was definitely the same guy.

Here in Romania, it was nearly midnight. For the past two hours, I'd been holed up in our latest hotel suite with my head buried in my notebook computer.

Anna was in her private bedroom talking to Flynn. On the other side of her closed door, I heard laughter and giggles – the kind that suggested I'd be smart to stay away.

Good.

The truth was, *I* didn't want to be interrupted either.

As far as the guy on my computer screen, I'd found his picture while scouring the local news sites within a two-hour radius of Worthington, New York – one of the last cities I'd visited with Jack.

In what couldn't be a coincidence, this also happened to be the city where I'd caught him with those naked pictures.

Now as I stared at the mug shot on my computer, I couldn't help but wonder what those lewd photos had to do with this latest development. They were definitely connected.

They *had* to be, right?

Above the guy's photo, the headline announced, *"Local Judge Arrested in Corruption Probe."*

When I read the news article, I learned that the guy had been caught accepting bribes for favorable outcomes. Allegedly, his customers included a whole slew of shady characters ranging from high-level drug dealers to a local businessman involved in some sort of human trafficking case.

The judge had been arrested just yesterday, which explained why I hadn't come across the story earlier. Until now, he'd apparently kept a fairly low profile.

It was no wonder.

Now as I stared at his mug shot, I racked my brain, trying to figure out Jack's role in all of this. He definitely had one. Of this, I was certain.

I read the article a second time, and then a third. When it netted no new clues, I changed my focus to other stops along the book tour.

During our time together, Jack and I had visited over a hundred cities – double that if I accounted for the fact that we rarely stayed in the same city as the actual book-signing.

As I considered the vast quantity of locations, I frowned. *And what about all those cities we'd driven through?*

There were a lot.

Feeling almost light-headed now, I started from the beginning.

I found nothing of particular interest in Atlanta. Or more accurately, I found *so* much news that it was hard to zoom in on a single thing.

And then I remembered, Jack's public appearance in *that* city had only happened because he'd been substituting for Flynn.

Still, I couldn't help but recall the time I'd spotted Jack in the hotel lobby at nearly four in the morning. He'd been carrying my stolen paperback.

How had he gotten it, anyway?

Was it the same way he'd gotten those lewd photos?

As far as the paperback itself, it had been months since Jack and I last discussed it. But I still had the book tucked into the inside pocket of my favorite suitcase.

Overcome by a wave of melancholy, I felt a sudden longing to see it. I wandered to the closet and dug it out. As I opened it to the signature page, I felt my eyes grow misty.

The original inscription was still there. *To Becka – a trouble-maker of the highest order.*

But underneath it, in a different color ink, was something new. *I love you. Don't forget that.* It was dated on the last day we'd seen each other.

As I stared at the new inscription, I blinked away more unshed tears. That was two whole weeks ago, and I hadn't heard from Jack since. *No phone calls, no texts, no email messages. No nothing.*

So much for love, huh?

Feeling more confused than ever, I returned to my computer with a renewed determination to solve the puzzle that was Jack Ward. This time, I focused only on the cities where I knew for sure that he'd slipped away during the middle of the night.

I found just a few items of interest – a few more bribery scandals, some drug deals gone bad, and some high-end robberies, but nothing I could tie to Jack for certain.

In the end, all I felt was exhausted and overwhelmed.

I didn't remember falling asleep, but as far as waking up, I remembered *that* perfectly.

I woke to the sound of my sister's voice, saying, "Hey, Becka – did you see the thing about Jack?"

CHAPTER 71

Becka

I sat up and rubbed at my eyes. "What?"

Anna stared down at me. "Why'd you sleep out *here*?"

I glanced around. Apparently, I'd fallen asleep on the sofa. On the coffee table in front of me was my notebook computer, still open. The screen was dark, but the room wasn't. Already, pale sunlight was filtering in through the suite's window blinds.

I asked, "What time is it?"

"Just past seven," she said. "But forget that. Did you see?"

I shook my head. "See what?"

"The thing about Jack." Her voice rose. "Did you see?"

"I, uh, don't think so." I squinted up at her. "What do you mean?"

She leaned forward. "Do you know who he is?"

It seemed an odd question. "Yeah. I mean, I think so." I was still trying to clear the cobwebs. "Sorry, but I have no idea what you're talking about."

She pointed to my computer. "Go to the news."

Oh, no. Bracing myself, I asked, "What news?"

"*Any* news," she said. "It's all over the place."

My stomach lurched. *Oh, my God.*

He'd gotten caught.

Doing what, I didn't know. But it was beyond easy to guess where this was going.

I grabbed my computer and fired it up to the same Web browser I'd been using last night. On the screen was the last Web site I'd visited – the main news page of a Seattle TV station.

In front of me, I saw nothing new.

Was that good or bad? I looked to my sister.

"Hit refresh," she said.

I wasn't sure I wanted to. Stalling, I said, "But this is just a local site. I mean, it might not have anything."

"I don't care," she said. "It'll be there."

With my heart in my throat, I did what she asked. And then I stared as relief coursed through me. It wasn't the kind of news I'd been expecting. *Thank God.*

He wasn't in jail or dead or any of the other awful scenarios I might've expected.

He was something else entirely.

Or more accurately, he was *someone* else entirely.

Right there on the screen in front of me was Jack's picture along with his name, or rather the name I'd always known him by. But according to the latest news, this *wasn't* his name at all.

With stunned disbelief, I read the headline out loud. "Jack Ward Revealed to be Only Son of Disgraced Senator Charles McBride."

Holy crap.

I knew who the senator was. *Cripes, everyone knew.* A few years earlier, he'd been busted in a huge corruption scheme involving a whole bunch of unsavory activities – bribery, extortion, prostitution, illegal gambling, and rumors of much worse.

He was still in prison.

As my heart raced, I skimmed the article in front of me. Jack's *real* name was Christopher. I said it out loud, "Christopher McBride?"

I looked to my sister. "Did you know?"

"No," she said. "Did you?"

I shook my head. "I didn't know anything."

Even to my own ears, the statement sounded truly unbelievable. *I loved him. And he loved me.* Or at least that's what he'd claimed.

Now I didn't know what to think about anything.

Hungry for more details, I devoured news story after news story until I had a better idea of what was going on.

Apparently, Jack had run away from home while still a teenager – even as the senator had told his friends and associates that his son was simply away at boarding school.

After that, the senator had stopped mentioning his son at all.

But I didn't care about the senator. *I cared about Jack.*

According to the news, the rest of Jack's official bio was surprisingly accurate. He'd worked construction during the day and wrote his novels by night, until they'd taken off like rockets, shattering sales records worldwide.

As the day progressed, I read countless news items from every source I could find. None of the articles contained any quotes from Jack whatsoever. Instead, they all included the same sort of generic statement. *Jack Ward was unavailable for comment.*

I almost scoffed out loud. *Welcome to the club.* As long as I'd known Jack, he'd been unavailable when it came to sharing personal details about his life.

Was *that* the reason?

If so, I guess I could see why. Still, I couldn't help but take it at least a little personally that he'd been so tight-lipped with *me*, the person he claimed to love.

And besides, I could keep a secret.

In spite of what Jack might think, I was no blabber. Even now, I hadn't said a single word about his strange behavior on the book tour – or the fact I'd seen those photos.

But now I was more curious than ever.

This afternoon, Anna and I were scheduled to tour yet another castle. Irresponsible or not, I couldn't see myself doing it. All I wanted to do was hunker down with my computer and read all about Jack.

In the end, I begged my sister to go without me and write up whatever she saw. *Was I shirking?* Maybe. But the truth was, I wanted to be alone with my thoughts, and I knew full well that I'd be crappy company, anyway.

Our Romanian research trip was scheduled to last for three weeks total. Two of those weeks were already gone, which meant that in just one week, I'd be seeing Jack again.

In theory, anyway.

Still, I couldn't resist trying to call him, if for no other reason than to see how he was doing with all of the publicity. But when I did, the call went straight to voicemail.

As usual.

I shouldn't have been surprised.

Apparently, that whole "no comment" thing applied to me, too.

Go figure.

I spent the whole afternoon in the hotel suite, desperately searching for all the news I could find, until I could probably write a giant news story on my own – not that I ever would.

And besides, I was too emotionally exhausted to write anything.

Throughout the day, my thoughts and emotions had been bouncing around like crazy – going from self-righteous anger to an odd kind of gratitude. *And why gratitude?* It was because I'd come up with a new theory, and I was pretty sure I was right.

After all, it wasn't just news about Jack that I'd been researching. It was news about all those cities, where corrupt people were being outed left and right.

If Jack was somehow involved – and I was pretty sure he *was* – that meant he'd been treading on some very dangerous ground over the past few months.

And yet, he'd somehow managed to keep me out of it.

That couldn't be an accident.

Finally at dinner time, I ventured down to the hotel lobby intending to dash out for a quick bite, only to stop in surprise at the sight of a familiar figure near the front desk.

It wasn't Jack.

It was Imogen, who sounded just as frustrated as *I* felt.

CHAPTER 72

Becka

The lobby was bustling with people coming and going. And yet, Imogen was talking so loudly that I noticed her the moment I got off the elevator.

She was standing near the front desk, hassling the concierge. At the sight of her, my steps faltered, and I stopped to stare. Her hair was coiled tightly atop her head, and she was wearing a long slinky dress and lots of jewelry.

Her face was flushed, and her stance was unsteady, as if she'd had way too much to drink or had just returned from a very long boat ride.

In that fake accent of hers, she announced, "But I'm quite certain that he's here."

I frowned. Even for Imogen, the accent sounded way off. *Was she slurring?* Between the accent itself and the chatter of the crowd, I couldn't be sure either way.

As for the concierge, his reply was too hushed for me to make out. Still, the set of his jaw told me everything I needed to know. *Whatever she was selling, he wasn't buying it.*

Imogen's voice grew shrill. "But surely you can tell *me*. I'm his fiancée, for God's sake."

I rolled my eyes. *Fiancée my ass.*

Okay, it was true that Jack and I hadn't spoken for way too long. And we might even be broken up. But I wasn't so stupid as to believe that he'd gotten engaged during the last two weeks, to Imogen no less.

I stalked up behind her and asked, "So, when's the wedding?"

At the sound of my voice, she whirled to look. From the

expression on her face, she was just as delighted to see *me* as I was to see her. She eyed me up and down before slurring, "What are *you* doing here?"

Her breath reeked of booze. What kind, I had no idea. But she was definitely drunk.

I crossed my arms. "I might ask the same."

"Don't bother," she slurred, half-forgetting the accent. "In case you didn't notice, I'm having a private conversation."

It hadn't been *that* private, considering that I'd heard her voice all the way from the elevators. Still, I couldn't help but smile. "Oh really? With who?"

She looked at me like I was a total idiot. "Isn't it obvious?" She turned around, only to belatedly discover that the concierge had mysteriously disappeared.

It wasn't a mystery to *me*. I'd seen him leave with my own two eyes. He hadn't been slow about it either.

Imogen whirled back to me and demanded in a drunken voice that was All-American, "Where'd he go? I *know* you know."

Yup, I sure did. While her back had been turned, he'd slipped into that big, private door behind the front desk.

But Imogen wouldn't be hearing this from *me*.

With a loose shrug, I replied, "Maybe he's getting dressed for the wedding."

Her brow wrinkled in obvious confusion. "Whose wedding?"

Seriously? Either she had no sense of humor, or she'd totally missed the point. "Yours," I said.

She gave a drunken scoff. "Well it's not like we'd get married *now*. It takes time to plan a wedding, you know."

I did know. But she was missing the point. I tried again. "So, where's your ring?"

She scrunched up her face for a long moment before replying, "Maybe at the jewelers? Getting resized?"

It was such a sorry excuse that I had to laugh. "Oh yeah? If that's the case, I'm the Queen of England."

She gave a drunken snort. "You are not. You're not even English."

"Yeah. And neither are you."

"So what?" she slurred. "It's called branding."

"What?"

"Branding," she repeated. "Just like Jack." She leaned closer to me and mumbled, "We're *so* made for each other. *He's* someone else. And *I'm* someone else." She gave a little sideways stagger. "See?"

Oh yeah. She was someone else, all right.

And why was she so convinced that Jack was here at the hotel? Or even in Romania at all?

Was it because he'd paid for my hotel suite? But how would Imogen know? *Did she have access to his credit card or something?*

It was a decent guess. And just when I'd decided that I might be right, she looked past me and hollered out something that sent me reeling all over again. "Jack! *There* you are!"

CHAPTER 73

Jack

Yeah. I was.

And I wasn't happy with what I saw.

I'd just gotten off the elevator, only to see Imogen and Becka facing off in the crowded lobby.

Becka, who was dressed in jeans and a casual white shirt, was a sight for sore eyes. Imogen, whatever she was wearing, was the last person I wanted to see, especially here, so close to Becka.

I strode toward them, making plans as I moved. *First step – get rid of Imogen.*

Second step – make it right with Becka. And third – well, that depended on steps one and two.

Imogen stumbled toward me, jostling people aside as she wove her way through the crowd. I stopped to stare. *Was she drunk?*

But forget Imogen. I looked to Becka. She didn't move as our eyes locked across the distance. I gave her a pleading look. *Don't leave.*

She didn't. *Thank God.* Instead, looking almost amused, she followed in Imogen's wake.

I was still looking at Becka when Imogen plowed into me and clutched me like a lifeline.

Shit.

I made no move to return the embrace. "What are you doing?"

With no trace of that English accent, she slurred, "Saying hello."

She reeked of perfume and gin – and desperation. As she clung to me, she said, "Aren't you gonna say hello back?"

I made a move to dislodge her. "Hell no."

She refused to be dislodged. With her arms wrapped around my waist, she leaned back and stared up at me. "Hey, you said it all wrong."

No. I'd said exactly what I'd meant. To clear up any confusion, I told her, "You need to go." As I spoke, I moved backward, hoping she'd take the hint.

She didn't. Instead, she held on tighter, letting me drag her along for several paces as she whined, "But I came all this way!"

Yeah. Me, too. But it wasn't to see *her.*

With growing frustration, I looked to Becka, who was still strolling toward us. As she moved, I drank in the sight of her, wishing I could stride forward and meet her more than halfway.

When she reached us, it was pure torture. To think, I could reach out and gather Becka into my arms, if only that space weren't occupied by a drunk interloper.

I gave Becka a pleading look. "Just wait, okay?"

She surprised me with an impish smile. The smile went straight to my heart, warming it all the way through. As I soaked up the sight of her, Imogen slurred, "I *knew* Tom wasn't lying."

Tom? I looked to Imogen and said, "Tom who?"

She gave a drunken giggle. "Your pilot. He's been *really* friendly."

My jaw clenched. "You mean Tim?"

"Yeah." She laughed. "That's what I said."

I didn't bother arguing. Tim was a substitute co-pilot while the regular guy was off having some minor surgery. Tim didn't know it, but he was fucking fired.

Not only had the guy talked, he'd obviously blabbed the moment I'd made my flight plans known.

I was still chewing on *that* when Imogen slurred, "I saw the news, the thing about your dad, the senator. I saw it."

She didn't need to say it twice. I'd been dealing with the shit-storm for the last twenty-four hours. I hadn't known the story was coming, which meant that I'd had no chance to tell Becka beforehand.

I'd been planning to tell her everything at the end of the tour. Timing aside, she should have heard it from me.

Too late for that now.

Against me, Imogen was still slurring, "You're like a prince or something."

Where she got *that*, I had no idea.

I was no prince. Not even close.

And she wasn't finished. "You know, like Prince Toros in your books? *He* had a secret history, too. And remember Lady Marielle?"

I did. After all, she was my creation. But that was fiction. And this was reality.

When I didn't bother with a reply, Imogen said, "When I go, I want to die just like her." She gave a happy sigh. "In *your* arms."

Oh, for fuck's sake. "Don't tempt me."

"Huh?" Her arms tightened as she pulled back to stare up at me. "What does *that* mean?"

From the sidelines, Becka said, "It's a joke. Like he wants to murder you." She gave Imogen a hopeful smile. "Get it?"

"Oh shut up," Imogen slurred. "Prince Toros didn't kill nobody." She looked back to me and mumbled, "And you and me? We're *totally* connected."

If she meant physically, yeah, we were. And right about now, I'd give just about anything to dislodge her – *without* resorting to actual murder.

Even if the thought was oddly tempting.

Imogen was still babbling. "I mean, *you've* got a secret identity, and *I've* got a secret identity." Her eyes were gleaming now. "Together, we're like Batman."

What the holy hell?

Through clenched teeth, I said, "No. We're not." *Because for one thing, my identity wasn't so secret anymore.*

With growing frustration, I looked to Becka.

There she was – the girl I loved, the girl I'd flown twelve hours to see, the girl who made me want to smile, even now.

But more than anything, I wanted her safe in my arms.

Earlier, when I'd arrived at the hotel, I'd gone straight up to the suite she shared with Anna. Finding the suite empty, I'd returned back down to the lobby to scour the sofas and armchairs for a certain someone who liked to curl up and read.

But instead of finding Becka alone reading, I'd found her arguing with another someone who still couldn't take a hint.

And now Imogen was saying, "And speaking of bats, I *really* like Romania. At the airport, I met this Count. He was *so* into me." Her shoulders slumped. "But he was old."

Looking amused as hell, Becka reached out and tapped Imogen on the shoulder.

When Imogen turned to look, Becka asked, "Just how old was he?"

Imogen frowned. "*Really* old, like ancient."

Becka's eyes sparkled. She leaned close and said in a loud whisper, "If he's a day over six-hundred, you'd better wear a scarf."

Imogen blinked. "Really? Why?"

Becka's eyebrows furrowed. She looked to me and said, "*You* got that, right?"

"Oh yeah." I got it all right. And I loved her all the more for it.

Still, her happy demeanor wasn't what I'd expected. I'd expected her to be mad as hell.

Aside from the latest news about my family, I'd been hiding things for months. And I'd been out of touch for two full weeks. And then today, I'd shown up with no warning, hoping to win her back.

But from the look in her eyes, I hadn't yet lost her.

How was that possible?

I didn't know. But I was determined to find out.

CHAPTER 74

Becka

"So then," I said, "I started looking at all those cities."

Jack and I we were sitting side by side on the sofa in my hotel suite. I was leaning against him, enjoying the feel of his hard body against mine.

He asked, "Which cities?"

"The ones where you disappeared in the middle of the night. And you know what I found?"

"What?"

I smiled. "Some pretty crazy stuff."

"Such as...?"

"Well, for starters, about the judge – you know, the guy you had pictures of? I saw the story of him getting arrested."

Jack's tone grew teasing, "Did you now?"

I nodded against him. "And I just *knew* you had something to do with it." I pulled back to study his face. "You *are* planning to tell me what happened, aren't you?"

He smiled. "Maybe."

I gave him a mock push to the chest. "What do you mean, maybe?"

"I mean, it depends."

"On what?"

He pulled me tight against him. "On if you're still mine."

I did my best Jack Ward impression. "You've gotta ask?"

"I do," he said. "No joke. I thought you'd tell me to go to hell."

I laughed against him. "Yeah, me too."

"But you didn't. Why?"

"Okay, yeah, I was pretty angry. But then I saw that news story about the judge, and I did a little more research, and then, there was that thing today with your family. And well...I finally remembered something."

"What?"

"Back at my condo, when you searched Nicky's room, you wouldn't tell me what you found in his dresser, remember?"

"I remember."

"And when I asked you why, do you recall the reason you gave?"

With a wry laugh, Jack said, "Plausible deniability."

"Right," I said. "And, after I thought about it, I realized why you didn't tell me what was going on during the book tour." My eyes grew misty as I explained, "It was because you didn't want to get me in trouble..." I hesitated. "...you know, if things didn't turn out so great."

Into my hair, Jack said, "You're pretty smart for a trouble-maker."

Once again, I pulled back to look at him. "But you're here now. Does that mean that everything turned out okay?"

"So far."

This wasn't *quite* the answer I'd been hoping for. "So...you're not sure?"

"A hundred percent? No." His gaze warmed. "But I *am* sure of one thing."

"What?" I asked.

"Make that two things," he said. "One—I love you, Becka."

I fought another urge to cry. And now I didn't know what to say, or rather, *how* to say it. I mean, I wasn't even sure what to call him. But that didn't change the way I felt. In the end, I settled on, "And I love *you. A lot.*"

He smiled. "And, two – no matter what happens, you won't be involved."

"So I was right?" I said. "That's why you sent me away? So I wouldn't be involved?"

"I should've done it sooner," he said. "But you want the truth?"

I nodded.

"I wanted you with me." His voice grew quiet. "It was selfish. Stupid, too."

"It wasn't selfish," I said. "And it was smart, *really* smart." I smiled through my tears. "And besides, it all worked out."

Jack didn't smile back. "There's no guarantee. You know that, right?"

"I don't need a guarantee," I said. "All I need is you."

Now, he did smile. "I know the feeling."

My own smile faded as I realized how much I still didn't know. I had a million questions. But first there was the most important question of all. "Are you okay? I mean, with the news about your family?"

"I'm more than okay." His eyes met mine. "And I want you to know something."

"What?"

"I would've told you."

I couldn't stop myself from asking, "When?"

"Soon. And it wasn't the only thing I wanted to say. I mean, I had a reason for waiting."

"Really? What?"

"No comment." He leaned his forehead against mine. "…yet."

"Oh come on," I said. "I mean, we've got time, right?"

"Not as much as you'd think," he said. "Your sister will be here in forty minutes."

"How do you know?"

"Let's just say she's not coming alone." He reached out and caressed my face. "I missed you."

His words, his touch, the look in his eyes – all of it was a balm to my battered soul. I leaned into his caress. "I missed you, too. And you know what?"

"What?"

"I'm thinking…" My pulse quickened like it always did. "Maybe we should talk later, anyway. I mean, forty minutes, that's not much time."

His eyes filled with humor. "For what?"

Yes, I knew we had a lot to talk about, but suddenly, all I wanted was to feel his body pressed tight against mine with nothing between us. I gave him a secret smile. "To see what you've been missing."

Now he was smiling, too. "Don't you mean what *you've* been missing?"

I stood and grabbed his hand. "That too."

CHAPTER 75

Becka

True to Jack's word, my sister arrived within the hour. She was accompanied by Flynn, who'd apparently flown in with Jack on his private jet.

When Anna and Flynn walked into the hotel suite, laughing, I wanted to laugh, too – even though I hadn't heard the joke.

As Jack and I watched from the sofa, Flynn pulled Anna close and told her, "I'll deal with *you* later."

She smiled up at him. "Promise?"

He grinned. "You know it."

With Jack at my side, and my sister looking so happy, I felt like everything was finally clicking into place. As for myself, I was weak-kneed and smiling from ear-to-ear, thanks to the amazing guy sitting next to me.

As Flynn shut the door behind them, Anna looked to me and said, "Guess who we saw in the lobby."

I gave a dramatic groan. "Oh, no. Don't tell me. Imogen?"

My sister nodded. "Yup."

I was almost afraid to ask. "What was she doing?"

"Arguing with the concierge," Anna said. "And she was drunk off her ass." Anna made a face. "She kept ranting about Batman. The whole thing was so bizarre. You should've seen her."

I tried to laugh. "I *did* see her." I looked to Jack. "I guess she didn't stay in her room, huh"

He shrugged. "I guess not."

"I know why," I said. "She was expecting you to join her."

He smiled. "Maybe."

I just had to know. "Did you tell her that? Or did she just assume?"

"She assumed," he said. "But hey, I would've told her anything to get rid of her."

"Anything?" I teased.

"It was either that, or kill her," he said.

It was an obvious joke. Still, it was a good reminder that Jack owed me some details that he'd promised earlier. *And it was time for him to pay up.*

So when he and I returned to my private bedroom to pack for the trip home, I asked, "So, are you finally going to tell me?"

"Tell you what?"

"Everything you did on the book tour. You said you would, remember?"

"You already know the most important thing."

"You mean with the judge?"

"No. I meant with you." He reached out and yanked me close. "I fell in love."

Even as I laughed, I told him, "I'm serious. If you don't tell me, I'll go crazy."

And, so he did.

It took him nearly an hour, and by the time he finished, I was staring in absolute shock.

Turns out, he'd planned the whole book tour as a cover for his secret activities, which included putting a whole bunch of corrupt people behind bars – or at least heading seriously in that direction.

And the funny thing was, Jack had done all of this in secret, without any cooperation from authorities.

As he rattled off the names and occupations of the people he'd exposed in one way or another, I sat in silent wonder. His list included two judges, a police sheriff, a couple of lawyers, three drug dealers, a banker, several corrupt businessmen, and more.

And now that I knew *who*, I was dying to know *how*. As we sat on the edge of my bed, I asked, "How'd you do it?"

"That depended on the person," he said. "Like take the judge. From those pictures, you might've guessed he was being blackmailed."

"Yeah, I guessed, but it didn't say that in the news."

"I know," he said. "It hasn't gotten out. But *he* knows."

"You mean the judge?"

Jack nodded. "Those pictures – he was storing them in his safe. They weren't the originals. And when the pictures started popping up around the court house, he didn't take it so well."

I felt my lips twitch with the sudden urge to smile. "And how exactly did they start popping up?"

Jack shrugged. "I might've mailed a few copies."

"To who?" I asked.

"A few lawyers, a couple of law clerks, their janitorial service–"

"But wait, why them?"

"Because they clean the court house," he said. "And, they've got plenty of employees. The point was, I wanted the guy to panic."

I recalled what I'd read in that first news story. During the last couple of weeks, the judge had been accusing all kinds of people of being "out to get him."

Between his strange behavior and the photos popping up in random places, it didn't take long for officials to open an investigation. And when they did, they quickly found more than they anticipated, including several judgments, along with sizeable bank transactions, that didn't make much sense.

I looked to Jack. "So who was blackmailing him? And how did you even know this was happening?"

"It wasn't just blackmail," he said. "He was accepting bribes, too. The guy had a pretty good business going."

"But still, how did you know?"

"It wasn't hard to figure out," he said. "If you saw some of the rulings this guy made, you'd know something was off. Then you see who benefits, and there's your answer."

He made it sound oh-so simple. But I knew it wasn't. "And how did he even come to your attention?"

"Because I'm a curious guy. When I see things that don't add up, I want to learn more." He gave me a look. "Funny, I know somebody else like that."

"You can't mean me."

"I can. And I do."

"But I'd never do anything like *you* did."

"Good," he said.

"Why is that good?"

"Because I don't want you anywhere near this."

"Oh, so it's good for you, but not for me?"

"Hell yeah."

I was almost offended. "Why?"

"Because for one thing, I'm better at it. And for another..." He leaned his forehead against mine. "You get in enough trouble already."

I wasn't even sure if he was joking. "Hey, can I ask you a serious question?"

"What?"

"This mission of yours, did it have anything to do with your dad?"

"Maybe."

"What do you mean, maybe?"

"It's complicated."

I had no doubt of *that*. "So you're not gonna tell me?"

"I will," he said. "But first, there's something I want to show you. And it's not here."

CHAPTER 76

Jack

Becka's mind was racing.

I could see it in the brightness of her eyes and the parting of her lips as she gazed out over the panoramic view. I wanted to pull her close and kiss her hard and heavy. But I'd been doing plenty of *that* already, and watching her reaction now felt nearly as satisfying.

Nearly, but not quite.

Still, we had plenty of time for *that* later. I smiled at the thought. If I had my way, we'd have years. *No. Decades. A lifetime.*

We were standing in my living room, gazing out through the floor-to-ceiling windows of my mountain-top home.

With laughter in her voice, she said, "So you call this a cabin, huh?"

"Hey, it's made of logs."

She snickered. "Yeah, but it's got like ten bedrooms."

"Oh yeah?" I teased. "How do you know?" It was a valid question. We'd been here for less than five minutes, and during that time, Becka had barely moved from the window.

She was smiling like a kid at Christmas. *And I loved it.*

She asked, "How many miles can you see?"

"On a clear day? Fifty-six."

She turned to face me. "Seriously? You know the exact number?"

I shrugged. "Hey, I'm not one to guess."

"I believe *that*," she said, turning once again toward the view. Outside the window, the fall colors were on full display in patches of orange and red in the trees below.

At this elevation, autumn came early, and spring came late. And, as far as winters, well, let's say it was a good thing I kept the place fully stocked for those times when the road became nearly impassable, even for me.

She said, "I bet this is great for entertaining."

"I wouldn't know."

"What do you mean?" she asked.

"I mean, you're only the second guest who's been here."

"Oh come on," she said. "You can't be serious."

"Wanna bet?"

She turned to study my face. After a long moment, she said, "Actually, no. I think I'll pass on that whole betting thing."

I smiled. "Smart girl."

"But only two people, huh? So who was the first? Imogen?"

I laughed. "Hell no."

"Really?" she said. "You dated her for a while, so I guess I just figured–"

"Sorry, but you figured wrong. You want the truth? You're the first girl I've brought here."

She beamed up at me. "Seriously? Why?"

The answer to *that* was easy. I reached out and took her hand in mine. "Because they weren't you."

She leaned forward and laughed against my shoulder. "Hah! I bet they just chickened out."

I knew what she meant. This place wasn't easy to get to. The private road leading up to the cabin was narrow and dangerous by design.

Unless the weather said otherwise, it wasn't dangerous to me. Over the years, I'd driven it hundreds of times. By now, I knew it like the back of my hand. But to someone else? The road was a good deterrent.

And if that didn't do the trick, I had hidden steel shutters, solid iron doors, and the best security system money could buy – plus a few other tricks here and there.

The place was virtually impenetrable, even if the log construction might suggest otherwise.

Becka pulled back and said, "So if I'm only the second person to visit, who was the first?"

"You wanna guess?"

She paused. "Flynn?"

I smiled. "See?"

"So, why all the seclusion?" she said. "Is it so you can write in peace?"

"It doesn't hurt," I said. "But no. That's not the reason."

"So….is it to avoid the media?"

It wasn't the primary reason, but it was a nice bonus, especially now.

The story of my real identity was still front-page news. Yesterday, we'd left Romania to a swarm of reporters, thanks to Imogen telling the whole world exactly where I was – and *who* I was with.

The Trollop.

Aka the girl of my dreams.

Becka.

In reply to her guess about the media, I said, "Nope. You wanna try again?"

"Actually," she said, "I'm out of guesses. You should probably tell me."

"All right," I said. "The truth is, the place wasn't paid for. And I don't mean with money."

CHAPTER 77

Becka

It wasn't paid for?

As I stared up at him, I tried to figure out what he meant. This wasn't as easy as it should've been.

We'd left Romania late last night and had spent most of the hours since then in the air. Oh sure, I'd slept a little on the plane, but not nearly enough.

Our first destination had been Michigan, where we dropped off Anna and Flynn before refueling and flying straight out to Montana, where Jack had a rugged SUV waiting in the airplane hangar.

The drive from the small, private airport had taken nearly an hour, and the last thirty minutes of that drive had been truly terrifying with steep drop-offs, single-lane roads, and unexpected curves in the strangest places.

But then, when we reached the top, it was all worth it. The first thing I'd seen was a small cabin nestled among trees within view of a nearby cliff. And the second thing? It was the largest, most elaborate log cabin I'd ever seen.

In fact, to call it a cabin was a massive understatement.

From the outside, it was absolutely stunning. And from the inside, it was even more impressive, with lofty ceilings, massive windows, and a surprising amount of warmth, given the size of the place.

But it was the view from the main living area that took my breath away. I swear, I could've stood at the window for hours, if not for the fact that Jack had just piqued my curiosity.

He'd just said something about the place not being paid for. *But not with money? What did he mean?*

I asked, "So if you don't owe money, what *would* you owe?"

"Deeds."

"You mean like property deeds?"

"No. The other kind."

I shook my head. "Like...good deeds?"

"Or bad deeds," he said. "Depending on how you look at things."

I tried to laugh. "Now I'm really confused."

"Lemme back up," he said. "This mountain – I own it."

"Seriously? The whole thing?"

He frowned. "Oh yeah."

I studied his face. "But isn't that a good thing? I mean, your books did *really* well, so it's not like you didn't earn it, right?"

Jake gave me a serious look, but said nothing.

As the silence stretched out between us, I suddenly realized what he was getting at. "Oh." I winced. "Unless you bought it *before* your books took off?"

He nodded. "Good guess."

"So I'm right? But that must've cost a fortune."

"It did."

"So...whose money did you use?"

He grimaced. "I think you know."

"Your dad's?"

"Right." As I listened, Jack went on to explain that when he left home as a teenager, he'd had access to one of his dad's many off-shore accounts. He'd drained it dry and then used the money to buy his own private mountain through a private trust.

I stared in shock. "Why a mountain?"

"I wanted to be alone." He gave a low scoff. "*And* I was a dumb-ass."

"Why? Don't you like it here?"

"I love it. But I don't like how I got it."

"You mean, because you took money that didn't belong to you?"

"No. Because I took money that didn't belong to *him*."

"You mean your dad?" When Jack nodded, I asked, "So who *did* it belong to?"

With a tight shrug, Jack replied, "Hell if *I* know."

"So what are you saying? He stole the money?"

"I'm saying that however he got it, it was earned off the misery of others." Jack's jaw clenched. "That fucker's hand was in everything."

I recalled everything I'd read. Jack's dad sounded more like a mob boss than anything else. But of course, if the stories were true, he practically *was*.

To Jack, I said, "But if it bothers you so much, why don't you just pay it back? I mean, you have the money, right?"

"And who would I pay?"

I tried to think. "Actually, I don't know."

"Yeah. And neither do I," he said. "That's the point."

At last, I understood what he meant. "Well, you could always just donate the same amount to charity or something."

"I could. And I did." He shrugged. "I still do."

"See?" I tried for a smile. "Then your account's settled, right?"

"It is *now*."

"How so?"

"The book tour," he said. "*That* was my payback."

And with those words, everything finally clicked into place. "So you were righting wrongs? As what? Some sort of penance?"

"Something like that."

"How many wrongs?" I asked.

"As many as I could. I had sixty people on my list. But some nights – hell more nights than not – I came up empty."

"What do you mean?"

"I mean, there was nothing to find. Like maybe the person wasn't as crooked as they looked. Or maybe they did a better job of covering their tracks. Or maybe they kept their stuff somewhere off-site. You never know 'til you get there."

I was staring now. "So on that book tour, you went out *sixty* times? Really?"

"More if I count repeat visits."

I was beyond stunned and just a little horrified. Sure, I'd known that he'd been slipping out, but I hadn't realized the full extent of it until now. "So you were doing this like what, three times a week?"

"Give or take."

By now, I hardly knew what to say.

At something in my expression, Jack said, "Hey, you noticed more than you missed."

"This isn't about me," I said. "It's about you. That was really dangerous. And for what? To pay some imaginary debt?"

"It wasn't imaginary to me."

"But—"

"But nothing," he said. "I made a promise. And I had to keep it."

"A promise to who?"

"Myself."

"But that doesn't count."

"It *always* counts."

"So the book tour was what? Just a cover story?"

"Pretty much."

"Speaking of books," I said, "how'd you get *mine* back from Darbie? You never *did* tell me."

He shrugged. "Eh, it wasn't hard."

"I don't believe *that* for one minute," I said. "And here's another question. Why didn't you return it to me right away? You know, on the night I saw you in the lobby?"

"Because I didn't have it."

"The book?" I said. "You did, too. I saw you carrying it, remember?"

Jack shook his head. "No. You saw me with the other one."

"Ohhhhh. You mean the replacement book? The one that *wasn't* signed? *That's* the one you were carrying?"

I smiled as I recalled the look on Darbie's face when she pulled that book from her suitcase, only to discover that Jack's signature was missing.

Disappearing ink? I gave a silent scoff. *More like disappearing book.*

Corny or not, it still made me smile.

Jack said, "That's the one."

"So why were you carrying it around?"

"That night?" he said. "Because I'd just picked it up."

"From where?"

"A used book store in Cleveland."

My jaw practically hit the floor. "Oh come on. You don't mean you flew to Cleveland to pick it up, do you?"

"Well, I didn't walk to Cleveland. I can tell you that." With a grin, he added, "What's the use of having a private jet if you don't use it?"

I could hardly believe it. "But why'd you go so far?"

"It wasn't that far," he said. "And, it was the closest place that had a matching book. Same creases, same cover, same print date. You know the drill."

Actually, I didn't. But I was still blown away. "And you're *just* mentioning this?"

He put on his innocent face. "Is that a problem?"

"Definitely," I said. "I should've thanked you."

"You did."

"But not enough," I said. "And not for that." And now I couldn't help but recall with embarrassment that I'd given Jack a pretty hard time about that very same book. "I'm surprised you didn't hate me."

He grinned. "Yeah. Me, too." But then, his gaze softened. "Trouble-maker."

I couldn't help but grin back. "You're one to talk. And you never did say. How'd you switch them out?"

"The books? It wasn't hard," he said yet again. "I just needed access to her suitcase, that's all."

I made a scoffing sound. "That's all?"

"Don't worry," he said. "She wasn't there. And with those locks? Hell, a kid could've done it."

"I seriously doubt *that*."

"Wanna bet?" he said. "Me? I could crack a safe by the time I was ten."

"You're joking."

"No joke," he said. "I learned all kinds of skills."

"From who?" I asked.

"My dad's associates."

I tried to laugh. "You mean criminals?"

"Hey, I was curious kid."

He made everything sound oh-so easy. But I knew it wasn't. *It couldn't be.*

Regardless, I was beyond relieved when he assured me that with the completion of the book tour and its related side missions, he considered his account paid in full.

Afterward, he gave me a tour of both cabins – the larger one and the smaller one that he'd built years earlier. I loved them both. But mostly I loved the guy who'd made it all happen – back then *and* now.

In the end, we decided to stay on the mountain for a full month, soaking up the fall colors and precious time alone, free from prying eyes and media speculation.

I felt like I was living a dream.

And it wasn't over, not even close.

CHAPTER 78

Becka

During our month alone on the mountain, Jack was the same amazing guy I'd come to love during the book tour, except now, there were no more secrets between us.

No more late-night excursions.

No more dodging my questions.

No more mixed messages and things that didn't add up.

During this time, I even learned more about the scars on his legs. The story was actually pretty funny – and horrifying at the same time.

He'd been only twelve years old.

And he'd fallen through a window, all right – except he'd fallen *into* the house, not out, while he'd been breaking into his dad's mansion through a second story window.

"But why'd you do it?" I asked. "Were you locked out or something?"

"Hell no," he said. "By that age? I was never locked out."

"Why not?"

"Because I could pick a lock in under ten seconds." He made a sound of derision. "And forget the alarm system. That was child's play." He grinned. "Literally."

I had to laugh. "But still," I persisted, "that doesn't tell me what you were doing on some second-floor ledge."

He shrugged. "Practice."

"For what?"

"For whatever. I mean, it's good to keep up your skills, right?"

Like so many other times, I didn't know whether to laugh or

scream. So instead, I let him pull me into his arms and make me scream and laugh in different ways.

And I loved every minute.

There was only one problem. I missed my sister like crazy. Oh sure, I talked to her all the time, and I'd just seen her in Romania, but that didn't change the fact that things were so much simpler when she and I lived in the same town.

Would I return?

I wanted to.

And I wanted to stay with Jack.

On the upside, Anna's wedding was just a few months away, and Jack and I were planning a nice long visit to help with the plans.

Plus Jack was scheduled to deliver that college lecture he'd promised Professor Greenberg way back in the beginning of summer.

He had, after all, promised. And, as I'd seen firsthand, Jack wasn't one to go back on his word.

As part of the visit, I figured we'd stay with Anna and Flynn. But as it turned out, Jack had another idea entirely.

CHAPTER 79

Jack

I felt like a bastard for keeping her away from home for so long. But the way I saw it, she deserved a surprise – a *good* one for a change. So when we turned onto the narrow road leading to Flynn's secluded estate, it was all I could do to keep a straight face.

We'd nearly reached his front gate when Becka said from the passenger's seat, "Oh man, Flynn must hate *that*."

I stopped the car. "Hate what?"

She pointed to the property directly across the street from Flynn and Anna's private domain. "Look," she said. "Someone's building right across from them."

I looked to where she pointed. Sure enough, a new driveway was leading into the wooded lot directly opposite Flynn's front gate.

She said, "I'm surprised it could even happen. I mean, Flynn's so private. I guess I always assumed that he owned *all* of the land around him."

At one time, he did.

Not anymore.

With a shrug, I said, "You know what? Let's check it out."

"I'm not sure we should," she said. "I mean, it's private property."

"I don't see a sign."

"Yeah, but it *must* be private," she said. "Why else would there be a driveway? It must lead *somewhere*."

She was right. It did.

I eased off the brake, and the car moved forward. Trying like hell not to smile, I said, "We won't know 'til we find out."

As I turned into the long, curving driveway that led into the woods beyond, I gave Becka a sideways glance.

Sometime in the last few seconds, her expression had changed from concern to suspicion. She turned in her seat to face me. "You know something."

"Do I?"

"Definitely. I can tell."

But it wasn't until we reached the nearest clearing and saw the small cabin that she said, "I knew it!" With a happy laugh, she turned to me and said, "You didn't."

I grinned. "Didn't what?"

"Is this *your* cabin?"

In reply, I opened my car door. "Don't move."

"Why not?"

"Just hang on, all right?" And with that, I got out of the car and strode around the front of the vehicle. The air was frigid with the promise of snow, but I felt nothing but warmth as I opened Becka's door and held out my hand. "Let's check it out."

She placed her hand in mine and practically leapt out of the car. "So it *is* yours?"

"No."

Her smile faltered. "Oh."

"It's ours."

She laughed. "Seriously?"

"On one condition."

"What?"

"Make that two conditions," I said. "First — you've got to help me build a new place."

She glanced toward the cabin. "What do you mean?"

"I mean, the cabin's awful small. Let's call it a guest house."

Her eyes were bright and beautiful with excitement. Laughing, she said, "Okay."

"So we'll need something bigger, right?" I pointed to a cleared spot off in the distance. "I'm thinking right there."

She turned to look, and her breath caught. "It's beautiful."

"Not as beautiful as you." I squeezed her hand. "Becka?"

She turned to face me. "What?"

"The second thing – it's a lot tougher."

"Really?"

"Really," I said. "And you wanna know why?"

"Why?"

"Because…" I said, going down on one knee. "…it'll take a lifetime." I smiled up at her. "So I want you to think long and hard."

From the look in her eyes, thinking was the last thing on her mind. Breathlessly, she said, "Oh?"

It was time. "Becka Burke?"

Her breath hitched. "What?"

Finally, I pulled the ring out of my pocket. I held it up between us and asked, "Will you marry me?"

Her eyes filled with tears. "Oh my God. Yes. A million times yes."

It was the answer I'd been waiting for, just like I'd been waiting for Becka all of my life, even if I hadn't realized it.

As I slipped the ring on her finger, I felt more happiness than a guy deserved.

And, as if I weren't lucky enough already, she leapt into my arms the moment I stood. "You know what we should do?" she said.

"What?"

"Celebrate." With tears in her eyes, she said, "I want you. Now and always."

I knew exactly how she felt. "Now and always," I repeated.

She gave me an impish smile. "And speaking of *now*… I don't suppose there's a bed in there?"

CHAPTER 80

Becka

Turns out, there was. Or at least, that's what Jack told me, just before sweeping me up into his arms and carrying me across the clearing toward the front steps of the cabin.

With one hand, he opened the front door and then carried me inside. As he did, I looked around in amazement. "Oh, my God. So it's done? Like *completely* done?"

I'd been half-joking about the bed. With the way I felt now, I would've gladly done it on the floor – or even in the car – and considered myself a very lucky girl.

But my yearning for him, even as strong as it was, couldn't dim my astonishment at the condition of the cabin. The place wasn't just furnished. It was decorated, too.

Everywhere I looked, there was something new and beautiful to look at. I saw throw-pillows and pictures, and fresh flowers everywhere.

There was even a cheerful fire going in the fireplace.

Breathlessly, I asked, "How'd you do this?"

"Do what?"

"The cabin, the furnishings, everything."

"By phone, email, you name it," he said. "And as far as the furnishings, I had plenty of help."

"From Anna and Flynn?"

"You know it."

I stifled a laugh. Part of me was dying to tell my sister right away about our engagement. But now, I had a sneaky suspicion that she already knew, which meant that I had all the time in the world to enjoy this moment alone with Jack.

I was still cradled in his arms. "Want to hear something funny?" I said. "I almost feel like a newlywed already." With an embarrassed laugh, I added, "You even carried me across the threshold."

"Say the word, and I'll carry you anywhere."

"Anywhere?" I teased.

"Anywhere."

I leaned my cheek against his shirt. "That rug in front of the fireplace looks pretty nice."

With a smile in his voice, he replied, "Yeah?"

I nodded against him and smiled with happy anticipation as he began heading in that direction. On his way to the fireplace, he grabbed a folded quilt off the back of the sofa and tossed it onto the rug before setting me down exactly where I'd wanted.

As he did, I pulled him close and kissed him softly at first, and then harder, with a need that felt too raw and hungry to be contained. I pulled back just long enough to tell him, "I love you so much. You know that, right?"

His eyes, so very blue, warmed with an expression that would've melted my heart if only it weren't already a gooey mass of pure bliss.

He smiled. "I love you, too, even if you *are* a trouble-maker."

I whispered, "Of the highest order?"

"Of the highest order."

The cabin felt warm and wonderful, but not half as warm as my thoughts and desires. Already, I was burning for him – to have him inside me, to feel his body against mine, to celebrate like only lovers can.

In my eagerness to get him undressed, I nearly tore his shirt. But he didn't object, and neither did I, not even when he *did* tear mine, sending buttons scattering in all directions.

With eager hands, I went for his pants while he went for my skirt. Soon, all of our clothes were scattered to who-knows-where.

~ might've been embarrassed by my desperation except for the fact he same way, eager and ready. *And boy, were we willing.*

As we kissed and caressed, naked in front of the fireplace, I let my hands roam and my mind drift as I considered just how many ways he'd made my life complete already.

Less than a year ago, he'd been a phantom, someone I'd admired from afar. But now he was mine to have and to hold no matter what.

Talk about unbelievable.

Overflowing with happiness, I rolled us over so I was on top. And then, I sat up, drinking in the sight of his handsome face and amazing body, along with the certain knowledge that he was mine for all eternity. *And I was his.*

As I guided his hard length to my opening, already slick with desire, I savored the sight of him, the feel of him, and even the sound of him when I lowered my hips and took him deep inside me.

As our eyes locked, and our hips moved, I felt so deeply connected that it barely seemed real. But it was. And it *always* would be, now and forever.

Afterward, I wasn't even sure how long we lay there, warm and sated in front of the fireplace. But I *do* know what made me sit up with a start. It was the sound of footsteps on the front porch, followed by familiar, hushed voices.

Anna and Flynn.

I looked to Jack and smiled. "Were you expecting company?'

He grinned. "Maybe."

I giggled. "And you didn't think to tell me?"

"And miss *that*?" he said, wrapping both of us up in the warm blanket. "Forget it."

Yup, he was a trouble-maker, all right. But he was *my* trouble-maker. And I was *his.*

For always.

THE END

Other Books by Sabrina Stark

(Listed by Couple)

Lawton & Chloe
Unbelonging (Unbelonging, Book 1)
Rebelonging (Unbelonging, Book 2)
Lawton (Lawton Rastor, Book 1)
Rastor (Lawton Rastor, Book 2)

Bishop & Selena
Illegal Fortunes

Jake & Luna
Jaked (Jaked Book 1)
Jake Me (Jaked, Book 2)
Jake Forever (Jaked, Book 3)

Joel & Melody
Something Tattered (Joel Bishop, Book 1)
Something True (Joel Bishop, Book 2)

Zane & Jane
Positively Pricked

Jax & Cassidy
One Good Crash

Jaden & Allie
One Bad Idea

Flynn & Anna
Flipping His Script

ABOUT THE AUTHOR

Sabrina Stark writes edgy romances featuring plucky girls and the bad boys who capture their hearts.

She's worked as a fortune-teller, barista, and media writer in the aerospace industry. She has a journalism degree from Central Michigan University and is married with one son and a pack of obnoxiously spoiled kittens. She currently makes her home in Northern Alabama.

ON THE WEB

Learn About New Releases & Exclusive Offers
www.SabrinaStark.com